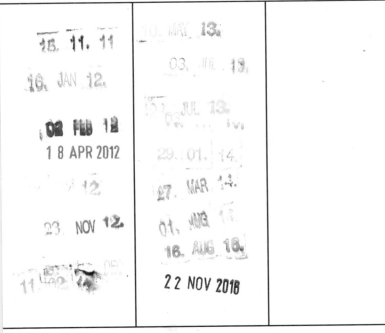

JUSTICE DENIED

The investigation of LaShawn Tompkins' murder seems straightforward. Just another ex-drug dealer caught up in turf warfare. Seattle investigator J.P. Beaumont is handed the assignment under the strictest confidence. But as Beau starts digging the situation becomes more complicated. It appears that LaShawn really had turned over a new leaf. Someone had targeted the man for death. Meanwhile, Beau's lover and fellow cop, Mel Soames, is given her own hush-hush investigation. A routine check on registered sex offenders has revealed a disturbing pattern of death by unnatural causes. The latest suggests an inside job and Mel isn't letting go. As Mel's investigation becomes entangled with Beau's, the two begin to uncover a nightmarish conspiracy involving people in high places — which could include their own.

Books by J. A. Jance
Published by The House of Ulverscroft:

LONG TIME GONE
DEAD WRONG
WEB OF EVIL

J. A. JANCE

JUSTICE DENIED

Complete and Unabridged

CHARNWOOD
Leicester

First published in Great Britain in 2008 by
HarperCollins*Publishers*, London

First Charnwood Edition
published 2009
by arrangement with
HarperCollins*Publishers*, London

The moral right of the author has been asserted

British Library CIP Data

Jance, Judith A.
  Justice denied.- -(A. J. P. Beaumont mystery)
  1. Beaumont, J. P. (Fictitious character)- -Fiction.
  2. Police- -Washington- -Seattle- -Fiction.
  3. Detective and mystery stories.
  4. Large type books.
  I. Title II. Series
  813.5′4–dc22

  ISBN 978–1–84782–877–4

Published by
F. A. Thorpe (Publishing)
Anstey, Leicestershire

Set by Words & Graphics Ltd.
Anstey, Leicestershire
Printed and bound in Great Britain by
T. J. International Ltd., Padstow, Cornwall

This book is printed on acid-free paper

In memory of Anne Medigovich and
Rachel Riggins; and to Dallas and Susie
and the old days at the DRBA

PROLOGUE

LaShawn Tompkins saw the sole white woman, a nun, huddled under her umbrella in the pouring rain as he turned the decrepit Windstar van off Rainier Avenue South onto Church Street. The cracked rubber on the wiper blade wasn't doing much to clear the windshield. Through puddled raindrops he caught only the barest glimpse of an anxious white face illuminated in the yellowish haze of a feeble rain-washed streetlight. His headlights flashed briefly on the gold-embossed lettering of the book she carried.

LaShawn didn't have to read the words printed there to recognize the book for what it was — the Holy Bible. It wasn't uncommon for fearless missionaries of many denominations to venture into this part of Seattle's central district to spread the word about their particular brand of salvation, but it was unusual for one to do so alone. LaShawn suspected that the nun's proselytizing companion or companions were merely out of sight somewhere, knocking on doors or chatting in someone's living room.

Not his mother's, though, LaShawn thought fiercely. Whoever these heathen-seeking women were, they had no business dragging their skinny white butts (he was teaching himself to weed the profanity out of his words, so he didn't even *think* the word 'asses') out here where they didn't belong. And where it wasn't safe. Didn't

1

they know their Bibles or their skimpy little *Watchtower* magazines would be zero defense against random violence or against the stray bullets likely to culminate any number of drug deals gone bad? Maybe they were counting on God to protect them.

'Well, good luck with that,' LaShawn muttered under his breath as he pulled into the short driveway of his mother's south Seattle cottage.

LaShawn was both a neighborhood pioneer and a survivor. As a juvenile he had been one of the original gangbangers who had helped turn the quiet of Church Street into a deadly drug-dealing no-man's-land. Most of the kids LaShawn had grown up with were either deceased or in prison by now. The fact that his mother still lived there — the fact that Etta Mae Tompkins refused to live anywhere else — was one of God's little practical jokes. It was like He was saying, 'See what you did, Shawny? You planted them weeds and now you gotta watch your momma live in that garden.'

Zipping up his bright yellow King Street Mission wind-breaker, LaShawn stepped out of the dented van into a wholesale downpour. This wasn't the usual dry drizzle — the gentle and ever-present rain — for which Seattle is famous. No, this was a warm, heavy spring rain, the kind the weathermen liked to call a Pineapple Express. If the heavy precipitation prematurely melted the mountain snowpack, there might well be a water shortage the next summer. Another one of God's little jokes. If He sent too much rain in March, Etta Mae's flowers would thirst to

2

death the following August.

LaShawn glanced up the street. The nun was still there, standing on the corner. Where were her buddies? Or was she maybe waiting for a ride to come collect her? *Fair enough*, LaShawn muttered under his breath. *Long as you don't come nosin' around here.*

If one of them tried knocking on Etta Mae's door, LaShawn would be there to send her packing. Etta Mae Tompkins may have been LaShawn's mother, but she was also the most godly woman he had ever known, bar none. She didn't need some busybody white lady coming around door-to-door and telling her what she should or shouldn't believe.

Ducking his head against the rain, LaShawn hurried up onto the porch. He came here twice a day, morning and night. So far Brother Mark had been good enough to let LaShawn use the shelter's van for these filial visits to care for his ailing mother. Unfortunately, the situation at the shelter seemed to be going downhill fast. LaShawn didn't know how much longer he would be at the mission, to say nothing of having access to the van. But for now he was still able to come by each morning to make sure Etta Mae was up and around and to fix her breakfast. During the day Meals-on-Wheels dropped off packets of fairly decent, already prepared food. In the evenings LaShawn came by again to make sure Etta Mae actually ate it.

The floor of the porch was firm and dry under his step. When he turned the knob, the solid core door swung easily open inside the jamb. The sturdy door and its well-made frame were also LaShawn's doing — or, perhaps, the Lord's, depending on your point of view. LaShawn had hired the contractors and had overseen the work, but it was his money — the out-of-court settlement won by LaShawn's lawyers in his wrongful-imprisonment suit — that had paid the bills for all that construction.

Considering that seven years had been erroneously deducted from LaShawn's life, the settlement wasn't much, but it was enough that he could have bought Etta Mae a nice place somewhere else. The problem was, she hadn't wanted to leave. She loved the neighborhood and her old familiar house. So LaShawn had fixed the place up for her as well as he was able. It wasn't one of those *Extreme Makeover* things like they did on TV, but it was enough to get the job done — enough to make the place livable and comfortable.

And now that the job was finished, LaShawn was relieved to see that Etta Mae's house didn't look all that different from the other houses on the street. Had the place been too upscale, it would have been nothing more than a magnet for roaming gang-bangers looking for something to steal. No, the cosmetic changes were subtle and understated.

New vinyl siding had replaced sagging clapboard. The rickety porch had been rebuilt with a wheelchair ramp added off to one side. Insulation had been blown inside what had once been skimpy, insulation-free walls. Dangerously old wiring and questionable plumbing had been

4

replaced, and the whole thing was covered with a brand-new standing-seam metal roof. Interior doorways had been widened enough to accommodate a wheelchair if and when the time came that Etta Mae might need one rather than her sturdy walker, and the bathroom had been fitted out with one of those easily accessible step-in bathtubs LaShawn had read about in *Guideposts*.

Why had LaShawn done all that? Because Etta Mae deserved it, that's why. Because all the while he'd been hell-bent on the wrong path, she'd believed in him and kept on praying for him anyway. Those seven long years he'd been stuck on death row she'd never missed a single month of visiting him. No matter what, she'd found a way to make the grueling six-hundred-mile round-trip journey from Seattle to Walla Walla, rising early enough on her one day off to catch the Sisters of Charity van that took prisoners' family members back and forth across the state. On those Saturdays she'd be there at the window in the visitors' room smiling at him and telling him how much she loved him and that God hadn't forsaken him. And now that Etta Mae's health was failing due to a combination of diabetes and congestive heart failure, LaShawn wasn't going to forsake her, either.

He believed with all his heart that Etta Mae was the only reason he was free. She was the one who had begged and cajoled until someone from the Innocence Project had finally taken an interest in his case. She was the one who had

5

pleaded with them to reexamine his trial and the evidence, including the exculpatory DNA evidence, previously concealed by the DA's office, that had eventually exonerated him of the brutal rape and murder for which he had been convicted.

Somehow, in the process of saving her son's life, Etta Mae had succeeded in saving his soul as well. Her unshakable belief had been strong enough for both of them. He had still been on death row when someone from the jail ministry had come to see him, bringing him the Good Word that Jesus had died for his sins. And for the first time ever LaShawn had been ready to listen and to turn his sorry life around. And when the miracle had finally happened, when God had sprung wide his prison doors and LaShawn Tompkins had walked out of Walla Walla a free man, he was also a changed man — a thankful and believing one.

His lawyers had won the settlement for him, but by the time the money came to him LaShawn had dedicated his life to doing the Lord's work. Rather than taking the money for himself, he had spent it on his mother. As for LaShawn? He lived full-time at the King Street Mission, devoting his days and nights to bringing God's Holy Word to the hopeless people he met there — to troubled, angry people using drugs and booze to mask their anger and pain — people not so different from the one LaShawn Tompkins had been not so very long ago.

'Shawny?' Etta Mae called over the blaring TV news. 'Is that you?'

'It's me, Momma. Come to make sure you eat your supper.'

'Well, come on in, then. Don't just stand there where I can't see your face.'

Hanging his dripping jacket on the coat rack, LaShawn kicked off his Nikes and stepped into Etta Mae's pristine living room. The volume on the TV set was so loud that it was nothing short of miraculous that she had heard the door open and close. LaShawn knew about his mother's worsening vision problems, but this was something else they needed to discuss — the possibility of Etta Mae's having her hearing checked. LaShawn didn't hold out much hope on that score. The first time he had brought up the subject, it hadn't gone well.

'What did Meals-on-Wheels bring you today?' he asked.

'Mac and cheese and green beans,' Etta Mae replied. 'At least that's what that nice Mr. Dawson said when he was putting it in the fridge. I do like their mac and cheese. Not as good as mine, but then I don't have to fix it, do I.'

He went over to where she sat and kissed the top of her head. Her hair was still wiry and springy, but he was surprised by how thin it was. And how gray. He was pleased to see that she was wearing her button, the emergency alert necklace he had bought for her. That way, if she needed help all she had to do was press one button to be connected to an emergency operator.

'I'll go heat up that mac and cheese,' he said.

7

'You want to eat it here or in the kitchen?'

'That depends,' she said. 'Will you eat some, too?'

LaShawn shook his head. 'You know better than that, Momma. Those Meals-on-Wheels are for *old* people. I ain't that old.'

'Then I shouldn't eat them, either.' Etta Mae sniffed. 'You're only as old as you think you are.'

'I'll eat at the mission,' he assured her. 'The nice ladies in the kitchen know that I'm over here feeding you, so they hold back a little something for me.'

'Well,' Etta Mae said. 'In that case, since you won't join me, I could just as well eat on a tray here in the living room.'

Out in the kitchen — also built to be wheelchair-friendly — LaShawn put the macaroni and cheese into the microwave and began counting out the evening's supply of pills. With morning and evening visits from him, they were making this work, but at some point there would be another decision to be made. LaShawn was hoping to hold that one off as long as possible. Etta Mae had told him that she'd rather die than go live in one of those awful assisted-living homes, and he knew she meant it.

He put the pills, silverware, and a napkin on the tray along with a bottle of Snapple. He was waiting for the microwave to finish reheating the food when the doorbell rang. 'You stay where you are, Momma,' he called. 'I'll get it.'

Expecting to find a missionary on his mother's doorstep, an annoyed LaShawn hurried to the door ready to send whoever it was packing. As he flung the door wide open, the first bullet, muffled by a silencer, caught him full in the gut. He never saw it coming. As he fell, the second bullet scored a direct hit on his heart. He was dead before he ever hit the surface of his mother's newly Pergoed floor.

'Shawny?' his mother called a little later. 'What was that noise? And I feel a breeze. Did you leave the front door open?'

A good five minutes after that, Etta Mae Tompkins used her emergency alert button for the very first time.

'Good evening, Mrs. Tompkins,' a disembodied voice called from somewhere behind her. 'How can we help you?'

It took a moment for Etta Mae to realize it was the emergency operator speaking to her from the box in the living room. 'My son!' Etta Mae wailed brokenly. 'My poor baby son Shawny is dead. Somebody's murdered him. They shot him right here in my front door!'

1

I was standing in my own bedroom minding my own business and knotting my tie when Mel Soames hopped into the doorway from her room down the hall. She was wearing nothing but a bra and a pair of panties, and she was doing a strange ostrichlike dance as she attempted to put one foot into a pair of panty hose.

'So what are you going to do about a tux?' she asked. 'Buy or rent?'

Some questions posed by half-naked women are more easily answered than others. This one had me stumped. *What tux?* I wondered.

Since I quit drinking, I find I'm in fairly good shape when it comes to remembering things. For example, we had spent most of the weekend on the road, driving down to Ashland, Oregon, to see my month-old grandson, Kyle Roger Cartwright. I remembered the eight-hour ride down, including our post-midnight arrival at the Peerless Hotel in the wee hours of Saturday morning.

I remembered spending all of Saturday alternately having my picture taken with and taking pictures of a month-old blanket-wrapped round-faced little kid who looked like he would have preferred sleeping peacefully to being passed from hand to hand during a nonstop day-long photo shoot. I clearly remembered having to explain to my precocious four-year-old

11

granddaughter, Kayla, that Mel was *not* her grandmother. And I particularly remembered how much of a kick my daughter and son-in-law, Kelly and Jeremy, had gotten out of my trying to dig my way out of that hole.

And I also remembered the eight-hour drive back to Seattle on Sunday afternoon, especially the part where I had managed to keep my mouth shut when Mel was pulled over by an Oregon state trooper for doing seventy-seven miles per hour in a posted sixty-five. (It could have been much worse. The alabaster-white S55 Mercedes sedan I bought used from my friend and lawyer Ralph Ames has five hundred horsepower under the hood, a top speed of 184, and is deceptively quiet.) But the motorcycle cop was a young guy. Mel gave him the full-press blonde treatment complete with a winning if apologetic smile and managed to talk her way out of the ticket. But then, that's Mel for you.

However, nothing in all those bits of memory even hinted at my needing a tux. For any reason whatsoever.

'Buy,' I said.

It was a desperate gamble, but I came up winners. Mel shot me a radiant smile. 'Good answer,' she said. 'We should probably plan on doing that at lunchtime, or maybe right after work. That way, if there's tailoring that needs to be done . . . '

Snapping her panty hose in place, she disappeared back down the hall to finish dressing. I finished knotting my tie and then went out into the kitchen to drink coffee and

12

contemplate my fate. Tux or not, Mel Soames brought something to the table that wasn't half bad.

We had met working for the Washington State attorney general's Special Homicide Investigation Team, the SHIT squad, as it's derisively known in local cop-shop circles. I had gone there after bailing out of homicide at Seattle PD. My former partner, Sue Danielson, had died in a shoot-out, and I had wanted to find a way to keep my hand in law enforcement without having to deal with the emotional stress of a partner. Ross Alan Connors, the A.G., had offered me just such a position. Mel, it turned out, had come to Washington State and to SHIT for a similar reason, only the partnership problem she was leaving behind was a bad marriage and a worse divorce. But then we got turned into partners anyway — unofficially and without either one of us necessarily meaning for it to happen.

In the course of several memorable days, Mel had ended up watching my back in not one but two life-and-death situations. It turned out she was damned good at it, too. And then when someone ran me through a greenhouse wall, cut open my scalp, and filled me full of tiny glass shards, she had brought me home from the ER and had stayed on to look after me. (Months later, little slivers of glass still pop up occasionally when I'm shaving.)

To begin with, Mel camped out in the guest room down the hall, but over the course of time that had changed, too. The only parts of the guest suite she now uses are the closet and the bathroom. We call it her dressing room.

It goes without saying that we're both well beyond the age of consent and old enough to know that working together and living together is a very bad idea. SHIT is a new-enough agency that nobody has ever quite gotten around to setting down in writing all the rules and procedures about what should or shouldn't be done. If they had, I'm sure cohabitation between fellow investigators would be close to the top of the prohibited list. But there's no fool like an old fool — or maybe even a pair of them.

And so, even though it's probably a bad idea, we do it anyway. Sometimes we stay at Mel's place in Bellevue, but mostly we stay at my high-rise condo in Seattle's Denny Regrade neighborhood. (Much better view from the penthouse at Belltown Terrace than from her third-story apartment in the burbs!) We car-pool together in the express lanes across Lake Washington and then pick up or drop off the other vehicle in the park-and-ride lot on the east side of the lake.

A word about my condo. New acquaintances are often curious about how a retired homicide cop happens to sit in the penthouse suite of one of Seattle's most desirable high-rises. The truth is, I wouldn't be in Belltown Terrace at all if it weren't for Anne Corley, my second wife, whose shocking death left me holding an unexpected fortune. I had never driven a Porsche until I inherited hers. And it was only after that one finally bit the dust — after being mashed flat by a marauding Escalade — that I had gone looking for something else.

My Mercedes S55 may have come to me used, but it's several years newer than Mel's BMW, so her 740 tends to be relegated to second-class status on most workdays. The only problem with sharing cars is my steadfast refusal to have talk radio playing in mine. Period. (In my opinion, a little bit of all-talk-all-the-time arguing goes a very long way.) So when we're in the Mercedes we tend to listen to KING-FM. I'm a latecomer to classical music, but it's the one inarguable alternative to perpetual arguing.

Once on the east side, we split up and drive on to the SHIT Squad B offices in Eastgate in our two separate vehicles. We park next to each other in the parking lot and ride up in the elevator together. Big secret — sneaky and subtle. It's a lot like thinking you're pulling the wool over parental eyes when you're in junior high and busy sneaking in and out of the house in the middle of the night. I suspect our boss, Harry I. Ball, knows all about it and simply chooses to keep his mouth shut on the subject. I believe it's a variation on the theme of 'Don't ask; don't tell.'

Mel showed up in the kitchen looking like a million dollars. She gave me a breezy kiss, filled our two thermos traveling cups with coffee, and we headed out. It had been sunny in Ashland over the weekend, but it had rained from Thursday on in Seattle and it was still raining like crazy that Monday morning.

'Did you call Beverly and Lars?' she asked.

Beverly, my ninety-something grandmother, lives with her second husband, Lars Jenssen, in an assisted-living facility up on Queen Anne Hill. Beverly was fading — they both were — and I dreaded calling for fear of hearing bad news.

'Not yet,' I said. 'Too early.'

That was nonsense, of course. Both Beverly and Lars were lifelong early risers who could have, individually and together, roused the birds out of bed.

'Try giving them a call later, then,' Mel advised. 'Kelly sent along that little framed picture of Kyle — the one they took in the hospital. She wanted to be sure we got it to them right away.'

'Right,' I said. 'Maybe we can see them after work tonight.'

We rode up in the elevator together. Mel ducked into her office and turned on her radio. I was surprised to see that Barbara Galvin, our super-efficient office manager, wasn't at her desk. I found her in the break room waiting for a pot of coffee to finish brewing.

'Heads up,' she said. 'The big guy's here.'

'The big guy,' of course, was none other than Attorney General Ross Alan Connors. In the two years I had worked for the man, I could count on one hand — more like one finger — the times the A.G. had sallied forth from his lair in Olympia and driven up the I-5 corridor to pay a personal visit to Squad B of his Special Homicide Investigation Team.

'What's up?' I asked.

'Who knows?' Barbara replied with a shrug.

16

'He turned up a few minutes after I did. He's been closeted with Harry for the last twenty minutes.'

I'm a guilt magnet — even when I haven't done anything wrong. In this case, I knew I was at fault. There was no doubt in my mind that Ross Connors had appeared in person to read me the riot act for carrying on with Mel. (Mel would insist I was being a sexist jerk since, in actual fact, we were both equally at fault.) Sexist or not, however, when Ross showed up outside my door a few minutes later, I was ready to take full responsibility for our little indiscretion.

'Hey, Beau,' Ross said. 'Do you mind?'

'Come on in,' I replied as casually as I could manage. 'Be my guest.'

Ross Connors is a big man, someone who fills up any room he enters. That goes triple for my tiny office. At six-four and two-eighty, he looks like what he was in high school and college, a top-drawer tackle. He's also an experienced politician with all the careful grooming, finely tailored clothing, and good looks that go with that territory. But Ross was beginning to show his age. His wife's very public suicide a year or so earlier had taken its toll. His hair, once a distinguished salt-and-pepper, was now solid gray, and there were dark circles under his eyes — as though he wasn't sleeping well. I could certainly relate to that.

Holding a cup of coffee, Ross settled back in my only guest chair. He took a tentative sip of the coffee and then heaved a contented sigh. 'Much better,' he said. 'I don't know who made

17

that first pot. It was like drinking crankcase oil.'

'That would be Harry,' I told him. 'His own personal witch's brew. The rest of us have learned to wait until Barbara Galvin makes the next pot.'

'Wise decision,' Ross said. 'Remind me next time.'

My office isn't much larger than a cubicle would be anywhere else. When Ross reached over and pushed the door shut, I figured he was building up to giving me my dressing-down, but he didn't. Instead, he took another measured sip of coffee.

'So what are you working on these days?' he asked.

This qualified as a disingenuous question of the first water because I was sure Ross Alan Connors knew *exactly* what each of his special investigators was working on. I decided to go with the flow.

'The missing persons thing,' I answered.

Harry I. Ball, with his usual flair for understatement, had shortened the handle to MPT, and MPT was definitely Ross Connors's own personal baby. In most jurisdictions, missing persons reports could just as well go into the round file to begin with. The reports come in and they go away almost immediately. Unless the missing person in question is a little kid or a good-looking babe who catches some media attention, nothing much happens. Most agencies don't have the time, money, resources, or inclination to follow up on them.

It had finally dawned on Ross, however, that it

18

was time for a systematic review of missing persons reports from all over the state. He had embarked on a program that included making the effort of tracking down and interviewing surviving family members, inputting all relevant information from Washington State's missing persons reports into a national database, and comparing our list to any nationwide reports of unidentified remains. This was all done in the hope and expectation that closing some of our missing persons cases would also help close some unsolved homicides. So far the results were disappointing.

For the past two months, from as soon as I came back from medical leave, that's what I had been doing — combing missing persons reports, entering the information into national and statewide databases, and seeing what came out the other end. For the most part it was dull, unrewarding work that could have been done by a well-trained clerk, but if the A.G. wanted full-grade investigators working the program, who was I to argue?

'How's that going?' Ross asked.

'It's a lot like looking for two halves of the same needle in several different haystacks,' I told him.

'No hits yet?'

'A few. I've found three where the people had turned back up, but, for one reason or another, never did get taken off the missing persons list. This afternoon I have an interview scheduled with a woman named DeAnn Cosgrove whose father went missing back in 1980.'

19

'Twenty-five years,' Ross mused. 'That's a long time.'

'That's what she said when I called her about it. Why bring it up now? I told her I had to — it was my job.'

Ross smiled and nodded. He didn't seem to be in any hurry, but I was ready for the other shoe to drop.

'So how are things between you and Seattle PD these days?' he asked.

This was not the shoe I expected. 'Seattle PD?' I asked stupidly.

Ross grinned. 'You know. Remember the place you worked for twenty-odd years?'

His 'how are things' inquiry should have been easy to answer, but it wasn't. Yes, I had worked in Seattle PD for a long time, most of it as a homicide detective. All the way along, though, I had rubbed the brass the wrong way, and the reverse had certainly been true. I hadn't liked them much, either. Something to do with my not being considered a 'good team player.' It turned out that working for Ross Connors had proved to be the one notable exception in a career marred by ongoing feuds with many of my commanding officers.

'So-so,' I said. 'Things improved a little after Mel Soames and I pulled Paul Kramer's fat out of the fire.'

Kramer was the brownnosing, ambitious jerk who had been a thorn in my side from the moment he first stepped foot in Homicide. His, in my opinion, undeserved promotion to captain had been the final straw in the whole series of

20

unfortunate events that had driven me off the force.

Months earlier, his singularly stupid episode of tombstone courage — of going into a dangerous situation without waiting for backup — had almost cost him his life, would have cost him his life if Mel and I hadn't ridden to the rescue at just the right moment. And, of course, that was the very reason he had done it in the first place. He had realized that we were following the same trail he was. In his eagerness to beat us to the punch and gain all the credit, he had committed an almost fatal error.

'Good,' Ross said. 'Glad to hear it, because we seem to have a little problem, and you may be able to help.'

So he wasn't here about Mel and me after all. I breathed what I hoped was an inaudible sigh of relief. 'What kind of problem?' I asked.

'Does the name LaShawn Tompkins mean anything to you?'

It took a minute but then I remembered. LaShawn was a hotshot, tough-guy gangbanger who had gone to prison years earlier for the rape and murder of a teenage prostitute. I recalled that some time in the last year or so, after sitting on death row for years, he had been exonerated through newly examined DNA evidence. After his release, the state had declined to retry him. Tompkins's release had been a huge media event, and his subsequent wrongful-imprisonment settlement had caused a storm of controversy that was now the centerpiece of what looked to be a knock-down, drag-out battle in the upcoming

21

campaign to elect a new King County prosecutor.

I nodded. 'Isn't that the guy the do-gooders managed to spring from death row last year?'

'The very one,' Ross agreed.

'What about him?'

'Someone shot the shit out of him last Friday evening,' Ross said. 'Plugged him twice, once in the stomach and once in the heart when he opened his mother's front door over in the Rainier Valley.'

That didn't sound so unusual to me. In fact, it's pretty much same old, same old. A guy gets out of prison, comes back, tries to go back to doing whatever he did before he went to the slammer. He soon finds out that times have changed. New thugs have taken over his old territory and his old contacts, and they don't like him encroaching on what they now regard as theirs.

'Turf war?' I asked.

'Maybe,' Ross said. 'Maybe not. That's what I'd like you to find out for me.'

'Why?' I said.

For the first time since he'd sat down in my office, Ross looked uncomfortable. 'I really can't say,' he said. 'Or rather, I won't. Not at this time. And given the fact that there have been leaks in my office before . . .'

I nodded. We both knew too much about those.

'I'm not about to put anything in writing,' he continued. 'Not in an e-mail. Not in a letter. Not in anything official. At this point it's strictly an informal inquiry.'

I wanted to ask how come, but I thought better of it. Ross gave me an answer anyway — a partial answer.

'It may be nothing at all. Then again, it could be a big deal,' he added. 'Until I have a better handle on what's going on, I don't want to leave any kind of a paper trail.'

It was more of an answer than I probably deserved. It was also as much information as I was likely to receive. 'Got it,' I said. 'I'll see what I can do. So this is under the radar?'

'Yes. Absolutely.'

'Can I use your name?'

'Let me know first.'

'Reports?'

'Nothing written,' he said. 'Nothing that goes through channels and across desks. I've cleared it with Harry, so he knows you're on special assignment. I'll check with you off and on in the next few days and see how it's going.'

For the first time I wondered if LaShawn Tompkins's murder didn't have something to do with whether Ross Alan Connors himself would stand for reelection.

'So I'm your secret agent man?' I asked.

Ross nodded. 'For the time being. I've got a good crew of people here,' he added. 'All of them are hand-picked, and all of them trustworthy, but you and I have a history, Beau. I'm counting on your discretion in this matter.'

'Okey-dokey,' I said. 'You want discretion, you've got discretion.'

'Thanks,' he said. 'And that includes your

special friend, by the way,' he added as he rose to his feet.

It was a long way from what I had expected and deserved, but it was clear Ross knew all about Mel and me, and now I knew he knew. And not telling Mel about what he had asked me to do would put me between a rock and a hard place.

Ross pulled the door open. As he stepped into the corridor, he turned and looked back at me. 'Life goes on, doesn't it,' he said.

That throwaway comment covered a lot of territory. Ross Alan Connors and J. P. Beaumont did have a history, one that included the pain of losing wives to suicide. This was the second time now that Ross had come to me personally when he needed something handled under the radar. In the world of SHIT, I was indeed Ross's secret agent man. He had just given me the handshake.

'Yes,' I agreed. 'Yes, it does.'

2

For a long time after Ross Connors left my office, I sat there and contemplated what it all might mean. Obviously, by limiting the scope of the investigation into LaShawn Tompkins's death to one officer and by disallowing any kind of a paper trail, the A.G. seemed to be looking for a certain amount of deniability with regard to whatever his interest might be in the homicide of a now-exonerated killer. I also gave some careful thought to what I would tell Mel when she got around to asking, as she inevitably would, what the hell was going on.

It happened at lunchtime as we were driving through rain-washed sunshine to the Men's Wearhouse in downtown Bellevue. 'So what did Ross Connors want?' she asked. 'Barbara told me the two of you were in your office for a closed-door meeting for a very long time.'

We were in the BMW and she was driving, so she wasn't looking at my face when I answered. There's a good reason I don't play poker. My face is always a dead giveaway of whatever's in my hand.

'Just chewing the fat,' I said casually. 'I don't think he's ever gotten over what happened to Francine.'

'His wife?' Mel asked, shooting me a questioning look.

All that had happened before Melissa Soames

had turned up at SHIT. I nodded, hoping she'd go back to watching traffic instead of watching me.

'That's understandable,' Mel said. The fact that she swallowed my lie without a moment's hesitation made me feel that much worse.

I had held out some hope that in the process of actually buying the damned tux I'd somehow manage to jar loose a little more information as to the whys and wherefores of my needing one. No such luck. Other than telling the alterations lady that we needed to have the tux in hand by Friday evening, Mel didn't let slip any additional details. By then I was in far too deep to ask.

After my ordeal by tux (the first one I ever purchased as opposed to rented, by the way), we hurried across the street to the California Pizza Kitchen to grab some lunch. Mel knows her way around downtown Bellevue the same way I know my way around downtown Seattle. The place was bright, busy, crowded, and noisy, which suited me just fine. I hoped that Mel would be preoccupied enough with her surroundings that she'd stop giving me the third degree about Ross's special project. Fat chance.

'So what are you up to later?' she asked.

'I have an MPT interview set up for this afternoon,' I said. 'Once that's over, I may end up having to go directly from there into Seattle.'

'So I'm on my own for getting across the water tonight?' she asked.

'Looks like.'

'That's all right,' she said. 'I had forgotten. I have a board meeting tonight. I'd need to bring

26

my car home anyway.'

That's when it finally dawned on me. Mel had been drafted onto the board of SASAC — the Seattle Area Sexual Assault Consortium. (Who makes up these names?) Their annual fund-raising auction was scheduled for Friday night. Since she's on the board, not appearing simply wasn't an option, and that's why I needed the tux. But my relief was short-lived.

'What about Beverly?' Mel prodded. 'Did you call her yet?'

'Not yet, but I will,' I promised.

'If you go see her tonight, be sure to take that picture of Kyle along. I left it on the hallway table with the rest of the mail.'

I was eager to move away from the uncomfortable subject of visiting my grandmother. 'What does your afternoon hold?' I asked.

Mel rolled her very blue eyes. For weeks she'd been working on a county-by-county analysis of violent crime. She'd been complaining about it for that long as well.

'As of this morning,' she said, 'I'm suddenly charged with creating a catalog of violent sex offenders, which is, if you ask me, a long way away from our primary mission.'

'A catalog?' I asked.

She took a bite of her pasta salad and nodded. 'More like a survey,' she answered. 'For the past five years. Ross wants to know where Washington's released sexual offenders have been — where they went once they got out of jail and

27

where they are now. Oh, and he also wants it ASAP.'

Considering Mel's extracurricular activity with SASAC, I could see why Ross Connors had drafted her for that particular job.

'Sounds like fun,' I said.

'Doesn't it just,' she agreed glumly. 'I guess I'll be letting my fingers do the walking.'

We had paid up and were headed toward the door when, over the noise of rattling crockery, I heard someone call, 'Melissa! Oh, Melissa.'

I turned and saw someone — a blonde — waving frantically from a table on the far side of the cashier stand. 'Is that someone you know?'

Mel's face broke into a smile. 'Come on,' she said. 'There's someone I'd like you to meet. It's Anita.'

Mel tends to refer to her friends by first names only. I knew that Anita was somehow related to SASAC, but in that moment I couldn't have remembered how for any amount of money.

Anita Nolastname stood up, held out a diamond-bedecked hand, and proffered a smooth perfumed cheek for an expected kiss. She was upper thirty-something, pencil-thin, and drop-dead gorgeous.

'Why, you must be the unparalleled Beau Beaumont,' the woman said with a smile. 'I'm Anita Bowdin. Mel talks about you all the time, by the way. Says you're wonderful.'

'I wouldn't believe everything I hear,' I told her. When I glanced in Mel's direction I saw she was blushing, and I have to confess that the idea of Mel's talking about me in my absence put a smile on my face.

28

'So you're coming on Friday?' Anita continued.

'Wouldn't miss it,' I said, faking for all I was worth with what I hoped sounded like sincere enthusiasm. 'Got my tux and everything.'

'Good boy,' Anita said. 'See there? You're every bit as wonderful as she says. And you'll be at the board meeting tonight?' she asked, turning to Mel.

'Yes, I will,' Mel answered.

We didn't say anything more until we were back in the BMW.

'So you talk about me when I'm not around?' I asked innocently.

'Don't press your luck, buddy,' Mel returned. 'Wouldn't miss it!' she repeated, mimicking my delivery. 'You're such a liar I'm surprised you weren't struck by lightning.'

'As a matter of fact, so am I,' I said, and we both burst out laughing.

When we arrived back at the office I got into my own car and headed out for my interview with DeAnn Cosgrove.

For years I went along with the self-congratulatory prejudice that causes people who live in downtown Seattle to maintain that the east side of Lake Washington is nothing but a vast residential wasteland. Driving across the lake and becoming instantly and hopelessly lost is a point of honor for some confirmed city dwellers. Now that I work in south Bellevue, however, I'm gradually getting over it. With the help of my newly purchased GPS, I had no difficulty making my way to the residence of

29

DeAnn and Donald Cosgrove on the western edge of Redmond.

The house was one of a number of small neat family homes tucked onto a quiet cul-de-sac. A tiny fenced and well-maintained front yard was graced by a number of plastic vehicles and a small swing set. When I rang the bell it was answered by a woman in her early thirties who carried a relatively new baby on one hip while being trailed by a pair of what looked to be three-year-old twins.

DeAnn Cosgrove had the wan, distracted look of someone suffering through months of sleep deprivation. She wore a long-sleeved denim shirt with distinct traces of baby burp dribbling down one shoulder. Her hair was pulled back in a ragged ponytail. Looking at her reminded me of Kelly. When we'd seen my daughter down in Ashland, she'd looked a lot like that, too — weary beyond words.

'J. P. Beaumont,' I said, holding out my ID. She glanced at it with no particular interest. 'I'm with the Special Homicide Investigation Team,' I added. 'Are you DeAnn Cosgrove?'

'Yes, I am,' she said, nodding. 'Come in. Please excuse the mess.'

She was right. The house was messy — not dirty but cluttered with laundered but unfolded clothes piled two feet deep on the couch, with the dining room table covered by a snarl of papers, and with a minefield of toys littering the carpeted floor. That, too, reminded me of Kelly and Jeremy's place, for many of the same reasons. Taking care of kids doesn't leave a lot of

30

excess time for anything else, most especially housekeeping.

'I meant to shower and have this all picked up before you got here, but . . . ' she began.

'Don't worry about it,' I assured her. 'I just came back from visiting my daughter and son-in-law down in Ashland. They have small kids, too.'

DeAnn gave me a sincere but haggard smile and then swiped an easy chair free of plastic toys so I could sit down. Then she settled into a rocker. Without practiced aplomb, she unbuttoned her blouse, covered herself with a tea towel, undid her bra, and began nursing the baby. She accomplished this while at the same time trying to cajole the twins — two impish little boys — into picking up their toys and putting them in a nearby toy box.

'So what's this about my dad?' she asked.

I glanced at the name on the folder I was carrying. The missing person's report for Anthony David Cosgrove had been filed by someone named Carol Cosgrove on May 19,1980. DeAnn, the daughter, had been listed on the form by name.

'Who's Donald, then?' I asked. 'Your brother?'

DeAnn shook her head. 'No,' she said. 'Donnie's my husband. Cosgrove's my maiden name. When Donnie and I were getting married, I told him I wanted to keep my name just in case Daddy ever showed up and came looking for me. Luckily for me, Donnie's a really practical guy. He said it made no sense to have more than one name in our family, so he changed his name to mine. His dad didn't like the idea very much, but Donnie said he was marrying me, not his father.'

It was clear that almost twenty-five years later, DeAnn Cosgrove was still grieving for her absent father and hoping against hope that someday he would return. That kernel of knowledge was enough to break my heart. It put a personal human spin on an assignment that had been, up to that point, nothing but a list of names.

'Sounds like your husband's got a good head on his shoulders,' I said.

An odd expression flitted across DeAnn's face. 'Yes,' she agreed finally. 'Yes, he does. But you still haven't told me. What's this about? Why are you asking questions about Dad after so many years?'

'It turns out there are literally hundreds of unresolved missing persons cases in this state that have gotten zero attention . . . '

'Tell me about it,' she said.

'I work for the Washington State attorney general, Ross Connors. He's asked my agency, the Special Homicide Investigation Team, to go through those cases and see if by cross-checking we can bring some of them to a close.'

'I've heard about cases like that,' DeAnn offered. 'Cold cases where they eventually figure out that an unidentified body somewhere else is someone who's been missing for a long time.'

'Yes, so if you don't mind . . . '

But I didn't even finish asking the question before DeAnn Cosgrove launched into her story. 'It happened the day Mount Saint Helens blew up,' she said at once. 'Daddy went fishing that weekend and never came home.'

The day Mount Saint Helens blew up. If you lived in Washington State or even anywhere in the Pacific Northwest at the time, those words conjure a day you remember — a beautifully clear Sunday morning in late spring when the mountain — one some Native Americans referred to as 'Louwala Clough,' or Smoking Mountain — suddenly roared back to life after being quiet for 123 years. The initial blast caused a huge avalanche and sent up an immense over-heated cloud of three-hundred-degree pumice and ash that killed every living thing inside a two-hundred-square-mile area.

'So your father was one of the fifty or so people who died?' I asked.

'The actual number was fifty-seven,' she said. 'Daddy wasn't ever counted in that official number because they never found any trace of him — no sign of him or his vehicle. But Mount Saint Helens is where he had told my mother he was going that weekend — he said he was going fishing on Spirit Lake.'

I had gone camping on the edge of that pristine lake myself years ago — long before the mountain blew up. In advance of the actual eruption — between the time of the first sizable earthquake underneath the mountain in March and when the first big eruption happened on the eighteenth of May — I remembered reading about a curmudgeonly old guy — memorably named Harry Truman — who had told interviewers that if the mountain ever exploded, he'd just go out on the lake in his boat and wait it out. There was only one problem with Mr. Truman's plan — the lake was vaporized in that initial explosion, and so was he.

It seemed likely to me now that if Anthony David Cosgrove had been anywhere near Spirit Lake at the time, he had most likely met a similar fate. But I remembered, too, that investigators had found traces of many of the human tragedies left behind in the volcano's aftermath. Etched in my memory were images of eerie shells of burned-out vehicles still smoldering in the devastated wilderness and testifying to the fact that for the people trapped inside those vehicles, there had been no escape.

In the decades since then, though, Mount Saint Helens and the surrounding area have been subjected to an almost microscopic examination as scientists study both what happened back then and what's happening now. The area where millions of board feet of timber were felled in one cataclysmic blast is now an ongoing laboratory of Mother Nature at work, reclaiming that which she has previously destroyed.

With that in mind, it seemed strange to me that no fragment of Anthony Cosgrove's vehicle had ever been found. Still, there was always an outside chance that something had surfaced and no one had bothered to notify his daughter. Bureaucracies are notoriously dim when it comes to taking the feelings of individuals into consideration.

By then the baby seemed to have fallen asleep.

She held him to her shoulder, burped him, and then went to put him down somewhere out of sight. The process made me wonder a little. I knew that Kelly had nursed Kayla when she was a baby. Kyle, on the other hand, seemed to be a bottle baby. When we had been down in Ashland, I had noticed this and wondered about it, but there are things fathers can ask and things they can't. This was one of the latter.

When DeAnn returned to the living room, she brought with her a small gold-framed photo of a young man wearing a vintage 1970s hairdo and equally dated horn-rimmed glasses. Grinning goofily for the camera, he held a tiny, red-faced, wrinkly baby — held her awkwardly and carefully, as though he was concerned she might break.

It was one of those standard set-piece types of photos that are part of most families. They're usually trite, poorly lit, and unoriginal, but they're wonderful all the same. They testify to the fact that no matter what may happen later — death or divorce, midnight arrests for shoplifting or wrecked first cars — at that point in time, that newly arrived child was a joyfully welcomed addition to his or her family.

'Your dad?' I asked, handing the photo back to DeAnn.

'Yes,' she said. 'It's the only one I have. After he was gone, Mom went through the house and got rid of most of his pictures. This is one my grandmother happened to have.'

She put the treasured photo up on the mantel, settled cross-legged on the floor, and then

35

gathered her rambunctious twins to her as if finding solace in their wiggly presence. Having corralled their toys into the toy box, spurred on by an amazing combination of motherly prodding and patience, they now cuddled up next to their mother on the carpeted floor. With their heads in her lap and their feet sticking out in opposite directions, they gradually settled down. One of them clutched the tattered corner of a faded yellow blanket while the other industriously sucked his thumb.

Waiting for them to drift off, I tried to remember if Scott and Kelly used to do that when they were little — just fall over and go to sleep like that, regardless of where they were or what was going on — but I didn't have a single memory I could focus in on. At the time, I wasn't that kind of a father. Driven, intent on earning enough money to support them and also intent on drinking too much, I had recklessly squandered my own children's childhoods. It's something I've come to regret every day of my life.

'How old were you when it happened?' I asked.

'When my father went missing? I was eight,' DeAnn answered. 'Old enough to be scared. It was bad enough that my father had disappeared into that awful place and didn't come back. I saw all those terrible pictures on TV. I kept worrying that if one mountain could blow up like that, maybe the others would, too. I mean, we were living in Kent back then. Whenever the sun was shining, Mount Rainier was right there with us.

At least, that's how it seemed.'

Karen and I had been living down by Lake Tapps when the mountain blew. It had felt the same way to me, too. If God decided to send an overheated avalanche of rock and ash roaring down a mountainside at 150 miles per hour, Mount Rainier was way too close for comfort. It didn't seem as if there would be nearly enough time to get out of the way.

'Since they never found any sign of him, I assume your father stayed on the missing list — permanently.'

DeAnn nodded again. 'That's right. I've always thought it would have been easier for me if we'd at least found something of him to bury. Maybe then I could have gotten over it and moved on. My mother did. She was impatient. She didn't bother waiting around seven years to have him declared dead. She divorced him, remarried, and made a whole new life for herself, but I just couldn't. They did declare him dead eventually, but it didn't change anything.'

She paused while tears welled in her eyes. She pursed her lips. 'He called me his princess,' she added brokenly, all the while struggling to control her emotions. 'He said that one day I'd be carried away by a prince on a white horse. My mother told me Dad was just being silly and making those things up. Donnie's a lot like him. Tells the kids stories. And he's an engineer, too. No pocket protector, though.'

Until right then I had been doing the job Ross Connors asked me to do, but I don't think I had really believed in it. As far as I and the rest of the

SHIT squad were concerned, Ross Connors's 'missing persons thing' had us off on a harebrained tangent that didn't make a whole lot of sense and wasn't worth either our time or our energy. But in talking to DeAnn Cosgrove I could see that the effort was making sense to her.

'So what happened after the report was filed?' I asked.

DeAnn shrugged. 'Not much,' she said. 'At least not as far as I was concerned. Everyone was too worried about the volcano and what was going on with that. But somebody finally came to the house and told my mother that it was hopeless — that my father wasn't ever coming home and she should just give up on it. And so she did. We had a little memorial service because like I said, there wasn't anything to bury.'

I could envision DeAnn Cosgrove as a brokenhearted little girl, lost and grieving, while the grown-ups around her, preoccupied with their own difficulties, walked away from hers and moved on.

'But you didn't give up, did you.'

'No,' DeAnn agreed. 'Never. I loved him too much. I couldn't.'

And you still haven't, I thought.

'I miss him every single day,' DeAnn added. 'I wish he could meet his grandkids — so he could tell them the same kinds of stories he used to tell me. I wouldn't tell him they were silly, though. I'd want them to believe everything he said.'

'Where's your mother these days?' I asked.

'Once my father was declared dead and the insurance money finally came through, she and

Jack, her new husband, bought a place up in Leavenworth,' she said. 'Just outside Leavenworth,' she added. 'I guess I shouldn't call Jack a new husband. He's been around for a long time. They celebrate their twenty-fifth anniversary next year. That's fifteen years longer than she was married to Daddy.'

So Mrs. Cosgrove hadn't spent much time waiting around for her missing husband to show up or playing the grieving widow. If they'd finally gone to the formality of having her former husband officially declared dead, it seemed to me as though someone in the world of officialdom should have noticed the transaction and removed Anthony Cosgrove's name from the list of officially missing persons.

DeAnn apparently read my mind about her mother's unseemly matrimonial haste. 'Mom and Jack got married in January of the following year,' she said. 'I don't like the man much — never have. He's an overbearing jerk. And we had our issues, especially when I was a teenager. That's why I ended up living with my grandmother — my father's mother — down in Kent most of the time I was in high school. But by then there was money coming in from Social Security, so it didn't seem like I was a burden.'

'But you said there was insurance?'

DeAnn nodded. 'Quite a bit,' she said. 'Some of it was group insurance and the rest of it was stuff Daddy owned. There was one smaller policy that was just for me. Donnie and I used that to make the down payment on this house.'

Insurance proceeds are often the motivator in

39

homicide cases, but not in this one. A payout accompanied by a seven-year delay seemed unlikely, but it was still worth checking into.

'What's your mother's name?' I asked.

'Lawrence,' DeAnn answered. 'Carol Lawrence. And her husband is Jack. Like I said, they live up in Leavenworth now. If you want to talk to them, I can get you the phone number, but I don't see that it'll do much good. I doubt they could tell you any more about what happened than I can.'

I made a note of their names anyway. I didn't bother taking down the phone number. I knew if I needed to reach them I'd be able to locate Jack and Carol Lawrence's phone number — listed or not.

I was about to put my notebook away, but then I looked at DeAnn Cosgrove and could see she wasn't done talking. Maybe after years of not talking about it, she was ready.

'Anything else you can tell me about your dad?' I asked.

'I was always surprised that he went fishing that weekend,' she said. 'As far as I know, he hadn't ever gone before. He didn't even like fish that much. What he liked were airplanes. He loved airplanes.'

'You mean as a hobby?'

'As in every way. That's what he did, you see. He worked for Boeing, too, designing airplanes. I'm not really sure what he did there. I wish now I'd been older so I could have known which planes he worked on and what he did. Maybe I've ridden on one of the ones he helped design.'

'You probably have,' I said.

'I hope so,' she replied. I put the notebook in my jacket pocket. 'So what happens now?' she asked.

'I'm not sure,' I said. 'I may check with the people down at Mount Saint Helens and make sure that they haven't learned something we don't know about. And I may want to speak to your mother as well. What about your grandmother, the one who lived in Kent?'

'Grandma died last year,' DeAnn said. 'Daddy was her only son, just like I'm my father's only child. That's the other reason I'm glad we kept my name. Grandma made me promise that I'd keep her ashes so that if they ever found my father, he and she could be buried together. She's out in the garage,' she added. 'Up in the rafters.'

When I stood up to go, DeAnn expertly eased the two sleeping kiddos off her lap without disturbing either one of them. Then she rose from the floor with an easy grace that my gimpy knees could never have tolerated.

'Thanks,' she said as she showed me to the door. 'And please tell your boss thank you for me, too. It means a lot to know that someone still cares about my father after all this time — that someone's still looking for him. It means more than you know.'

The last thing I did before I left was to hand her a business card. 'This is how you can reach me,' I said, jotting my cell number on the back. 'That way, if you happen to think of something you may have forgotten . . . '

'Okay,' she said, stuffing it into the pocket of

her jeans. 'Thanks.'

As I walked back to the Mercedes parked just outside the small front yard with its plastic Big Wheels and swings, I had a whole new idea about that daunting list of missing persons. Every single one of them had left behind family members for whom life had gone on. There were children and grandchildren who had never seen those missing people. There were parents who had died with their child still lost to them. And there were spouses who had been forced to move forward on their own, making the best of the hand they'd been dealt.

Everybody at SHIT had sneered when Ross had announced his missing persons directive, but having met DeAnn Cosgrove and witnessed her pain, I could see that this was a situation where the attorney general was right and everybody else was wrong.

3

After leaving DeAnn Cosgrove's place in Redmond I started back to Seattle and then thought better of it. Since I was going to be approaching the LaShawn Tompkins situation pretty much without portfolio, I needed to track down whatever information was out in public — as in the news media. Since Mel and I had been gone all weekend, whatever had been on local television or radio news had passed me by. As for newspapers? That's another story.

In the old days, I never subscribed to one. I bummed them, used, in restaurants and coffee shops so I could work the crossword puzzles, but as far as having one show up outside my door on a regular basis? Never. Until Mel Soames turned up in my life, that is.

She's a news junkie. She listens, watches, and reads. I finally got tired of her griping about not having a morning paper. When I said fine, let's have one, then, she went ahead and ordered two — both the *Seattle Post-Intelligencer* and the *Seattle Times*. (Give the girl an inch and she thinks she's a ruler.)

We are, however, newspaper-compatible and divide our consumption into two separate but unequal parts. I own the crosswords; she reads everything else. If she came home and discovered I had been scrounging through her dead newspaper collection for actual news, she

43

would know at once that something was up. Instead, I stopped off at the Starbucks on Rose Hill, bought myself a latte, settled into one of the easy chairs, and logged on to the Internet to read the weekend newspapers online.

LaShawn Tompkins's murder had indeed been big news over the weekend. Not so much on Saturday when the victim's name had yet to be released and the death had been reported simply as a shooting in Rainier Valley. No biggie there. But by Sunday, word was out. In the Sunday paper, which is still supposedly a joint endeavor by the staffs of both the *Times* and the *P-I*, there were three separate stories, all viewable on the virtual front page — one about the murder itself, one rehashing the flawed case that had sent LaShawn to prison years earlier, and a third under the byline of my old nemesis, columnist Maxwell Cole.

Max and I have never been friends. A very long time ago, however, we were fraternity brothers when we were both students at the University of Washington, known locally as the U. Dub. Everything was fine until he showed up at a mixer with a cute blond girl named Karen Moffitt. Much to Max's dismay, Karen and I hit it off immediately, and eventually we ended up getting married. Years passed. Karen and I eventually divorced and she subsequently died, but Max has never gotten over the fact that I stole her away from him in the first place. I think his long-running feud with anyone and everyone at Seattle PD is

44

symptomatic of his long-running feud with me. But then maybe I'm suffering from delusions of grandeur on that score.

Naturally, I harbor no ill will at all about any of this. Right. Of course not. Which is why I read Max's piece first. It was prominently placed, right there below the virtual fold.

LaShawn Tompkins: 1975–2005
A life transformed; a life destroyed

by MAXWELL COLE
Special to the *Times*

LaShawn Tompkins was nineteen years old when he was arrested and charged with the brutal rape and murder of a fifteen-year-old prostitute named Aleta Princess Jones. He was twenty-one when he was convicted of aggravated first-degree homicide and sentenced to death. He was twenty-eight when DNA analysis of the evidence in that flawed case caused him to be released from his cell on death row with no new charges filed against him. Now, at age thirty, he's dead, gunned down execution-style in the doorway of his mother's Rainier Valley home.

I've always been amazed how Max can dredge up yesterday's news and turn it into fodder for one of his bleeding-heart columns for which someone actually pays him money. I could tell from the opening paragraph this one would be no exception.

45

As a child, LaShawn was a bright student who got good grades and a series of Sunday school perfect-attendance records from his neighborhood church, the African Bible Baptist Church. By junior high, though, Sunday school was a thing of the past. He was running with the wrong crowd — a much older crowd — that automatically put him on the wrong side of the law. By fifteen, he had dropped out of school, had several juvenile offenses on his record, and was on the fast track as an up-and-coming lieutenant in the local Crips organization. From there it was only a short hop and a skip to death row.

Yes, Sunday school kiddo goes bad. Yadda, yadda, yadda. Had I been reading a hard copy of the story, I would have been tempted to wad up the newspaper and pitch it across the room. There was no way, however, I was going to throw my laptop, so I gritted my teeth and kept reading.

'Despite being convicted of a crime he didn't commit, LaShawn used the time in prison to turn his life around completely,' says Mark Granger, executive director and pastor of the King Street Mission where Tompkins had worked as a counselor since his release from Walla Walla two years ago.
    'After being wrongly convicted, he could easily have become hardened and bitter. Prison, especially a death row existence,

46

tends to do that. Instead, LaShawn devoted his life to Christ and to helping those he considered less fortunate than himself.'

Yes, and the crippled shall walk and the blind shall see, I thought. So which one of those 'less fortunates' plugged him full of lead?

It was his wrongful conviction in the death of fifteen-year-old murder victim Aleta Jones that put LaShawn Tompkins on death row. According to Philippa Jones, Aleta's mother, LaShawn had, in the years since his release, gone out of his way to befriend her and other members of Aleta's family.

'Two months ago, on the anniversary of her death, we held a prayer vigil in my daughter's honor. LaShawn was right there with us the whole night,' Ms. Jones said. 'I'm sorry he got sent to prison for something he didn't do, and I'm real sorry he's dead. He was a good man.'

That's why detectives investigating Tompkins's apparent homicide are so puzzled by his violent death last Friday. 'As far as we've been able to learn, Mr. Tompkins has had zero involvement in criminal activity since his release from prison,' says one Seattle homicide detective close to the case who wished to remain anonymous.

That last comment caught my attention. I wondered which Seattle PD detective Maxwell Cole had managed to cozy up to and co-opt now. The people at Media Relations are the ones who are supposed to talk to reporters. Homicide detectives, even anonymous ones, are expected to keep their mouths firmly shut.

Tompkins had come to his elderly mother's home on Friday, as he did twice every day, morning and evening, to check on her, to help dispense her medications, and to prepare her meals. There was no sign of forced entry. Indications are that Mr. Tompkins willingly opened the door that allowed his killer access to the home.

'Shawny went out into the kitchen to heat up my Meals-on-Wheels mac and cheese,' said the victim's bereaved mother, Etta Mae Tompkins. 'The next thing I know he was lying there on the floor by my front door with blood everywhere. He was such a good boy, and he was doing the Lord's work. The only good thing about this is that I know my son was saved and he's gone home to Jesus.'

Ms. Tompkins may be sustained by faith in this difficult time, but the same can't be said for many of her Rainier Valley neighbors, who fear some new killer now stalking their streets.

Ms. Janie Griswold, who has lived next door to Etta Mae Tompkins for the past twenty-five years, is very disturbed by what happened last Friday. 'It's one thing for drug dealers to go around killing other drug dealers,' she said. 'But when they can walk right up to someone's front door and just start blasting away, it's scary.'

Attorney Amy Duckworth, who now works for Gavin, Gavin, and Plane, a Bellevue area law firm, was one of a number of students who worked on LaShawn Tompkins's case as part of the Innocence Project, an organization devoted to post-conviction examination of DNA evidence. It was their efforts that revealed Mr. Tompkins had been wrongly accused and wrongly convicted.

'I was there in Walla Walla the day LaShawn walked out of prison,' a tearful Ms. Duckworth said in a telephone interview. 'It was so inspiring. He just hugged me and thanked me for everything we had done. He was glad to have a second chance. We all put so much work and effort into this, and now to have him end up murdered is a real tragedy.'

He probably had plenty of second chances, I thought. *This one turned out to be his last second chance.*

And so, while friends and coworkers grieve over the death of LaShawn Tompkins and while investigators try to piece together what happened, plans are moving forward on funeral services that are expected to be held sometime later this week — most likely at the King Street Mission where he worked.

To have a young life redeemed and then

so senselessly lost is, I believe, a peculiarly American tragedy.

I was about to go on to the next article when my cell phone rang. As soon as I saw the Queen Anne Gardens number on the readout, my heart fell. Lars Jenssen is an old-fashioned kind of guy. He doesn't like cell phones, and I knew he would call me on mine during work hours only as a last resort and for the worst possible reason.

'It's Beverly,' he said.

'How bad?' I asked.

'*Ja*, sure,' Lars answered. 'It's pretty bad. I hated to call and worry you, but I t'ink you should probably come now.'

Lars is an old Norwegian, a retired halibut fisherman, whose accent gets markedly worse the moment he comes in contact with a telephone.

'I'm on my way,' I said. 'I'll be there as soon as I can.'

Driving down 405, I called Mel at work and told her what was going on. 'I'll let everyone here know,' she said. 'If you want me to, I'll drop everything and meet you there.'

'No,' I said. 'That's all right. I'm okay.'

Which wasn't exactly true. This was hitting me very hard. Beverly Jenssen was my last surviving elder. She and my grandfather had been estranged from my mother and me for many years both while I was growing up and long into adulthood. My grandfather, a man of unbending principles and scant human kindness, had thoroughly disapproved of the fact that my mother had not only gotten herself pregnant

50

outside the bonds of holy matrimony but had also adamantly refused to 'do the right thing' and give me up for adoption. It was only in the past ten years or so — and long after my mother's death — that I had established a connection with them at a time when my hard-nosed grandfather had been on his last legs.

It was then, after all those years, that I had learned how my grandmother, forbidden by her husband to have any contact with either my mother or me, had faithfully followed as many of my exploits as she could. She had kept voluminous scrapbooks that included clippings of everything to do with J. P. Beaumont. Some had been as early as Cub Scout endeavors. They included high school athletic competitions and later news mentions drawn from my long career at Seattle PD. There had been copies of Scott's and Kelly's newspaper birth announcements as well as a mention of Karen's and my divorce proceedings. Wifely duty had kept Beverly from contacting me against her husband's wishes, but seeing those secret scrapbooks, ones my grandfather had known nothing about, had told me everything I needed to know about Beverly Beaumont's selfless love and constancy.

And then she met Lars. That had been an incredible bonus for all of us. Widowed by then, Beverly had come to help out at the memorial service for my late partner, Sue Danielson. Somehow my grandmother and Lars, my AA sponsor, ended up doing dishes together in the party-room kitchen at Belltown Terrace and had hit it off. They had married within months of meeting, and everything had been fine. Until now.

At Queen Anne Gardens I parked in the visitors' lot and then signed in. 'She's not in their apartment, you know,' the desk clerk told me. 'She's been moved to our Care Center.'

Euphemistically speaking, Care Center was assisted living code for ICU. I thought they should have called it IWU — intensive waiting unit. There were two beds in the room, but only one was occupied. Lars, leaning on his cane and staring off into space, was seated next to Beverly. When he saw me he smiled and made an effort to rise.

'Sit,' I told him. 'What's happening?'

He shrugged and sank back down. 'She's sleeping now,' he said. 'But she was asking for you earlier. That's why I called.'

I looked at Beverly sleeping. I had never before seen her without her false teeth. That alone made her seem less dignified and far frailer. Somehow she appeared to be much smaller than I remembered, even though I had seen her only a few days earlier, shortly before Mel and I left for Ashland. At the time she had still been in their apartment. There she'd had Lars to see to it that she got wheeled back and forth to the dining room and to make sure she was eating. I doubted she was taking much nourishment now.

'Is she in any pain?' I asked.

'No,' he said. 'She's yust tired. We both are.'

A glance at Lars's weathered face told me that was true. His eyes were red-rimmed and watery.

'We had some good times,' he added. 'But she's ready to move on.'

I looked around the room. There was no heart monitor. No oxygen equipment. 'Isn't there something we should do? Some treatment? Something?'

Lars shook his head and gestured toward the bright yellow DO NOT RESUSCITATE placard that had been affixed to the door. 'No.' he said. 'There's nothing. She yust needs to rest a little.'

'And so do you,' I said. 'I'm here now. Why don't you go take a nap?'

I was surprised by his ready agreement. '*Ja*, sure,' he said, getting shakily to his feet. 'I t'ink you're right.'

Left alone in the room with Beverly, I sat there for a long time simply watching her sleep. She seemed serene, untroubled, and unafraid. Leaving her asleep, I went out into the corridor and placed the necessary calls, telling Scott and Kelly what was going on. They both wanted to know if they should drop everything and come home.

'I don't think so,' I said. 'When I figure it out, I'll let you know.'

'Have you talked to her doctor?' Kelly demanded. How my daughter somehow had transformed herself from a headstrong, dippy teenager into an amazingly practical adult is one of the mysteries of the universe, and it never fails to surprise me.

'Not yet,' I told her. 'But I will.'

Ten minutes after I finished giving the news to my son Scott, my cell phone rang. 'Sorry about this,' Dave Livingston said. 'Anything I can do?'

Dave is my first wife's second husband — Karen's official widower. He's also my children's stepfather. I suspected that Kelly was the one who had seen fit to call him and let him know, but it could just as easily have been Scott. Dave is a likable guy and both my kids look up to him. Either way, I was glad someone had notified Dave, and I was touched that he had gone to the trouble of calling.

'No,' I said. 'For right now, I guess it's just a matter of waiting.'

'Waiting's tough,' he said. I understood without anything more being said that the man knew whereof he spoke.

Back in Beverly's room I castigated myself for not stopping by Belltown Terrace on the way and picking up Kyle's picture. Not that it would have made any difference. She was asleep, and I doubted if she would ever waken enough to see the framed photo Kelly had wanted Beverly to have.

My grandmother had been a young bride when she had my mother, and my mother had been a very young not-bride when I was born. And so at a time when other men my age were losing their mothers, my mother, who had died young, was already gone, and I was losing my grandmother instead.

I sat there for the rest of the long afternoon listening to Beverly breathe, thinking about the few short years we'd had together, and regretting the many years we'd spent apart. I was glad for the happy times she and Lars had shared and felt sad when I realized how much it would hurt for him to lose a second well-loved wife.

In his day, Lars had been a serious drinker (that's why he was my AA sponsor, after all). He had loved his first wife, Hannah, but I knew from things he'd told me over the years that he'd also neglected her — the way alcoholics often do, not out of any particular malice but because nothing's more important to them than booze. Lars had done much better by Beverly, and losing her would be hard on him. I wondered, in fact, if he'd survive it.

Lars came limping back into the room and resumed his bedside watch about the time the sun went down behind the grain terminal out in Elliott Bay. The sky was layered with banks of clouds that turned pink, purple, and finally gray as the setting sun sank beneath the western horizon. I went down the hall to the nurse's station and brought back a second chair.

'No matter what,' Lars said quietly, 'I wouldn't have missed this.'

I nodded. That's always the bottom line where love is concerned. Is loving someone ever worth the ultimate price of losing them?

'And she's very proud of you, Beau,' Lars added. 'Always has been.'

That got me. 'I know,' I said, blinking back tears.

Mel turned up about then, bringing with her Kyle's missing photo. I was grateful she had gone to the trouble in the few spare minutes she had between the end of work and the start of her evening board meeting. After showing Kyle's photo to Lars, who was suitably unimpressed, I placed the small framed photo on the nightstand next to Beverly's glass and water pitcher. Mel was smart enough not to ask how I was doing or how long I'd be because I had no idea.

I badgered Lars into going down to the dining room for some dinner just before they closed. He offered to take me along, but I wasn't hungry. He had barely left the room when Beverly's eyes popped open. She looked first at the chair Lars had just vacated, then gazed anxiously around the room.

'It's all right,' I assured her. 'He went downstairs for some dinner.'

'Oh,' she said.

Then she mumbled something I couldn't make out. For a moment I wondered if she even knew who I was. When I asked her to repeat what she'd said, she opened her eyes and looked at me impatiently.

'Where's Mel?' she demanded.

That was clear enough. It left no doubt about whether she recognized me, and it told me plainly enough that my grandmother was in full possession of her faculties.

'Mel had to go to a meeting,' I said. 'She'll be back later.'

'Lars said you were on a trip,' Beverly mumbled a few seconds later. 'Did you marry her?'

So that was it. Beverly had evidently decided that Mel's and my trip to Ashland had been something it wasn't.

'No,' I said. 'We drove down to Ashland to see Kelly and Jeremy and their new baby . . . ' I reached for the photo to show Beverly her new great-great-grandson. Ignoring Kyle, Beverly stared directly into my face.

'Marry her,' she commanded forcefully. 'Mel's a good girl, and she's good for you. Don't let her slip away.'

That single fragment of forceful and lucid conversation seemed to sap all Beverly's strength and energy. She soon drifted off to sleep once more and was still asleep when Lars returned from the dining room.

'How is she?' he asked.

'Still sleeping,' I said. Somehow I didn't mention to him what she had said earlier. I didn't say anything then and I didn't later as the night wore on and Beverly's breathing grew more and more shallow. I didn't want to admit to Lars that she'd roused herself long enough to give me one last set of marching orders. And I didn't want him to know that, in what might well be her last waking moments, Beverly had been thinking about me rather than him.

By midnight it was over and she was gone. I stayed with Lars long enough to see him settled in the apartment he and Beverly had shared. By the time I left Queen Anne Gardens the clouds had returned and it was raining again. A little past one, I let myself into the condo at Belltown Terrace. Mel, with her feet tucked under her, was curled up in my recliner, sound asleep. I stood there for a long moment or two watching her — stunned by how amazingly beautiful she was and wondering how much time we might have to be together, or if we even should. Finally

I reached out and touched her gently on the shoulder. She awakened instantly.

Mel searched my face and read what was written there. 'Beverly's gone, then?' Mel asked.

I nodded.

'I'm sorry,' she said.

'So am I,' I agreed. 'Sorrier than I would have thought possible. Let's go to bed.'

4

When Mel woke me up in the morning it was with a cup of coffee and a goodbye kiss. She was almost dressed and ready to go to work.

'I already called Harry and told him you won't be in,' she said.

'Thanks,' I said.

'He wanted to know when the services would be.'

'I'm not sure. Lars says that's all handled, but we didn't really discuss it last night.'

'There's handled and then there's handled,' Mel declared. 'And I'm sure there will be lots of loose ends that need tying up. And if all the kids are coming home,' she added, 'we should probably make some hotel reservations for them. I don't think having all of us stay here together is a good idea.'

'Yes,' I told her, savoring the coffee and enjoying watching her button her blouse. 'Living in sin does have its little complications, especially if you're blessed with serious-minded young adult children who make no bones about knowing right from wrong now that the shoe is somehow, inexplicably, on the other foot.'

Mel smiled. 'You can thank your lucky stars that we have only one set of disapproving young adult children. If I'd had kids, too, it could have been a lot worse.'

There was no point in calling Scott and Kelly,

59

or my good friends Ron and Amy Peters, either. Not right then — not until I had a firmed-up schedule from Lars. I was out of the shower and toweling dry when he called.

'Hate to bother you,' Lars began. 'But you said you probably wouldn't be going in today. If you could take me to the mortuary and to a flower shop . . . '

'Whatever you need, Lars. All you have to do is ask. I can be there in half an hour.'

'An hour's fine,' he said. 'They don't open until ten.'

It was sometime during that hour that I realized Beverly had done both Ross Connors and me a huge favor. By dying when she did, she afforded both of us the luxury of cover — time off the clock when I'd be able to pursue the LaShawn Tompkins matter with no one, Mel Soames included, being the wiser.

I used that hour of privacy to cull through Mel's newspapers, carefully putting them back the way I'd found them when I finished. I didn't find much. News about LaShawn had been relegated to the second page of the local section, and that was comprised mostly of nothing new to report. In the obituary section there was a brief announcement that gave a quick overview of LaShawn's short-circuited life. The service for him would be held on Thursday morning at 10 A.M. at the African Bible Baptist Church on Martin Luther King Jr. Way.

For a moment or two I considered putting in a call to Seattle PD and seeing if I could worm any information out of some of my old compatriots. I

60

thought better of it, though. It would be more useful for me to do some of my own investigating. To that end I located an address and a phone number for E. M. Tompkins on Church Street and stuffed it in my pocket. If I had time after I finished helping Lars, I'd stop by and pay a call LaShawn's grieving mother.

I found Lars hobbling back and forth in front of Queen Anne Gardens's sliding glass door. He looked agitated. I assumed he was still upset about Beverly. He was, but that wasn't the only problem.

He climbed in beside me. 'Those old ladies,' he muttered, slamming the car door behind him and shaking his head.

'What old ladies?' I asked.

'Back there,' he said, gesturing back toward Queen Anne Gardens. 'Beverly's not even in the ground and here they were all over me at breakfast, wanting to sit with me and bring me coffee. *Ja*, sure, they was treating me like I was . . . fresh fish.'

It was hard not to smile. It occurred to me that since Lars was in his nineties, he had a hell of a lot of nerve calling anyone else 'old.' And only a lifelong fisherman would confuse 'fresh meat' with 'fresh fish' in that particular context. The very idea of Lars suddenly cast in the role of a sought-after and eligible bachelor was one that was difficult to grasp.

'They were probably just concerned about you,' I said.

'No,' he declared heatedly. 'I'm old enough to know better than that!'

61

I had to give him that one. If he thought the randy ladies at Queen Anne Gardens were on the make, he was probably right.

'Where to?' I asked.

'Bleitz,' he muttered.

I knew where that particular funeral home was with no need of additional directions. It was where services had been held for Ron Peters's estranged first wife back in January. We went up and over Queen Anne Hill and down the back side to Florentia near the Fremont Bridge.

Dana Howell, Lars's funeral consultant, greeted him warmly. 'I'm so sorry to be seeing you again so soon,' she said.

Lars nodded. '*Ja*, sure,' he said, 'but I'm glad we got it done.'

And it turned out it was done. All of it, down to what would be printed on the program as well as what music would be sung and played. Beverly had already been brought to the mortuary from Queen Anne Gardens. There was an opening for a service at noontime on Thursday, if that was appropriate, and Lars allowed as how it was.

'You still want two urns?' Dana asked.

Lars shot me a sidelong glance and then nodded. 'Half her ashes go into the lake with her first husband. The other half goes with me. That's fair.'

That was the first I knew that when the weather cleared, I'd be required to make another pilgrimage to Lake Chelan to scatter a second set of ashes. This time I hoped I'd have brains enough to wear the sea-sick bracelets Beverly had given me. That way I wouldn't turn green the first time *The Lady of the Lake* hit rough water.

'My arrangements are here, too,' he added in an aside to me while nodding in Dana's direction. 'Dana here knows yust what I want, and it's paid for, too. You won't have to worry about a t'ing.'

After leaving the funeral home we stopped by a florist on top of Queen Anne Hill where Lars blew all of seventy-five bucks on a floral arrangement and then worried about having spent too much. I made a note to call back later and add a few more arrangements to the floral end of things. Beverly Piedmont Jenssen's memory certainly deserved much more than a single bouquet with a less-than-a-hundred-dollars price tag.

'Anything else?' I asked him, once we were back in the car.

Lars hesitated for a moment, then he nodded. 'I t'ink I'd like to find a meeting.'

I wasn't surprised to hear that, even after years of sobriety, Lars might be thinking about falling off the wagon. If your lifelong coping mechanism for dealing with grief is to numb the hurt with booze, than it's easy to want to drift back into bad old habits. I made a few calls and located a noontime AA meeting at the back of an old-fashioned diner up on Greenwood. When it came time to repeat the Serenity Prayer, I saw the white-knuckled grip Lars had on his cane and knew right then he was having a hell of a struggle accepting what he couldn't change. I was in pretty much the same boat.

When I took him back to Queen Anne Gardens, I went around to the passenger side of the car to let him out. Once he was upright, he surprised me by giving me a heartfelt hug. 'T'anks,' he said. 'T'anks for everything.'

'The kids will all be here tomorrow,' I told him. 'Kelly and Jeremy are driving up from Ashland in the morning. They'll be here in time for dinner tomorrow night, and Scott and Cherisse will be flying in about the same time. But what about tonight? Would you like to have dinner with Mel and me?'

Lars shook his head sadly. 'No,' he said. 'I'll be all right.' With that, he hobbled away.

I glanced at my watch. It was only a little past one. Mel wouldn't be back on this side of the water anytime before six. That meant I had several relatively free hours. I suppose I should have felt guilty about using that time to pursue the LaShawn Tompkins homicide, but I didn't. After all, Beverly had been proud of the job I do. I thought she would have gotten a kick out of having a one-time-only chance to be part of what was close to an undercover operation.

With that in mind I got back into the S55 and headed for Rainier Valley. When I arrived at the Tompkins place on South Church Street, I looked around for any official-looking cars. Other than a battered eight-passenger van with the words KING STREET MISSION lettered on the door, I didn't see any. As far as police presence was concerned, I was it.

Etta Mae Tompkins's house was small but

tidy-looking, with a well-kept fenced front yard. A few traces of the earlier tragedy were still visible. A scrap of yellow police tape lingered on a gatepost. When I stepped onto the porch, I could see that someone had gone to the effort of trying to scrub the fingerprint dust off the door frame, but a practiced eye could still see grubby gray traces marring the otherwise white trim around the doorbell. A mop and bucket filled with dingy reddish water reeking of Pine-Sol sat next to the doorway. The screen door was closed, but the inside door stood slightly ajar. As I raised my finger toward the bell, I heard the sound of a female voice coming from inside.

'I know he was important to you and your people, Pastor Mark, and you're welcome to have whatever kind of memorial service for Shawny you like,' the woman was saying. 'And if I can get a ride, you can bet I'll be there. But the funeral is mine, and that's final. It don't matter what LaShawn would or wouldn't have wanted, neither. He's dead, you understand me? LaShawn is dead and gone and he gets no say in the matter. Oh, you're right. King Street Mission was his place and all, but it's not *my* place. Funerals is for the living. Bible Baptist is my church, with my pastor and my people. That's where I'm having it, and that's final!'

A man spoke then. I couldn't make out the individual words, but his tone sounded conciliatory.

Just then a second white van pulled up outside the little house's front gate and parked just behind the first. A magnetic sign affixed to the van's door announced: MEALS-ON-WHEELS. A tall black man with a bald head and amazingly wide shoulders stepped out. Then he reached back inside and lifted a small cooler out of the backseat. Excusing himself, he shouldered past me on the front porch, pulled open the screen door, and stepped inside.

'It's me, Etta Mae,' he called. 'Mr. Dawson with Meals-on-Wheels. I'm here with your food.'

'Come on in, Mr. Dawson,' she replied. 'You know the way. Janie, Mr. Dawson's here from Meals-on-Wheels. Could you help him put it away?'

Janie, I surmised, was likely to be Etta Mae Tompkins's longtime neighbor, the one Maxwell Cole had interviewed. Obviously this was a very full house. It seemed to me one more uninvited guest probably wouldn't make much difference. After only a moment's hesitation, I followed Mr. Dawson inside.

The small entryway also reeked of Pine-Sol. I wondered if Pastor Mark's most likely unanticipated arrival had interrupted someone intent on the grim task of trying to erase from his mother's walls and floors the bloody evidence of LaShawn's untimely passing. Dried blood isn't easy to remove, however, and subtle remnants of stains and splatters still lingered. I guessed that it would take new plaster, paint, and tile to do the job completely. A framed poster depicting Jesus in His crown of thorns hung on the wall next to the door. Real blood now marred the printed surface, meaning that would have to be replaced as well.

Beyond the entryway I could see a white man with long, flowing gray locks. He seemed to be in full retreat. 'I'll be going, then,' the man I assumed to be Pastor Mark said. 'I'm sorry for your loss.'

'And I'm sorry for yours,' Etta Mae conceded. 'I know Shawny was a big help to you.'

As Pastor Mark made for the door, I had to step into the living room in order to allow him to pass. I knew I'd need to interview Pastor Mark eventually, but now was not the time.

The living room was tiny, just big enough for two chairs. Between them was an occasional table with a single lamp. A small color TV set with no sound sat perched on top of an old-fashioned and apparently dead console set. And that was all. A large black woman with a halo of wiry gray hair was seated in one chair with a sturdy walker positioned close at hand.

Squinting to see me better, Etta Mae Tompkins raised an implacable finger in my direction. 'Who are you?' she demanded. 'And where did you come from?'

I dug out my ID and handed it over. 'Homicide,' she mused, squinting some more and holding it up to her face in order to read it. 'I've been talking to homicide people for days now. Can't you-all get together and talk to each other and leave me alone? And what are you staring at?'

Embarrassed, I realized I was staring. I knew LaShawn Tompkins had been thirty years old. Human biology being what it is, his age gave me a rough idea of how old his mother would be

— probably close to my age or younger. This woman was much older than that.

'You think I'm too old to be Shawny's mama?' she asked. 'Is that it?'

I was reminded yet again why it is that I don't play poker.

'My daughter died a few days after Shawny was born,' Etta Mae explained without my having asked. 'He was a breach baby, and they had to do a cesarean. She ended up dying of an infection — sepsis, they called it. I'm the one who brought Shawny home, and I'm the one who raised him. I'm the only mother he ever knew. You got a problem with that?'

'No, ma'am,' I told her.

She reached over to the table and picked up a folded copy of the front section of Sunday's *Seattle Times*. 'That's what this here man, this Mr. Cole, thought, too!' She sniffed. 'Elderly! Where does he get off calling me elderly?'

I realized then that Max was losing his touch — that he must have phoned in his interview rather than actually meeting with Etta Mae. If he had seen her in person, he would have noticed the same thing I had and he certainly would have mentioned it, but if Etta Mae wanted the world to think LaShawn was her son, far be it from me to say otherwise.

'So what do you want then, Mr. Policeman? Why are you here?'

I was the one who was supposed to be asking the questions. By then my fellow visitor, Mr. Meals-on-Wheels, had off-loaded his food. He stood in the kitchen doorway observing the proceedings between Etta Mae and me with a good deal of satisfaction and no small amount of amusement. As soon as she sent one of her fearsome glances in his direction, however, Dawson seemed to think better of hanging around.

'I'll be going then, Mrs. Tompkins,' he said hastily. 'See you tomorrow.'

'I want to find out who murdered your son,' I said.

She nodded. 'You and me both,' she said. 'So sit down then. Take a load off.'

I sat.

'What's your name again?'

'Beaumont,' I said. 'J. P. Beaumont.'

'Your mama didn't give you no first name?'

'Jonas,' I said.

Etta Mae nodded sagely. 'A good Bible name,' she observed. 'Like in the whale.'

Not exactly, but close enough that mean-spirited boys plagued me with that from the time my mother signed me up for kindergarten. It was due to a bellyful of whale jokes, if you'll pardon the expression, that I pretty much abandoned my given name by the time I hit junior high.

'So are you saved, Mr. Beaumont?'

I thought about the blood-spattered picture of Jesus by the front door and realized that the interview wasn't going at all the way I had intended. Where was Mel Soames when I could have used her to run interference?

My grandfather's moral superiority, suppos-edly based on religious principles, had driven his daughter, my mother, away in disgrace. It was

69

also the main reason I had grown up largely unchurched. Faced with Etta Mae Tompkins's piercing stare, I decided that an honest answer was better than attempting to dodge the issue.

'Probably not according to your lights,' I said.

'You might be surprised about my lights,' she replied. 'But I'll tell you this: My son was saved. He went into prison one way, and, praise Jesus, he came out another. He wasn't doing drugs,' she added. 'And he wasn't selling drugs, neither. Shawny wasn't doing nothin' wrong. He was here fixing my supper, looking after me. Why would someone want to kill him like that?'

'I have no idea.'

'And who did you say you work for again?'

'Ross Connors. The Washington State attorney general.'

'And why's this Mr. Ross interested in who killed my Shawny?'

'I'm not sure.'

'Maybe he thinks those detectives from Seattle PD won't do a good job?' she suggested.

That was, of course, a distinct possibility.

'That Detective Jackson seemed nice enough,' Etta Mae added.

I was happy to have that piece of information. Detective Kendall Jackson, who is probably as tired of wine jokes as I am of whales, is one of the newer guys in Homicide, but he's also someone I know and respect. I was glad to hear he was on the case. I figured he was someone I could go to with a few discreet questions.

'What do you want from me?' Etta Mae asked.

'Maybe you know something,' I said. 'Maybe

your son said something to you that would have some bearing on what happened. For instance, did he mention anything to you about having any difficulties with people at work?'

Etta Mae shook her head. 'If he had any troubles like that, he never said nothin' to me about 'em.'

'What about friends from around here?' I asked. 'Did he take up with any of his old pals from the neighborhood once he came home?'

'I already told you, Jonah,' she said firmly. 'LaShawn came out of prison a changed man. He didn't go back to any of his old friends or his old habits. He knew them for what they are, the way of the devil. So he stayed away from them. If you make a habit of standing in the way of temptation, you just might get run over.'

I didn't bother correcting the Jonah bit. There was no point. 'What about a girlfriend?' I asked. 'Did he have one?'

'Not that I know of.'

'What about difficulties with money?' I asked.

Homicidal violence often has its origin in some combination of drugs, women, and/or money, and I'm not just talking about homicides in the Rainier Valley area of Seattle, either.

'He didn't have no money,' Etta Mae declared. 'Didn't need it, neither, because he was giving his life over to the Lord and to the King Street Mission. When he got that settlement from the state, I think Pastor Mark thought Shawny would turn right around and drop the whole thing in the collection plate, but he didn't. Instead, LaShawn spent it on me, fixing this place up all nice and cozy so I'd have myself a comfortable place to live.'

I didn't remember the exact amount of LaShawn Tompkins's wrongful-imprisonment settlement. I wondered how much of it was left, and was it enough to provide a motive for murder?

'If your son had no money, what did he do for food and clothing?' I asked.

'He ate his meals at the mission. As for clothing? I don't know nothing about that. You'll have to ask Pastor Mark.'

I'll do that, I thought, *just as soon as I get a chance.*

I said, 'You and the good pastor seemed to be having a slight difference of opinion when I first got here. What was that all about?'

'Oh, that,' Etta Mae said. 'Pastor Mark is under the impression that just because Shawny worked for him, it was like he owned him or something, and that he could say how and where the funeral was gonna be and all that. I had to set him straight on that score, and I did.'

Yes, Pastor Mark and the King Street Mission would bear some scrutiny. It would have been nice to think that LaShawn Tompkins and Pastor Mark had both seen the light and that the two of them subsequently had devoted themselves to lives of selfless service to others. But I just didn't happen to think that was true. It was likely there was something else at work here. If I ever managed to figure out exactly what that was, I'd most likely know who had gunned down LaShawn Tompkins and why.

72

5

I left Etta Mae's house about midafternoon. Before leaving I had been introduced to Etta Mae's neighbor, Janie Griswold, who had eventually emerged from the kitchen and resumed her thankless task of trying to clean up the blood-spattered entryway.

Walking back to the car, I felt frustrated. What should have been an uncomplicated, straight-up interview had ended up being more of a prayer meeting, one in which I had been on the defensive far more than I should have been. I came away knowing that Etta Mae's belief in her son's miraculous transformation was utterly unshakable. I, on the other hand, had my doubts.

When I had first pulled up in front of the house on Church Street, I had turned off my cell phone. It would have been more than a little awkward if Mel had called and asked what I was doing when I was in the midst of interviewing an important witness in a supposedly nonexistent case. As soon as I turned the phone back on, it was bristling with a collection of messages and missed calls.

I dialed Mel immediately. 'Where are you?' she wanted to know.

'Headed home,' I hedged. I was in fact driving back toward downtown Seattle at that very moment — just not from the direction she might have anticipated.

'How's Lars?' she asked.

'Medium,' I said.

'Did you invite him to dinner?' she said.

'Did,' I said. 'He turned me down.'

'He probably shouldn't be alone right now,' Mel said. 'He should have people with him.'

I thought about the gaggle of unattached Queen Anne Gardens dames Lars had claimed were hovering around him, all of them circling for a premature landing. 'I doubt he'll be all that alone,' I said.

'Still,' Mel said. 'He should be with family at a time like this. Do you think I should call and ask him?' she wanted to know.

Mel probably could have talked Lars into coming out for dinner, but if she did, we might end up having a discussion of exactly when I had dropped him off and what I'd been doing in the meantime, et cetera, et cetera. What was it my mother always used to say? 'Oh, what a tangled web we weave when first we practice to deceive.'

'He seemed pretty tired,' I said. 'Let's leave well enough alone.'

I gave her the arrangement details for Beverly's services so she could pass them along to Barbara Galvin and Harry. She extracted a promise that I'd order more flowers. She also told me that she'd made arrangements for the kids to stay at the Homewood Suites a few blocks away from Belltown Terrace at the bottom of Queen Anne Hill. Once again I appreciated Mel's attention to detail. Making room reservations was something I probably wouldn't have remembered — until it was too late.

'What are you going to do now?' Mel asked.

'Go home and put my feet up,' I said. 'It was a pretty short night.'

On the way, I listened through a string of condolence calls — from Ron Peters, a former partner and a good friend; from Ralph Ames, my attorney; from Ross Connors along with several other members of the SHIT squad. In other words, Mel had put out the word.

When I got as far as downtown, I thought briefly about stopping by Seattle PD, but decided against it. It would create far less of a stir if I phoned Kendall Jackson than it would if I showed up on the premises in person asking questions. And since Ross seemed to want deniability, less of a stir would be far preferable to more of one.

Back at the condo I settled into the recliner, picked up the phone, and dialed that old familiar number that took me straight to the heart of Homicide. In the old days I couldn't have made such a call without spending several minutes chewing the fat with Watty Watson, who was, for many years, the telephone-answering nerve center for Seattle PD's homicide squad. But now Watty had moved on — either up or out. The phone was answered by someone whose name I neither caught nor recognized. I was put through to Detective Jackson with no chitchat and no questions asked.

'Hey, Beau-Beau,' Kendall boomed into the phone. 'How're you doing these days? Did they finally get all that glass out of your face?'

Jackson had been first on the scene after I

went through the shattered wall of that greenhouse. The last time he had seen me I had been a bloody mess on my way to the ER.

'Pretty much,' I said. 'Although I still find shards of it now and then.'

'You're doing better than Captain Kramer,' he said. 'You know he's still out on disability? Everyone says he's coming back soon now, though, probably sometime in the next couple of weeks.'

Mel and I might have saved Paul Kramer's sorry butt, but that didn't mean I liked him any better. 'Glad to hear it,' I lied.

The words came to my lips almost effortlessly. Maybe I was starting to get the hang of it. After all, I had managed to lie to Mel. Now it looked as though I might be able to spin believable whoppers at the drop of a hat for anybody at all, no exceptions.

'What can I do for you?' Jackson asked.

'I understand you're working the LaShawn Tompkins case.'

'Yup,' Jackson said. 'Hank and I drew that one.'

Hank was Detective Henry Ramsdahl, Jackson's partner.

'How's it going?' I asked.

'Is that an official 'how's it going' or an unofficial?' he returned.

'Unofficial,' I replied. 'After the state made that payout in the Tompkins case, Ross Connors wants to be sure everything is on the up-and-up, but he also doesn't want to make a big fuss about it, if you know what I mean.'

'We're not making much progress so far,' Jackson admitted. 'From everything we've been able to learn, Tompkins had been keeping his nose clean. We've turned up no sign that he was involved in any illegal activities. According to what we've been told, LaShawn found God while he was in prison. Once he got out, he straightened up and flew right — right up until somebody shot him dead, which, if you ask me, sounds pretty iffy,' Jackson concluded. 'Old bad guys mostly don't go straight.'

We were on the same wavelength on that score.

'With the possible exception of the girlfriend angle, though,' he added, 'we haven't found anyone with a beef against him.'

'What girlfriend?' I asked. The fact that LaShawn might have a girlfriend was news to me, and it would no doubt be news to Etta Mae as well.

'Name's Elaine — Elaine Manning. That would be Sister Elaine Manning.'

'Sister as in she's black?' I asked.

'That, too, but mostly sister as in that was her title at King Street Mission. Also an ex-con. Spent five years at Purdy for armed robbery. From what I can tell, that's pretty much the prerequisite for becoming a counselor at King Street — you've already done your crime and your time. It's a cachet that gives you more credibility with the clients.'

'What about Elaine Manning?' I prompted.

'We're hearing bits and rumors that she and Brother Mark may have had something going, but that was before Brother LaShawn turned up on the scene. Once that happened, Sister Elaine more or less spun out of Brother Mark's orbit.'

'So we could be dealing with a simple love triangle?' I asked.

Of course, love triangles are hardly ever simple.

'Maybe,' Jackson agreed. 'Problem is, so far we haven't been able to locate Ms. Manning.'

'You're saying she's gone missing?'

'Yup. No one's seen her since sometime Saturday morning. Took off right after breakfast. Since then, she hasn't shown up at work and hasn't called in, either. No one seems to know where she is or how to reach her. We consider her a person of interest.'

Someone close to a murder victim who goes missing about the same time as the murder is *always* a person of interest, especially if there are hints of a love affair gone bad. Jackson made it sound like it was no big deal, but I guessed that the full powers of Seattle PD were being brought to bear on locating Sister Elaine Manning. It was probably better if I just sat back and let them do the heavy lifting. There would be plenty of time for me to talk to her once she was found.

'Tell me about Pastor Mark,' I said. 'What's his deal?'

'That would be Brother Mark or Pastor Mark, depending on who you talk to,' Kendall said. 'Last name's Granger. Former druggie. Did a fifteen-year stretch for second-degree murder. Been out for the past five years. Another unlikely prospect for a Goody Two-shoes award, but we haven't been able to find anything new on him, either. Everybody at King Street seems hellbent on keeping their noses clean — no drugs, no booze, no illegal activities. They don't even allow cigarettes.'

'They just aren't making ex-cons the way they used to,' I said.

'I guess not,' Jackson agreed with a laugh.

I started to ask him if he had any details on the payout Tompkins had received from the state. I stopped myself just in time. If my cover was that Ross Connors was worried about it, I'd better have the details of that at my fingertips. And I jotted a note to myself to make inquiries about the settlement on my own.

'So there's nothing on the street about who might have done this?' I asked.

'So far not a word,' Jackson replied, 'and believe me, we've been asking.'

'What about forensics?' I asked.

'A thirty-eight,' Jackson said. 'We ran the bullet through NIBIN. Nothing turned up.'

NIBIN is the National Integrated Ballistics Information Network, which keeps track of bullets the same way AFIS (the Automated Fingerprint Identification System) keeps track of fingerprints. The fact that the bullet used to kill LaShawn Tompkins hadn't shown up in the database meant that the weapon was clean — that it hadn't been used in any other crime prior to his murder. Now that it had been entered into the system, however, if it was used again, it would be noticed. When or if that happened, it would make the killer easier to

79

trace. Right now, though, it didn't do us any good.

'So you'll keep me in the loop on this one?' I suggested.

Jackson laughed. 'Unofficially in the loop, that is.'

'Yes.'

'Only if you do the same,' he returned. 'Quid quo pro, whatever. If you dredge something up, I want to hear about it, too.'

'Fair enough,' I said.

I put down the phone, leaned back in the recliner, and closed my eyes. I may even have drifted off for a second or two before the phone rang, startling me awake if not to full consciousness.

'How come we have to stay in a hotel?' my daughter demanded. 'Why can't we stay with you? Is it because of *her*?'

And there, in a nutshell, is why men find women so baffling — daughters included. Or perhaps, daughters especially.

I'll be the first to admit that I wasn't always the best of fathers when Scott and Kelly were kids, but in the years since I stopped drinking I've gone to great lengths to undo as much of that damage as possible. Maybe I've made more progress with Scott than I have with Kelly. Still, I've done my level best, and I thought we were doing fine. The previous weekend, when Mel and I had been down in Ashland, she and Kelly seemed to get along fine — at least fine as far as I could see. I remembered Kelly even teasing Mel about whether or not we were going to get married. Now Kelly uttered the word *her* in regard to Mel with such vivid contempt that it caught me by surprise. Between Sunday morning and Tuesday afternoon, what could possibly have changed?

'I just talked to Mel,' Kelly continued. 'She told me we'll be staying at Homewood Suites and gave me the confirmation number.'

I still didn't get it. My first thought was that since Kelly and Jeremy live on a very tight budget, maybe she was worried about having to pay a hotel bill.

'I'm paying for the room,' I said, trying to fight my way out of a mess not of my own making. 'You don't have to be concerned about that.'

'This has nothing to do with money!' Kelly exclaimed, her voice trembling with outrage. She seemed on the verge of tears. 'It's bad enough that we have to come all the way from Ashland to Seattle with a month-old baby in the car. Is it asking too much to expect that we'd get to spend some time with you instead of being carted off to a hotel like a bunch of strangers?'

Let it be said that Mel and I had just finished squandering the better part of three reasonably pleasant days in my daughter's company. On the face of it, her sudden antipathy made very little sense.

'Scott and Cherisse will be staying there, too,' I offered lamely. 'And it's only a couple of blocks from here.'

From Kelly's point of view the hotel could have been on Pluto. 'It's all about Mel, isn't it,' she raved on. 'Mel this and Mel that. She's shacked up with you there and has you completely under her thumb. Mel's doing this because she doesn't want to share you with anyone, not even with your granddaughter, who's crazy about you, by the way!'

By now this amounted to the most bizarre conversation I'd ever had with my daughter — in terms of turning tables, that is. Because the truth of the matter was, having my children come stay at Belltown Terrace with Mel and me when we were obviously living in sin was a big deal — in my book, anyway. And I suspected it was in Mel's, too. Of course I could have pointed out that Kelly and Jeremy hadn't exactly tied the knot in a timely fashion. In actual fact, Kayla's birthday predates her parents' wedding anniversary by several months.

People say that there's nothing worse than a reformed drunk, and the situation here was probably similar. Maybe now that Kelly had finished sowing her wild oats, she wanted her father to shape up and do the same. It occurred to me that Kelly's great-grandmother, Beverly Jenssen, had been of the same opinion. DNA will out.

On the other hand, I wasn't about to send Mel packing back to her apartment in Bellevue for the duration of the kids' visit, either.

'I'm sure it'll be fine,' I said soothingly. 'I won't be going in to work. We'll be able to spend plenty of time together.'

'We will *not!*' Kelly insisted. With that, she hung up on me. I didn't call her back. There wasn't much point.

Mel came home a little while later. She whipped out of her work clothes, put on a jogging suit and sneakers, and dragged me with her down to the running track.

Belltown Terrace is one of the few buildings in Seattle actually constructed under an interesting, short-lived, and amazingly complicated set of residential/mixed-use zoning rules. The bottom five stories are office building. The sixth floor — including the rooftop of the office building — is a common recreation area for the taller residential structure. It includes a party room, a swimming pool and hot tub, an exercise room, as well as a sport court. Much of the outdoor rooftop area is devoted to gardens, which Mel tells me include an award-winning collection of hydrangeas. (Since I know zero about flowers and/or gardens, I more or less have to take her word for this.)

A rubber-mat-covered running track runs the full perimeter of the sixth floor — about a quarter of a mile in all. When the building was first built, this running track was supposed to be a big selling point, and maybe it still is, but what looks and sounds good on paper sometimes misses the mark when it comes to actual delivery.

What the architects and planners had failed to take into consideration was the wind-tunnel effect from nearby high-rise buildings. Even in the dead of summer you can be out on the Belltown Terrace running track with a chill gale blowing into your teeth. Since this was March and a long way from the dead of summer, it was downright frigid out there.

I've often said that my major form of exercise is jumping to conclusions. Mel had set out to change that. At least three times a week she dragged me, usually kicking and screaming, down to the running track, where she literally ran circles around me while I walked. (All knees are not created equal.)

Afterward, sitting in the hot tub, she leveled a blue-eyed stare in my direction.

'What's wrong?' she said. 'You're a million miles away. Are you thinking about Beverly?'

I was sad about losing Beverly, but what was really bothering me right then was the fact that Mel's good deed of making hotel reservations for Kelly and Scott was about to blow up in both our faces. I knew I'd have to tell Mel about the situation with Kelly eventually, but not right then. I nodded and sighed as convincingly as I could manage.

'It is sad,' Mel agreed. 'Especially for Lars. Widowers often don't fare too well when they're left on their own.'

Which gave me something else to worry about entirely.

'How was your afternoon?' I asked in an attempt to change the subject.

Mel frowned. 'More interesting than it should have been,' she said. 'I started tracking down locations on those released sex offenders. I just barely scratched the surface, but already two of them are dead.'

'Dead?' I asked.

Mel nodded. 'One suicide and one accident.

It's too bad I didn't know about this over the weekend. We could have stopped off in Roseburg on the way coming or going and made some inquiries. Feet on the ground instead of phoners.'

'What's in Roseburg?'

'Outside of Roseburg, actually,' she said. 'A guy named Les Fordham got sent to prison for molesting his girlfriend's twelve-year-old daughter. When he got out he went to live in southern Oregon. That's where he was from originally. Got a job working in a sawmill there and seemed to be doing all right. Then, last summer, for no apparent reason he turned on the gas on his stove and ended up blowing himself to kingdom come. Started a mini forest fire in the process. Fortunately it rained like hell the next day, and the fire didn't turn into a major one.'

'And the accident?' I asked.

'You may remember it,' Mel said. 'The guy's name was Ed Chrisman. He was living up in Bellingham. Got all drunked-up on a Sunday afternoon last December. The investigators theorized that he stopped off at one of the rest areas on Chuckanut Drive to take a leak. It was cold, so he left the car running while he got out to do his business . . . '

'I remember,' I said. 'He also left his car in gear. It hit him from behind while he was standing there with his fly unzipped. Knocked him off the edge of a cliff into the water. The car went into the drink right along with him — on top of him, as I recall. Smashed him flat.'

Mel nodded. 'That's the one. Nobody

bothered to report him missing until several days later. With the weather the way it was, his vehicle wasn't found at the foot of the cliff until almost a week after it happened. The transmission was still in gear when they fished it out of the water.'

'Sounds like he was still in gear, too,' I said.

I admit, it was a tasteless joke — but dying with your pants unzipped *is* a tasteless joke. Mel glared at me. 'Not funny,' she said.

'No,' I agreed. 'I suppose not. But if those two guys were already dead, how come they're still on Ross's sex-offender list?'

'I believe that's why Ross has me updating the list.'

'Right,' I said. 'Makes sense to me. Sounds like me and missing persons. Now let's go see about dinner.'

6

One of the things Mel and I share in common is that we're both terrible cooks. Yes, we can make coffee. And toast on occasion. And, according to Ron Peters's girls, I could brew a mean cup of hot chocolate in my day. So we don't eat at home, unless it's carry-out or carry-in, as the case might be. Mostly we go out. Fortunately, since the Denny Regrade is full of restaurants, trendy and otherwise, we're in no danger of starving to death.

Our current favorite is a little French place called Le P'tit Bistro two blocks up the street. I know, I know. Over the years I've developed a well-deserved reputation for unsophisticated dining, and some of my old Doghouse pals would choke at the very idea of me hanging out in a French dining establishment. But now that the Regrade has morphed into Belltown, that's how much things have changed around here in the past few years. Maybe that's how much I've changed, too.

I'm guessing Le P'tit Bistro comes close to being the French approximation of an old-fashioned diner. The food doesn't put on airs, and neither does the waitstaff. Just for the record, real men do eat quiche — and crepes, too, for that matter.

'Maybe I should stay in Bellevue while the kids are here,' Mel suggested as she sipped a glass of red wine. I was having Perrier. As I said, the place is French.

It was almost as though Mel had implanted a listening device in my head and overheard my disturbing conversation with Kelly. 'No way!' I responded.

Mel ignored me. 'With the funeral and all,' she continued, 'emotions are bound to be running high, and daughters can be . . . well, let's just say they can be a little territorial.'

'Did Kelly say something to you about this?' I demanded.

Mel shrugged. 'Not in so many words,' she replied. 'She didn't have to. I got the message.'

That's another thing about women. You're damned by what they do say and you're damned by what they don't say. For a guy, it's lose/lose either way. It would have been nice to be able to change the subject again — to talk with Mel about something easy, like murder and mayhem and who blasted LaShawn Tompkins to smithereens, but that would have gotten me in trouble with Ross Connors, so I soldiered on.

'Look,' I said, 'it's bad enough that we have to play hide-and-seek with the guys at work, but I'm damned if I'm going to play the same game with my kids. You're in my life because I want you in my life. Everybody's just going to have to get used to it — Kelly and Scott included.'

Under the circumstances that seemed like a perfectly reasonable thing to say, but the next thing I knew Mel was crying, mopping away tears and mascara with her cloth napkin while the lady who's the co-owner of the restaurant shot daggers at me from her station behind the dessert case. Some days you really can't win.

Mel was pretty quiet — make that dead-quiet — the rest of the time we were eating. I thought I was in more trouble with her than I was with the lady at the restaurant. On our two-block walk back to Belltown Terrace, however, Mel slipped her arm through mine, then leaned into my shoulder. 'I think that's one of the nicest things anybody's ever said to me,' she said.

We went home. It was still early, but we went to bed anyway, and not to watch Fox News Channel, either. Later, with Mel nestled cozily against my side and sleeping peacefully, I lay awake for a long time. I realized that there were many things I was more than willing to give up for the sake of my children, but Melissa Soames wasn't one of them. With a smile on my face I finally drifted off to sleep as well.

My mother was perpetually whipping out little aphorisms in the hope, I suppose, of turning me into an upright citizen. Some of them are still imprinted in my brain: 'Save the surface and you save all.' 'A stitch in time saves nine.' 'God helps those who help themselves.' At four o'clock the next morning, when I was wide awake and Mel wasn't, the saying that came most readily to mind was 'Early to bed; early to rise . . . ' I was up early, all right. Not wanting to awaken Mel, I bailed out of bed. Out in the living room I dredged my laptop out of my briefcase, booted up, and logged on.

Less than two months ago I had been down in the morgue at the *Seattle Post-Intelligencer* personally combing through brittle rolls of old microfiche on the trail of a case that had been cold for more than fifty years. Between then and now, though, SHIT had entered the information age. Ross Connors had sprung for an agency-wide subscription to LexisNexis, which meant that with my secret password (well, maybe 'doghouse' isn't all that secret), the whole world of cyber news and public records was open to me without my having to do all the searching myself. With a click of a mouse, as they say.

In reality it took a little more than that, but before long I had the information on LaShawn's payout from the state — $250,000. Not that much, considering he'd been wrongfully imprisoned for seven years. And much less when you took into account the fact that his attorney probably walked off with half the settlement. Etta Mae had told me her son had spent his money on fixing up her house. The house on Church Street wasn't large, but remodeling anything costs a bundle these days. It seemed safe to assume that there probably wasn't a whole lot of LaShawn's windfall left for anyone to fight over. Which probably took money out of the murder-motive equation.

Next I went looking for Elaine Manning, LaShawn Tompkins's girlfriend at the King Street Mission. She had been sentenced to prison in North Carolina for robbing a Krispy Kreme. A doughnut shop, for God's sake? And then, after some kind of difficulty inside the prison in Raleigh and for some inexplicable reason, she was shipped off to Washington State to complete her sentence. People who watch *Cops* on TV are always amazed that the crooks are so amazingly stupid. It's no surprise to me. And someone who would use a weapon to rob a Krispy Kreme most likely wasn't a mental giant.

On to Pastor Mark Granger, the head of the mission. His story was a little less typical because he was maybe a little smarter than that. Came from a good middle-class background. Got screwed up on drugs in college and went to prison for second-degree murder from a drug deal gone bad when he was twenty years old. Got a mail-order degree — in divinity, of all things — while he was still in prison. So Pastor Mark really was a pastor.

It turns out there are lots of King Street missions in this country. The one in Seattle was housed in what had once been a derelict flophouse near the railroad. In the mid-nineties it had been purchased and refurbished by an outfit called God's Word, LLC. My searches on them led me from one blind real estate trust to another. Only lawyers' names appeared on the documents I was able to track down. Whoever was behind God's Word was anonymous and fully intended to stay that way. Goody Two-shoes ex-cons are suspicious enough, but I can accept that they exist. Anonymous do-gooders? Not likely. Those are, again as my mother would have said, scarce as hens' teeth.

I was still looking for traces of God's Word when I heard the toilet flush. It's one of those newfangled power-assisted things that sound like somebody is strangling a cat. The racket gave me enough warning that I was able to log off LexisNexis. By the time Mel started the coffee and came into the living room, I was perusing the online edition of the *Seattle Times*.

'Good morning,' she said, kissing me hello. 'You're up early. Why do you insist on reading those things online? The paper's right out in the hall. All you have to do is open the door, pick up the paper, and take off the rubber band.'

'I seem to remember you prefer finding your newspapers in pristine condition,' I replied. 'I'm only thinking of you.'

'Thanks,' she said.

When it comes to lying, I'm getting better all the time.

Mel collected her papers. Then she went over to the window seat, wrapped a throw around her shoulders, and settled down in one corner to read the headlines and await the end of the coffee-brewing cycle. On a clear day someone sitting in the window seat can see Mount Rainier to the south and east and the Olympics to the north and west, with a vast display of water and/or city in between. This was March. The only thing visible was rain — lots of it.

'Did you get the flowers?' she asked.

The puzzled look on my face must have been answer enough.

'For Beverly's funeral,' she reminded me. 'You were going to order more, right?'

'Right,' I said. 'But Ballard Blossom isn't open right now. It's too early. I'll have to call later.'

'And then you should probably drag home

some groceries. The kids will be here at least part of the time.'

'What kind of groceries?' I asked.

'You know. The usual. Sodas, cereal, milk, bread, peanut butter, animal crackers.'

'Where the hell do they keep animal crackers these days?'

'Same place they always have, but when you get to the store, ask,' she said patiently. 'Someone there will be able to tell you.'

Mel left for work a little past seven. I went back to surfing the net, where I was still trying to track down principals in God's Word when Ross Connors called me at home a little after eight.

'Sorry to hear about your grandmother,' he said. 'Harry told me you weren't coming in.'

Since he had called on my home number and not on my cell, I had already figured that out. 'Thanks,' I said. 'But I'm still working. It would be a hell of a lot easier on me if I could talk to Mel about this Tompkins situation. I don't like sneaking around on her. It feels like cheating.'

'Indulge me,' he said. 'I'm not ready to start connecting the dots yet. What have you found out on LaShawn so far?'

'According to Detective Jackson at Seattle PD, it could be nothing more or less than an old-fashioned love triangle with both LaShawn and Pastor Mark from King Street Mission going after the same girl.'

'Who also happens to be missing at the moment,' Ross supplied.

In other words, I wasn't telling him anything he didn't already know. So why did he need me?

Ross answered the question without my asking it. 'Find her,' he said. 'There is nothing that would make me happier than to know LaShawn Tompkins is dead because he fell in love with the wrong girl.'

This was not a throwaway comment. There was an urgency in Ross's voice that I recognized. Something was going on — something Ross was not yet prepared to divulge — and LaShawn Tompkins's murder, inconsequential as it might seem in the big scheme of things, was somehow the tip of that iceberg.

'You know,' I said, 'it might be easier to fix this problem if I knew what the hell was really going on.'

'Just find the girl,' Ross said. 'Find Elaine Manning. Maybe this is nothing more than what Kendall Jackson says it is, a love story gone awry, and maybe I'm just over the hill, full of crap, and pushing panic buttons for no reason. That's what I'm hoping.'

I knew for certain that Ross Connors was anything but over the hill and full of crap, so I kept my mouth shut. When he hung up, he left me with the sure knowledge that I'd better hit the road and do what I'd been ordered to do — find Elaine Manning. And the first place to look was King Street Mission.

For years Ross Connors has been a big-time political player in the state of Washington. That means he comes complete with lots of connections — political, financial, and otherwise. The fact that God's Word wasn't up-front about who all was involved made it seem likely to me that we were dealing with some pretty heavy hitters. Otherwise why would Ross be worried — or personally involved?

So I closed the computer, showered, dressed, and headed out for the King Street Mission. It's not the kind of place you stumble into by accident. The only way to get there is on purpose — because that's where you mean to go.

The mission was situated in a squat, unimposing old brick building set in a mostly industrial and dying warehouse area that was so far out of the downtown core that parking was actually free. It faced a generally freight-bearing rail spur. With its back pressed up against the noisy roar of I-5's southbound lanes, the building itself as well as the neighborhood as a whole would probably defy all efforts of gentrification for generations to come. It was located too far from the easy panhandling of tourist-teeming Pioneer Square and the sports-crazed fans that populate the area around Safeco and Qwest fields. King Street Mission was clearly a place for people serious about recovering from whatever ailed them.

The hand-lettered sign over the front door, complete with crosses on either end, exhorted new arrivals to 'Abandon all dope ye who enter here.' I took that to mean King Street Mission was probably one of those trendy faith-based organizations that sets out to rehabilitate folks the state gave up on long ago — probably for good reason. There was no stand-alone ashtray next to the outside door and no scatter of nearby cigarette butts, either. The one or two I saw in the gutter had probably come from passing vehicles. I remembered what Detective Jackson had said about King Street not tolerating smoking. From the looks of the front entrance the people inside were making that rule stick both inside and out.

I stepped into a brightly lit multipurpose room that served as dining room, lobby, and library. The white tile floor was polished to a high enough sheen that it would have put most hospital corridors to shame. At one end of the room was a series of tables equipped with several desktop computers. Behind them were shelves lined with books and a series of couches and easy chairs. If somebody had been selling lattes, that part of the room could have passed for a Starbucks franchise. At the other end was a dining area already set with two dozen or so places. Behind a pair of swinging doors came the sounds of a kitchen crew hard at work, most likely preparing what would be the noon meal.

Directly in front of me was a battered hotel desk that looked as though it had been through several wars. Behind the desk sat a young dark-haired woman who might have been attractive had it not been for her mouth — the missing and blackened teeth and swollen gums that are routinely called meth-mouth these days. Her name tag said she was Cora. Her awful visage made me glad I don't do meth and that I see my dentist regularly. It also made me wonder what else she had done that had landed her first in prison and then here.

'Something I can do for you?' she lisped

through her missing teeth.

'Yes,' I said. 'I'm looking for Pastor Mark.'

'He's conducting a Bible study right now,' she said. 'You're welcome to wait. He should be done in ten minutes or so.'

'I'll wait,' I said.

Cora returned to her computer keyboard. She didn't exactly put a pretty face on the King Street Mission's mission, but then maybe she was emblematic of what they were doing — and the kind of raw material they started out with. These people were coming from way behind GO.

The wall next to the front desk was lined with a series of bulletin boards. I wandered over to them and studied the contents. One contained what looked like a duty roster and included things like cooking shifts, sweeping, bathroom cleaning, garbage takeout, et cetera. So this was a cooperative effort. People who lived here were expected to keep the place clean and running. That was refreshing.

There was also a schedule of classes — computer skills, resume writing, GED, literacy, et cetera, although I'm not sure how someone who was illiterate would have found his or her way to that last class. There were also three different Bible studies — one Old Testament and two New — on every day of the week: morning, afternoon, and evening. And there were AA and NA (Narcotics Anonymous) meetings as well. This was a very busy place, with supposedly uplifting stuff happening at all hours of the day and night.

A handwritten note next to the class and

meeting schedule announced that an in-house memorial service would be held Thursday at 7:00 P.M. I made a note of that, but I already knew I had a conflict in terms of my grandmother's services. Maybe Kendall Jackson could cover it.

'Funeral services for Brother LaShawn will be held on Friday from 2:00 to 4:00 P.M. at African Bible Baptist on MLK Jr. Way,' the posting continued. 'Anyone needing bus transportation to or from the funeral should sign up on the sheet below.'

It was only Wednesday morning. Already fifteen names appeared on the list. I wondered if people were planning on attending LaShawn's funeral because they wanted to go, or had they been ordered to attend . . . or else?

'May I help you?'

I turned around to see Pastor Mark standing behind me. He had arrived soundlessly in a pair of white tennis shoes that were a stark contrast to his black pants, black short-sleeved shirt, and stiff clerical collar. His graying hair was pulled back in a ponytail. His wire-framed glasses gave him the jaunty look of a with-it college professor. The array of jailhouse tattoos that cascaded down both bare arms told another story.

I held out my hand. 'My name's Beaumont,' I said. 'J. P. Beaumont. I'm an investigator for the Washington State Attorney General's Office. I believe I saw you yesterday at Mrs. Tompkins's home, but we were never properly introduced.'

'You're a cop?' he asked.

Considering Pastor Mark's divinity degree was

98

of the jailhouse variety, his question was entirely understandable. Ex-cons and cops have a way of recognizing one another on sight. We tend to run in the same circles.

I nodded.

'Then I'll need to see your ID,' he said.

He studied it for a long time. 'Special Homicide Investigation Team — SHIT. This is a joke, right? But it's a little too early for April Fool's.'

Displaying my SHIT ID tends to have that effect on people. Once they go down that road, it's hard to get them to take you seriously.

'It's no joke,' I said. 'I'm looking for Elaine Manning.'

'I'm afraid I can't help you, then,' Pastor Mark replied. 'Sister Elaine's not here.' Something steely came into his tone. I recognized that as well.

'You have no idea where she might be?' I asked.

'None at all.'

'When did she leave?' I asked.

'Sometime Saturday morning. I'm not sure when.'

'And what about Friday evening?' I continued. 'Where were you around seven P.M. or so?'

Kendall Jackson had told me that was the approximate time LaShawn Tompkins had been shot.

Pastor Mark gave me a slow but confident smile — a Cheshire cat kind of smile, as though he knew way more than I did. 'I was right here,' he said. 'I was here with everyone else eating dinner between six and seven. Seven sharp is the beginning of Evening Bible Study, which I conducted myself that evening. New Testament, Book of John, chapters six and seven. Cora can give you a list of the people who were at dinner as well as the people in my study session if you wish. Beyond that, however, I've been advised to answer no additional questions without my attorney being present. And now, if you'll excuse me, I have work to do.'

Clerical collar or not, Pastor Mark Granger was an experienced but oddly polished ex-con, a felon who knew exactly when it was time to lawyer-up. I noticed something else about him, too. Underneath that polished exterior lurked a seething anger that he managed to hold in check — but only just barely. And men like that — the ones with explosive tempers lurking right beneath the surface — are often the most dangerous, especially when thwarted in any way.

Knowing all that, recognizing the reformed Pastor Mark for what he really was, I couldn't help wondering how it was that Etta Mae Tompkins had managed to send the man packing in full retreat the day before. It could have been the power of her considerable righteousness. On the other hand, it could have been due to my turning up just when it did. The outcome might have been entirely different had I not arrived on the scene during their somewhat heated discussion.

There are times I despair of ever being in the right place at the right time, but maybe that wasn't true regarding my visit to Etta Mae

Tompkins's house. No, on that one occasion at least, I had somehow managed to stumble into arriving at exactly the right moment.

Sometimes things just work out.

7

People who go missing of their own volition usually do so because they've got something to hide. People who go missing against their will usually disappear because someone else has something to hide. At that point I had no idea which of those causes applied to Elaine Manning. But if I was going to find her — as I had been ordered to do — then it made sense to start asking questions in the last place she'd been seen.

On my way to the King Street Mission I had been concerned about what I'd say to the Seattle homicide cops I was liable to run into who would also be there working. Turns out I needn't have worried on that score. No one was there. It was Wednesday. LaShawn Tompkins had died on Friday. His death may have made a big media splash over the weekend, but by Wednesday his death was old news. Not only that, the clock had ticked far beyond those first critical forty-eight hours when a case is most likely to be solved — if it's ever going to be solved. Homicide cops don't necessarily have a short attention span, but police departments can and do, especially if something else comes up in the meantime.

So J. P. Beaumont had the King Street Mission pretty much to himself. When Pastor Mark turned his back on me and then disappeared into an office on the far side of the front desk, he didn't tell me I should move along. So I didn't. I went into questioning mode, starting with the almost toothless Cora.

On the one hand, it was hard to look at her. On the other hand, it was hard not to stare. For her part, Cora seemed to be totally unaffected by her tragically flawed physical appearance. She had finished doing whatever she had been doing on the computer. An open Bible now lay on the desk in front of her.

'I'm looking for Elaine Manning,' I said. Cora glanced cautiously over her shoulder, as if to make sure Pastor Mark's door was closed before she answered my inquiry.

'Like Pastor Mark said,' she told me, 'Sister Elaine left.'

'Did she say where she was going?'

Cora shook her head. 'No. She just took off.'

'Are you here at the desk most of the time?' I asked.

'Oh, no. Just today. It's my chore for the day — minding the front desk.'

'And who was minding it when Ms. Manning left?'

'Sister Elaine, you mean. That was Saturday morning. As it happens, I was on the desk then, too. I had lunch-cooking duty and I traded with Brother Samuel. I hate cooking.'

'What time was it?'

'Right after breakfast. Around nine or so. The cops had come by the night before and talked to Pastor Mark. They told him what had happened to Brother LaShawn. The rest of us didn't hear about it until breakfast, when Pastor Mark made the official announcement.'

'And how did Sister Elaine react to that news?' I asked.

'About the way you'd expect. She was very upset, crying and everything,' Sister Cora said. 'But then we all were. Brother LaShawn was just the nicest person you'd ever hope to meet.'

'And Ms. Manning left right after that?' I asked.

'Almost right after,' Cora verified with a nod. 'She left the table while the rest of us were still there. When she came back downstairs, she had a suitcase with her. Well, not a suitcase, actually, a duffel bag. She went into Pastor Mark's office and talked to him for a few minutes. I was sitting here at the desk by then, so I heard them — their voices, anyway, not exactly what they were saying. They were yelling. I heard her say something about how dare he do something or other, but I didn't hear the rest of it.'

'Could it have been related to Mr. Tompkins's death?'

Sister Cora shrugged. 'I suppose so,' she said. 'A few minutes later Sister Elaine came out and asked me to call her a cab. Then she left.'

'Did she happen to mention to you where she was going or where the cab would be taking her?'

Sister Cora shook her head. 'She just said 'Get me a cab,' and I did. It was green, I think.'

But I happen to know that cab companies have records. They keep track of where and when they pick up fares; they also know where they drop them off.

'Tell me about Friday night,' I said. 'Were you here at dinner?'

Sister Cora nodded. 'We all were. The only excuse for missing dinner is if you're working at an outside job. With Brother LaShawn it was different, though. He was taking care of his mother, so that was all right. He had an excused absence, but everyone else was supposed to be here, and they were.'

'How many people is that?' I asked.

'Without Brother LaShawn and Sister Elaine, we're down to thirty-six. We can hold forty max.'

'The King Street Mission isn't exactly on the beaten path. How do people find this place?' I asked. 'How do they know to come here?'

'My parole officer told me about it,' she said. 'Praise God for that,' she added. 'Otherwise I'd probably be dead by now.'

But LaShawn Tompkins is dead, I thought. So that was small comfort.

'How does this place work?' I asked.

'Work?' she asked.

'Do you pay rent, or what?'

Sister Cora shook her head. 'There's no rent,' she said. 'But we have to obey all the rules. If you break one, you're gone — O-U-T.'

'And the rules are?'

'No booze. No drugs. No cigarettes. You do your assigned chores. You attend classes, work at the thrift store, do whatever needs to be done. We're here to better ourselves. To learn to make better choices.'

'How long do people stay?' I asked.

'As long as it takes,' Sister Cora answered.

105

'Sometimes it's only a couple of months. Sometimes it's longer. I'll be leaving in another month or so, after I get my new teeth.'

'New teeth?'

'I get fitted for them next week. A dentist volunteered to fit me for free. I can hardly wait.'

Without teeth Sister Cora looked like an old woman, although she was probably only in her midthirties. I tried to imagine how she'd look with new teeth. She'd most likely still look like she'd been rode hard and put up wet, but not as bad as she did right now.

'What about money?' I asked. 'If you're doing all this volunteer work and taking classes and studying the Bible, what do you do for spending money?'

'We don't need spending money,' she said simply. 'The Lord provides for our needs while we're here. We earn credits for the chores we do and for however many classes we take. If we do work at outside jobs, we turn that money over to the treasurer, who holds it until we leave. Then, when it's time to go, we have that money and whatever is in our credit account to use to get started outside — for an apartment deposit or whatever. It's like a little savings account.'

Yes, I thought. *At the bank of Pastor Mark.*

I wondered what kind of interest rate the good pastor paid, or if he paid any at all. Sister Cora's impending teeth notwithstanding, I kept trying to figure out if this wasn't some kind of scam. Maybe King Street Mission was the sort of place where if Pastor Mark directed the residents to swill down a cup of arsenic-laced Kool-Aid, they would all say 'Bottoms up' and guzzle away.

The front door opened. A man in a suit and properly knotted bow tie slammed his way in through the door and then strode across the room. I had him pegged for an attorney long before he opened his mouth.

'Is this man disturbing you, Sister Cora?' he demanded.

She looked at him in some confusion. 'Not at all, Mr. Ramsey. He was just asking a few questions.'

I recognized the name. That would be Dale Ramsey, of Ramsey, Ramsey, and something else, a name I vaguely remembered from some of the published legal papers regarding God's Word, LLC. Which meant Pastor Mark had run up the flag for help and here was Mr. Ramsey riding to the rescue.

'I'm afraid you'll have to leave now, Mr. Beaumont,' he said. (Pastor Mark's careful study of my ID had obviously allowed him to remember my name with uncanny accuracy. He had also duly reported it.)

'Sister Cora has work to do,' Ramsey continued. 'You've kept her from it long enough. Furthermore, Pastor Mark tells me that you're from the attorney general's office. Our people have spent all weekend answering questions for investigators from Seattle PD concerning the unfortunate death of Brother LaShawn. Unless Ross Connors's office has some reason for horning in on someone else's jurisdiction, I see no reason for this to continue.'

Ramsey was pushy in a stilted, officious, and

107

overly formal way. It's no wonder I took an instant dislike to the man. But for Ross Connors, deniability was still everything. If I made even the slightest objection, phone calls would be made to Seattle PD downtown. Questions would be asked. Attention would be paid.

'Of course,' I said, equally formally, and bowed slightly in Sister Cora's direction. 'You've been most helpful.'

Pastor Mark emerged from behind his closed office door in time to watch me leave. With his tattooed arms folded across his chest, he stood and smiled — smirked, really — at my being ejected. I nodded and sent my own half-baked smile in his direction, just to make sure we were even.

It doesn't matter if we're talking bars or missions. I don't like being run out of places before I'm ready to go. It rubs me the wrong way. In this case it made me think that God's Word, LLC, had something to hide. But thanks to Sister Cora, I wasn't walking away empty-handed. I knew which Seattle cab company had green cabs, and since they keep records, that meant that, whether the folks at God's Word liked it or not, I also had a lead on Elaine Manning's whereabouts.

I had left my cell phone in the car while I visited King Street Mission. I had been inside for far longer than I had anticipated, and again the phone was awash in messages. I hurried through them one by one.

'Hi, Dad,' Scott said cheerfully. 'Mel wanted me to call you with our flight information, but we'll be renting a car, so you don't need to worry about coming to pick us up. By the time we get our luggage, it'll probably be close to six-thirty or so. Are there dinner plans? Should we go there directly or just check into the hotel and wait for marching orders?'

The next caller was Mel: 'Where are you?' she asked. 'Why aren't you picking up? Did you remember to order the flowers?'

Next was one from my son-in-law: 'Hello. It's me. Jeremy.' He sounded nervous, and I can understand why. We hardly ever talk on the phone. 'We're in Salem at the Burger King,' he continued. 'Kelly's in the restroom changing Kyle's diaper. We'll probably be in Seattle around two or so. I guess we'll be coming straight to the house. I think that's what Kelly wanted me to tell you. If it isn't, I'll call back.'

If Kelly had charged her husband with calling me, did that mean she and I weren't speaking, or at least she wasn't speaking to me? If that was the case, it would make the occasion of my grandmother's funeral more than a little awkward.

Mel again: 'Harry wants to know if the funeral is a private affair or if it would be all right if some of the SHIT guys came along,' Mel said. 'I told him it was fine, but now I'm wondering. Should I have checked with Lars? Do we know how many people really are coming? Had we better order some food and reserve the party room? Call me.'

Awkward and complicated. This was beginning to sound like putting on a wedding

109

— minus the bride and groom.

Next was Men's Wearhouse: 'Mr. Beaumont, when you were in on Monday, we were told that you needed your tux in time for Friday. It's ready now. Could you please stop by at your convenience and try it on? That way, if any additional alterations are required . . . ' Checking on a tux for Friday seemed like a very low priority.

Mel again: 'I've been trying to think of where we should go to dinner with a new baby and all. I finally decided that we'd be better off eating at home. So I've called that new catering place, Magical Meals, and I've cleared it with the doorman. They'll deliver a roast beef dinner with all the trimmings to the condo, complete with someone to serve and clean up. They'll be at the house at six. If you think that's a bad idea . . . ' In fact, it seemed nothing short of brilliant.

Then a message from Lars: '*Ja*, sure,' he said. 'If you have time, give me a call . . . '

I hadn't been writing anything down, and by then my head was spinning. I called Lars back first. 'What's up?' I asked.

'I t'ink I'd like to go to another meeting,' he said. 'If it's not too much trouble.'

'I'm on my way,' I said.

I called Mel back and breathed a small thank-you when I reached her answering machine instead of her. 'Busy with Lars,' I said. 'Taking him to a meeting. Dinner sounds great.'

I forgot about the tux, but on the way to Queen Anne Gardens I remembered to call the flower shop and got the flowers ordered. Several different arrangements. Big ones. Spare no expense. So I may not be great, but at least I'm not entirely useless. In between all that I even managed to call the cab company and started the process of tracing Elaine Manning's Saturday-morning ride.

Lars came out to the car looking like death warmed over. I'd managed to find another noontime meeting, this one over on the east side at a place called Angelo's. I'd been there before, years ago. So had Lars.

'Thank you,' he said, once he got in the car.

'What's going on?' I asked.

He shook his head. 'I cannot believe t'ose women,' he said. 'The first one knocked on my door this morning to see if I needed someone to help me with breakfast. *Ja*, sure, I can eat my own breakfast! And it's been that way all day long, one of them after another.'

Are we going to a meeting just to get away from a bunch of pushy women? I wondered. Or is he afraid one of them will haul out a bottle of booze and slip some to him?

So we went to the meeting. Then, because Lars was in no hurry to go home, we went by and picked up my tux. And then, because he still didn't want to go back to Queen Anne Gardens, I took him along on a jaunt through the grocery store to stock up on essentials and then home to Belltown Terrace with me, where he settled into my recliner and snored like a jackhammer for the remainder of the afternoon.

I did my best to work around him. The dispatcher from the cab company called to say

111

Elaine Manning had been dropped off at the YWCA on Fifth. I called there and made inquiries, but to no avail. It's a lot easier to tell someone to buzz off when you're talking to them on the phone than it is when they're standing right there in front of your desk. So I figured I'd try talking to the ladies at the YWCA another time when I didn't have Lars Jenssen underfoot and a whole contingent of company bearing down on me from every point of the compass.

Then, because the house was still quiet — relatively quiet due to Lars's Olympian snoring — and because I couldn't think of anything more to do about LaShawn Tompkins right then, I called up LexisNexis one more time and, just for the hell of it, typed in the name Anthony David Cosgrove.

All right. So I complained about computers for years. Resisted using them. Griped about having to use them. But now I'm a believer. Within seconds of typing the name, there it was — a whole list of hits concerning Anthony David Cosgrove. To my surprise one of them was only two months old. It came from an obscure magazine called *Electronics Engineering Journal*. It was a long, amazingly dull article on corruption and payoffs among defense contractors. The reference to Cosgrove came near the end of the article.

According to industry analyst Thomas Dortman, payoffs with dollar signs on them are the ones that gain big headlines, but payoffs that result in job offers are almost

112

standard operating procedure. One of the earliest Dortman recalls happened at Boeing in the early eighties. In that instance charges came to nothing, however, when the alleged whistle-blower, electronics engineer Anthony David Cosgrove, disappeared in the Mount Saint Helens explosion.

That was it. But still, it was intriguing. The missing persons report had said nothing about Cosgrove being involved in any kind of at-work investigation. And DeAnn hadn't mentioned anything to me about it either, but she had been a little girl at the time. Something could well have been going on at work without her having any knowledge of it. The wife would have known, however, and I was interested to see that she had made no mention of it.

I jotted down Thomas Dortman's name. If, as he claimed, he had personal knowledge of what was going on at Boeing in the early eighties, maybe he had personal knowledge of Anthony David Cosgrove as well.

The next listing for Anthony Cosgrove predated the previous one by almost twenty years. It turned out to be the 1988 announcement in which the man was declared legally dead. It seems to me that being declared legally dead would be enough to get your name removed from a missing persons list, but bureaucracies really are bureaucracies, and the right hand often has no idea what the left is doing.

I would have plowed on. I was about to put Dortman's name into my search engine when the phone rang.

'Okay,' Detective Kendall Jackson said. 'Thought you'd want to know that you've flunked Miss Congeniality one more time. You're back on everybody's bad list again.'

'Me?' I asked with feigned innocence. 'What have I done this time?'

'Stepped on somebody's toes hard enough that we've been told we're not to share information about LaShawn Tompkins's murder with anyone, most especially anyone with the initials J.P. So what did you find out?'

'I found out that the King Street Mission gives me the creeps,' I replied.

'I hear you loud and clear on that one,' Jackson said.

'And I wouldn't trust Pastor Mark any farther than I can throw him.'

'Ditto on that,' Jackson agreed.

'I learned that King Street Mission will be holding a memorial service for LaShawn on Thursday night, and I know I can't attend.'

'No problem,' Jackson said. 'Hank and I already have that one covered.'

I had saved the best for last. 'And I've traced Elaine Manning as far as the YWCA on Fifth Avenue, arriving at ten-oh-six on Saturday morning. I have no idea where she went from there.'

'That's something I didn't know,' Jackson said. 'Thanks for the heads-up. I'll check it out.'

'So you and I are still good, then?' I asked.

'As far as I know,' he replied. 'Your name's Beau Beaumont, right? Never heard of anyone named J.P.'

Detective Kendall Jackson was indeed my kind of guy.

About then I thought everything was in good shape, but before I could return to LexisNexis, the phone rang. It was the doorman calling to let me know that my daughter and her family were downstairs. Could he send them up?

'Of course,' I said. After that, everything went straight to hell. In a handbasket. –

I expected Kyle to be a handful. After all, he was only a month or so old. And Lars? Of course he would need attention. His wife had just died. And Kayla? She's four. What could you expect, especially considering the fact that my penthouse condo is anything but kid-proof. (Then again, when it comes to four-year-olds, is anything ever really kid-proof?) What I didn't anticipate was that Kelly would be more of a pain in the neck than all of the rest of them put together.

Because, as I had gathered from our nonphone conversation, she really wasn't speaking to me. She spoke to Lars. She spoke to Jeremy, who looked as though he would much prefer being anywhere else in the universe to being cooped up in his father-in-law's domicile. Kelly spoke to Kayla. When she went into the guest room to feed Kyle and put him down for a nap, I went gunning for Jeremy. I found him hiding out in the family room with Kayla, who was watching a cartoon about someone named Elmer or Elmo — something like that. Kayla and Lars were both engrossed in watching the TV. Jeremy was dozing. Like Kelly, he, too, had that dim, chronically sleep-deprived look which, as I remember, is part and parcel of having a newborn in the house. I woke him up.

'What's going on with Kelly?' I asked.

Jeremy shook his head and shrugged. 'Beats me,' he said miserably. 'All I know is I can't do anything right.'

'That makes two of us,' I said.

At which point Kelly suddenly reappeared in the doorway. 'Let's go,' she announced.

Jeremy said, 'Where?'

'To the hotel,' Kelly said. 'Obviously that's somebody else's room! I wouldn't want to be in the way.'

'No!' Kayla wailed. 'I don't want to go!'

In actual fact, it was someone else's closet. Mel didn't use the bedroom at all, but with Mel's clothing and makeup clearly evident in both the bathroom and the closet, I could see how Kelly might have gotten that mistaken idea into her head.

'I thought we were going to stay for dinner,' Jeremy objected.

'We'll eat at McDonald's,' Kelly said firmly. 'Kayla will like that better anyway.'

'I don't wanna go!' Kayla said. 'I want to stay here. With Gumpa.'

Lars said, 'Is there a problem?'

Dutifully Jeremy began collecting things — the diaper bag, the baby carrier, and all the other little necessaries that go with being parents of young children — while Kelly simply headed for

116

the door with the blanket-swaddled Kyle in her arms. By then Kayla was wailing at the top of her lungs and stamping her feet. 'Don't wanna go. Don't wanna go.'

At which point the telephone rang again. 'Your caterer is here,' the doorman announced. 'Should I send her up?'

Why the hell not? I thought. 'By all means,' I said.

Kayla was still screeching as the elevator headed for the lobby. It was enough to make me long for the old days and the relative peace and quiet of the Seattle PD homicide squad — even if Captain Paul Kramer was the guy running the show.

8

The catered dinner was not a huge success. In fact, although the food itself was excellent, the company was lacking. Kelly and Jeremy did not attend. Lars wasn't hungry. Scott and Cherisse showed up an hour and a half later than expected due to their Seattle-bound aircraft having had some kind of mechanical problem while it was still on the ground at SFO. Their food was cold. Mel didn't show up for dinner at all. And she didn't call.

This should probably be filed under the heading of 'Just Deserts,' because if my ex-wife Karen were still alive, I'm sure she could recount, chapter and verse, the many times I missed meals — and didn't call, either. But knowing it was payback time didn't make me feel any better. About 9:00 P.M., when I came back from returning Lars to his digs at Queen Anne Gardens, Mel was home. I found her at the dining room table. Still damp from taking a shower and clad only in a robe, she was chowing down on leftovers.

'How'd it go?' she asked.

'Could have been better,' I muttered. 'Where've you been?'

'Crime scene,' she replied. 'Out by Mount Si. We were out in the boonies far enough that we ended up in a telecommunications black hole. Cell phones don't work there.'

'What kind of crime scene?' I asked.

'Homicide,' she said. 'What did you think it would be?'

Barring unusual circumstances, SHIT isn't often called in on homicide crime scenes. First response usually falls to local agencies and jurisdictions.

'Whose case is it?' I asked. 'And how come you took the call?'

'It happened in rural King County,' Mel explained. 'But it turns out the victim is one of mine — one of my registered sex offenders, that is. So we're running a joint investigation. The guy's name is Kates — Allen Christopher Kates. That's still tentative, even though it's based on ID we found on the body. We'll need dental records to get a positive, and we won't have those from the Department of Corrections until tomorrow at the earliest.'

The call for dental records implied that the body had been there for a while. I've been to grim crime scenes like that. The fact that Mel could come from a sickening homicide investigation with her appetite for dinner still intact said a lot about who she was — and why I liked her.

'Kates lived by himself in a little camper shell out in the woods, sort of like the guy down in Oregon,' Mel continued. 'He wasn't big on friends and family, since he'd been dead for a month or longer before anyone bothered to report him missing.'

'Meth lab?' I asked.

People who live by themselves in the woods often participate in the manufacturing sector.

119

Mixing up batches of meth is a growth industry in rural areas all over the country.

'Nope,' Mel said. 'No sign of meth. He was growing plenty of grass, however.' And she didn't mean Bermuda.

'What did he die of?' I asked.

'A single bullet wound to the head. It was fired from point-blank range. Blew out most of his skull.'

'Self-inflicted?' I asked.

'Not likely,' she answered, 'since no weapon was found at the scene.'

'And how did you get dragged into it?'

'Like I said, he was one of the guys on my list. I happened to be checking on him at the same time someone else was busy finding the body.'

'That makes what, now — three of your guys, as you call them — dead? One in Oregon, one in Bellingham, and now this?'

'More like seven,' Mel said as she stood to clear her plate and carry the remaining containers of roast beef, mashed potatoes, and gravy back to the fridge. 'I thought Ross wanted me to verify addresses of living sex offenders. I had no idea so many of them would have croaked. And the dead guys are all over the map — literally. Two now in Washington, one each in Idaho, Oregon, and Montana, and two more in Arizona.'

It didn't surprise me to think that any given list of ex-cons, violent sexual predators or otherwise, would have a high mortality rate. They're not exactly the kind of folks who avoid what insurance actuaries like to call 'risky behavior.' Accidental overdoses of illegal drugs routinely take out far more bad guys these days than executioner-administered lethal injections ever will.

'So your guys are dying like flies. What of?'

Mel smiled at my inadvertent rhyme. 'Three car accidents,' she said. 'The guy on Chuckanut Drive and the two in Arizona. Ricardo Fernando Hernandez and Felix Andrade Moreno were cell mates in Monroe and later roommates down in Phoenix. Their vehicle ended up upside down in an irrigation canal outside Phoenix. Hernandez was behind the wheel and drunk. That one's been ruled an accident. Idaho and Montana were both overdoses, most likely suicides, although no notes were found.'

'Maybe they couldn't write,' I suggested.

'And maybe there was too much pressure,' Mel said. 'At least that's how it looks for some of them. Once they're out of the slammer they're required to register with local authorities and their information is posted on the Internet. The guy in Pocatello, Frederick Jamison, lost his job and was being evicted once his information became public. Pretty much the same thing happened to Ray Ramirez in Helena, Montana. There was a huge public outcry from the neighbors about him coming back there to live with his parents.'

'Pardon me while I don't go all warm and fuzzy over a bunch of loser sexual predators,' I told her. 'And what's the matter with you? Sounds like you're saying 'evil, nosy neighbors' and 'poor, pitiful sexual predators.' '

Mel looked troubled. 'I'm not saying anything of the kind, but it does strike me as odd. I've only worked my way through a hundred and fifty names or so, and seven dead strikes me as a pretty high number. These are reasonably young guys, mostly in their thirties and forties. I think something's amiss here, and I don't know what. I also think that's why Ross has me looking into it — because, as you said, they are dying like flies.'

I was starting to feel better by then, lulled by the simple normality of talking shop with Mel, of discussing the nuts and bolts of her several cases. I have no doubt that my visit to the King Street Mission would have benefited from a dose of Mel Soames's insightful analysis, too, but asking for her help on that one would have meant admitting I was working a case when I was supposedly off work on bereavement leave and looking after Lars. The same went for Anthony David Cosgrove. Since I wasn't supposed to be working, I didn't bring that one up, either.

We went from the table to the window seat, where Mel moved a cushion and unearthed one of Kayla's toys, a red hand puppet that looked a lot like the cartoon character she'd been watching on TV earlier in the afternoon. Obviously Jeremy's rushed toy-collection mission hadn't been entirely successful.

'Elmo,' Mel said, slipping the puppet onto her hand.

'I never heard of him,' I told her. 'How do you know this guy's name is Elmo?'

Mel laughed. 'I'm a detective, remember?' she said, whacking me playfully on the noggin with

Elmo's semi-hard head. 'I get paid for knowing things. Actually, my niece loves anything Elmo. What's your excuse for not knowing? And where did everybody go? I expected to come home to a houseful of company.'

And so I gave her a blow-by-blow description of my disastrous 'family' afternoon and evening, including the part about Kelly decamping in a huff once she found Mel's personal items lurking in the guest room closet and bathroom.

'Sounds like she's suffering from a severe case of separation anxiety,' Mel said. 'She's afraid of losing you to me.'

'That's ridiculous,' I argued. 'Kelly isn't losing me. I'm not going anywhere.'

'She just had a baby,' Mel pointed out. 'I'm guessing her hormones are all out of whack at the moment. You need to be patient.'

'She's the one who could use some patience,' I grumbled.

Shaking her head, Mel changed the subject. 'Did you ever get around to making some kind of arrangements for a post-funeral reception for Lars?' she asked.

I had been playing social director all afternoon, but this one responsibility had somehow fallen off the radar. 'Damn!' I said.

'I take that to mean no?' Mel asked.

I nodded. She immediately reached for her cell phone. 'I'll call Rita, then,' she said. 'I'm sure she'll do it.'

'Who's Rita?' I asked.

'Rita Davenport. She runs the same catering company that served dinner tonight. She and I

123

are both board members of SASAC. That's how I knew to call her. Why don't you check with the manager on party room availability. I'll see what I can do about rounding up some food.'

Luckily, the party room was open for early Thursday afternoon. While I reserved it via the landline, Mel made arrangements for Magical Meals to provide food and beverages. In less time than I would have thought possible, Beverly Jenssen's post-funeral reception was a done deal.

'You do good work,' I told Mel when she put the phone back down.

'Thank you,' she said, turning to give me a long, inviting kiss. 'I'm actually a multitalented girl.'

And that was absolutely true.

I awakened the next morning to the smell of brewing coffee and to Mel's voice on the telephone telling Harry I. Ball in no uncertain terms that Allen Kates or no Allen Kates, Mel was taking the day off.

'The man's already been dead for more than a month,' she said. 'If King County comes up with anything today, I'm sure they'll be more than happy to bring me up to speed tomorrow.'

Harry Ignatius Ball was fearless, except when it comes to dealing with irate women. He's liable to say something politically incorrect in the process, but he always capitulates. This was no exception. Harry buckled.

'Now that I'm not going in,' Mel said, handing me my coffee, 'do we have a schedule?'

We didn't, but Mel managed to organize one in short order. Scott and Cherisse were dispatched to Queen Anne Gardens to collect Lars and bring him to the Shanty on lower Queen Anne for a family breakfast. Despite the risk of occasionally running into Maxwell Cole, I've come to appreciate the Shanty in the past few months. It's old enough for me to feel comfortable there, and I know Lars likes it, too. It had the added advantage of being within easy walking distance of the kids' hotel.

I expected breakfast to be another disaster, but it wasn't. Mel disarmed Kelly's emotional Molotov cocktail by charming Kayla with a pocketful of stickers and by holding Kyle and cooing over him in a way that would have dumbfounded her fellow SHIT officers, Harry I. Ball included. And while Mel and I looked after the kids, Lars had everyone else's undivided attention as he passed around Beverly Piedmont Jenssen's treasured scrapbooks.

On that particular day, that collection of yellowed newspaper clippings served as my grandmother's parting gift to me — and an incredible blessing. It amounted to pretty much a hard-copy LexisNexis report on the life and times of J. P. Beaumont, but this one had been done the old-fashioned way, with scissors and Elmer's glue.

Back in the days when names meant business for local community newspapers, Beverly had culled all kinds of bits and pieces of my life from the pages of the now-defunct *Ballard Dispatch*. There were items about Cub Scout activities and high school athletic events, all of them carefully clipped and dated. I don't think either of the kids had ever seen Karen's engagement photo or our wedding announcement. (Our divorce announcement was there, too, but that was much later. Beverly wasn't one for editing out bad news.)

Later on, the stories shifted away from the *Dispatch* and onto the pages of the *Seattle Times* and the *P-I*, as my career as first a Seattle PD beat cop and later as a detective took off and occasionally became newsworthy. There were secrets lurking among my grandmother's treasures that neither of my children had ever known or suspected about their father. It turned out Beverly had managed to glean things about Kelly and Scott as well — their published birth announcements, for example. Beverly had continued keeping her loving long-distance vigil even after I had reconciled with her and my grandfather.

And at the very last, tucked into the first empty page in the most recent notebook, was the cardboard-framed hospital photo of Kyle. I'm sure Lars put it there for the simple reason that he needed to put it away. I don't know if his choice of the notebook was deliberate or accidental, but I gave him credit for a stroke of pure genius when I saw the tearfully grateful look Kelly shot in my direction when she found it. The look was utterly priceless — and due entirely to Mel's efforts rather than my own.

By the time we left the restaurant it was almost time to go to the funeral home.

I don't like funerals, probably because I've been to far too many of them in my time. And I expected this one to be bad news. I realized it was going to be different, however, as soon as we walked into the chapel, where an invisible organ was playing 'Love Is Lovelier the Second Time Around.' The back two rows were packed with people — mostly women and one lone man — from Queen Anne Gardens. Also near the back was the contingent from SHIT — Harry and the two other guys from Squad B, Brad Norton and Aaron Oliver. Close to the front were my friends Ron and Amy Peters, along with their three kids. Ralph and Mary Ames were also in attendance.

The whole front of the chapel was arrayed with floral arrangements. Maybe I had overdone it a little, but not that much. As Beverly had specified, there were two separate boxes of cremains on the altar. Between them stood a color photo of a beaming Beverly Piedmont Jenssen, dressed, for once in her life, in sparkling formal attire.

The photo had been one of those shipboard rites of passage taken prior to the formal-night dinner on the *Starfire Breeze* during their honeymoon cruise to Alaska. Seeing Beverly's very sophisticated upswept hairdo, I remembered the firefight that had resulted when Lars had made the tactical blunder of comparing Beverly's hairdo to the fender on a '57 Cadillac. If you studied the photo closely, you could see the edge of Lars's glasses where someone, using one of those computerized photo-editing programs, had excised him from the formal pose.

Lars leaned over me. '*Ja*, sure,' he said. 'Yust

look at all the flowers. Who do you t'ink sent them?'

'No idea,' I said.

Robert Staunton, the chaplain from Queen Anne Gardens, officiated at the ceremony and did a credible job of it. It was clear from his remarks that he knew Lars and Beverly well, and that he had liked and respected them. What he had to say was in fact a celebration of the love and caring they had brought to each other late in life.

Toward the end of the service Staunton opened the proceedings for comments from friends and family. I was surprised when Kelly handed Kyle over to Jeremy and stepped up to the microphone.

'I didn't meet my great-grandmother at all until just a few years ago,' Kelly said. 'But I know she loved us even when we weren't together, and I'm grateful to have known her at all. And I'm grateful to Lars for making her so happy.'

That pretty well said it for me. There wasn't a single thing I could have added to that statement, so I didn't try.

When it came time to leave the chapel, Lars handed the two boxes of cremains over to Scott for safekeeping. Then he picked up the photo and carried it with him for the remainder of the day, clutching it to his chest as though it were a talisman that would drive away the several elderly women who did tend to cluster around him. As far as they were concerned, however, Lars Jenssen's opinion to the contrary, I never saw anything at all in the women's behavior that was the least bit inappropriate. They seemed like nice, ordinary women who were clucking in order to express sincere concern for someone who had lost his mate. Period. If one of them was dead set on maneuvering Lars into the sack, I didn't see any evidence of it. –

Scott and Jeremy loaded all the flowers into the back of Scott's rented Taurus to take back to Belltown Terrace for the reception. As they were doing the loading, Lars was busy obsessing about how he'd manage to write all the thank-you notes.

'Not to worry,' Mel assured him. 'I'll handle it.'

Thus saving my bacon one more time.

We made it through the reception in fairly good shape. I had been prepared to take the whole group out to dinner, but Scott let me know that wasn't necessary. 'Jeremy and Cherisse haven't spent much time in Seattle,' he said. 'And, according to them, Kayla spent her whole day's worth of good behavior at the funeral. We're going to go out for pizza and then tomorrow we're going to go sightseeing. If you want to come along . . . '

Somehow the idea of my kids' spending some adult time together because they wanted to, without squabbling and without parental enforcement, was an idea that warmed me. 'I think I'll take a pass on pizza and sightseeing,' I said. 'But maybe we can have dinner together tomorrow night.'

Mel caught my eye. 'We're booked tomorrow evening, remember?' she said. Then she added, 'Although, if you want to spend time with your kids, I can go alone.'

Then I remembered — the fund-raising auction and the tux. I also knew that the day had gone as well as it had due, in no small measure, to Melissa Soames's efforts. I owed her.

'How long are you staying in town?' I asked.

Scott grinned. 'The desk clerk said our bill is paid until Sunday, so we aren't going home before then. Really, though, Sunday is when our plane leaves, and that's when Kelly and Jeremy plan to head back, too.'

'Saturday, then,' I said. 'We'll make a day of it and have dinner together on Saturday.'

By six everybody was gone. Lars had returned home. The floral arrangements had been dispersed — some to Queen Anne Gardens, some to the front lobby of Belltown Terrace, and some to our living room. I was in the recliner with my feet up. Mel had just kicked off her shoes and curled up on the window seat to browse through Beverly Jenssen's scrapbooks when her cell phone rang. She had to get up and track down her purse in order to answer.

I listened in on her part of the conversation, but her noncommittal yeses and uh-huhs didn't tell me much. By the time she ended the call, though, she was visibly upset.

'Who was that?' I asked.

'Lenny Kessleman,' she said. 'Head of CSI for King County.'

'What's the matter?'

'The bullet from the Kates homicide scene is missing.'

'Maybe one of the detectives who was there

130

yesterday picked it up and failed to put it in the log.'

'It's missing from the wall,' Mel clarified firmly. 'We all saw the hole in the wood paneling inside the camper. Since it didn't penetrate the outside of the camper shell, we assumed it was lodged between the paneling and the shell and was probably stuck somewhere in the insulation. We decided to leave the paneling as is until after the CSIs had finished up with the other evidence.'

When a bullet exits a human skull, there's always plenty of biological evidence — blood, bone chips, and brain matter — left behind. I understood why detectives on the scene would have left the bullet undisturbed until after all that evidence, including blood spatter and possible shoe prints, had been properly photo-graphed, collected, and cataloged.

'So today they cut out that chunk of paneling and dug through the insulation, but the bullet wasn't there,' Mel continued. 'And from what Kessleman just told me, when they took the piece of paneling in for processing, they found evidence that would be consistent with the bullet having been removed from there at the time of the shooting.'

I've done plenty of head-shot crime scene investigations in my time. Encountering the physical evidence of one of those can be a soul-shattering experience — even long after the fact. If Allen Kates's killer had been tough enough to wade through fresh blood and gore in order to retrieve damning evidence of his crime,

131

it was likely we were dealing with someone who was appallingly cold-blooded. Most murderers don't come equipped with the presence of mind to clean up after themselves. Most of them aren't that smart.

'What about shoe prints?' I asked.

'What I saw would be consistent with a killer who wore booties.'

That meant the guy was definitely crime-scene savvy.

'Sounds like you're dealing with somebody who's watched way too many CSI programs on TV.'

'There is one more possibility,' Mel ventured after a pause. 'Maybe our killer is a cop.'

Unfortunately, given the circumstances, that conclusion wasn't at all outside the realm of possibility.

'That would certainly explain why Ross Connors is involved.'

'Wouldn't it just,' Mel agreed. With that, she once more reached for her phone.

9

Ross Connors's SHIT squad is the first place I've ever worked that isn't all hung up on everybody going through channels and across desks. I find that very refreshing. Yes, Harry I. Ball runs our unit, but Ross values the handpicked people he's chosen as his investigators and he trusts them. He's made it abundantly clear that we all have direct access to him whenever and wherever we deem it necessary. So it didn't surprise me that the call Mel placed was to the attorney general. Nor did it surprise me when he called her back five minutes after she left him a message.

She gave him a brief rundown of what Kessleman had told her, then she started hedging. 'I suppose I could meet you at the office or else my place in Bellevue in about twenty minutes.'

Mel paused while he said something in return. After a glance in my direction, she replied, 'Ten minutes? Sure. That'll be fine. One of us will be downstairs to let him in.'

To my astonishment she was blushing as she closed her phone. 'So who told Ross we were living together?'

'I sure as hell didn't!' I exclaimed.

'Well, somebody did,' she said. 'He's at a meeting at the Fairmont. He'll be here in ten minutes.'

'He's coming here?' That did surprise me. The mountain usually doesn't go to Muhammad, and the fact that he was coming to Belltown Terrace for a late-evening personal visit meant something was up — something that couldn't wait until regular business hours.

With only ten minutes' worth of warning there wasn't time to stand around speculating about it. I'm on the wagon. Have been for years. Washington State attorney general Ross Connors is definitely not on the wagon. Anything but.

In the old days — the pre — Melissa Soames days — an unexpected evening visit from him would have necessitated my knocking on my neighbors' doors in search of a borrowed cup of spirits. Now that Mel was living here, however, we had a moderately decent wine cellar. The best I could do was offer Ross a glass of wine from a twenty-dollar bottle of imported French Bordeaux purchased from Mel's wine merchant of choice — Costco.

While Mel went downstairs to collect our visitor I opened the bottle, set out some glasses, and poured myself a tonic and tonic over ice.

When Ross showed up, he looked surprisingly distressed and I could tell he'd already had a drink or two. 'This is ostensibly a condolence call,' he said brusquely as Mel led him into the room. 'Other than that, no meeting has taken place. Got it?'

So Beverly Jenssen was still providing cover — this time for the A.G. himself.

'Got it,' I said. I poured him a glass of wine. He took a long sip without really tasting it.

'So let's go over this Kates thing again,' he said to Mel. 'From the top.'

He listened without comment as Mel recounted the story. 'Any ideas?' he asked when she finished.

'Beau and I were speculating just before you got here,' Mel replied. 'We're wondering if maybe Kates's killer could be a cop, or at the very least someone with a law enforcement background.'

Ross shifted uneasily in his chair, and since he had appropriated my recliner, I knew it wasn't that uncomfortable. 'Could be,' he said. Then he sighed and continued. 'Our killer could be a cop or an ex-cop or maybe even a correctional officer who's systematically targeting ex-cons who did their time in Washington State. We need to know if this is an inside job. That's why I put both of you on the two separate cases — with Mel running the sexual-offender roundup and you on the LaShawn Tompkins incident. That way, if the two cases do link up, I'm hoping to localize the problem.'

Mel gave me a look. Hers said clearly, 'Who the hell is LaShawn Tompkins?' which meant that whatever more Ross might say in that regard was going to put me in deeper — in the other kind of shit — with Melissa Soames.

Hoping to divert her attention, I spoke up. 'Are you saying you think we're dealing with two separate issues, or one?'

Ross nodded. 'I'm not sure,' he said, 'but it's possible they're not separate at all.'

He peered bleakly at Mel over the rims of his glasses — the one in his hand and the pair

135

perched on his nose. 'The report you sent me yesterday morning, prior to finding Mr. Kates's body, indicated you had found six dead victims. Let's assume for argument's sake that the two guys who ended up in the irrigation canal in Phoenix really were involved in a drunk-driving incident and their deaths aren't related. But the rest do seem suspicious, not so much when taken individually — as I'm sure was intended — but certainly when taken together. So what have you learned so far?'

'Les Fordham is the victim from down near Roseburg,' Mel answered. 'Arson investigators found nothing amiss with any of the gas appliances or gas lines in the trailer. The burners were simply left on without being ignited. Eventually enough gas built up inside the mobile home for the pilot light on the hot water heater to set it off. Roseburg effectively closed the case by assuming it was suicide, but Fordham's parole officer swears his client was doing well. He had a good job and a new girlfriend. There was nothing going on that would account for his committing suicide.'

'Any note?' Ross asked.

'No note,' Mel told him.

'What about the guy on Chuckanut Drive?' Ross asked.

'That would be Ed Chrisman,' Mel answered, without having to resort to looking at the notebook she had retrieved from her briefcase. 'That, too, was officially designated an accident. The problem with that is that when the vehicle was recovered, it was still in gear. How many times in your life did you get out of a car to take a leak and leave the damned thing in drive?'

Mel's question was directed at Ross, but I was the one who answered.

'Never,' I said.

Ross nodded, reached for the bottle, and poured himself a second glass. I didn't say anything, but my concern must have been obvious. 'Don't worry,' he said, glancing at me. 'I have a car and driver waiting downstairs.' Then he turned back to Mel. 'What about the others?'

Mel scanned her notes. 'Frederick Jamison died of an accidental overdose in Pocatello, Idaho. Ray Ramirez succumbed to the same thing in Helena, Montana.'

'Were each of those cases thoroughly investigated?' Ross asked.

'I can't say one way or the other,' Mel answered. 'I certainly don't have access to all the files at this point, but my guess is probably not. They were labeled suspicious deaths. The reports I've seen so far are pretty sketchy. Maybe whoever did this counted on that — on the idea that local authorities wouldn't expend a lot of time, energy, or expense in resolving these cases. After all, who gives a damn about one dead crook more or less?'

Clearly Ross Connors did. These guys were all dying on his watch.

'Someone else is bound to pick up on this and start making connections. It's going to explode once it hits the media,' he said glumly. 'At that point there'll be hell to pay regardless of who's actually doing the killing here. And guess who's going to have to shoulder the blame?'

For the better part of twenty years Ross Connors had navigated Washington State's stormy political seas with apparent impunity. I suspect that, for the first time, he was encountering a crisis that could leave him vulnerable. That explained his wanting to keep our investigation under wraps, at least in these preliminary stages.

'So what we need to know is who is behind this,' Ross said. 'Who he is and how he's locating and targeting his victims.'

'Finding them is easy,' Mel said. 'So far all the dead guys on my list are sexual offenders with their addresses posted on the Internet.'

'But that doesn't explain LaShawn Tompkins,' Connors said. 'He wouldn't be on any registered sexual offender list because he's not a sexual predator per se since he was actually exonerated on the rape charge.'

'If he's not listed,' I said, 'maybe his death has nothing to do with the others.'

Ross heaved a sigh. 'But Tompkins was imprisoned here,' he said. 'He may not have been guilty, but the fact that he's out of prison now makes him an ex-con. What neither of you know is that three more dead ex-con cases turned up today — one in New Mexico, one in Nevada, and one more here in Washington, down in Vancouver. None of them would have ended up on Mel's list because they're not sexual predators. Two are grand theft auto and the other one is a bank robbery. Two died of unexplained drug overdoses and one of carbon monoxide poisoning in a closed garage.'

I remembered Mel saying her cases were all over the map. These were even more so, not only geographically but also in terms of murder weapon. The more I heard, the more unlikely it seemed that we were dealing with a single killer.

'We've got someone twisted here,' Ross continued morosely, 'some egomaniac who's appointed himself judge, jury, and executioner. From what you've told me, whoever killed Allen Kates is familiar with crime scene investigation and forensics.'

'That's true in the other cases as well, at least as far as I've perused the files,' Mel said. 'In each case the assailant left behind almost no trace evidence.'

'So he's wily,' I said. 'And careful. And he is also someone who has access to prison-release records,' I added.

'That's why I'm saying it's a rogue cop,' Ross concluded. 'That's what I've been thinking ever since Todd brought it to my attention. Either a bad cop or a corrections worker gone postal.'

I know all the guys who work for SHIT — at least I thought I did. But the name Todd didn't ring a bell.

'Todd who?' I asked.

Ross squirmed in his seat once more. 'Todd Hatcher,' he answered. 'A guy who works in my office.'

'An attorney then?' I asked.

'No,' Ross said. 'Actually, he's an economist.'

I almost choked on a sip of icy tonic. When I was in college I washed out of only two classes

— economics and philosophy. I ended up taking incompletes in both of them. Since then I've looked on practitioners of either profession with a somewhat jaundiced eyeball.

'An economist?' I croaked. 'Are you kidding?'

'Not at all,' Ross returned. 'Ever heard of forensic economics?'

Mel and I shook our heads in unison.

'It's relatively new,' Ross said. 'Before last summer, neither had I, but then Todd turned up and told me all about it. He had just picked up a Ph.D. in economics from the University of Washington. He claimed that by doing a statistical analysis of our current and recent prison population he could create a computer model that would predict our recidivism rates, tell us how many prison beds we would need in the future — where, when, and what kind. For instance, he thinks he can sort out the exact number of geriatric facilities we'll eventually need as our prison population ages.

'Believe me, those kinds of studies can cost big bucks. But here was this one very motivated guy who wanted to do it for practically nothing. He had made a similar proposal for his dissertation, but his faculty adviser had turned him down. I think he came to me because he was still pissed at his adviser. The fact that the university had axed the project made him that much more determined to do it, so much so that he offered to work for a pittance as long as I gave him unlimited access to our data. Truth be known, he probably has a book deal waiting in the wings somewhere. Why wouldn't he? He's an economist, for God's sake. But in terms of cost to the state of Washington, it was an irresistible offer.'

'So you took him on,' Mel said. 'An economist, not a cop.'

'That's right,' Ross agreed. 'So I hired Hatcher. I gave him an office and a computer and turned him loose with oodles of information. Shortly after he started doing his study, however, Todd hit on an anomaly — a sudden spike in mortality rates among recently released inmates, one that didn't fit inside the expected actuarial norms for that particular population. That's his area of expertise, you see — demographics.'

'How recent a spike?' I asked.

'In the last year and a half or so. Before that, the death rates were pretty steady and followed predictable patterns. Many of those deaths were clearly age-, behavior-, or illness-related. But the dead guys in this new group are all fairly young — twenties, thirties, and forties — relatively healthy, and they all seem to have died under mysterious circumstances that aren't necessarily homicides. Several of the deaths have been labeled simply suspicious. So I asked Todd to start looking into it. He's been at it for only two weeks now and he's already come up with the ones I told you about tonight as well as with the ones Mel found. You can see why I'm leaning in the direction of a cop gone bad, and if it turns out he's someone who's worked for me . . . ' Ross shook his head, lapsed into a moody silence, and stared into the depths of his almost empty wineglass.

Now I began to fathom why Ross Connors was so gun-shy about news of our investigation getting out. A previous leak from the A.G.'s office had resulted in the death of a woman in the witness protection program — someone it had been his professional obligation to protect. I knew that failure on his part still weighed heavily on him, especially since it had eventually led to the death of Ross's own wife. No wonder he was so concerned. If it turned out a serial killer with close to a dozen victims could be traced back to his administration, Ross's days as attorney general were probably numbered. Still, it irked me to think that Mel and I were working as glorified fact-checkers for some hotshot economist.

'If we discover present or former law enforcement personnel are involved,' Ross resumed after a pause, 'I'll have to bring in the feds, no question, but I don't want to do that until I'm reasonably sure what we're dealing with. On the other hand, we simply must put a stop to this. Yes, the victims are some pretty bad dudes, but they've also served their time and paid their debts to society. According to the Constitution, even scumbags have a right to due process.'

'What about Mr. Tompkins?' Mel said.

On the surface her question was directed at Ross, but the look she sent in my direction said otherwise.

'What's the story with him?' she continued. 'Whatever it was must have happened before I came to town.'

That was true. LaShawn Tompkins had been both wrongly convicted and rightly released long before Melissa Soames turned up in Bellevue as Ross Connors's latest addition to SHIT.

'Ask Beau here,' Ross said helpfully. 'At this point I'm sure he knows far more about it than I do.'

So I told them what I knew, pretty much. I left out the part about Kendall Jackson working with me on the q.t. as far as attempting to locate Elaine Manning was concerned. If Ross needed deniability, so did Detective Jackson. After all, he still has to survive inside Seattle PD.

The problem was, the more I told the more I could see Mel didn't like the fact that I had used Beverly's death as a smoke screen to hide what I was doing.

'I'm still hoping maybe it is a love triangle,' I finished somewhat lamely. 'Maybe, when we locate the girlfriend — '

'I hope so, too,' Ross interrupted. 'But I'm not holding my breath. You can see why I turned to the two of you, though. I wanted this situation investigated with as little fuss as possible. Of all my people, you two are uniquely situated for keeping something like this quiet.'

Every time the man opened his mouth he made things worse for yours truly.

'Yes,' Mel agreed, sending yet another scathing glance in my direction. 'I can certainly see why you might think that.'

I wanted to turn the focus away from us and back onto something less dangerous — like the victims themselves. 'What do our dead guys have

143

in common?' I asked. 'Were any of them locked up in the same facility?'

'Todd is working on putting together a spreadsheet analysis of all that. As far as facilities are concerned, we have only so many prisons,' Ross said. 'Since these guys were all incarcerated at more or less the same time, it stands to reason that some of them would have served time in the same facility. If it turns out they all were, then that's another story.'

'The irrigation-canal victims were locked up together,' Mel offered. 'They were actually cell mates up in Monroe.'

'What about their crimes? Any similarity there?' I asked.

'With the exception of Mr. Tompkins, they're all multiple offenders,' Ross replied. 'Their crimes run the gamut of your regular felonies — grand theft auto, armed robbery, bank robbery. You name it, they did it.'

'What about gang affiliations?' Mel asked.

Connors shrugged. 'They all had some, of course. If they didn't have them when they went into prison, they sure as hell did when they came out. That's one of the things Todd assures me he's great at, data mining — once he has it. That's where you come in, Mel. You'll need to gather up all the information we have on these offenders from all applicable jurisdictions so Todd will be able to organize the information for us. Once we look at all the cases together, we may find there are common denominators, details no one has noticed.'

Ross Connors reached for the bottle and

144

emptied it into his own glass without offering any to Mel. I knew he was drinking way too much way too fast. I was glad he had a driver.

'I count ten victims so far,' Mel said. 'It seems to me that's worthy of a task-force approach. If it comes to light that you've only put three investigators on this and one of them is an economist instead of a cop, it's not going to sound like you're taking this seriously.'

'Oh, I'm serious, all right,' Ross said. 'Very serious. What I'm hoping is that the two of you will point me in the right direction. If it turns out our prime suspect is a cop, let me know.'

'There's more than one state involved,' Mel pointed out.

'I know all that,' Ross said impatiently. 'As I said, I'll call in the feds when it's time — once I understand the full extent of the problem.'

I had always respected Ross Connors. Politics had always been one of his considerations, but never the top one. This time things were different and I wondered why.

'I still think we need a task force,' Mel insisted.

'We're already dealing with a task force,' Ross returned. 'A task force of killers — a syndicate, if you like. If they're plugged into the law enforcement community, as soon as we start putting together a large-scale investigation, they'll know what we're doing and when we're doing it. At that point they'll go to ground, and we'll never find them.'

With that, Ross rose unsteadily to his feet. 'I'll call Harry in the morning,' he said. 'Tell him that you two are working a special project for me for the foreseeable future. And, considering the situation, it might be better if you worked from home instead of the office.'

Control freak Harry I. Ball was going to love that.

Mel escorted Ross downstairs in the elevator and hooked him back up with his car and driver. When she returned, just as I expected, she took me to the woodshed over the Tompkins situation.

'Maybe you'd better tell me about your friend LaShawn,' she said. 'This time don't leave anything out.'

I have no idea how she knew I had left something out, but she did. And so I told her the whole story, including the parts about working sub rosa with Detective Kendall Jackson. I expected all hell would break loose, but it didn't. When I finished, Mel stood up and stretched. 'Time to go night-night,' she said. 'This turned into a hell of a day, and tomorrow isn't going to be any better.'

A little while later we were lying in bed. I was almost asleep when Mel said, 'So how do you feel about all this?'

Even half asleep and without having any idea of the actual topic of discussion, I was smart enough to recognize this as a trick question — almost as volatile as the age-old 'Do I look fat in this?'

'Feel?' I asked dimly.

'About our being partners,' she said. 'That was the first thing Barbara Galvin told me about you when I showed up at SHIT. She said, 'Beau

146

doesn't work with partners.' Of course, we already did that once — unofficially, yes. But it sounds to me as though this time Ross is making it official — in an under-the-table kind of way.'

Mel was right about my wanting to avoid investigative partnerships. During my time in Homicide at Seattle PD, I felt I had been exceptionally hard on partners. Ron Peters and Big Al Lindstrom had both sustained line-of-duty life-changing injuries. Much later, Sue Danielson had died in a hail of bullets. In all three instances subsequent departmental inquiries had exonerated me of any fault. Officially, Seattle PD had concluded that I was blameless. Undeterred by facts and official findings, however, I had continued to hold myself accountable in each and every instance. As far as I was concerned, my partners' biggest problem — their single common liability — had been their star-crossed association with me.

My relationship with Melissa Soames, however, was entirely different from the ones I had shared with each of those other partners. For one thing, I sure as hell hadn't been in love with Ron Peters and Big Al Lindstrom. I hadn't been in love with Sue, either. I had felt protective of her, had wanted to be her mentor, but there had never been any romantic overtones on my part or hers.

But I definitely was in love with Mel. On the surface of it, that should have made me that much more reluctant to put her in any danger. But I had seen how Mel reacted when she was under fire. I knew that if things got tough I could trust her implicitly. When you're out in the real world dodging bullets, it doesn't get any better than that.

'Ross Connors is a little behind the times,' I said, pulling her close. 'We were partners long before he got around to saying so.'

10

When you awaken to the enticing smell of freshly brewed coffee it's easy to think that all's right with the world. Mel's side of the bed was cool to the touch. There was a hint of floral fragrance lingering beneath the aroma of coffee. That would be her shampoo. So Mel had been up long enough to shower and make coffee. I got up and wandered out into the dining room, where I found my two daily crossword puzzle pages, removed them from their (for me) completely extraneous newspapers, and laid them out on the dining room table. Mel came down the hall a moment after I poured my first mug of coffee. She was fully dressed.

'I'm going to go see Lenny,' she announced, slipping on a pair of low-heeled pumps.

I knew that meant she was on her way to visit the crime scene folks at King County to check out the missing-bullet situation.

'I've talked to Todd,' she added. 'He's on his way here.'

'Here?' I'm sure I sounded more than a bit territorial. After all, a man's home is his castle, and the idea of having an itinerant economist show up on my doorstep along with my first cup of coffee did not compute.

'Yes, here. Ross doesn't want us working on this in the office, remember? Todd's bringing abstracts of the files on all the cases Ross

149

mentioned last night, and the ones on my list, too.'

'Has anybody told Harry about our new working arrangements?'

'Already handled,' Mel said with a smile. 'Ross took care of that bright and early this morning. What about the kids? Have you heard anything from them?'

'As far as I know they're sightseeing today.'

'So you're off 'Gumpa' duty?' she asked.

'Looks like,' I said.

She gave me a goodbye kiss and left, steaming travel cup firmly in hand. We Seattleites don't go anywhere or do anything without our personal jolt of java.

Able to ignore the cross-lake traffic reports for once, I settled in at the table with my own hit of caffeine. I doubted Ross Connors would begrudge me the time it would take for me to whip through the Friday *New York Times* puzzle. I was making excellent progress when my cell phone rang. I figured it was either Mel, who had forgotten something, or else the kids, who had decided they wanted to take me up on my offer to buy breakfast after all, but the number wasn't one I recognized.

'Mr . . . ' It was a male voice — a relatively young male voice. 'Beaumont,' he said uncertainly, butchering my name by pronouncing the 'Beau' part the same way you'd say the B-U in 'Butte' instead of the way it's supposed to be pronounced, Beau as in 'go.' If this had been my landline phone, I would have expected to hear a recorded spiel offering to sell me vinyl siding for my nonexistent house or to pick up my household castoffs to benefit the blind. But this was my cell phone. Solicitation calls aren't supposed to intrude on my cell phone minutes.

'The name is Beaumont,' I said, pronouncing it properly for him but all the while trying to sound as cantankerous and off-putting as possible.

'My name's Donald,' he said nervously. 'Donnie, actually. Donnie Cosgrove. I think you talked to my wife earlier this week.'

Was that just this week? I wondered. So much had happened that it seemed eons ago, but I realized it had only been a few days earlier, on Monday, when I had stopped by the Cosgroves' neat little Redmond rambler.

'Of course,' I said, at once modifying my tone. 'DeAnn. What can I do for you, Mr. Cosgrove?'

'I told her I was going to go clean the jerk's clock, but DeAnn begged me to talk to you instead.'

'Wait a minute,' I said. 'Slow down. What are you talking about?'

'Jack,' he said. 'Jack Lawrence, DeAnn's stepfather. He came roaring through here yesterday while I was at work, yelling and raising hell. Woke the kids up in the middle of their naps. Threw our whole household into an uproar.'

'What was he upset about?' I asked.

'That DeAnn had talked to you. Wanted to know how dare she bring this back up after all these years. Told her she should learn to mind her own damn business and let sleeping dogs lie.

151

Didn't she know when she was well off. Stuff like that. Can you believe it?' Cosgrove demanded, his voice shaking in outrage. 'He actually said that to her about her father — called him a 'sleeping dog'! And in our own home, too.'

I gave Cosgrove a moment to get a grip on his emotions before asking, 'You're saying Mr. Lawrence seemed to think your wife had something to do with instigating our renewed interest in Anthony Cosgrove's disappearance?'

'Evidently.'

'How did he find out about it?'

'DeAnn called her mother to see if you had contacted them. Carol is DeAnn's mother, after all, so we try to maintain some kind of normal relationship with her — as normal as you can with a nutcase like Jack lurking in the background. Carol said you hadn't called or stopped by, or at least not yet, but she must have mentioned the conversation to Jack. He hit the roof and drove all the way down from Leavenworth to bitch DeAnn out about it. I just wish I'd been there when it happened, but of course Lawrence is such a coward, he'd never tackle someone like me. He'd rather terrorize DeAnn and the kids.'

'Maybe you should consider swearing out a restraining order against him,' I suggested.

'What good would a piece of paper do?' Cosgrove wanted to know.

'For one thing, if he came back and caused trouble, DeAnn could call the cops and have him put in jail.'

'I've read about what happens to women with

152

restraining orders,' Cosgrove said bitterly. 'A lot of them end up dead.'

'Has your father-in-law been violent toward DeAnn in the past?' I asked.

'Why do you think she moved out of the house when she was in high school?' Donnie returned. 'That's why she went to live with her grandmother.'

'What about his wife?' I asked. 'Does he beat her, too?'

'I'm not sure. She hasn't ever come right out and said so,' Donnie conceded, 'but that doesn't mean it hasn't happened. She's shown up with oddball bruises from time to time, but she always has one lame excuse or another for what's happened to her.'

Domestic-violence victims almost always have excuses, I thought. *They don't want to say what has really happened to them, probably because they don't think people will believe them, or maybe because they're afraid they will.*

'Anyway,' Donnie continued, 'the man's scary as hell. What I don't understand is why your looking into Tony's disappearance all those years ago would send Jack off the deep end.'

Observed over- or underreactions on the part of near and dear relatives or even those who are near and not-so-dear always raise red flags for homicide detectives. They indicate that something is out of whack with the relationship — that all isn't as it should be. In this case I couldn't help but be struck by Jack Lawrence's over-the-top response to learning that we were reexamining a case that, on the surface, had

153

opened and closed twenty years ago.

'What can you tell me about the man?' I asked.

'About Jack? You mean other than the fact that he's an asshole and a bully?' Cosgrove returned.

'Other than that.'

'Jack Lawrence is a my-way-or-the-highway kind of guy,' Donnie answered. 'Ex-marine. Tough as nails. Very opinionated. Always knows everything about everything. I can't stand the guy and don't want him in my house. And up until yesterday, he never had been. Like I said, we've tried to maintain a relationship with Carol, but Carol without Jack. Just being around him upsets DeAnn too much.'

'Is there a chance that Jack is distressed about our investigating Tony Cosgrove's disappearance because he was somehow involved in it?'

There was a long pause before Donnie answered. 'Maybe,' he said finally.

'What do you mean?' I asked.

'I've heard rumors that Jack and Carol were romantically involved long before Tony went fishing at Spirit Lake. It always struck me as a little too convenient that Tony disappears and the next thing you know, Jack and Carol are a couple. But it all happened long before I was part of the picture. When I heard the rumors I kept quiet about them for DeAnn's sake.'

'You don't accept as fact the idea that Tony Cosgrove died in the eruption?' I asked.

'Not really,' Donnie said. 'It never made sense to me that a man who hardly ever went fishing would just happen to be doing that very thing on

Spirit Lake the day the mountain blew up. And I always thought it was strange that nobody ever turned up even the smallest trace of him or his vehicle. When vehicles get burned up or when people do, there are usually some traces — some little bits and pieces — that are left behind.'

I had to agree with him there. The destruction of the World Trade Center came to mind.

'A few years ago,' Donnie continued, 'I happened to see a program on TV about a similar case, one that took place somewhere back east — in Chicago, I think.'

'They have volcanoes in Chicago?' I asked.

Donnie paused uncertainly. Then, realizing I was attempting a halfhearted joke, he allowed himself a hint of a chuckle. 'No, it's just that a woman was murdered on the same day an airliner went down in that same general area. I think the jet was flying out of O'Hare. The killer tried to maintain that the dead woman had been a passenger on the plane, but the airline didn't have any record of her because she'd never been on the plane in the first place. She was already dead.'

'If you don't buy the official story about Tony Cosgrove's disappearance,' I said, 'have you ever tried to do anything about it?'

'I don't make a big deal of it, but I do check with people down at the Mount Saint Helens Visitor Center from time to time,' Donnie answered. 'Just in case — just to make sure nothing's turned up in the meantime. I guess the last I spoke to them was months ago — last summer sometime. The mountain had started

155

burping again, and there was a lot more interest in it than there had been previously. I thought that maybe, with a lot more activity and attention, someone might stumble across something of Tony's — if there was anything to find.'

'But there wasn't.'

'Not so far.'

'Does your wife know you've been making those kinds of inquiries?' I asked.

Donnie Cosgrove sighed. 'No,' he said. 'I never mentioned it to her.'

'Why not?'

'I didn't want to get her hopes up,' he said. 'Or kill them, either. There's a part of DeAnn, the little-girl part, who believes Tony Cosgrove is still alive and that someday he's going to turn up — that one fine morning she'll open our front door and he'll be standing on the front porch.'

I knew Donnie was right on that score. I, too, had heard the unrealistic longings — the dreamy wishful thinking of an abandoned little girl in DeAnn Cosgrove's voice. No doubt that had been the overriding consideration behind her wanting to keep her maiden name.

'I believe DeAnn mentioned something to me about Jack Lawrence working for Boeing at about the same time her parents were there,' I said. 'Was that the case?'

Donnie nodded. 'Tony started working there sometime in the late sixties or early seventies. That's where he and Carol met, at some kind of company event — a Christmas party, maybe. Jack turned up later. After retiring from a twenty-year hitch in the military, he hired on

156

with Boeing in sales. Carol ended up being his secretary.'

'Carol told you this or DeAnn?' I asked.

'Neither one,' Donnie answered. 'I worked for Boeing for a little while back when I first got my degree and before I moved over to Fluke, which is where I am now. But back then, when people at Boeing heard I was the guy who had married Tony Cosgrove's daughter, a couple of them took me aside and hinted around that maybe Tony's disappearance wasn't an act of nature after all; that maybe someone should have taken a closer look at what was going on at the time he disappeared.'

'Did you ever ask anyone to look into it?' I asked.

'No. I was just out of school and new on the job. I couldn't afford to risk drawing attention — rocking-the-boat kind of attention. So other than talking to the folks down at Mount Saint Helens periodically, I haven't dared raise the issue.'

'Why not?'

'Despite what people think, the aerospace industry is actually a surprisingly small, closely knit group, and these days electronics engineers are a dime a dozen, especially in India. That's why I'm calling you on my cell, Mr. Beaumont. And not from my office, either. But to have Jack come charging into the house the way he did yesterday . . . was just . . . too much.'

That's about when I figured it out. Donnie Cosgrove was upset that his father-in-law had stopped by and raised hell with DeAnn, but

Donnie wanted someone else to do something about it — namely me. The fact of the matter is, raising hell with scumbags is a big part of my job description.

'I'm glad you called,' I told him. 'This is all very interesting, and I'll be looking into it. Do you happen to remember the names of any of the people who talked to you back then about Tony Cosgrove's disappearance?'

'Not offhand,' Donnie said. 'It was just sort of break-room BS. I'll think about it, though. If I remember anyone in particular I'll let you know.'

'Thanks,' I said. 'Do that.'

But by then I was already one step ahead of him. I had read the article in *Electronics Engineering Journal*, and I had a pretty good idea that a 'defense analyst' named Thomas Dortman had been one of Anthony Cosgrove's coworkers at Boeing in the late seventies and early eighties. All I had to do was track him down.

'So what are you going to do now?' Donnie asked. 'Will you go talk to him?'

For a moment I thought Donnie was asking if I was going to talk to Dortman. Then I realized he was actually referring to his erstwhile father-in-law — stepfather-in-law — Jack Lawrence.

'I'm sure I will eventually,' I assured him. 'But not until after I check out a few things first.'

'And you'll let us know what you find out?' Donnie asked. 'I mean, you'll let DeAnn know?'

'Believe me,' I told him, 'I'll let you both know.'

Call-waiting buzzed just then. I ended the call

with Donnie Cosgrove.

'Mr. Hatcher to see you,' the doorman announced when I switched to the other line.

'Good,' I said. 'Send him up.'

I'll confess right now to having had certain preconceived notions about our visiting economist — none of them very flattering. I had envisioned someone with a fairly wide-load build, horn-rimmed glasses, and a mop of long greasy hair. Todd Hatcher failed to meet those specifications — on every count.

For one thing, he was tall and lanky — scrawny, in fact. And he looked like a cowboy just in off the range in boots and Levi's and wearing a dripping Stetson and a soggy leather jacket. In one hand he carried a bulging backpack that was just as damp as he was.

'Mr. Beaumont?' he asked as I opened the door.

I nodded. 'Welcome. Come on in,' I said. 'Make yourself at home.'

Removing his hat, he banged some of the excess water off it out in the hallway before stepping into the apartment. His blond hair was cut in a short but not quite military buzz cut. Without even shedding his jacket, Hatcher, like every other visitor to the penthouse, was immediately drawn to the windows on the far side of the living room.

'Wow,' he exclaimed, looking out on the gray expanse of water that was Elliott Bay and Puget Sound. 'What an amazing view!'

'It's even more amazing when it isn't raining,' I told him. 'Can I take your coat?'

He peeled it off and handed it over, revealing the unapologetic pearl-buttoned Western shirt underneath. As I walked away with the jacket I noticed that the only part that wasn't wet was the part that had been under the backpack. Rather than putting the wet jacket in the closet, I draped it over the back of one of the kitchen bar stools in hopes of letting it dry.

'Coffee?' I asked.

'If it's not too much trouble,' Todd replied, 'coffee would be great. Black, please.'

By the time I returned to the living room he had abandoned the view in favor of sitting in the window seat and examining the room itself. 'Growing up in Benson, I never could have imagined a place like this.'

'Benson?' I asked.

'Benson, Arizona.'

'I think I've been there,' I said, handing him his coffee. 'Isn't Benson just down the road from Bisbee?'

He grinned. 'You've actually heard of it? Most people never have. Benson is actually down the road if you're in Tucson and up the road if you're in Bisbee, and relative elevations have nothing to do with it.'

I went back to the kitchen and poured a second cup of coffee for me. First impressions are important. The fact that he looked like a hick just off the farm — or ranch, as the case may be — didn't inspire a whole lot of confidence, but we needed to know something about him. I took my coffee and returned to my recliner.

'What brought you to Washington?' I asked.

'An Ingmar Hanson Fellowship in economics,' he said. 'I came here to finish my Ph.D.'

I didn't know Ingmar Hanson from a hole in the wall, but clearly Todd Hatcher was a hell of a lot smarter than he looked.

'It's done now,' he said. 'My degree was awarded last June. I had a couple of offers to teach, but I wanted to do this first.' He glanced down at the sodden backpack.

'By 'this' you mean the study for Ross Connors?'

He nodded. 'I had hoped to be able to use it for my dissertation. That would have broken new ground — a dissertation about something useful, for a change — but my adviser wasn't having any of it. He told me no one's interested in analyzing the need for geriatric prison beds, which, of course, is patently stupid, since prisons are still one of this country's growth industries, and the prison population is aging everywhere.'

I tried to picture Todd Hatcher in his cowboy boots and Stetson sauntering across the U. Dub's beloved Red Square. Talk about out of place! It came as no surprise to me that Todd and one or more of his professors wouldn't have seen eye to eye.

'Presumably you are interested, though,' I said. 'Mind if I ask why?'

Hatcher uncrossed his legs and gave me a speculative look. 'I mind,' he said, 'but since we're going to be working together, I could just as well tell you.'

It appeared that we were starting our working relationship based on a certain level of mutual distrust. Maybe that was a good thing.

'Nobody ever expected me to amount to much,' he said. 'My mother was a waitress; my father was a failed bank robber. When I was four, he went to prison for shooting a security guard in the course of an attempted bank robbery. Those are the first memories I have of my father, taking that long ride up to Florence every once in a while to visit him on weekends.

'Growing up, all my friends were fascinated with Luke Sky-walker or Spider-Man, but we were too poor to go to movies. My mother took me to the library instead. While my friends were still playing with Transformers, I was working my way through Sherlock Holmes. By the time I was thirteen or so, I wanted to be Alan Greenspan when I grew up. My mother and I survived on almost no money, and Greenspan seemed to be someone who knew all about money and how to get it. While other kids were focused on high school sports, I was spending my summers working as a ranch hand and reading Ayn Rand on the side. I won a full scholarship to the University of Arizona. That's where I got my B.A. and my master's. I came to the U. Dub to earn my Ph.D.'

He stopped, but that clearly that wasn't the end of the story.

'And?' I prompted.

'My father was sentenced to life in prison,' he said after a pause. 'Five years ago they released him, sent him home to my mother in Benson. Claimed it was because the prison was overcrowded and they had determined he was no

162

longer a danger to himself or others. That's what they *said*. The reality turned out to be they had diagnosed him with early-onset Alzheimer's and they didn't want to have to take care of him, so they sent him home to my mother to die.

'She had never divorced the man for the simple reason that she loved him. She had health insurance — major medical for herself — but not for him. There was no way for her to add him onto her policy, and he was too young for Medicare. She applied for disability Social Security benefits for him, but they kept turning her down. So she took care of him to the best of her ability. He died two years ago, and she died six months later. He would have died anyway. Sending him home like that was a death sentence for her.'

Now Todd Hatcher's doggedly persistent interest in the aging prison population made a whole lot more sense. It was much more than just a 'study' for him. It was a labor of love.

'If this country really buys the three-strikes-you're-out mentality, then we'd better be prepared to pay the piper,' he added after a pause. 'If we say someone's going to prison for life and mean it, we'd better get ready.'

'So that's why you're here, then,' I said.

He nodded. 'In order to know how many geriatric prison beds will be needed, I hope to create a computer model that will predict exactly how many current prisoners will end up dying there. In order to be accurate, however, I need to have some idea of how many new offenders will land in the prison system on a permanent basis

163

as well as how many ex-cons are likely to reoffend and be returned to prison. Recidivists, of course, are far more likely to fall under three-strikes provisions and end up with lifetime sentences. That's my expectation.'

'And everything was going along fine and dandy until you stumbled across a whole bunch of young dead ex-cons who screwed your so-called model all to hell.'

'Right,' Hatcher said. 'If they're dead, they won't reoffend, and they won't need geriatric prison care, either. The problem is, in the normal course of events some of them will be dead long before they grow old in prison, but they shouldn't be dead yet. It struck me that this whole cluster of deaths was some kind of an anomaly. When I brought the situation to Ross's attention he asked me to look into it in more detail. And here I am.'

I recalled Ross Connors's somewhat cynical remark about Hatcher probably having a book deal waiting in the wings. From what I could see, the man's motivation was much less self-serving than that — and a lot more understandable.

'So what's the plan?' I asked.

'Mel told me I should work on the spreadsheet here. That way, I can consult with one or the other of you as I go along. If we're all going over the files and picking out what strikes each of us as important, we'll probably come up with better data. Once we have that, we'll run a paradox analysis and see if anything pops.'

For all the sense it made to me, that last sentence could just as well have been uttered in

Russian. Or Chinese.

'So what do you need from me?' I asked.

He opened the backpack and took out a slim laptop. His boots may have been on their last legs, as it were, but his computer was absolutely state-of-the-art.

'A place to spread out and work,' he said.

I pointed toward the granite counter of the breakfast bar. 'Will that do?' I asked.

He nodded. 'Sure,' he said. 'What about logging on?'

There I had him. 'We've got a WiFi network complete with a broadband connection.'

'Cool,' he said.

That remark came with no need of translation. I was gratified that our telecommunications system measured up to his expectations. And I was also glad that, despite the considerable difference in our ages, cool was still cool.

Somehow I found that reassuring.

11

Todd Hatcher was hustling around and setting up shop when my phone rang. 'Hey, you are there,' Detective Jackson said. 'I tried calling your office and they said you were off.' Off wasn't quite the same as out, but I let it pass. 'How was the memorial service?'

'Pretty low-key. Naturally Manning didn't show, but we've got a lead on her this morning. According to our sources, she's staying in a shelter up on Aurora. Hank and I are on our way to interview her right now. I'll let you know what we find out.'

'Maybe I should talk to her, too. Want me to ride along? Meet you there?'

'Considering your persona non grata status around here, maybe that's not such a good idea,' he said. 'I can give you a rundown of what we learn — '

'I want to talk to her myself,' I said. 'What's the address?'

'You're not listening,' he said irritably. 'I'll give you a call when we finish up the interview and let you know where to find her. I don't want you showing up while we're still there.'

'No,' I agreed. 'Of course you wouldn't.'

'And remember,' Jackson added, 'no matter what, you didn't hear any of this from me.'

That I understood completely.

My next order of business was to see about

tracking down Thomas Dortman, but before I got to square one on that, Jeremy called.

'Wanted to say thanks for everything,' my son-in-law told me. 'We really appreciate the hospitality, but we're headed back to Ashland as soon as Kelly gets out of the shower and we can get packed up.'

Once again Jeremy had been drafted into doing the dirty work and talking with Kelly's ogre of a father. I assumed that meant I was still in the doghouse.

'But I thought you were staying until Sunday . . . ' I began.

'Kyle was awake most of the night last night, and so was everybody else,' Jeremy said. 'We've decided we'll all be better off if we're back in our own place. At least that way we'll have a little privacy when the baby is crying or Kelly is yelling.'

In terms of needing privacy, I suspected that the former was less of a problem than the latter. 'My daughter can be a handful at times,' I said.

Jeremy's sigh of agreement was heartfelt. 'Yes, sir,' he said. 'She certainly can be that. I'm really sorry about not coming to dinner the other night. I don't know why she was so upset about Mel.'

'Don't worry about it, Jeremy,' I told him. 'Mel can take it and so can I.'

'Thanks,' he said. 'Oops, gotta go.'

Kelly's shower had evidently ended and so did Jeremy's phone call. I know I should have been sorry at the idea that they were taking off two days early, but I wasn't. Call me an old curmudgeon, but I was losing patience with Kelly's theatrics. And that's all I thought it was — theatrics. Kelly's mother had certainly been good at pitching a royal fit in her time, and Kelly seemed to have inherited the same tendency.

I went out to the kitchen, poured the last cup of coffee, and made a new pot. With Todd now ensconced at the bar, I took myself and my laptop to my recliner and went looking for Thomas Dortman. He turned out to be a freelance writer and sometime Fox News contributor whose Web site's home page said he lived in the Seattle area, although his 728 phone prefix hinted at a downtown location. I called the number and left a message, telling him who I was and asking him to call. And then, because there was always a chance he was off gallivanting around somewhere, I shot him an e-mail as well.

Hoping for Kendall Jackson to call me back, I spent the remainder of the morning working side by side with Todd Hatcher. We finally decided that we'd both go through the documents and make our own separate notes, which Todd would then transcribe into the spreadsheet. That way Mel could come along later and do the same thing. The resulting document would contain all of our impressions of what we each had read, hopefully boiled down into one readily accessible document where, with any kind of luck, the most important points would somehow bubble to the surface.

I concentrated primarily on the file concerning Ed Chrisman, the genius who had been taking a leak when his own vehicle knocked him off a cliff and into the drink several hundred feet below. I learned Chrisman was anything but a Boy Scout, with several increasingly serious scrapes with the law before he'd finally been sentenced for sixteen years after brutally raping his ex-wife. He'd been released early — ten percent off for good behavior — and had been free for just over a year when he took his nosedive. It chilled me to glean from his file that for the past six months he had worked as an in-store security guard. (Doesn't anyone bother checking résumés anymore?)

Much of the police report simply didn't make sense. As Mel had pointed out the day before, most people aren't stupid enough to relieve themselves while standing in front of a vehicle that is still in gear. I thought maybe this was a weird accident, one of those situations where a vehicle somehow takes on a mind of its own and slips itself into drive from neutral. But the vehicle had been examined in great detail once it had been hauled from the water, and there had been no sign of mechanical failure.

Some attempts had been made to follow up on Chrisman's activities in the days before his death, but those efforts had come up short. The evening before, he had been seen drinking in a bar in Fairhaven in the company of a still-unidentified woman. All efforts to trace her had also come to nothing. Several people said they thought she was a hitchhiker Chrisman might have picked up the day before driving back from Seattle, but even with the help of a composite drawing they had been unable to come up with any kind of identification.

The passage about the unidentified and so far unreachable woman made my blood run cold. What were the chances that Chrisman had assaulted this unnamed woman and left her either dead or dying somewhere in a winter-bound forested landscape that might never yield up either her remains or her identity?

Reading an abstract has its shortcomings. It's not nearly the same as reading an actual file. And reading about evidence isn't the same as seeing it with your very own eyes. According to the record, Chrisman's smashed vehicle remained in the Skagit County Sheriff's Department impound lot. After several weeks underwater, very little usable forensic evidence had remained in the vehicle. The keys had been found still in the ignition. Chrisman's wallet had been stuffed under the seat, with money and credit cards intact. If anyone else had been involved in what happened to him, robbery had not been part of the program.

The file did reference a single scrap of dark material — not matching any of Chrisman's clothing — that had been found caught in the front passenger door. Other than saying the cotton broadcloth was either blue or black, there was no way of telling if it had been lodged there on the day Chrisman had taken his last Sunday drive or if it somehow predated the day of his death. As I made my notes I realized that sometime soon someone in our group — Mel or me or even Todd — might have to travel north to Bellingham and see the evidence for ourselves.

I kept looking at the clock, hoping Mel would

come home or that Kendall Jackson would call me in time for me to go see Elaine Manning prior to LaShawn Tompkins's funeral. By noon, however, it became clear that neither of those things was going to happen. I gave Todd carte blanche to rummage through our two-day-old leftovers, but he was so absorbed in his work I doubted he'd notice I was gone — to say nothing of remembering to eat.

Weather in Seattle can turn on a dime. By the time I finally pulled out of the garage the morning rains were gone and the sky directly overhead was a brilliant blue. The sky was clearing, although the pavement was still wet. The sun glinting off it was blinding in spots. As I drove toward the I-90 bridge, even Mount Rainier was gradually emerging from its wintertime cocoon of low-lying clouds. I tried calling Mel as I drove, but her phone went straight to voice mail.

Down in the Rainier Valley I was early enough that I was able to park close to the church. I was so early, in fact, that the doors to the African Bible Baptist Church were not yet open, so I walked the length and breadth of Church Street and talked to any number of Etta Mae Tompkins's neighbors.

Mostly I got nowhere fast. No one had seen anything, or, at least, no one would *admit* to having seen anything. Finally I branched out and wandered up and down MLK. Two blocks to the north I spoke to a gas station attendant from a BP station who reported having noticed a single white woman — a nun — walking in the neighborhood shortly before LaShawn Tompkins was shot. I didn't ask him if he had happened to mention any of this to the other detectives because I was sure he had. It turns out the other detectives hadn't happened to mention it to *me*. In this business, though, you can't afford to take that stuff personally.

'Did she look suspicious?' I asked.

The man laughed outright. 'Are you kidding? I figured that nun was just like one of those Jehovah's Witnesses babes that are always coming around here — scary but not suspicious.'

'She was wearing a habit, then?'

'You mean one of those black robe things? Yes, she was, carrying her Bible and her umbrella. When I saw her there, all by herself in the dark and the rain, I remember asking myself, 'Man, what is that woman thinking?''

'Did you get a good look at her?'

'Naw. Just because she was dumb enough to stand outside in the rain didn't mean I was, but I know she was white if that's what you're asking.'

It was what I was asking, and I made a note of his comment. If a nun had been out there on the street at the time LaShawn Tompkins was shot, there was an outside chance that she might have seen a vehicle coming or going. I needed to track the woman down and talk to her. Other than that, I learned nothing. Zero. Zip.

By one-thirty and still on foot, I made my way back up Martin Luther King Jr. Way to the African Bible Baptist Church. This was, as I remembered, Etta Mae Tompkins's home church. It was also her neighborhood church and within walking distance of her home. Even though the neighborhood had changed and there was a far greater Asian presence there now, the congregation of African Bible Baptist — at least the members assembling there that afternoon — was primarily black. And although I certainly didn't blend, I was made to feel welcome.

A media van pulled up to the curb. I was intent on keeping a low profile. Having my mug show up on local television newscasts didn't seem like a good idea, so I headed for the door to the church, where a smiling usher in a shiny charcoal-gray suit greeted me and led me into the sanctuary.

I sat near the back. From there I was able to spot Etta Mae seated alone in the first pew. With unwavering dignity she gazed at LaShawn's open, flower-bedecked casket.

Moments after I was seated, a group of people led by Pastor Mark Granger made their way up the aisle. Among them I caught sight of both Sister Meth Mouth Cora and the King Street Mission attorney of record, Dale Ramsey. The group commandeered two full pews directly behind Etta Mae.

She turned and looked at them as they filed in. With a scowl of distaste and a slight shake of her head, she looked away again. I suppose she was thinking much the same thing I was. She had given King's Mission free rein in how they did their own send-off for her Shawny, and I think she was worried that Pastor Mark and his flock wouldn't allow her the same courtesy.

By the time the appointed hour of 2:00 P.M.

rolled around, the church was packed. Detectives Jackson and Ramsdahl came in during the first hymn — a moving rendition of 'Swing Low Sweet Chariot.' By then, late arrivals were having to be shoehorned into extra chairs that had been hauled out and placed in the aisles. Jackson's chair was at the end of the pew I was in; Hank Ramsdahl was seated two rows ahead of us.

Having attended Beverly Jenssen's memorial service the previous afternoon, I couldn't help thinking that her send-off suffered in comparison to the one given LaShawn Tompkins by Etta Mae's African Bible Baptist Church. It was her show from beginning to end. Even though this was early on a Friday afternoon, the funeral service played to a capacity crowd. Not only was the full congregation in attendance, but so was a top-notch, full-throated choir.

Funeral or not, attendees and choir alike came prepared to make a joyful noise unto the Lord. I noticed that the visitors from King Street Mission held their hymnals open, but they looked uneasy and didn't seem to be singing along with everyone else. This may have been due to the fact that they didn't know the words to the various hymns, or maybe they were accustomed to practicing a somewhat more subdued version of Christianity.

Good for Etta Mae, I thought.

The Reverend Clarence Wilkins officiated. When it came time for the eulogy, he spoke movingly of LaShawn as a cute but mischievous little boy who had regularly attended Sunday school. The minister also spoke of LaShawn's years in the wilderness when he had been lost in a world of drugs and gangs. Finally, to a chorus of heartfelt 'Praise Gods' and 'Amens,' Wilkins related how, in the end, LaShawn had come back to Jesus. Wilkins made only the slightest nod in Pastor Mark's direction as he told that part of the story, and the reverend made no mention at all of LaShawn's work at King Street Mission. I wondered if that was an accident or a deliberate oversight.

The service came to an end rather abruptly after that, closing with a final hymn and with no chance for attendees to come forward and make comments of their own. Maybe I have an overly active imagination or possibly it was simply prejudice on my part, but I assumed Etta Mae had precluded any additional speakers in order to keep Pastor Mark from taking to the pulpit. Since he had seemed intent on hijacking the entire service, I could hardly blame her for that.

Out on the street, while we waited for the casket to be carried out of the church and transferred to the waiting hearse, I tracked down Kendall Jackson. Hank Ramsdahl was nowhere in sight.

'I thought you were going to call me,' I said.

Jackson was busy scanning the crowd. 'That's right. I said we'd call when we finished interviewing Elaine Manning.'

'Well?' I asked.

'We never finished,' he said, 'because we never found her. I was hoping she'd show up here. So far no such luck.'

'She wasn't at the shelter?'

'She probably was there,' Jackson corrected. 'If so, she wouldn't come out to talk to us. And the woman who ran the place was pissed as hell that we had any idea that's where Elaine was staying in the first place. It's a domestic-violence shelter, you know.'

'But if LaShawn was her boyfriend and he's dead, who's she running from?'

'Good question,' Jackson said. 'For right now, my money's on Pastor Mark.'

'But he has an alibi for the time of LaShawn's murder,' I said. 'At least he claims to have an alibi.'

'He also has an attorney,' Jackson said.

Who also happens to be in attendance, I thought, but somehow I didn't mention that fact to Detective Jackson. This wasn't a grudge match, but since he hadn't told me about the nun, I figured that made us even.

By then the front pews of the church were finally emptying. When the King Street Mission people emerged, most of them wandered off toward three eight-passenger vans parked down the block. Pastor Mark and Dale Ramsey walked off together toward a black Lincoln Town Car that came complete with a driver in a black suit. The vans may have been good enough for Pastor Mark's flock, but they evidently weren't good enough for the shepherd himself.

'I guess that means he's not going to the cemetery,' Jackson said to me. 'And I guess that means Hank and I won't be going either. We'll just follow along and ask him if he has any idea why Elaine would have left King Street and

176

taken up residence in a DV shelter.'

'My guess is he won't say a word.'

'Mine, too.' Jackson grinned. 'But it doesn't matter. Sometimes silence speaks louder than words.'

Hank showed up in their car right then. Detective Jackson hopped inside and they headed down MLK Way behind the retreating Town Car.

It took about fifteen minutes to get the funeral procession formed up and ready to travel. I walked back to my Mercedes. Once the procession rolled past, I pulled into what I assumed was the caboose position as we headed south for Renton and the Mount Olivet Cemetery. A block or two south of Church Street I noticed that another vehicle, an older-model Honda, had pulled in behind me. There was only one occupant in the Honda, a woman. She didn't turn on her headlights, but as the procession made its way south, it was clear she was part of LaShawn Tompkins's funeral cortège.

Homicide detectives always look for things that are slightly out of the norm, slightly off. Funerals aren't fun, and most of the people who bother showing up for them want full credit for doing so. They sign guest books. They chat with grieving friends and family members. They *want* survivors to know they were there, almost as though they were storing up stars in their crowns or putting in markers for when the time comes for *their* own funerals. But the lady in the Honda clearly wasn't looking for credit, and the fact that

177

she was deliberately avoiding attention captured mine.

So before we reached the gates to Mount Olivet, I peeled off onto a side street. Most of the cars in the procession followed the hearse on into the cemetery and stopped close to a canopy-covered grave site. The Honda, on the other hand, stopped just inside the gate.

The woman who exited the vehicle was sturdily built. She was black, in her mid-thirties, and wore her shoulder-length hair in a cascade of tiny braids. She was dressed in boots and a long denim skirt. She went over to the grassy edge of the road, far enough to see the people clustering around the grave site. The woman watched the funeral attendees, but none of them noticed her, and she wasn't seeing me, either. I stepped out of the Mercedes and walked up behind her.

'Ms. Manning?' I asked.

Startled, she jumped and then spun around to face me. 'Who are you?' she demanded.

'My name's Beaumont,' I told her. 'J. P. Beaumont. I'm an investigator with the Washington State Attorney General's Office.' I held out my ID, but she kept her eyes on my face rather than on my identification or my badge.

'I shouldn't have come,' she said simply.

'From what I've been told, you and LaShawn Tompkins were an item,' I returned. 'Why wouldn't you come to his funeral?'

'I don't want to talk to you,' she said. 'I don't want to talk to anybody.' She dodged away from me and headed back toward the Honda, but I managed to beat her to the driver's door.

'We're trying to figure out what happened to him,' I said. 'Don't you want to help us?'

'Somebody shot him.' She was crying now. Tears streamed down her cheeks, leaving glistening tracks on her skin.

'Do you know who killed him or why?' I asked.

She shook her head. 'All I know for sure is that LaShawn is dead.'

'Why did you leave King Street Mission, Ms. Manning?' I pressed. 'And why are you staying in a domestic-violence shelter? What are you afraid of? Who are you afraid of?'

Without answering she tried to reach around me to grasp the door handle, but I was in the way. When the attempt failed, instead of falling back she leaned into me, weeping uncontrollably on my shoulder. For a moment I didn't quite know what to do. Eventually, with no other choice, I wrapped my arms around her and held her close.

'Shhhh,' I said, patting her. 'It's going to be all right.'

Finally she drew back, wiping fiercely at her eyes. 'I'm sorry,' she said. 'That was stupid of me.'

'Grieving isn't stupid,' I said. 'But not talking to me about this would be. Please, Ms. Manning, that's all I'm asking you to do — just talk to me. Tell me what you know or even what you think you know. Don't you owe LaShawn that much?'

'Yes, but not here,' she said, turning back toward the group clustered around LaShawn

Tompkins's open grave. 'Let's go somewhere else.'

'My car or yours?' I asked.

'It's not mine,' Elaine answered. 'It belongs to a friend of mine — from the shelter. But I can't leave it here. I saw a Burger King on the way here, down by 405. What if I meet you there?'

'That'll be fine,' I said. 'You lead the way.'

12

I thought Elaine might try to skip out on me, but she didn't. We drove straight to the Burger King and parked side by side. Inside she went to one of the window booths while I placed our order — coffee for me, Diet Coke for her.

By the time I got to the booth she was putting away a compact, having repaired the damage her tears had done to her makeup, and she seemed to have her emotions well in hand.

'I didn't see Pastor Mark get out of any of the buses at the cemetery,' she said.

'That's because he didn't go there,' I told her. 'He was at the funeral, but I think he was annoyed because he didn't get to run that show. He left the church and drove off in the opposite direction with Mr. Ramsey.'

'Oh,' Elaine said.

'Is Pastor Mark the one you're afraid of?' I asked.

She nodded. 'Is it that obvious?'

'I'm a detective, remember? But what isn't obvious is why.'

'Pastor Mark has a temper,' Elaine said.

'I already figured that out,' I interjected.

'And he didn't approve.'

'Of you and LaShawn?'

She nodded. 'Pastor Mark claimed we were setting a bad example for the other people at the mission, and he made it pretty clear that if

LaShawn and I insisted on being a couple we'd have to leave King Street.'

'Would that have been a problem?' I asked.

'More to Pastor Mark than for us,' Elaine returned.

'Why's that?'

'Because we were his best worker bees. LaShawn did a lot of the physical labor around the place, in addition to much of the active counseling. He was the one who made sure people were doing the work they needed to be doing.'

'You mean work as in jobs — as in the duty roster I saw?'

'I ran the household end of it — made up the duty roster and ordered supplies,' she said. 'And I handled client intake. Yes, Pastor Mark is the one with the degree in divinity, but LaShawn was way better than Pastor Mark at doing the kind of spiritual work it takes to turn lives around. After all, LaShawn had actually *been* there. He knew what it was like to be cast into the lion's den and walk out unscathed because it happened to him. His was an example other people could relate to and copy.'

'You still haven't answered my question,' I insisted.

'About why I'm afraid of Pastor Mark?'

I nodded. She sipped her Diet Coke for several thoughtful seconds. 'I think he was jealous of LaShawn,' she said finally. 'And I think he did it.'

'Wait a minute,' I said. 'You're saying you think Pastor Mark is responsible for LaShawn's death?'

It was Elaine's turn to nod.

'But he has a foolproof alibi,' I returned. 'At least he claims to have one. He says he was teaching a Bible study class at the mission at the time LaShawn was shot and he says he has a list of participants to prove it.'

'Pastor Mark knows a lot of people,' Elaine said. 'Not very nice people,' she added. 'Ones who may have come to the mission at one time or another but who, for one reason or another, have gone back to their old ways.'

'So he knew people and could put out a hit. But would he have done that over you? Would he gave gone that far?'

'I think he was afraid LaShawn and I would go out on our own and start a new mission somewhere else.'

'In competition with Pastor Mark?'

'He's not good at competition of any kind,' she answered. 'Yes, he was jealous of LaShawn and me, but I think he was even more jealous of the relationship LaShawn had with some of the clients. Thought it was undermining his authority somehow.'

'Was it?' I asked.

'Yes,' Elaine said simply.

'What happened Saturday morning?' I asked. 'I heard you and the good pastor did a few rounds in his office.'

'The cops had come to talk to him the night before, but he never said a word to me about it until Saturday morning, when he made the public announcement at breakfast. He knew what LaShawn meant to me. I couldn't believe he'd be that cruel. I went to talk to him about it and things . . . got out of hand.'

'What do you mean?'

'I accused him of having something to do with LaShawn's death. And he just snapped. Told me if he heard I'd even hinted to the cops that he might be responsible, that the same thing could maybe happen to me.'

'He threatened you?'

Elaine nodded again. 'So I went to the shelter. A friend of mine runs it. I knew she'd take me in.'

I knew that this tale of joint romantic and professional jealousy was one that would gladden Ross Connors's heart. If Pastor Mark had set out to clear the field of competition, at least it couldn't come back to bite the state of Washington in the butt. In order to prove that to be the case, I needed more information — and so would Kendall Jackson.

'What can you tell me about God's Word, LLC?' I asked.

Elaine shrugged. 'It's an umbrella 501-C corporation. Donations go to that. God's Word pays the mission's bills, owns the property, that kind of thing. And that's something else — the money. I've heard rumors that some zoning changes are in the works that might alter the makeup of the neighborhood. I'm guessing if that happened, God's Word would stop being a mission and start making money.'

'What would LaShawn have thought about that?' I asked.

'He was never in it for the money,' she said.

'That wasn't what he was about.'

But it was certainly another possible bone of contention between the dead man and Pastor Mark.

'Do you have any proof that Pastor Mark might be responsible for LaShawn's death?' I asked.

'I know he's a dangerous man,' Elaine responded. 'He went to prison for murder.'

'LaShawn went to prison, too,' I pointed out.

'Yes,' she agreed. 'But he was innocent.'

'How about you?' I asked. 'You went to prison for armed robbery. Are you dangerous?'

It was probably unfair of me to bring up Elaine Manning's checkered past. Listening to her speak, it seemed clear she was smart enough. As far as I could tell, it appeared that in her case, the King Street Mission had worked its magic.

'That was different,' she said at once. 'I got into drugs when I went to college — into them in a big way — and I stayed screwed up for a long time. I was high as a kite and looking for my next hit when I robbed that Krispy Kreme. I don't do drugs anymore, Mr. Beaumont. I don't do them at all.'

I believed her on that score, just as I believed she could very well be right about Pastor Mark's being responsible for LaShawn Tompkins's murder. But if I wanted to prove it, I would have to have someone else besides Sister Elaine telling the story and making the connections.

Elaine Manning's concerns about Pastor Mark sounded good, and they might have convinced me, but whether she was well-spoken or not, a

185

jury looking at her most likely wouldn't look beyond the fact that she was a convicted felon. Unsupported allegations from a reformed armed robber/druggie wouldn't carry much weight on a witness stand. I doubted they'd make the grade with Ross Alan Connors, either.

As I left Renton and headed home, it was after four-thirty, and I was in the throes of Friday-afternoon rush-hour traffic. After half an hour of stop-and-go driving just to make it from the Renton entrance onto 1-5 up to Boeing Field, I finally bailed and resorted to using side streets. By then they weren't much better, but at least they gave me the illusion of movement. I had visions of getting home late and finding Mel dressed and ready to go to the shindig. I shouldn't have worried.

On the way I called Detective Jackson to let him know I had connected with Elaine Manning. He was not a happy camper. 'You mean, after I went chasing that woman all over God's creation you ended up tracking her down after I left the funeral?'

'What can I say? I just lucked out.'

'What's the deal?' he said, grumbling. So I told him what Elaine had told me, ending by letting him know that I had cleared the way for him and Ramsdahl to stop by and see her the next day. That made him a little less grumpy.

'All right, then,' he said. 'You think she's credible?'

'I think she definitely believes Pastor Mark Granger had something to do with LaShawn Tompkins's death.'

'We'll take a closer look at his alibi, then,' Jackson said. 'And we'll also start looking around at some of his associates.'

'Did he talk to you?'

'Are you kidding? His attorney wouldn't let him say a word. But thanks for the help, Beau. I appreciate it.'

'Any luck tracking that nun that was seen in the neighborhood the night LaShawn was shot?' I put the question out there just to let him know that I knew and to see what he'd do about it.

'Not much,' he said. 'We've been looking into it, but nothing so far.'

'You let me know if you do,' I said, 'and I'll do the same.'

When I finally walked in the door at a quarter to six I was astonished to find Mel dressed in the clothing she had worn to work much earlier that morning. She glanced up at me from the kitchen counter, where she and Todd were still hard at work.

'How's it going?' she asked.

'Slow,' I said, kissing her hello. 'Very slow. What about you?'

'Pretty much the same,' she said. 'There's a lot of material here.'

Todd roused himself from his computer and sent an unabashedly admiring look in Mel's direction. 'If you want me to hang around and work on this over the weekend . . . ' he began.

But Mel jumped in to send him packing. 'No,' she said. 'You go right ahead with your plans. We have more than enough here to keep us busy all weekend. Besides,' she added, pointedly glancing at her watch, 'we have an engagement this evening. If we don't head out soon, we'll be late.'

Todd Hatcher took the hint. 'All right, then,' he said, closing his computer and starting to stuff it into his backpack. 'I'll go. Should I take the abstracts or leave them?'

I shrugged. Mel said, 'Leave them. We may have time to work on them over the weekend.'

'All right,' Todd agreed. 'But if you need anything, call me. And here's a fax number. If you have more notes for me to add to the spreadsheet, you can fax them down to me.'

Mel ushered him to the door.

'You're sure you don't want me to . . . ' he began.

'No,' Mel said firmly. 'Take the weekend off, Todd. You work too hard.' Once he was outside the apartment she looked at her watch. 'Better hurry,' she told me.

We went into our separate bathrooms to shower and dress. I hadn't tried on the tux after it had been altered — not with Lars Jenssen waiting out in the car — but the changes had been done expertly enough that the tux fit perfectly, sleeve length, shoulders, and all. At twenty after six Mel appeared in my bedroom door looking gorgeous in a long black beaded dress with a slit that showed a length of exquisitely formed leg. She held up a single-strand pearl necklace.

'Can you fasten this?' she asked.

Complying, I brushed her perfumed shoulder with my lips as I did so. 'You're beautiful,' I told her. 'Poor Todd. The guy was practically salivating every time he looked at you.'

'I noticed,' Mel said.

'Did he tell you about his parents?' I asked.

'What about them?'

We were in the elevator and on our way to the car and I was starting to tell her the story when we were interrupted by a phone call from Jeremy letting me know they were safely back in Ashland.

'Good,' I said. 'Glad to hear it.'

I thought that would be the end of the conversation, but it wasn't.

'She's upstairs right now,' he added. 'Putting the kids to bed, but I don't know what to do with her, Beau. She cried all the way home.'

'Kayla?' I asked, remembering that traveling with cranky preschoolers can seem like a long-term jail sentence at times.

'No,' Jeremy said tersely, 'Kelly. I kept asking her what was wrong, but she wouldn't tell me or couldn't tell me. From Seattle to here, she just cried and cried.'

I felt a rush of impatience. It seemed to me that sometimes twenty-something daughters and tantrum-throwing toddlers had a lot in common. After all, I hadn't put all kinds of roadblocks in the way of Kelly's romance with Jeremy, one that, to all outside observers, had seemed destined to fail. Now here she was raising hell over my relationship with Mel. It didn't seem fair. If I was willing to treat her as an adult, didn't I deserve the same courtesy? And eight straight hours of crying seemed to be overdoing it.

'Look, Jeremy,' I said. 'This makes no sense. Kelly's mother and I divorced years ago. Karen's been dead for almost four years now, and I can't for the life of me imagine why, all of a sudden, Kelly should take such an intense dislike to Mel. I mean, last weekend everything was hunky-dory. Now, less than a week later, Mel is evil personified. How can that be?'

'I don't understand it either,' Jeremy agreed miserably. 'Gotta go.' He hung up, just like that. Obviously Kelly had finished putting the kids to bed.

'What was that all about?' Mel asked as we climbed into the Mercedes.

I shook my head. 'Kelly's still mad at me, I guess, but she'll just have to get used to it. I'm not giving you up.'

Mel gave me a radiant smile. 'Good,' she said. 'I'm glad to hear it.'

'Now tell me about tonight,' I said. 'What am I in for exactly?'

'The pre-gathering gathering is in the Presidential Suite up on the thirty-fourth floor of the Sheraton,' Mel told me. 'That's for SASAC board members and their spouses and/or partners only. It's the time when we all stand around having drinks and congratulating our-selves on what a great job we did. Then, at eight, we'll go downstairs for the fund-raising banquet itself. That's in the ballroom.'

My tux, which had fit perfectly only a few short minutes before, suddenly felt too tight. 'I'm going to a cocktail party?' I groused. 'Oh, goody.'

'I talked to the catering staff,' Mel assured me. 'They'll definitely have nonalcoholic beverages available.'

'Right,' I muttered. 'I can just imagine. God save me from the nincompoop who invented virgin margaritas.'

Back in my drinking days I pretty much regarded myself as the life of any given party — after I'd had a couple of shots of McNaughton's, that is. Give me enough booze, and I'd overcome my natural aversion to small talk. I could chitchat away with the best of them, and swap off-color jokes with wild abandon. I always thought my party behavior above reproach, although, if my first wife were still alive, I'm sure Karen would have a few choice words on the subject.

Riding the elevator up to the Sheraton's Presidential Suite without having had the benefit of any liquid courage I found myself having second thoughts about the whole thing — second thoughts and very damp palms. Mel must have been reading my mind, or maybe she noticed my hands were so sweaty I could barely manage the elevator buttons.

'Don't worry about it,' she said. 'It's going to be fine.'

And it was. I stepped into the spacious but crowded room and discovered, to my immense relief, that I was properly attired. Thanks to Mel's timely intervention, my tuxedo held its own with every other tuxedo in the room. That definitely improved my outlook. And Mel didn't just measure up to the other women — she outshone most of them. That made me feel even better.

She knew everyone, of course, and was immediately caught up in first one conversation and then another. Wanting to make myself useful, I wandered over to the bar and ordered a tonic with a twist for me and a glass of Merlot for her. Then I settled in by the windows and stared out over the surrounding glowing high-rises to the distant darkened mass of Elliott Bay, twinkling now with moving ferries and a border of reflected city lights.

'Great view, isn't it?' someone said.

I turned to look. The man standing beside me was about my age and size. Since there were no conveniently placed tables, he, too, was holding two drinks — a rocks glass with an amber liquid that was probably Scotch and a glass of white wine.

'Name's Beaumont,' I told him. 'J. P. Beaumont. Since we both seem to be functioning as window dressing at the moment, I guess we'll have to shake hands later.'

The man chuckled. 'Cal Lowman,' he said. 'You'd think they'd be able to spring for a couple of tables at things like this so we wouldn't have to stand around looking like a pair of idiots. I always wanted to be a drink stand when I grew up, didn't you?'

Cal Lowman was a name I recognized. He was a senior partner with one of the big-deal corporate law firms in town — Henderson, Lowman, Richards, and Potts.

I grew up on the wrong side of the tracks in

Seattle's Ballard neighborhood, raised by a single mother who supported us by working as a seamstress. She made a meager living by sewing knock-off copies of designer dresses for Seattle's social elite. All through grade school I had to endure endless teasing over showing up each day in one or another of my mother's homemade shirts. Eventually I fought back, winning some and losing some and being sent to the principal's office on an almost daily basis. The fights didn't stop for good until I was in high school and was old enough to get an after-school job at the local theater. Only then did I achieve the pinnacle of sophistication by showing up at school in a store-bought shirt.

But America's a great place. Here I was, decades later, having a tuxedo-clad male bonding conversation with one of Seattle's prime movers and shakers.

'Your wife's on the board?' Lowman asked.

This is one of the reasons I'm no good at chitchat. If I couldn't explain Mel Soames's position in my life to my children, how would I manage with this stranger? Mel most definitely was not my wife, but the more dispassionately accurate U.S. Census Bureau term, POSSLQ — a person of opposite sex sharing living quarters — just didn't do it for me. And we were both far too long of tooth for the old standby terms of boyfriend/girlfriend to apply.

'Mel Soames is my partner,' I said finally. 'And yes, she's on the board.'

Just then the woman we had met days earlier at the California Pizza Kitchen arrived on the scene. She was dazzling in a strapless green silk gown topped by an amazing emerald necklace. 'Hello, there,' she said to me. 'We've got to stop meeting like this.' Then, reaching past me, she collected the glass of wine Cal Lowman had been holding.

'So you've already met my Anita?' Cal asked with a possessive smile.

As I said, Cal was about my age. Mel is fifteen years younger than I am, and this delectable piece of arm candy was far younger than that.

I brushed off my conversational skills as best I could and tried to measure up. 'Briefly,' I said. 'But I'm not up on exactly what you do.'

'I'm retired,' Anita told me, sipping her wine. 'And trying to make the world a better place. That's why I started the SASAC in the first place.' She turned to Cal. 'Okay,' she said, 'time to go to work. There's someone I want you to meet.'

She dragged him away so unceremoniously that I was surprised Cal didn't object. Their abrupt departure left me wearing the conversational equivalent of two left feet.

About that time Mel showed up and relieved me of her glass of wine. 'So let me guess,' I said, nodding in Anita and Cal's direction. 'Now that Anita's hooked up with a sugar daddy like Cal Lowman she can forgo working for a living and can afford to devote herself to charity.'

Mel gave me a bemused look. 'There you go,' she said. 'You've fallen back into that age-old trap of gender stereotyping. You've got this story upside down and backward. If anybody's a sugar daddy, it would have to be Anita. She left Microsoft at age thirty-three with a pocketful of loot. That's where she met Cal — at Microsoft. She plucked him off Microsoft's team of corporate legal beagles and took him home to play house. A lot like you and me, babe; only, in our case, you're the one with the moolah. Anita could probably buy and sell Cal Lowman a dozen times over.'

That's when it came home to me. Times had changed; women had changed. My second wife, Anne Corley, had died and left me with an armload of money, but tux or not, I was still that unsophisticated hick from Ballard. No amount of money in the world was going to fix that.

'And plan on being nice,' Mel added. 'I'm pretty sure we're seated at the same table.'

Convinced I had somehow bungled that initial encounter, I was dreading sharing dinner with Cal and Anita, but then I got lucky. When we went down to the cavernous ballroom and made our way through to the table directly in front of the speaker's podium, I caught sight of someone I actually knew — Destry Hennessey.

I had encountered Destry years earlier, when she had been a lowly criminalist working on a master's at the U. Dub during the day and toiling away in Seattle PD's crime lab by night. Once she earned her degree, she had taken a job somewhere else — I wasn't sure where. Sometime in the course of the last several years, Destry had returned to the West Coast as the newly appointed head of the Washington State Patrol Crime Lab.

I went up and shook her hand. 'Des,' I said, 'long time no see. What are you doing here?'

'I'm the speaker,' she said. 'I hate doing public speaking. In terms of phobias, it's supposed to be right up there with fear of dying. With a room this big I can tell you I'm scared to death.'

'You'll do fine,' I said.

'Thanks,' she said. 'It's nice to have a friend in my corner.'

When I went to introduce her to Mel, I was surprised to learn they already knew each other. 'We're both on the SASAC board,' Mel explained. 'We roomed together at a retreat down in Mexico last fall.'

'Funny,' I said. 'You never mentioned it.'

Mel shook her head. 'You and I weren't exactly an item back then, remember?'

While the two of them chatted I checked out our table, where I was dismayed to discover someone had taken the liberty of assigning seats. The good news was that Destry was on my right. On my left was a dragon lady named Professor Rosemary Clark, who, I soon learned, turned out to be the University of Washington's distinguished professor of women's studies. Since the good professor was far more interested in talking to Cal Lowman than she was to me, Destry and I spent dinner exchanging small talk.

We brought each other up to date on what had happened in our lives since we'd last crossed paths. After leaving Seattle PD she had worked for several years as second in command for the state crime lab in Massachusetts. However, her kids, now in high school, and her husband had all hated living on the East Coast. When the opportunity had arisen for her to come back home to Washington as head of the state patrol's crime lab, she had jumped at the chance.

'Heard you're working for SHIT now,' she said.

I nodded, glad that for once I was dealing with a fellow bureaucrat who didn't have to make a joke of the agency's name.

'How do you like it?' she asked.

'Not bad,' I said. 'Ross Connors is a pretty squared-away guy.'

As we started in on the salad course, I asked Destry about the talk she would be delivering.

'It'll be on our DNA pilot program,' she said.

Her answer left me entirely in the dark. 'What pilot program?' I asked.

'I'm sorry,' she said. 'You're here at the major donor table, so I figured you knew all about it. SASAC is paying the freight for a full-time DNA profiler in the crime lab. There's so much DNA evidence coming in now that we're falling further and further behind. If we raise enough money tonight, we may be able to fund another one. Someday we may be able to start making progress on that backlog of rape kits that have sat untested in evidence rooms for years on end.'

DNA's impact on crime solving has changed significantly in the last few years. Cold cases that were once deemed unsolvable were now being cleared as new techniques came online.

'With all this high-tech stuff,' I said, 'pretty soon old-time detectives like me will be completely obsolete.'

Destry Hennessey laughed and patted my hand. 'That would be a shame,' she said.

'Why?'

I thought she'd say something about society losing the benefit of our law enforcement experience and cunning and skill, and maybe even our flat-out stubbornness, but she didn't.

'Because some of you old guys are so darned cute,' she said with a smile.

I did not want to be cute! And I certainly didn't want to be old! What I really wanted was get up and stalk out of the ballroom without waiting around for the main course or for Destry Hennessey's upcoming speech, either. But I didn't. My mother raised me to be more of a gentleman than that — at least she tried to. So I plastered a phony smile on my face, chatted civilly with the professor when called upon to do so, and stayed right where I was.

I'm doing this for Mel, I thought glumly. *And she damned well better appreciate it!*

13

If you fall in love when you're young, you stake a claim on that other person's life. You want to know everything about them. But Mel and I fell in love later. We both had a past — maybe more than one each — and we arrived at the conclusion that the other person's past wasn't anybody else's business. For one thing, you can't change the past. And since we couldn't change what had happened to us before we met, it didn't make sense to go into all of that in any great detail, either. To that end we made a mutual and conscious decision to live in the present. We didn't go digging around in each other's personal history. So far that had worked for us.

But just because we didn't sit around jawing about our pasts didn't mean there was some big secrecy program going on, either. For instance, Mel knew about what had happened to Sue Danielson because Sue's death was work related. And I'm sure she could have found out about Anne Corley's death for the same reason. It had been big news in all the local newspapers at the time. Mel is, after all, a detective. I have no doubt she had picked up bits and pieces both good and bad about my relationship with Karen by paying attention to what my kids said about our marriage and subsequent divorce.

Mel's and my unspoken agreement did mean that Mel hadn't ever asked me about the whys and wherefores of my going to AA, although, come to think of it, that's pretty obvious. It also meant that I hadn't ever delved into her involvement with SASAC, although I have to admit to a certain amount of curiosity. My hands-off attitude on that score ended the night of the dinner at the Sheraton.

There was a lot about the evening that made me uncomfortable. For one thing, there was a whole 'Male Evil; Woman Poor Victim' theme to the event that rankled. Yes, I know that most victims of sexual assault are women, the major exception, of course, being generations of traumatized and equally victimized altar boys. But it turns out the villains there are also male, so being a nonabusing heterosexual male in that particular Sheraton ballroom was not a comfortable fit.

Still, I was expected to sit there and share the guilt and blame while a lineup of women revealed a litany of abuse that was enough to curl your hair. As a man, I was automatically under indictment. Whatever had happened to those women was somehow *my* fault. I was also expected to haul out my wallet and make a sizable donation to the cause, which included the funding of a twenty-four-hour rape hotline and Internet site, funding for victim advocates and victim counseling, as well as continuing to fund the rape-kit examination project that was, it turned out, Anita Bowdin's special focus.

That rankled even more. It was bad enough that Ross Connors was now passing off police work to underemployed economists. But to find out that the crime lab was outsourcing DNA profiling as well was enough to make this old cop feel like a member of an endangered species — an exceedingly cranky endangered species.

So I handed over my credit card number, kept my mouth shut, and just tried to make it through.

'What's the matter?' Mel asked.

We had finally escaped the overheated ballroom and were standing outside the hotel in a crush of people waiting for an outnumbered and overwhelmed crew of parking valets to retrieve the Mercedes from the garage.

'How did you ever get mixed up with that bunch of women?' I asked, thinking most particularly of the good professor of women's studies who had given me an earful of invective over the dessert course.

Okay, my comment was more of a growl than anything else. And it could have been phrased far more diplomatically. But I didn't expect what happened next. Mel simply turned and walked away. Make that stalked away. The manner in which she took off was far more definitive than mere walking.

'Where are you going?' I asked, trailing after her.

'To catch a cab,' she said over her shoulder.

'But . . . ' I objected.

'I'm going home,' she added. 'To Bellevue.'

I guess our voices were somewhat raised, and people started to gawk. Just then the valet showed up with my car and honked twice from the curb. By the time I tipped him and retrieved the Mercedes, Mel was nowhere in sight.

So, since she had said she was going to Bellevue, I drove there, too. There were no lights on in her apartment, so I parked outside and waited. And waited. Finally, forty-five minutes later, and needing to use the facilities, I headed back to Seattle. When I drove down into the underground garage I realized the error in my thinking. Her BMW was gone. So she had ridden the cab back to Belltown Terrace to pick up her car so she could drive herself across the lake to Bellevue. No wonder I had missed her.

Up in the apartment I soon discovered that her briefcase and her computer, along with Todd Hatcher's stack of abstracts, were all among the missing. So were her nightgown, bathrobe, and makeup. I glanced in her closet. I'm sure some of her clothing was gone as well, but I couldn't tell how much. If I could have sorted that out, it might have told me if I was dead or really dead. By then it was too late to consider driving back to Bellevue. I tried calling both her cell and her landline, but she didn't answer. Finally I gave up. I removed my newly purchased tuxedo, which hadn't exactly done me a hell of a lot of good, and took myself to bed.

When the phone rang bright and early the next morning, I grabbed for it eagerly, hoping Mel would be on the other end of the line. She wasn't.

'Hi, Dad,' Scott said. 'How's it going?'

Medium, I thought. 'Fine,' I said. 'How was your day yesterday?'

'Great!' he said. 'I took Cherisse out to Lake

Tapps and showed her our old stomping grounds. Geez, there are lots of houses out there now. I mean, our house used to be way out in the country. And the lake's a lot smaller than I remembered.'

'But it was fun?' I asked.

'Sure. We had a blast. This morning we're going to pick Lars up and take him to breakfast at the Mecca. Do you and Mel want to come along?'

I looked at Mel's empty pillow. 'I think we'll take a pass on that,' I said.

'And then we're going to go on playing tourist,' he said. 'The Arboretum, Snoqualmie Falls, the aquarium. Care to join us for any of that?'

If I ever go back to Snoqualmie Falls, the place where Anne Corley died, it will be way too soon. 'No,' I said. 'I'm working on a case. I should probably spend some time on that, but a man's got to eat. What are your plans for dinner?'

'Don't really have any,' Scott said, sounding a bit abashed. 'We've pretty much blown our budget.'

I remembered what it was like to be young and broke and wanting to impress your new wife but worrying about whether or not you'd be able to pay next month's bills if you did so. Thanks to Anne Corley, my financial situation had taken an amazing turn for the better since those tough old days.

'Dinner's on me, then,' I said. 'What sounds good?'

'Steak?' Scott asked hopefully.

'We'll go to El Gaucho, then,' I said. 'They have some of the best steaks in town, and it's only a couple of blocks from here. Say around seven or so. I'll call for a reservation.'

'What happened to Kelly and Jeremy?' Scott asked. 'I called to invite them to breakfast. The guy at the front desk said they'd checked out.'

'I guess Kelly wanted to go home.'

'She was acting weird,' Scott said. 'Even for Kelly. I mean, if this is all because of Mel, it's ridiculous. You do get to live your own life, don't you?'

My sentiments exactly, I thought, although looking at Mel's empty pillow made me wonder if her presence in my life was still an issue.

'Seems like I should,' I said.

'See you this evening,' Scott returned. 'Where's the restaurant, by the way?'

'Just come to the house,' I said. 'We can walk from here.'

Missing Mel, I rolled out of bed and went out into the kitchen to make my own coffee. Then, while the coffee brewed, I called Nick down at El Gaucho. Mel and I go there enough that I have the number programmed into my cell phone. No one answered that early on a Saturday morning, but I left my name and a message. I brought in the newspapers from the front door, but I didn't bother opening them. For some reason I didn't feel up to working a crossword puzzle.

Instead, I sat in my recliner, sipping coffee and brooding. Finally I threw caution to the winds and dialed Mel's cell.

Much to my surprise, she answered. 'I'm not speaking to you, remember?'

This seemed like an egregious overreaction to whatever I had or hadn't done, so I decided to ignore it. 'If you were speaking to me,' I countered, 'what would you say?'

' "Those women"!' she said, repeating my ill-chosen words with an inflection I recognized all too well. 'How did I get hooked up with 'those women'?'

'Mel, look. I'm sorry. I'm sure I was out of line, but you're not seeing this from my point of view. I spent dinner stuck next to that dreadful professor, who really does hate men, by the way, and listening to all of those awful stories. It seemed like every story and every single one of the women there said pretty much the same thing — that whatever had happened to them was all my fault. That I was somehow responsible. I'll bet even Anita Bowdin's husband . . .'

'Calvin Lowman,' Mel supplied. 'And he's not her husband.'

'Whatever,' I said. 'I'll bet even he was squirming in his seat. Every man there was probably doing the same thing.'

'Is there a purpose to this call?' Mel asked.

Her crisp tone would have deflected even the most determined of life insurance salesmen. 'I invited Scott and Cherisse to dinner at El Gaucho tonight at seven,' I said hurriedly. 'I was hoping you'd come, too.'

'What about Kelly and Jeremy?'

'They went home,' I said. 'To Ashland.'

There was a pause. 'I'll think about it,' Mel said. 'But don't hold your breath. And there is a reason,' she added.

'I'm sorry?'

'A reason I'm involved with 'those women.' A reason I'm on the board. I just don't like to talk about it, but maybe I'll tell you sometime. If I start speaking to you again, that is.'

With that she hung up, leaving me with no clear idea of where I stood. She claimed she wasn't speaking to me, but she had been. And the other part — the part she had left unsaid — about the reason behind her involvement with SASAC put a hole in the pit of my stomach. I had never even considered that someone as slick as Mel might have some dark corner in her past where she, too, had been gravely mistreated. If something like that had happened to her, I wasn't sure I was ready to hear about it. Once I did, would I feel obliged to go out, track the jerk down, and throttle him with my bare hands? That would make a lot more sense than sending donations to SASAC!!!

I called Mel right back. 'I know you're still not speaking to me,' I said quickly, 'but if you wanted to come back to the house and work together on Todd Hatcher's stuff, I promise I won't say a single word out of line.'

'I'll think about it,' she said, 'but I need some space, Beau — space and time.' She hung up again.

Rebuffed, I knew I couldn't afford to spend the day sitting around thinking about Mel and what I did or didn't know. I needed to do

206

something, to take some kind of action. Twiddling my thumbs wasn't an option when what I really wanted to do was go out and knock a few heads. So I did the next best thing. I called the DMV and ran a check on Carol and Jack Lawrence. Once I had their address information, I headed for Leavenworth, two and a half hours away, on the far side of the Cascades.

Many small used-to-be logging towns in rural Washington have drifted into almost ghost-town obscurity. Several of the burgs along Highway 2 run perpetual going-out-of-business sales in the form of retired churches, which, now devoid of parishioners, live on in a tawdry, makeshift fashion as threadbare antique malls.

Leavenworth, too, was once headed in that direction and might well have suffered the same fate had not some enterprising city fathers — and mothers, I'm sure — decided to reinvent the place. They slapped on layers of Bavarian facades, dressed everybody and his uncle in lederhosen, and declared the city a tourist attraction. Such is the magic of self-fulfilling prophecies that the ploy worked remarkably well. Now thousands of people flock there for their faux Octoberfest and for their annual Christmas-lighting ceremonies. For authenticity's sake, it helps that Leavenworth is high enough in the mountains that this holiday extravaganza usually takes place in frigid snow, with the occasional blizzard thrown in.

If I sound somewhat churlish about all this, let me say that the one time I bravely went there is also when the 'occasional' blizzard happened.

That storm resulted in a combination of record snowfall in Stevens Pass and an avalanche on I-90 at Snoqualmie Pass, a one-two punch that brought most of Washington's east-west travel to a halt. Karen and the kids and I didn't make it back over the mountains until Tuesday afternoon, two days late for both work and school. Since this was March instead of November or December, however, I figured I was safe enough on the weather score. And since it wasn't Christmas, there was no need for me to be brimming over with peace on earth and all that jazz — especially when it came to Mr. Jack Lawrence.

During the long solitary drive from Seattle across a still snow-bordered Stevens Pass I had plenty of time for thinking. Gradually I was able to let go of the Mel situation and turn my attention to the problem of Jack and Carol Lawrence. As I drove I realized this would probably be nothing more than a useless fishing expedition. In fact, if Lawrence hadn't given his stepdaughter such a tough time, I probably wouldn't have bothered trying to interview him at all. It turns out, though, that I'm a great believer in giving people like him the opportunity to reap what they sow. Besides, I found his interest in *not* discussing Tony Cosgrove's decades-old disappearance most interesting.

It was late on a sunny but surprisingly chill morning when I pulled up at the Lawrences' mailbox on Lavetta Road south of Leavenworth proper. Lavetta Road isn't so much a road as it is a very angular circle. Maybe they should have

208

called it Lavetta Oblong. With the help of my trusty GPS, I managed to locate the long winding driveway marked 'Lawrence,' which took off from the southernmost curve of Lavetta and headed off into the forest.

The house itself was one of those some-assembly-required log cabins where someone else cuts up, notches, numbers, and fits together all the tree trunks necessary to build the house. They're then taken apart, loaded onto a truck, and hauled to wherever the house is being built. At that point the hapless homeowner has to reassemble the pieces himself or pay someone else to do it. Since Lawrence was an engineer type, I figured he would have done the work himself.

This one was a large two-story affair with a steeply pitched roof and a covered porch that ran across the entire front of the house. A single vehicle was parked outside — a muddied Subaru Forester that seemed much the worse for wear. Out of force of habit, I jotted down the license number, then started up the walkway. In true Leavenworth fashion, the metal door knocker had been fashioned to resemble a nutcracker. I gave it a good bash and waited to see if anyone would answer.

The door was cracked open the distance of a short length of fastened security chain. 'Yes?' a woman asked questioningly, while remaining mostly out of sight behind the partially opened door.

Carol Lawrence was about my age. Her silver hair was pulled back in a ponytail, but even that small glimpse revealed a resemblance between her and her daughter that was nothing short of striking. She looked as if she had been crying, and I wondered what about.

'What do you want?' she asked.

I held up my ID. 'Mrs. Lawrence,' I began, 'if you have a few moments, I'd like to speak to you.'

By the time the words were out of my mouth she was already trying to slam the door. My foot, schooled by years of actual door-to-door Fuller Brush salesmanship, was firmly planted in the way.

'Go away,' she ordered. 'I'm not talking to you and neither is Jack. Tony's been gone for a quarter of a century. There's no reason to bring it all back up.'

'But your daughter — '

'My daughter disapproves of me,' she said. 'I didn't wait the whole seven years, and she's never forgiven me for that. But you know what? I'm the mother. I get to live my life the way I want to. Now go away.'

'Are you aware that your husband went to see DeAnn yesterday?' I asked. 'That he was off the charts and threatened her? She was very upset.'

'Look,' Carol said impatiently, 'Jack is DeAnn's stepfather. They have never gotten along and never will. Not only that, I've finally figured out that I can't fix it. So please go away and leave me alone before my husband comes home and finds you here.'

'You're saying he would be upset by my being here? Why's that? We're just doing a routine

210

follow-up on your missing first husband. I can't see why Mr. Lawrence finds that so disturbing — unless he has something to hide, that is.'

'Jack's a very private man,' Carol insisted. 'He doesn't like people nosing around in our private lives. We want to be left alone. Just go away.'

'The way he's acting is enough to make me think maybe the two of you were an item long before Tony went fishing up on Spirit Lake.'

'So what if Jack and I were an 'item' back then, as you call it?' Carol demanded hotly. 'We've been married for twenty-five years now. That should count for something. You don't have any idea what my life was like then, and you have no right to judge me now. Neither does my daughter. My husband is a very private man. The idea that DeAnn brought this up — '

'She didn't,' I interjected. 'DeAnn had nothing to do with it. The attorney general's office is doing routine follow-ups on missing persons cases from all over the state. That's how your former husband's name came up. Period.'

'Oh,' Carol said, sounding somewhat subdued. 'We thought . . . '

I took a business card from my pocket and passed it through the door. I didn't expect her to take it, but she did.

'I don't care what you thought,' I told her curtly. 'We are conducting an active investigation at this time. Please let your husband know that I am going to need to talk to both of you sooner or later. You can make it easy or you can make it hard.'

She studied the card, then unlatched the

chain. 'All right.' She sounded resigned. 'Come on in. Like I said, Jack isn't home right now. You probably passed each other somewhere between here and Seattle. What do you want to know?'

For the next hour or so we went over the same ground I had covered with DeAnn days earlier. I asked many of the same questions and heard the same answers, but with one telling difference. I had left DeAnn Cosgrove's home convinced she was telling the truth, or at least the truth as she knew it.

When my interview with Carol was over I left the Lawrences' sprawling log house living room with the distinct impression Carol had been lying through her teeth. I didn't know why, not for sure, but I had my suspicions. All I had to do now was to learn enough about the case to catch her in one of those lies.

Like Donnie Cosgrove, I was beginning to believe that Mount Saint Helens had nothing at all to do with his first father-in-law's disappearance.

'Have Jack give me a call,' I told Carol the last thing before I stepped off her front porch to return to my car. 'You have my number.'

'Okay,' she said, 'I'll tell him.'

We both knew he wouldn't call. Most likely Jack Lawrence would play hard to get. That didn't bother me, though. Tony Cosgrove had been gone for a quarter of a century. I had all the time in the world.

Without Mel there to ride herd on me I had missed breakfast, so I stopped off at the Brewery Pub in Leavenworth to grab some lunch before heading back to Seattle. As I waited for my hamburger, I was thinking about DeAnn Cosgrove and her mother. DeAnn evidently still disapproved of her mother's moving on twenty-five years after it had happened. That certainly boded ill for me and Kelly.

The waitress was delivering my hamburger when Kendall Jackson called.

'Just left Elaine Manning,' he told me. 'Thanks for that, by the way. What she had to say was interesting, and we'll follow up on some of the leads she suggested, but I'm not holding my breath. Without something more solid than her suspicion . . . '

'That's pretty much where I am on that, too,' I told him. 'What about the nun? Any luck tracking her?'

'All bad,' Jackson returned. 'But I seem to remember that your boss has way more high-level connections inside the Catholic Church than I do. Here's an idea. How about if you see what *you* can do to find that missing nun?'

I was still pissed that he hadn't mentioned the existence of a possible eyewitness without my having to find it out on my own, but there was no sense arguing over it, especially not when I still needed Detective Jackson in my corner on occasion.

'Thanks for the suggestion,' I told him. 'I'll give it a whirl.'

Ross Connors is a lifelong Catholic, and one of his best friends from O'Dea High School is now a special assistant to the bishop at the

213

Seattle Archdiocese. So I called Ross. It was March and nippy, but it was also that rarest of rare northwest commodities — a sunny Saturday. I had no doubt Ross was out on a golf course somewhere.

I left him a message to call me back. Then I put my phone away and tucked in.

14

On the drive back to Seattle, LaShawn Tompkins's murder slipped to a back burner as I concentrated on what my trip across the mountains had produced concerning Tony Cosgrove's disappearance. If nothing else, talking to Carol Lawrence had upped my suspicion level significantly. I was convinced that she and her husband did have something to hide, even though I wasn't sure what.

To my mind there was now a whole new urgency in my wanting to track down Thomas Dortman, the defense analyst. If, as I suspected, he had worked at Boeing during the seventies and eighties, there was a chance he had actually known Tony Cosgrove or maybe even Jack Lawrence. What I needed more than anything right then was to talk to someone who would either confirm what Carol Lawrence had told me — or blow her out of the water.

It wasn't until I turned south on 405 that I started thinking about dinner — and about Mel. I wasn't looking forward to going to dinner with Scott and Cherisse and having to explain why Mel wasn't joining us. I thought briefly about calling her. I glanced at my cell phone, but there hadn't been any calls. Then I thought about going by her place in Bellevue on the way home to Seattle. But I didn't want to show up outside the security door at her apartment only to be told I wasn't welcome. So I drove onto State Route 520 and straight home.

On the parking garage ramp leading down to P-2, however, I was astonished to see Mel's 740 parked in its customary spot. I headed up to the penthouse, not the least bit sure if it would be safe to open the door without wearing a flak jacket. When I stepped inside, however, I found Mel at the far end of the living room. The window seat was covered with stacks of papers, which I immediately recognized as excerpts from Todd Hatcher's abstracts. She was seated cross-legged on the floor in front of a yellow pad, reading glasses perched on her nose. She stood up as soon as I came into the room, walked over, and kissed me hello.

'Sorry,' she said. 'I was out of line.' I kissed her back. I would have done more, but she dodged out of my arms before I could get a good grip on her. She returned to the window seat and began gathering the papers. 'I should have talked to you about this a long time ago,' she added.

'Should have talked to me about what?' I asked.

'About why I'm involved with SASAC,' she replied.

I felt a funny twist in my gut. If this was something Mel didn't want to tell me, it was also probably something I didn't want to hear.

'Look,' I said, 'I was out of line, too. Whatever it was must have happened a long time ago. It's none of my business. You don't owe me an explanation of any kind.'

'But I do,' she said. 'What happened back then

216

is why I'm involved in sexual assault issues today. It's also why I'm a cop. Coffee?'

I recognized that her offer of coffee was nothing more or less than a diversionary tactic. I accepted it for the same reason. We were waltzing around something important and uncomfortable, and we needed to get past it. Mel's face looked so troubled — so hurt — that I wanted to take her in my arms and hold her, but she wasn't having any of that. She went back to the relative safety of the window seat and perched there, coffee cup in hand. I, on the other hand, retreated to my sturdy recliner. We both knew that whatever was coming wouldn't be easy to discuss, and maintaining some physical distance would serve us both in good stead.

'Did you ever have something happen to you where it wasn't your fault — I mean, you *know* it wasn't your fault — but you still hold yourself responsible?' Mel asked.

Let me count the ways, I thought.

My mother died of cancer. My ex-wife died of cancer. Sue Danielson died of gunshot wounds. Anne Corley died of gun-shot wounds. Only with Anne did I personally fire the weapon that killed her, and even that ended up being ruled justifiable homicide — self-defense. In all the others I was held blameless — as far as the world was concerned, but not on my own personal scorecard.

'Once or twice,' I conceded.

'Have I ever mentioned Sarah Matthews to you?'

I racked my brain and came up empty. 'I don't

think so. Who's she?'

'She was my best friend in high school — Austin High School in El Paso. Her father was a staff sergeant in the army and my dad was a major at the time. We were in the same homeroom.'

I was scrambling to pull together what little I did know about Mel Soames's background. She had grown up as an army brat. Her dad, William Majors, was retired military who now lived somewhere in Italy with his second wife, Doris. Mel's mother, Katy, was living in Florida with a long-term boyfriend, name unknown, whom she had so far declined to marry. I knew there had been bad blood all around during the breakup of their almost thirty-year marriage. As a result I had yet to meet any of Mel's parental units.

'Major Majors?' I asked, trying to inject a little humor. 'That must have been fun.'

Mel didn't respond in kind, and her grim expression didn't change.

'Sarah and I were in the same homeroom for three years,' she continued. 'My senior year Dad was transferred back to D.C. Sarah and I stayed in touch for a year or so — through graduation and for the first semester of our freshman year in college. She committed suicide a few days before Christmas of that year. She shot herself.'

'Where?' I asked.

'In the head,' Mel answered. 'Blew her brains out.'

'No. I mean where was she when she died?'

'She was still in Texas — University of Texas at El Paso.'

218

I knew Mel had graduated from the University of Virginia. 'So you weren't anywhere around when it happened?' I asked.

'No,' Mel said. 'Sarah was in El Paso. I was in Charlottesville.'

'So how could her committing suicide possibly be your fault?' I asked.

For an answer, Mel picked up a small book that had been sitting on the floor beside her. She got up, walked across the room, and handed it to me.

'What is it?' I asked.

'Sarah's diary,' Mel replied. 'I'm sure she was afraid someone at home might find it, so she must have hidden it on my bookshelf. When we moved, it got stuck in a box of books that stayed in storage until after my parents bought the house in Manassas at the beginning of my sophomore year. Mom found it and gave it to me. It pretty much explains everything.'

I was holding the book, but I didn't think Mel actually intended for me to read it.

'What does it say?' I asked.

Mel's eyes filled with tears. 'Her father molested her,' she said. 'From the time she was little. She tried to tell her mother, but her mom didn't believe her.'

'Did she tell you?' I asked.

Mel shook her head. 'Not in so many words. I think she tried, but I was too naive to understand what she was really saying. But if I had bothered to read the book . . . '

'You just told me that you didn't know about the diary until after she was already dead.'

219

'Right, but . . . '

'But what?'

'If I had been a better friend, I would have listened more. And when her father tried to put the moves on me — '

'He went after you?' I demanded.

Mel nodded. 'It was at a Christmas party at a neighbor's house. He caught up with me out in the backyard. He was drunk enough that I was able to get away, and I never told anyone about what had happened. I was too embarrassed.'

'He was what,' I asked, 'in his thirties?'

'Around there,' Mel conceded.

'And you were in high school? Whatever happened has nothing to do with you,' I declared. 'It was his fault, not yours.'

'It's not so much what happened before I read the diary,' Mel interjected. 'It's what happened afterward.'

'What did happen?'

'Nothing,' Mel answered hopelessly. 'Not one damned thing. I kept my mouth shut and didn't say a single word. By then Sarah's mother, Lois, was already sick, crippled by MS and confined to a wheelchair. She was totally dependent on the man. If he'd gone to the slammer then, I don't know what would have become of her. Sarah was already dead. What difference did it make? Even now, I doubt the diary itself would have been enough to convict him. So I just kept quiet.'

Mel sat in the window seat. She seemed to be staring out at the water, but I doubt she was seeing any of it.

'Where are Sarah's parents now?' I asked gently.

'Lois Matthews died about seven years ago. Sarah's father, Richard, is remarried and lives somewhere in Mexico. When I heard he was marrying again, I wrote a letter to his second wife. I told her I was a friend of Sarah's and that she had told me about being abused by her father as a child. I warned her to be careful — to make sure that he wasn't allowed around young children, especially young girls. She never wrote back. I don't know if she believed me or not. Maybe the letter never got through.'

'So you did do something,' I said.

Mel nodded. 'I suppose,' she agreed. 'But I didn't do enough, not about him. What I did, instead, was get involved in the sexual assault community. By my junior year in college I was volunteering at the rape crisis center in Charlottesville once a week. That's also when I decided to become a cop and changed my major from English to police science. I've been involved ever since,' she added. 'So now you know. That's how I became one of 'those women.''

The very idea of incest disgusts me. The fact that someone could do such a horrible thing — that a man could repeatedly violate his own child — is something I can barely comprehend. Still, I was slightly relieved. I had been afraid Mel was going to relate something horrific that had happened to her personally. When Richard Matthews had come after her, she had managed to elude him, so at least the worst of the

221

nightmare had happened to someone else. But Mel had been victimized, too. Her hurt was collateral damage to her friend's lifelong violation and eventual death.

For the first time I found myself wondering about some of the other women in that glittering ballroom at the Sheraton. What had propelled each of them to enter the sexual assault fray? Maybe there was something similar lurking in the lovely Anita Bowdin's background that would account for her involvement in SASAC, something all the silk and emeralds in the world couldn't quite erase. Maybe even the doyen of women's studies, the daunting Professor Clark herself, had suffered some similar circumstance that had marred her very existence. Maybe all the women on the board were, in one way or another, deeply damaged.

Mel had fallen silent and seemed to be waiting for some response from me.

'I'm sorry for your friend,' I said quietly. 'And I'm sorry for you, too. It's an awful thing to have carried around on your own for all these years.'

'Thank you,' she said. 'But I haven't been that alone. When I'm with the women from SASAC, none of us is alone.'

I've been a cop all my adult life. I know the statistics — six out of ten girls and one out of four boys are molested prior to age eighteen. And I had certainly seen the irreversible damage a history of child abuse leaves in its wake. I had seen the deadly results of the years Anne Corley spent watching her father routinely abuse her developmentally disabled sister. But I don't think

I had ever internalized it in the same way as I did when Mel made that one quiet and very simple statement about not being alone. And it gave me a whole new perspective on 'those women' at the Sheraton — the gutsy, determined, well-dressed women who had somehow moved beyond whatever had befallen them personally and who were striving to help others. It made me embarrassed to think how churlish I'd been with Mel afterward. And it made me wish I'd made a larger donation.

'Being involved in something like that changes you,' Mel said after a long pause. 'It changes your whole outlook on life. That's why I don't dwell on it and why I don't talk about it very often — and it's why I couldn't talk about it last night, not after all the stories we'd just heard. It brought it all back, and it hurt too much.

'But I really want you to understand where I'm coming from,' she continued. 'Working for SASAC and for organizations like it — raising money and raising awareness — means a lot to me. It makes me feel like I'm doing something in Sarah's honor even though it's too little too late to help her. Maybe I'm helping prevent what happened to Sarah from happening to some other unfortunate little girl. Or maybe when it does happen she'll realize that there are places she can turn to for help, where someone will really listen to her. The only help Sarah could see was turning a gun on herself.'

Mel needed comforting, and I did what I could. 'It sounds to me like you've accepted what you couldn't change and you're changing what you can,' I told her. 'That's part of what we talk about in AA. It's how we learn to go on. Thank you for telling me,' I added. 'I know it wasn't easy.'

Mel gave me a bleak smile. 'Thank you for listening,' she said.

'So now that I'm back in your good graces, what should I do?' I asked. 'Make a bigger donation?'

'No,' she said. 'What you contributed is fine. Listening is better.'

'What about dinner, then?' I asked. 'Are you going to join us?'

'Yes,' she said. 'But I missed you last night, and there's something I'd like to do first.'

And that's exactly what we did. It wasn't until much later — after we were showered, dressed, and waiting for Scott and Cherisse to show up — that we actually started talking about work. She told me how far she'd gone in making notes on the abstracts, and I told her about my semi-fruitful trip to Leavenworth.

'What's the defense analyst's name again?' Mel asked thoughtfully, reaching for her laptop.

'Dortman,' I said. 'Thomas Dortman. He lives here in Seattle. I already Googled him.'

Mel did several quick keystrokes and then studied her screen. 'And he has a new book coming out at the end of the month, *The Whistle-blower's Survivor's Guide*. Want me to order you a copy from Amazon.com?'

'Don't bother,' I said. 'From what I read in the article, Tony Cosgrove was supposed to be a whistle-blower. Or maybe he would have been, if he hadn't disappeared when Mount Saint Helens blew up.'

'So obviously Cosgrove didn't live long enough to benefit from the book,' Mel observed.

'No, he didn't,' I agreed. 'I sent Dortman an e-mail asking him to give me a call, but it's the weekend. I'll give him until Monday before I try doing anything else about finding him.'

We were still waiting for Scott and Cherisse to show up when the phone rang. Caller ID identified the call as coming from Kelly and Jeremy's place in Ashland.

'She took off,' Jeremy blurted the moment I answered.

'Who took off?'

'Kelly.'

'Where did she go?' I asked.

'That's the problem,' Jeremy answered, 'I have no idea. She tried to grab the car keys out of my pocket. When I wouldn't give them to her, she lost it. She screamed something about the kids and me being better off without her, then took off on foot. What am I going to do?' Jeremy added miserably. 'I can't take care of these two little kids all by myself. I wouldn't know where to start. What's the matter with her, Beau? What's going on?' He sounded utterly mystified and despairing.

'Are you saying you think she's left you for good?' I asked.

'I have no idea,' he returned. 'I told you what she said, but I don't know what it means. Do you?'

From the sound of things, it was probably a

good thing Kelly wasn't behind the wheel of a vehicle.

'Did the two of you have a quarrel of some kind after you got home?' I asked.

'How could we argue?' Jeremy said. 'She wasn't even speaking to me.'

Yes, I thought. *I know how that works.*

'Before you left Seattle then?' I asked. 'Did something happen while you were here that upset her?'

'You saw how she was,' Jeremy answered. 'She was upset the whole time we were there — upset and on edge. The thing is, what am I supposed to do now? Go looking for her? Let her go and hope she cools off? Call the cops?'

I hadn't the foggiest idea of what to tell him.

'What's going on?' Mel asked in the background.

'It's Jeremy,' I explained. 'Kelly cried all the way home from Seattle back to Ashland. Now Jeremy says she told him he and the kids would be better off without her and took off on foot.'

'Let me talk to him,' Mel said. I handed over the phone. She switched it to speaker mode. 'How long ago did she leave?'

'A few minutes,' Jeremy answered. 'I called as soon as she was out the door.'

'So she's probably still in the neighborhood somewhere,' Mel said. 'Take the kids with you, get in the car, and go find her.'

'But — '

'And when you do, take her straight to her doctor and tell him exactly what's going on.'

'But what is going on?' Jeremy asked.

226

'Have you ever heard of postpartum depression?' Mel asked.

'Yes, but I always thought it was some kind of joke.'

Jeremy's thinking on the matter wasn't that far from my own. As far as I knew, postpartum depression was right up there with mother-in-law jokes as fodder for stand-up comedians.

'It's no joke, Jeremy,' Mel told him. 'It's serious, and it can also turn deadly on occasion. If that's what's going on, Kelly needs to see her doctor right away so she can be diagnosed and treated.'

'She's not crazy or something, is she?' Jeremy asked. His voice was subdued. And scared. The deadly seriousness of Mel's demeanor had me scared, too.

There was a call-waiting alert on the phone, but Mel ignored it and so did I. 'Kelly may be acting crazy,' Mel countered. 'But having a baby is hard work. It probably left her internal chemistry totally out of whack. Since she's not nursing . . . she isn't, is she?'

'No.'

'Then having her doctor prescribe medication to counter that chemical imbalance shouldn't be a problem, but you'll have to find her first.'

'Should I call the cops?' Jeremy asked. 'Tell them that she's missing?'

There were plenty of reasons not to do that. Filing a police report could well give rise to questions about whether or not domestic violence was part of the equation. An official report might also bring Child Protective Services into the fray with questions asked about Kelly's suitability for motherhood. The idea that someone might step in and try to take Kayla and Kyle away from them froze my heart.

Before I could say anything on that score, however, Mel said it for me.

'No,' she told him urgently. 'In the long run that'll only make things more complicated. Just go find her. What's her doctor's name?'

'Howell,' Jeremy answered. 'Dr. Faye Howell here in Ashland.'

'I'll call the doctor and let her know what's going on,' Mel told him. 'Once you find Kelly, call back here. I'll tell you what the doctor says and where you should take her.'

While Mel busied herself with dialing information, I was summoned by the doorbell. I found Scott and Cherisse waiting outside in the hallway.

'The doorman tried calling to let you know we were on our way up,' Scott said as I let them into the apartment. 'Is something the matter with your phone?'

I waved him to silence so I could listen to Mel. By then she had used her law enforcement officer persona to mow down whatever gatekeepers stood between Dr. Howell and her patients.

'All right, then,' Mel was saying. 'As soon as Jeremy locates her, I'll tell him to bring her directly to the hospital, that you'll wait for them at the ER.'

Scott looked worriedly from Mel back to me. 'What's going on?' he asked.

'It's Kelly,' I said. 'She took off and left Jeremy

228

and the kids behind. He's frantic.'

'It's postpartum depression, isn't it,' Cherisse said.

Mel nodded. Cherisse turned back to Scott and poked him in the ribs. 'See there?' she said. 'I told you so.'

Scott and I exchanged long-suffering glances. That's what's so mystifying about women. Neither Mel Soames nor Cherisse Beaumont had ever had a baby themselves. Still, they somehow knew what was going on with Kelly, even though Kelly herself didn't seem to.

I've long maintained that women are born knowing things it takes men a whole lifetime to figure out. This was simply one more case in point.

15

Two nights earlier, Kelly's temper tantrum had spoiled one dinner. Now, from hundreds of miles away, her situation cast a pall on this meal as well.

We were halfway through our entrees when my phone rang. I could tell it was Jeremy calling, but it was too noisy for me to hear inside the restaurant. I excused myself and went outside to stand among the crew of waiting parking valets.

'Did you find her?' I demanded.

'Yes,' he answered, relief apparent in his voice. 'She was sitting on a bench down by Lithia Creek. It was cold as hell down there. She wasn't even wearing a sweater.'

I felt as relieved as Jeremy sounded. 'She's all right, then?' I asked.

'I guess,' he said. 'I did just what Mel told me to do. I took her to see Dr. Howell. She prescribed something to help her sleep. I don't think she's slept in days, but she's upstairs resting right now. Dr. Howell gave her some antidepressants. I guess it's a good thing Kelly decided against nursing.'

'I guess so,' I agreed.

'Is Mel there?' Jeremy asked.

'She's back inside the restaurant.'

'Tell her thank you for me,' he said. 'I kept thinking it was something I had done wrong, but Dr. Howell says it's something that happens to some women after they give birth. It can happen sooner rather than later, and this is definitely sooner. Dr. Howell said it was really smart of me to figure it out and let her know, but it wasn't me at all. It was Mel.'

'I'll tell her,' I said. 'But remember to give yourself some of the credit, too, Jeremy. You had brains enough to ask for help, and we're lucky it just happened to be someone smart enough to know what was going on.'

Unlike your father-in-law, I thought.

A baby wailed in the background. 'Gotta go,' he said.

I went back inside. I greeted Mel's anxious glance with a thumbs-up. 'Dr. Soames's diagnosis is correct,' I announced. 'The patient is back home. With the help of a sedative, she may be sleeping peacefully for the first time in days. The doctor also prescribed some antidepressants. Jeremy says thank you, and so do I.'

After the group heard Jeremy's good news, the remainder of the dinner was a lot more festive. We made arrangements to meet the kids and Lars for one more brunch extravaganza before their scheduled departure the next day, then Mel and I went home and fell into bed. It was amazing to realize how much better I slept with her there beside me. I awakened the next morning to the smell of brewing coffee. There was a note next to the pot. 'Taking a run in Myrtle Edwards,' it said. 'Back in a few.'

I had been thinking about Thomas Dortman as I fell asleep, and this seemed as good a time as any to continue my LexisNexis research on him. With my first cup of coffee in hand and waiting for the computer to boot up, I happened to think of something else. And so, out of idle curiosity, instead of typing in the defense analyst's name, I typed in something else — 'Richard Matthews, Mexico' — and waited to see what, if anything, would show up.

It didn't take long. What popped up first was an article dated November 14, 2004, from the *El Paso Herald*.

Two weeks ago, Candace Matthews kissed her husband Richard Matthews goodbye as he left to go on his regular morning walk near their beachfront retirement home in Cancún, Mexico. She hasn't seen him since. Although Mexican authorities say they have launched an investigation into Mr. Matthews's disappearance, information on the progress of that investigation is difficult to come by.

'No one will talk to me,' Ms. Matthews said. 'No one will answer my questions or tell me what's going on. They seem to think he just decided to leave me, but Rich would never do that. I'm sure he's dead.'

Richard and Candace Matthews were newly-weds four years ago when they purchased their dream home. It was a second marriage for both of them. Richard had retired from a career in the U.S. military and Candace was a former Realtor when they met at a dance club in El Paso,

Texas. They married two months later.

'It was love at first sight,' Candace said, choking back sobs during a telephone interview from Cancún. 'And it still is. No one here seems to take this seriously. They act like he's just wandered off somewhere and it's no big deal.'

'The investigation is progressing,' says Sergeant Ignacio Palacios of the Cancún Metropolitan Police Department. 'We are treating this as a missing persons situation, but so far there is no indication of foul play.'

That was as far as I had read when the door opened and a winded Mel bounded into the room. 'On my way to the shower,' she said. 'What time's brunch? I'll be glad when the company leaves. I feel like we're just bouncing nonstop from one meal to the next.'

She disappeared down the hall. I turned back to the computer.

Richard Matthews came to the El Paso area with his first wife and daughter when he was posted to Fort Bliss as a noncommissioned officer with the United States Army. He stayed on after his retirement, even though his life here was dogged by tragedy. This is where his only daughter, Sarah, died of a self-inflicted gunshot wound while a fresh-man at the UTEP. His first wife, Lois, spent the last twenty years of her life with limited mobility due to the crippling effects of MS. It wasn't until after her death that Richard's life seemed to take a turn for the better.

Five years ago, on a dare from a coworker, Richard Matthews signed up to take lessons at Tango-Rama, a short-lived ballroom dancing school where divorced Realtor Candace Sanders was a part-time instructor. The rest is history. After a whirlwind romance, the two married and spent their week-long honeymoon in Cancún. When they returned to El Paso they sold their respective homes and resettled in Mexico, where their joint real estate dollars went much farther than they would have in the States.

'This was our dream home and our dream life,' says Candace Matthews. 'There's no way Rich would just walk away from everything we've built together.'

Frustrated by a lack of official response, Ms. Matthews has posted a $5000 reward for information leading to her husband's safe return.

It probably only looked like a lack of response, I thought. What was actually going on was no doubt a spasm of legal infighting across jurisdictional boundaries — not the least of which was the international border. That would immediately translate into investigative paralysis. Mexican authorities, wanting to underplay anything that might adversely impact the tourism industry, were probably stalling for all they were worth, just as the guys in Aruba did when that teenage girl went missing.

Down the hall the shower stopped running and I heard the hair dryer whine to life as I struggled to fend off the intense sense of foreboding that suddenly gripped me. I looked back at the computer screen and double-checked the date: November 14. Mel and I hadn't been involved then, but I did remember Mel's returning from a week's worth of vacation sometime late in the fall — sometime prior to Thanksgiving. I recalled that she had come back to work in high spirits looking tanned and fit and bringing with her a gift for Barbara Galvin's son, Timmy — a huge sombrero with his name embroidered on it. Had she been to Cancún? That I didn't know.

I called up the next entry, dated November 18:

Unidentified human remains, discovered washed up along the base of a beachside cliff near Cancún, Mexico, are thought to be those of former El Paso resident Richard Lowell Matthews, who disappeared almost three weeks ago while on an early-morning walk. While confirming that remains have been found, Mexican authorities say that a positive identification will have to await the arrival of dental records that are expected in Cancún sometime tomorrow.

Sergeant Ignacio Palacios of the Cancun Metropolitan Police Department reported that the autopsy had revealed the presence of a gunshot wound that was most likely the cause of death. The case is being investigated as a possible homicide.

235

Candace Matthews, former El Paso real estate agent and wife of the missing man, expressed frustration at the lack of urgency surrounding the investigation. 'They didn't even bother calling me until after they'd already done the autopsy. How can that be? With Rich already reported missing, shouldn't they have come to me first?'

So Richard Matthews was dead, possibly of a gunshot wound. Down the hall the hair dryer switched off and on as Mel wielded hot air and a brush to force her hair into submission. In the weeks and months Mel and I had lived together I had learned to welcome the dryer's ungodly racket. It was an audible and daily reminder of how my life had suddenly changed for the better. It announced to me and to the world at large that another person had come into my previously solitary life. This morning, though, that hair dryer felt more like a screeching buzz saw slicing into my heart.

Surely not, I told myself. *Surely it couldn't be happening again, could it? Maybe I'm mistaken. After all, Mexico is a big place. There are lots of resorts she could have gone to that weren't Cancún. Or maybe I'm wrong about the timing. Then again, maybe I'm not.*

Once before I had fallen for a beautiful but flawed woman, one who had transformed herself into a one-woman vigilante brigade for both convicted and suspected child molesters. Smitten, I had been blind to Anne Corley's inexplicable interest in the death of a young girl at the hands of members of a local religious cult. My inability to grasp the seriousness of the situation had led inevitably to Anne's death — and almost to mine as well.

Now history seemed to be repeating itself. Only yesterday Mel had told me that she was still haunted by learning too late of her best friend's incestuous relationship with her father, a relationship that had eventually resulted in Sarah Matthews's tragic suicide. Mel had told me that she still agonized over having done nothing to avenge her friend's death. But was that true? That friend's pedophile father had now turned up shot to death. I had personally witnessed the fact that Mel Soames knew her way around the business end of a handgun. How could I be sure she had nothing at all to do with Richard Matthews's death, especially since there was a chance Mel had been in the same area at the time of his murder?

You're jumping to conclusions, I admonished myself. *You've got no proof she was involved. Give it a rest.*

The hair dryer switched off permanently. The bathroom door opened, freeing a cloud of steamy air. A heady combination of fragrances wafted down the hallway. There was shampoo, hair spray, and perfume — in short, all the individual fragrances that worked together to make Mel Mel.

Guiltily, like a kid caught reading prohibited *Playboy* magazines, I closed the screen containing the most recent *El Paso Herald* article and hurriedly typed Thomas Dortman's name into the search field.

Mel emerged from the bathroom wearing a short silky robe, the hem of which skimmed the bottom of her equally silky panties. She came over to where I was sitting and brushed the top of my head with a kiss as she collected my empty coffee cup from the end table at my elbow. 'Refill?' she asked.

'Thanks,' I mumbled.

'What are you working on?'

I could have asked her about Richard Matthews right then, but coward that I was, I didn't. I wasn't ready. The idea that history might be repeating itself was too appalling.

'Dortman,' I lied.

Mel stood in front of me, with my cup in one hand and the other on her hip. 'Look,' she said reprovingly. 'Anthony Cosgrove has been missing and/or dead since 1980. And most of the guys on my list have been gone for months if not years. This is Sunday. Other than last night at dinner, we've been so caught up in work that we've neglected Scott and Cherisse the whole time they've been here. We also haven't been very diligent about keeping tabs on Lars. How about if we give ourselves the whole day off and pay attention to people instead of cases?'

Concerned that Mel's womanly wiles might somehow allow her to see into the workings of my computer and divine what I had been doing prior to typing in Dortman's name, I immediately capitulated.

'Great idea,' I said, slapping shut the laptop's

238

lid. 'It's the weekend. Let's forget about work for a while. It'll do us both a world of good.'

Mel disappeared into the kitchen and returned with my replenished coffee cup, which she handed over to me. As she did so her forehead knotted into a puzzled frown. 'You look upset,' she said. 'Is something the matter?'

'No, nothing,' I said, probably a tad too quickly. 'I'll go shower — if you've left me any hot water, that is.'

The last was a joke. My condo is equipped with an instant hot water heating system that can replenish itself almost as fast as someone can use it. And Mel joked right back.

'A cold shower might be good for you now and then.' She grinned.

The shower wasn't cold, but it could just as well have been. I stood in the powerful flow that cascaded down from a ceiling-mounted showerhead while my body was pounded with spray from a collection of wall-mounted showerheads as well. Steam may have been circling upward toward the ceiling, but I felt chilled.

Surely she wasn't involved in the death of Richard Matthews, I told myself. *Surely not. It was probably a robbery gone bad, a fatal but otherwise ordinary mugging. Or maybe Matthews got involved in the drug trade to supplement his retirement income.*

But there was a part of me that held otherwise — part of me that was afraid my worst nightmare was about to happen all over again.

The easiest thing and probably the best thing would have been to come straight out and ask

Mel about it right then. But cops don't ask questions unless they have a fairly good idea of what the real answers should be. Anne Corley had lied to me with utter impunity, and I was determined not to be that stupid again. So before I asked Mel any questions I needed to find out some of the answers. To do that, I'd be operating solo. Mel may have been my partner in every sense of the word, but if she had somehow stepped onto the wrong side of the thin blue line, I was the one who would have to figure it out — and do something about it.

Standing there with the punishing water pummeling my body, I was suddenly struck by an idea. There was one other person in the world who had been betrayed by Anne Corley in much the same way I had been; one other sucker who, if I told him my suspicions, would immediately grasp all possible ramifications. After all, my friend and attorney, Ralph Ames, had been Anne Corley's friend and attórney long before he became mine, and she had suckered him, too.

Leaving the shower running full blast, I stepped out onto the bath mat, hotfooted it into the bedroom, retrieved my cell phone, and took it back into the bathroom, where I dialed Ralph's number.

'Where are you calling from?' Ralph asked once he was on the line. 'You sound like you're standing in the middle of a torrential downpour.'

'I am,' I said. 'That's the shower.'

'Here's an idea,' he said. 'How about if you call me back *after* you finish your shower.'

240

'Please, Ralph,' I said. 'There's a problem. Listen to me.'

And he did. I explained it all while the shower continued to roar. 'So what do you want me to do?' he asked when I finished. 'Try to find out whether or not the remains really do belong to Richard Matthews?'

'That would be a big help,' I said. 'And what, if any, progress has been made in finding out who killed him.'

'Anything else?' Ralph asked.

One of the good things about Ralph Ames is that he doesn't require a lot of explanation. He gets things. And then he goes to work and gets things done. And since he doesn't necessarily have to concern himself about maintaining chains of evidence and fruit of poisoned trees and all that jazz, he has avenues of investigation that aren't necessarily open to sworn police officers.

'Mel's full name is Melissa Katherine Majors Soames,' I replied. 'I'm pretty sure she went to Mexico sometime last November. I don't know for sure when she went or where she traveled, but I think it was sometime before Thanksgiving.'

'I'll see what I can do,' Ralph said. 'Meantime, watch yourself.'

That was another thing I appreciated about Ralph. He didn't stand around jawing or dishing out a bunch of phony platitudes. Since I was worried, he was worried, and he would simply shut up and go to work. That meant a lot.

Mel knocked on the closed bathroom door. I

241

was so startled it's a miracle I didn't drop the cell phone into the toilet. 'Lars is on the phone,' she said. 'Do you want to take it?'

Without saying goodbye to Ralph I pressed the call-ending button. 'Tell Lars I'm in the shower. I'll call him back when I get out.'

Still disturbed by the staggering possibilities, I was disgusted to find that my right hand shook uncontrollably. In the process of shaving I nicked my neck twice and the bottom of my ear once, and I emerged from the bathroom with tiny scraps of toilet paper stanching the flow of blood to keep it from ruining my collar.

Once I was dressed I stood for a few minutes looking at my cell phone on the bathroom's granite countertop. Part of me wanted to have it with me at all times so I'd be able to hear from Ralph the moment he learned anything. But I didn't want to have to take a call like that — regardless of his news — in Mel's presence. She was a cop. She'd be too curious. She'd want to know what the call was about. She'd want to know exactly what was going on.

But I had spent a lifetime living on call. It was too late to change that now. After a wavering moment of indecision I brought the phone along with me. Leaving it behind really wasn't an option.

Out in the living room I found Mel dressed and ready to go. 'Lars was calling to double-check on who was picking him up for breakfast — Scott and Cherisse or the two of us. He also wanted to know if you thought Scott and

242

Cherisse would mind if he brought a friend along to breakfast.'

'A friend?' I asked. 'What kind of friend?'

'Her name is Iris,' Mel answered. 'Iris Rassmussen. According to Lars she was a good friend of Beverly's.'

'Wait a minute,' I said. 'Are you telling me that we buried Beverly on Thursday and Lars wants to bring someone else along to brunch on Sunday?'

'I don't think he meant it like that,' Mel returned. 'I'm sure it's nothing romantic.'

I wasn't convinced. I thought about Lars's protestations earlier in the week about how all the single ladies in Queen Anne Gardens were camped out at his front door and jockeying for position before Beverly was even cool to the touch. And now this?

'What did you tell him?'

'I told him that as far as I knew, Scott and Cherisse were supposed to pick him up,' Mel answered. 'As for the rest of it, I said I was sure it would be fine but that you'd call him back as soon as you could.'

'It isn't fine,' I grumbled.

'Come on,' she said. 'He probably just wants to have someone along who's his age, someone who's on the same page he is.'

'I'll bet Iris is on the same page, all right,' I told her. 'Let's go.'

'But I thought you were going to call him back,' Mel objected.

'Why bother?' I said. 'You already told him he could bring her. He doesn't need to hear it from

243

me.' Even I was aware enough to see the irony of the situation. Kelly didn't have a thing on her old man.

Mel shot me an exasperated look. 'What's the matter with you this morning? Did you get up on the wrong side of the bed, or what?'

The wrong side of the universe is more like it, I thought. 'Nothing's the matter,' I said. 'What are we waiting for? We could just as well see what that randy old coot is up to.'

16

Breakfast wasn't nearly the disaster it could have been. Despite my misgivings about her, Iris Rassmussen turned out to be the life of the party. She was full of one off-color Sven and Ole joke after another, and she told them with all the verve and style of an aging stand-up comedienne. She kept all of us in stitches, me included, and that was pretty remarkable in view of the fact I wasn't in much of a joking mood. Lars laughed along with the rest of us, and chowed down on his oyster omelet with his customary enthusiasm. Laughing seemed to do wonders for his appetite.

Iris was tuning up to deliver yet another punch line and the waitress had yet to drop off the check when my phone rang. The Fisherman's Restaurant is low on six-tops, and I was stuck in a corner with my back to the window, which meant I couldn't very well leave the table to take the call. I was relieved when a glance at the readout displayed an unfamiliar number. At least it wasn't Ralph.

'Mr. Beaumont?' a woman asked. The voice wasn't one I could place, but she sounded upset. I excused myself and made my way outside.

'Yes.'

'It's me — DeAnn Cosgrove,' she said. 'There's someone here who needs to talk to you.'

I heard her passing the receiver to someone

else. 'Mr. Beaumont? I'm Detective Tim Lander of the Chelan County Sheriff's Department. I understand from Ms. Cosgrove here that you intended to go see Jack and Carol Lawrence in Leavenworth yesterday.'

'Yes,' I said. 'That's right, and I did go there. Why?'

'I'm investigating a double homicide,' he said. 'Carol and Jack Lawrence were found shot to death in the yard outside their home early this morning. A kid delivering their Sunday paper found the bodies.'

When husbands and wives perish together, it's usually pretty easy to fill in the blanks, and the outcome is one that would come as no surprise to 'those women' gathered in their evening finery at the Sheraton. A husband or ex-husband or boyfriend or ex-boyfriend murders the woman who was once the love of his life and then turns the weapon on himself.

'Murder/suicide?' I croaked.

'No,' Lander answered. 'That's not how it looks so far, since no weapon was found at the scene. Would it be possible to meet with you this morning? I'd like to discuss the purpose of your meeting with them yesterday. I'd also like to know what the outcome was.'

Lander had made his approach in an offhand way, but I knew there was nothing casual about his invitation. Both the Lawrences were dead. Now it seemed likely I was one of the last people to see Carol Lawrence alive. In the eyes of homicide investigators, that automatically made me a person of interest, if not an outright suspect. It also meant that Detective Lander wanted to talk to me, and he wanted to talk to me now. No doubt DeAnn had mentioned that I was with the attorney general's office. That explained why Lander's request for an interview was couched in a way that made allowances for professional courtesy. It was incumbent on me to respond in kind.

'I didn't meet with both of them,' I corrected. 'Jack Lawrence wasn't home at the time. I only spoke to Mrs. Lawrence, but of course I'll be glad to meet with you. Just tell me where and when. I'm in Seattle right now. Where are you?'

'Redmond,' Lander answered. 'Talking with DeAnn Cosgrove and her husband at their house.'

'I could meet you at the Special Homicide offices in Eastgate, if you like.'

'Where's that?' Lander asked. 'And how soon can you be there?'

I glanced at my watch. 'Depending on traffic, half an hour to forty-five,' I said. Then I gave him Special Homicide's street address as well as driving directions. When I returned to the restaurant, Iris Rassmussen was still holding forth. The only other person paying any attention to my phone call was Mel, who was giving me what I've sometimes heard my son-in-law refer to as 'the stink eye.'

'What's up?' she asked.

'Work,' I said, flagging down our harried waitress. 'I'm going to have to go into the office.'

'Good,' she returned. 'I'm coming along.'

I had been hoping to have a chance to confer

247

with Ralph Ames in relative privacy, but telling Mel she wasn't welcome to ride along would have caused an immediate uproar, especially since we had arrived at the restaurant in the same vehicle. We made our way out to the parking lot and said our goodbyes to Iris and Lars and to Scott and Cherisse as well.

'What's wrong?' Mel asked as soon as the Mercedes's doors shut behind us.

'What makes you think something's wrong?'

She rolled her eyes. 'Something's bothering you,' she said. 'And don't try blaming it on whoever called you just now. You were wound tight long before the call came in.'

That's one of the most disconcerting things about Mel. I sometimes think she understands me better than I understand myself. Or that she can read my mind. But she was absolutely right — I had been wound very tight. I screwed my courage to the sticking place and tackled the issue head-on. Well, more or less head-on.

'Where did you go when you went to Mexico last fall?' I asked.

'Cancún,' she said, sounding surprised.

Cancún. Bad answer. There it was — out in the open. My heart did a flip-flop at the very sound.

'Why do you want to know about that?'

I ignored her question. 'When were you there?' I asked.

'The end of October through the first week in November,' she said. 'But I don't understand. What's this all about?'

The dates she mentioned hit me like a second

blow to the gut. The end of October coincided exactly with the time when Richard Matthews had reportedly disappeared from his early-morning beachside walk. In Cancún. Having launched this disturbing conversation without waiting for any kind of confirmation from Ralph Ames, I realized there was no turning back.

'Remember your dead friend's father?' I asked. 'The one you told me about yesterday?'

'Richard Matthews, Sarah's father?' Mel asked. 'Of course I remember him. Why?'

'He disappeared in Cancún on the first of November.'

'Disappeared?' she asked.

'His body was found later. He died from a single gunshot wound.'

She chewed on that one for a while. 'And you think I had something to do with what happened to him?'

'Did you?' I asked.

We were on Mercer by then, headed for I-5. 'Why don't you stop the car and let me out,' she said. 'I'll walk back to the house.'

'We need to talk about this,' I said.

'It sounds like I'm a suspect here,' she said. 'Like maybe you need to read me my rights. Maybe I should have an attorney present. Or do you want to pick up my weapons and turn them over to ballistics?'

'Mel, please,' I said. 'It's not like this hasn't happened to me before.'

'So that's what this is all about?' Mel demanded after a pause. 'It's all about Anne Corley, isn't it? Since she went off the rails and

249

killed somebody, you automatically assume I must have done the same thing. Is that what you think?'

Of course she had me dead to rights on that one, and the similarities between the two cases in terms of motivation and deadly results was far too close to ignore. I didn't answer her question immediately, not aloud, and that in itself was answer enough. A glance in Mel's direction showed me that she was sitting on the far side of the car with her arms folded across her chest. When Melissa Soames folds her arms, it is not a good sign.

'What happened to Richard Matthews?' she wanted to know.

'I've told you everything I know. He went for a walk on the beach on the morning of November first and never returned. His wife filed a missing person's report right after he disappeared. His badly decomposed body was found sometime later, and an autopsy revealed he had died of what I believe was a single gunshot wound. I'm not sure whether or not a bullet was recovered.'

'I may have been in Cancún at the time he was shot,' Mel said, 'but I had no idea that's where he lived. And no matter what you think, I'm not responsible for what happened to him.' She paused briefly and then added, 'When did you learn all this?'

'This morning,' I said. 'I stumbled across it on the Internet while you were showering.'

'And you immediately leaped to the conclusion that since Richard Matthews was dead, I had to be the one who killed him?' Mel shook her head. 'That doesn't speak very highly for whatever it is I thought the two of us had going.'

'Mel,' I began. 'It's just . . . '

'Don't bother with the apology bit,' she said. 'I don't want to hear it.'

My phone rang then, right in the middle of the I-90 bridge. The way my luck was going, there was no need to check the caller ID readout. I knew it had to be Ralph as soon as the phone rang and before I answered.

'Mel flew in and out of Cancún along with seven other women on board a private jet that belongs to someone named Anita Bowdin,' Ralph said. 'They stayed at a beachfront home called Casa del Sol owned by Ms. Bowdin. They arrived on Thursday, October twenty-eighth, and returned to Seattle on Wednesday, November third.'

'Thanks,' I said, hoping to cut short the conversation. 'I appreciate it.'

But Ralph was just tuning up. 'If the guy disappeared on November first, she would have been there at the time. So we're definitely talking opportunity. I'm printing out whatever I can find on the guy on the Web. Is there anything else I can do to help right now?'

'No,' I said. 'Thanks for the invite, but I don't think we'll be able to make it to dinner tonight.'

'She's with you, then?' Ralph asked. For a guy, Ralph Ames is remarkably perceptive.

'Right,' I said. 'Maybe later this week. I'll have to get back to you on that.'

'Okay then,' he finished. 'Give me a call when you can.'

'What was that all about?' Mel wanted to know as soon as I hung up.

'Ralph and Mary were inviting us over to dinner tonight,' I lied. 'It didn't seem like such a good idea.'

'I'll say,' Mel said. And that was the last thing she said to me for the remainder of the trip. It was a very long and quiet six miles.

When we reached Eastgate, Detective Tim Lander's unmarked Chelan County patrol car was parked in a visitor's spot in the garage. While I went to greet him, Mel bailed out of my car without a word or a backward glance and headed for the elevator. I let her go on ahead.

'Mr. Beaumont?' Lander asked, exiting his vehicle.

I nodded. We shook hands and I led him onto the elevator and then upstairs to the SHIT squad offices on the third floor. He paused at the hallway door where the offending acronym was emblazoned in large gold letters on the glass. The sign guy had wanted to spell out the words in full. Harry I. Ball, for perverse reasons all his own, had insisted on putting the more objectionable shorthand version there for all to see.

Lander stopped in his tracks. 'Are you shitting me?' he wanted to know.

'Special Homicide Investigation Team,' I explained. 'We never close. Our official motto is: 'All shit all the time.''

I led him inside. We walked past Barbara Galvin's empty desk. Beyond that, the door to Mel's office was shut. The merest hint of

252

Sunday's edition of talk radio penetrating from there to the outside world posted a not quite audible but entirely understandable message: KEEP OUT. Or maybe even KEEP THE HELL OUT!! We kept right on walking.

'This is all part of the attorney general's office?' Lander asked as I cleared off the guest chair in my cubicle-sized space so he could sit down.

I nodded. 'There's a squad here, one down in Olympia, and a third one over in Spokane to cover eastern Washington.'

'And what exactly do you do?' Lander asked.

'We investigate whatever Ross Alan Connors asks us to investigate. When I first got here we were doing a lot of work on the Green River killer. At the moment he has me working on cold missing persons cases from all over the state. That's why I went to see DeAnn Cosgrove and Carol Lawrence — looking into the case of a man who disappeared twenty-plus years ago.'

Lander pulled out a notebook and consulted a page of scribbled notations. 'That would be Anthony David Cosgrove?' he asked. 'Disappeared on May eighteenth, 1980.'

'Correct,' I said. 'DeAnn's father and Carol Lawrence's first husband.'

'And you said you actually saw Carol Lawrence? You spoke to her?'

I nodded. 'Yesterday,' I said. 'Up in Leavenworth.' This was stating the obvious, since he clearly already had this information, but we needed to go over the basics anyway.

'What about her husband?' Lander asked. 'Did you see Jack?'

'No. He wasn't home at the time,' I replied.

'And what time was that?'

'A little before noon.' I took out my phone and scrolled through my incoming calls until I found the one from Kendall Jackson. 'Here,' I said. 'I had lunch in Leavenworth after I talked to Carol. This call came in about the same time my food showed up, and the call record says it came in at twelve-ten. I must have arrived at the Lawrences' house around eleven or so. After that I came back to Seattle. By seven-thirty or so I was having dinner at El Gaucho with my kids.'

'And we'll find your prints in the house?'

I nodded. 'In the living room. I sat on a couch with wooden arms. So my prints should be there. I doubt they'll show up anywhere else. And they're on file. Eliminating them won't be a problem.'

'Did Carol Lawrence tell you anything about the Anthony Cosgrove disappearance that you didn't already know?'

'Only that she and Jack were already involved before Tony went missing.'

'Involved as in having an affair?'

'Yes.'

'Anything else?'

'Other than that, she told almost exactly the same story DeAnn told.'

'Almost?'

I liked the way Lander caught my effort at hedging. He focused in on the wobbly modifier with laser precision.

'Look,' I said, 'we're talking perceptions here. As I said, Carol told me the same story her daughter did. In fact, the two versions were virtually identical. The problem is, when DeAnn told me the story, it seemed like she was telling the truth. When Carol told me the same thing, I got the feeling she was lying. We're talking gut instinct here,' I added. 'I have no proof of this whatsoever. None at all.'

'Lying or not,' Lander returned, 'what exactly did Carol Lawrence tell you?'

'That Tony Cosgrove was fishing on Spirit Lake the morning Mount Saint Helens blew up and that he died in the eruption.'

'Do you think that was a lie?'

'He may have gone fishing, but I don't think he died in the eruption. His body was never found.'

'Nobody ever found Harry Truman, either,' Lander pointed out.

Lander looked to be somewhere in his early thirties. I doubted he was old enough to remember much about the eruption itself or the curmudgeonly old guy named Harry Truman who had lived there. In the face of a possible eruption, Truman's adamant refusal to leave his home — his stubbornness and innate stupidity — had taken on a life of its own. Mount Saint Helens may have blown Harry Truman to bits, but his death-inducing exploits remained a part of Pacific Northwest lore and legend. Dead or alive, Tony Cosgrove didn't have nearly the same kind of media staying power.

'So you're saying you don't think Cosgrove's

really dead?' the young detective continued.

'I didn't say he isn't dead,' I answered. 'Carol admitted that she and Jack Lawrence were involved before Tony's disappearance. DeAnn told me that once Tony was out of the picture, Carol moved on in a hell of a hurry. Instead of waiting around long enough for Tony to be declared dead, she divorced him and married Jack Lawrence within months of Tony's going missing. That's the real reason I wanted to see the Lawrences yesterday — to assess if the two of them might have had something to do with what happened to him.'

'According to DeAnn, her stepfather seemed very disturbed to think that anyone would be revisiting Tony's disappearance,' Lander said. 'Did Carol give you any idea why that might have been the case?'

'You mean other than the fact that they might have been behind it? No, she claimed Jack was upset because he's a 'very private man.' That struck me as a load of crap. He may have been private, but I don't think that's the whole story.'

'How did you leave things with Carol Lawrence?' Lander asked.

'I handed her one of my cards and asked her to have Jack give me a call. I told her I needed to talk to him, but I figured it would be a cold day in hell before he ever called me back. In fact, I was a little surprised Carol even bothered to take my card in the first place.'

'Not only did she take it,' Lander told me after a pause, 'she kept it, too. The CSI guys found your business card in her hand. Her cell phone was on the ground next to her body. We know for sure that Carol Lawrence tried to call you on it. Your office number here at the office is the last one listed under dialed calls. She placed that call at eight fifty-seven P.M., which is about the same time the preliminary coroner's report estimates as the time of death.'

The idea that Carol Lawrence had tried and failed to reach me left me feeling half sick.

'It was the weekend,' I muttered. 'The office was closed. After-hours calls to SHIT go to our general voice mail. I can call our office manager and have her check to see what was left — '

'Don't bother,' Lander interrupted. 'I'm sure she didn't leave a message. The duration of the call is just over thirty seconds. Long enough to show that the connection was made but not enough to for her to make it through the voice mail prompts. Believe me, I already tried it.'

'How did this whole thing go down?' I asked.

Lander considered the question for a moment, weighing how he should proceed. Either he'd treat me as a suspect or as a fellow investigator. Considering that my dinner in Seattle made it impossible for me to be the killer, I figured he'd come down on the investigator side, and he did.

'The scene's a little chaotic,' Lander said at last. 'We made casts of several different sets of tire tracks going in and out. We already know that one of those sets belongs to the kid who found the bodies. We've located an area where a car pulled off the road and sat for a while. We found several empty beer bottles and some discarded gum there in the dirt.'

'So there could be fingerprint and/or DNA evidence?' I asked.

Lander nodded. 'If it turns out the shooter is the one who chewed it. We think he parked on the shoulder waiting for something, maybe for Jack Lawrence to come home. After that, it appears there was some kind of confrontation in the yard next to Jack Lawrence's vehicle. All three of them were involved, including the two victims. In the course of the struggle several shots were fired. Jack was hit once in the right shoulder and once in the gut. We believe Carol tried to flee and was shot in the back.'

'Did you find any brass?' I asked.

Lander nodded. 'That's where we got lucky.' He grinned. 'Nine millimeter. The killer was smart enough to go around picking it up but he missed one. Looks like that one bounced off something and rolled under Lawrence's RAV4. We didn't find it until early this afternoon, after the vehicle was towed.'

I closed my eyes and tried to envision Carol and Jack Lawrence's yard with its peaceful-looking log home tucked in among towering fir trees. It was hard to turn that idyllic setting into part of a deadly crime scene, one that had left two people dead.

'Another vehicle was parked in the Lawrences' yard when I was there,' I said, pulling out my notebook. 'A Subaru, I believe. A Forester. I'm pretty sure I jotted down the plate number — '

'That would be Carol's car,' Lander interjected. 'As far as I know it's still there.'

I was disappointed that my one little snippet

of information wasn't going to be of any help in solving the case. I returned the notebook to my pocket.

'So who killed them?' I asked at last.

'That's what we were hoping you could tell us,' Lander replied. 'For instance, what can you tell me about the son-in-law?'

'About Donnie Cosgrove?' I asked. 'I haven't met him. I've only talked to him on the phone, but he sounds like a good guy. He's an engineer of some kind and works for Fluke up in Everett. Makes enough money that his wife can be a stay-at-home mom.'

'Did you call him or did he call you?'

'He called me,' I said. 'Lots was going on. I don't remember exactly when he called, but I think it was Friday morning.'

'What was said?'

'He was mad as hell. Jack Lawrence had come to the house the day before and made a scene. Jack was convinced DeAnn had somehow jump-started our renewed interest into Tony Cosgrove's disappearance.'

'Had she?'

'No, not at all. DeAnn Cosgrove had nothing to do with it. According to Donnie, Jack told DeAnn she didn't know when she was well off — whatever that means.'

'Did Donnie come right out and threaten Jack Lawrence?'

'Not in so many words. He mentioned something about tearing Jack's head off. He certainly didn't say he was going to shoot him. I told him he should swear out a restraining order.

But it sounds like you're thinking Donnie's responsible.'

Lander gave me a grim smile. 'Are we talking proof or gut instinct here?' he asked. 'The man was nervous as hell when I was there talking to them this morning. He could barely sit still, his hands were shaking, he looked like he was about to puke.'

The symptoms sounded familiar. 'Maybe he was just hungover,' I suggested.

'That's what he told me,' Lander said. 'Claimed he had been out late last night, drinking with his buddies and tying one on. I'll be checking his alibi. I'll also be checking the gum. And as I was leaving, Donnie Cosgrove's SUV just happened to be parked out on the street and I just happened to have a camera with me, so even if he goes out this afternoon and buys a new set of tires, I've got a copy of the tread to match up with our plaster casts.'

I thought about DeAnn Cosgrove — her little house in Redmond and her three little babies. I hated to think that her husband might be responsible for any of this. But a homicide detective's suspicions often count for something, whether they're mine or someone else's. I had to give Detective Lander his due.

'What about getting the Lawrences' phone records?' I asked. 'Finding out who they've called and who's called them in the past few days would probably be a help.'

Lander frowned. 'We're working on it,' he said glumly, 'but of course that's going to take time.'

I know that drill all too well. When I used to

send requests for phone information from Homicide at Seattle PD, getting a response usually took forever. Now that I worked for the A.G.'s office, however, that was no longer true. Requests for information that had been signed by Ross Alan Connors were usually handled with surprising alacrity. Not only that, I suspected that giving Tim Lander a leg up in his double homicide investigation now was something that could possibly serve me in good stead in some future investigation of my own.

'Ross Connors could probably speed up that process for you,' I suggested.

Lander looked at me sharply. 'He could?'

I nodded.

'And would he?' Lander asked.

'If you and I made a joint request.'

Lander looked astonished to think that I might be able to bring the power of the Washington State attorney general to bear on his investigation. Since I've never been much of a team player, I couldn't quite believe it either.

'How long would it take to do that?' Lander asked.

For an answer I picked up my phone and scrolled through my phone book. I located Ross Connors's cell number and punched 'send.' Ross himself answered after the fourth ring, and he didn't sound the least bit fazed by the fact that my call was interrupting his Sunday-afternoon golf. From the sounds in the background he was already ensconced at the nineteenth hole.

'So you think the new double homicide up in Leavenworth is related to your old missing persons case?' Connors asked once I finished.

'No way to tell that for sure,' I told him, 'but it's a distinct possibility. I drove up to Leavenworth thinking the Lawrences might have had something to do with Tony Cosgrove's disappearance and they had simply used the Mount Saint Helens eruption as convenient cover. Now, though, with both Jack and Carol Lawrence dead, there's a possibility someone else was involved as well, someone who doesn't want us looking into Tony's disappearance any more than Jack did.'

'All right, then,' Connors said. 'Fax over the paperwork. I'll see what I can do.'

'He must be a pretty good guy to work for,' Lander commented after the call was finished.

'He is that,' I agreed. 'Ross is all about getting the job done. He doesn't much care who gets the credit.'

'Where do I sign on?' Lander asked.

'We're full up right now,' I told him. 'But I'll tell Harry I. Ball about you and ask him to keep you in mind.'

'Harry who?' Lander asked.

'Harry I. Ball,' I told him. 'My boss.'

'You're kidding me. That's his name, no shit?'

'Yes,' I said. 'Harry middle-initial-I Ball.'

Detective Lander shook his head in wonder. 'Sounds like you guys have a great time working here.'

'We do,' I said. 'It's a barrel of fun.'

'Anything else I should be tracking?' he asked as he stood up to leave. 'Any other leads?'

Since we were working together, there was no

reason to hold back. 'I've got a call in to someone named Thomas Dortman,' I said. 'He's a defense analyst who years ago used to work at Boeing with Carol Lawrence's first husband, Tony. I called him looking for background information more than anything. Since I haven't heard back, he's probably out of town.'

'If you find out anything useful from him, you'll let me know, won't you?'

'You bet,' I told him. 'I'll be glad to.'

17

Because the elevator is key-controlled on weekends, I had to escort Detective Lander back down to the parking lot. On our way I noticed that Mel's door was open and the lights and radio were both off.

Here we go again, I told myself. *She's probably gone AWOL just like she did yesterday.*

I had visions of her walking back to Seattle, striding purposefully through the bike traffic on the I-90 bridge. Back upstairs, I tried calling her cell phone and was surprised when she answered.

'Where are you?' I asked.

'Outside,' she said. 'In the smokers' hut.'

Last year the Washington state legislature passed its most recent rendition of the statewide no-smoking ban. The rules and regs not only prohibit smoking inside public buildings, they also forbid smokers from congregating within some arbitrary number of feet from any building entrance or exit. Knowing that some smokers, including our office manager, Barbara, will never quit no matter what, SHIT's compassionate landlord had handled this legal bump in the road by installing a two-car-wide canvas-topped vehicle canopy just outside the prescribed boundary. He had stocked this rain-proof shelter with ashtrays, trash cans, and picnic tables. In other words, banished outdoor smokers would still freeze their butts off (in every sense of the word), but at least they wouldn't be wet.

I hurried downstairs. With a brisk wind blowing down off the snow-covered Cascades, it was clear and sunny outside but cold as hell. Mel was huddled inside one of the collection of just-in-case outerwear she keeps in her office — a hooded, fleece-lined jacket. She sat at the table with a lighter and a package of Marlboros and a huge glass ashtray in front of her. An unlabeled file folder lay next to the ashtray.

'I didn't know you smoked,' I said, taking a seat across from her as the chill of the picnic bench bit into my backside.

Mel blew a column of smoke skyward and watched it drift off toward the traffic speeding past along I-90. 'I don't,' she said. 'I borrowed these from Barbara.'

It seemed mean to point out that she was indeed smoking. For once in my life, I had brains enough not to say anything.

'The last time I smoked before this was the day I came home from work early and found Greg in bed with my best friend,' Mel continued. 'I walked into the bedroom and there they were, both of them stark naked. I didn't say a word to either one of them. I stripped off my work clothes, put on a pair of sweats and tennis shoes, and went jogging. Threw my cigarettes into the bedroom trash can on my way out. I knew I couldn't jog and smoke. Never smoked again — until today.'

These were gory details from Mel's past that I

265

had never heard before, but knowing her, especially knowing her when she's mad as hell, I could see it all in my mind's eye. In another time and place I might have made a joke about it, but she was hurting way too much for me to make light of her pain. I didn't want to make it worse than it already was.

'Why today?' I asked.

'Someone's trying to frame me for murder,' she said. 'And it must be one of my so-called friends. It's so damned close to what happened to me before, with Greg and Gina, that it really set me off. Brought up all those bad old times; sent me looking for some of my bad old friends — one of these, for instance.' She pointed at the pack of Marlboros.

I wasn't surprised. This is the kind of emotional setback that can send long-sober drunks bellying up to the nearest bar.

Mel stubbed what little was left of her smoldering cigarette into the ashtray. I pushed the ashtray aside and covered her icy hand with mine.

'Which so-called friend do you think is involved?' I asked.

She shrugged. 'One way or another, it's all tied in with SASAC. I came down here to work up my courage before calling Ross. I'm sure he'll want to put me on a leave of absence before somebody in the media gets wind of this rather than after, the way he had to do with Destry.'

'Destry?' I asked. 'Destry Hennessey?'

'Sure,' Mel said. 'It was three years ago, just after she came back here but before I showed up.

266

Don't you remember?'

I did remember, but only vaguely. I wasn't involved with a news junkie back then; current events tended to get by me. 'Something about her grandmother?' I asked.

'Yes,' Mel answered. 'The shorthand version of the story goes like this. The grandmother had been widowed for several years and was living alone in Salt Lake City when a sixteen-year-old punk broke into her house one night, robbed her, raped her, and left her to die. But she didn't die — not right then. A neighbor saw the kid running out of the house and reported it. He was only two blocks away and still on foot when the cops managed to nail him with some of the grandmother's personal goods still in his possession. When the case went to court, the kid's defense attorney finagled a plea bargain. Juan Carlos Escobar went to a juvie facility up in Logan until he was twenty-one.'

'And Destry's grandmother?' I asked.

'She was left with permanent internal injuries. She had been independent right up until then, but after the attack she was no longer able to live on her own. She ended up first in an assisted-living facility and later in a nursing home, where, two years later, she died. The doctors were convinced that the infection that eventually killed her came about as a result of her original injuries, but the D.A. refused to amend the charges against the punk. He was released on his twenty-first birthday.'

The more she told me of the story, the more it jogged my memory.

'And he was killed that night, right?' I asked.

Mel nodded. 'On his way home to his own grandmother's place in Salt Lake. Someone ran him down in a vehicle. It wasn't an accident, either. They ran over him several times and left him to die in an irrigation ditch.'

'How do you know so much about this?' I asked.

'For one thing, Destry and I roomed together when we were down in Cancún. We sat up late one night on our balcony watching the moon on the water and drinking margaritas. That's when she told me about it. What happened to her grandmother was what propelled her into SASAC, the same as what happened to Sarah did me. For another, that's what I was doing upstairs — a LexisNexis search on the case.'

She tapped the file folder, but I didn't reach for it or ask to see what was inside.

'What about Ross?' I asked. 'You said something about what happened before?'

'Naturally Destry was a person of interest in that case. All of her relatives were as well, but on the night it happened, Destry and her husband were actually in Washington, D.C. She had been to a Homeland Security meeting and was at a dinner at the White House when Escobar died.'

'Talk about a gold-plated alibi,' I said.

Mel gave me a faint smile. 'That's what Ross Connors thought. He saw no reason to put her on administrative leave while the investigation ground on. And that's just as well since the case has yet to be solved. But some investigative reporter from the *Seattle Times* raised all kinds of hell about it. Thought Destry was being given special treatment. And that's why I'm going to go call Ross right now — to give him a heads-up.'

She started to rise, but I held her hand and stopped her. 'No,' I said. 'Not yet. Let's talk about this.'

'What's there to discuss?' she asked. 'I owe him. When I needed a job that would get me out of D.C., Ross Connors was the only guy who would give my résumé a second glance.'

'No, wait a minute,' I said. 'You said you thought someone was trying to frame you. Assuming that's true, there must be a reason. Has someone tried blackmailing you, for example?'

Mel looked me straight in the eye when she answered. 'No,' she said vehemently. 'Absolutely not.'

'So if they're not looking for something from you, then maybe whoever's behind this did it just for the hell of it. Because they could.'

'It doesn't really matter why they did it,' Mel returned. 'The point is, they did. And they're getting away with it.'

'Just like whoever took out Destry's grand-mother's killer is getting away with it,' I pointed out. 'What do you think the chances are that lightning strikes twice in exactly the same spot in exactly the same way?'

Mel shrugged and didn't answer.

'Right now,' I continued, 'the people respon-sible for all this think they're getting away with it. You haven't been notified that you're a suspect

269

in the Matthews case, have you?'

Mel shook her head. 'Of course not. How could I? I knew nothing at all about it. Until you brought it up this afternoon I didn't even know Richard Matthews was dead.'

'Exactly,' I said. 'The cops in Mexico haven't made the connection, and as far as the killer is concerned, neither have we. As long as nothing happens to change the status quo — Ross putting you on administrative leave, for example — no one will know we've caught on, either. And that gives us our best chance of catching Matthews's killer.'

Mel said nothing.

'I suggest we tackle this case the same way we would any other. First, let's go upstairs and put Barbara's cigarettes where they belong. Then let's go back home and work the case. I'll interview you the same way I would any other victim.'

'Or suspect,' Mel interjected.

'Victim,' I repeated firmly. 'We'll make a list of everybody who was on that trip with you and find out as much as we can about each of them. And we'll also check to see exactly what the cops down in Cancún have going for them on this case.'

'What if the killer used my weapon?' Mel asked.

'You had it with you?'

'My back-up Glock,' she said. 'We were flying on Anita's private jet. There wasn't an issue with security.'

That gave me pause. If forensics ended up

linking Mel's 9-millimeter to Richard Matthews's death, it was going to be a hell of a lot harder to make all this go away.

'Did you have the Glock with you all the time?'

'Not when I was swimming — or jogging,' she added. 'It's hard to carry a concealed weapon when you're wearing a bikini.'

'Amen to that!' I said.

She smiled at me then. 'Let's go inside,' she said. 'I'm freezing.'

We went back upstairs only long enough to return the cigarettes and lighter to Barbara Galvin's top desk drawer.

As we headed back to Seattle, Mel sat on the far side of the car, holding the file folder tightly against her chest. 'I tried to do some checking on the Matthews case,' she said. 'What little I could find was in the El Paso papers.'

'I saw that, too,' I told her.

'So how are you going to find out what the Cancún cops have without leading them straight to me?'

'You don't know about my secret weapon,' I said. 'Whatever Ralph Ames can't find out isn't worth knowng.'

'But Ralph's *your* attorney,' Mel objected. 'Whatever he found out wouldn't be protected . . . '

I handed her my phone. 'Look under 'incoming calls,'' I told her. 'His number should be one of the last ones that came in. Call him and tell him you're hiring him and that he should come by the house later this evening and

271

pick up his retainer.'

'But I can't afford someone like him.'

'This is too serious, Mel,' I said. 'You can't *not* afford someone like him. We can't afford it.'

Mel stared at the phone. 'What do I tell him about what's going on?' she wanted to know.

Mel's state of mind was still too fragile to tell her that I had already run up the flag to Ralph. By now he probably knew more about the case than Mel and me put together.

'Say we have a situation here and that we're sure you'll be needing his services.'

'Isn't that a little vague?' Mel asked.

'Believe me,' I told her, 'Ralph can handle vague better than anyone I know.'

So she made the call. Concerned Ralph might inadvertently blow my cover, I was relieved when he didn't answer and she left him a voice-mail message.

'Who all was at the retreat in Cancún?' I asked.

She rattled off a list of names. 'Anita Bowdin, Professor Clark, Destry Hennessey, Rita Davenport, Abigail Rosemont, Justine Maldonado, and me. Seven of us altogether. Then there was Sarah James, Anita's cook, and the two pilots. The cook stayed at Anita's place. The pilots went to a hotel. Anita had her own room. The rest of us shared.'

I remembered meeting the first four women Mel mentioned. The others were names only.

'And was there any kind of disagreement among you?' I asked. 'Hard feelings of any kind?'

'No. Not at all. We spent a lot of time

272

brainstorming about the upcoming fund-raiser. That was the whole point of the retreat. We were determined to raise more money than last year, and we did — raise more money, that is. But we had fun, too. We walked on the beach. Went into town for shopping. Did the whole tourist thing. And the food was wonderful. Sarah is a marvelous cook.'

'And did any of the women know your story — about what had happened between Sarah Matthews and her father?'

'All of them did,' Mel answered. 'Anyone who was on the board, and we all were, would have known about it.'

I tried to quell the sudden flare-up of anger I felt, but it didn't go away.

'How can that be?' I demanded. 'I didn't find out about any of it until yesterday, when you finally told me. But in the meantime, you're saying the rest of the world already knew?'

'It's part of the board of directors' selection process,' Mel explained. 'Prospective members are encouraged to write individual essays explaining how and why they came to be involved in sexual assault prevention programs. Once the essays are written they're circulated among existing board members.'

Maybe that was part of what had made me so uncomfortable at the SASAC banquet. Maybe the group's ultimate aim was to help people affected by sexual assaults, but there had been that exclusionary sense about the organization — an in-crowd, private-club chumminess about the women, 'those women,' an us-and-them mind-set, that had left me cold while at the same time leaving me out.

'So you have essays for all the other women on the retreat?' I asked.

'I've read them,' she said, 'but I didn't keep them. They're painful stories, Beau, all of them. When I was finished reading, I ran them through the shredder.'

'Would anyone else still have them?' I asked.

'Maybe. Why?'

'Because we need to check. If the guy who attacked Destry Hennessey's grandmother is dead and if Richard Matthews is dead, maybe some of the other responsible parties have met the same fate.'

For a moment Mel didn't answer. Then, with no further explanation to me, she dredged her own phone out of her pocket, scrolled through some numbers, and pushed 'send.'

'Hey,' she said breezily when someone answered. 'Mel here.'

There was a pause. 'Oh, no. The food was fine. Great. Not to worry. No complaints on that score whatsoever.'

Which told me Mel was calling Rita Davenport, her fellow SASAC board member and the lady who ran the catering company.

'So I was calling with a favor,' Mel continued. 'You wouldn't happen to have a copy of all the board member essays, would you? I'm one of those people who unload that kind of stuff as soon as I read it, but now I need to see one of them . . . You do? Hey, that's great. If you could just shoot them to me in an e-mail . . . sure

. . . that's terrific. Appreciate it. Wrong? Oh, no. No, nothing's wrong, and it's no big deal. I just wanted to compare notes on a couple of things. Fine. Thanks.'

Mel closed her phone and heaved a sigh. 'I suppose I'll go to hell for lying,' she said, 'because it is a big deal.'

Indeed it was.

Once back at Belltown Terrace, we did just what I'd said we would. Mel started a new pot of coffee. Then, armed with computers and notebooks, we began to go over what we knew and what we didn't know.

We had barely figured out where to start when Ralph called. 'What's going on?' he asked.

'Hold on,' I told him. 'This is Mel's story. You'd better hear it from her.'

I punched the phone onto speaker and handed it over to Mel. My trust in Ralph is well founded. He listened to the whole story without ever hinting that very little of what she had to say was news to him.

'What do you need from me?' he asked when she finished.

Mel sighed. 'I guess I'd like you to find out whatever you can about the ongoing investigation down in Cancún.'

'And if they haven't tumbled to your possible involvement, you'd just as soon I didn't mention it,' Ralph concluded.

'Yes,' Mel said.

'Give me a while,' Ralph said. 'But if you don't mind, I probably should swing by in a little while so you can give me that retainer. With a situation this serious, I don't want there to be any question at all about my being your attorney of record.'

One of the good things about working with a partner is that you gradually come to terms with a division of labor. Without our even having to discuss it, Mel opened Rita's e-mail containing the SASAC board member essays. While she started studying those, I opened the file she had brought home from the office.

Mel had given me the broad outline of Destry Hennessey's grandmother's case, but the collection of articles gleaned from various newspapers laid out the story in much greater detail. I skimmed over the ones that dealt with the physical attack on Destry's grandmother, Phyllis Elaine Hammond, and focused instead on what had happened to her attacker. Taking detailed notes, I was gradually able to gain a reasonably clear picture of the chain of events.

After serving four years for one count each of rape and robbery on seventy-nine-year-old Phyllis Elaine Hammond, Juan Carlos Escobar had been released from the North Utah Juvenile Correctional Institute in Logan on October 6, 2003. On the day of his twenty-first birthday, he had been driven to the bus terminal in Logan and handed a Greyhound ticket to Salt Lake City, where his own grandmother, Maria Andrade Escobar, had been expecting him. His bus ticket was never used, however, and he never arrived in Salt Lake, either. Several witnesses had reported seeing him in conversation with a nun near the Greyhound terminal an hour or so before his scheduled departure. Two days later, Escobar's battered body had been discovered in an irrigation ditch on a deserted blacktop road outside Bountiful.

At the time Escobar was sentenced to serve his time in a juvenile facility, several relatives of his victim had appeared in public strenuously objecting to his having received special treatment. One or two of them had even gone so far as to vow seeking revenge.

'With that kind of history, naturally that was the first place we looked,' the lead investigator, Bountiful homicide detective Ambrose Donner, reported. 'Members of Mrs. Hammond's family were initially considered persons of interest, but at this point they've all been questioned and cleared of any involvement.'

Investigators continue in their efforts to locate the unidentified nun who was seen speaking to Escobar shortly before he disappeared. They're also trying to locate the vehicle involved in the incident, reportedly a dark blue Buick Riviera with a broken front headlight and extensive front end damage.

The mention of a nun's possible involvement was an immediate red flag, but for right then I let it go because I finally had what I needed. Flipping open my phone, I set about finding Detective Donner. He had been investigating a homicide that involved a dead sexual predator, which, it so happened, was what SHIT was doing, too. More or less.

It took a while. 'Sorry to interrupt your Sunday,' I said when I finally reached the man at home and had introduced myself. I was worried he'd give me the third degree and want to know all about me — who I was and why was I horning in on his weekend, to say nothing of messing around in one of his cases.

'No big deal,' he said. 'I'm watching golf. Tiger's cleaning everybody's clock, as per usual. What can I do for you?'

'I'm looking into one of your old cases,' I said. 'Wondering whether or not you ever closed it.'

'Which one?'

'Juan Carlos Escobar.'

Donner didn't even hesitate. 'That punk? No, we never closed it. Doubt we ever will. Near as we can figure, he pissed someone off while he was in juvie and they took care of him as soon as he got out. He was sent up because he raped and robbed some helpless little old lady,' Donner added. 'The victim died eventually and probably because of what Escobar did to her, but he was never charged with murder like he shoulda been.'

'And none of her relatives were involved in his subsequent death?' I asked.

'We thought so at first, but they all came out squeaky clean. We ended up settling on the gangbanger theory. What can I tell you?'

'Did you ever find the vehicle?'

Donner hesitated. 'Yes,' he said. 'As a matter of fact, we did. Two weeks after the fact, this guy

278

comes home from taking his wife to Europe for their fortieth wedding anniversary. He gets off the plane and his car is missing from the airport parking lot.'

'Let me guess, a blue Buick Riviera.'

'You got it. The parking lot attendant figures the guy just forgot where he parked, so he gets a security guard to drive him around. When they find it, it's there in the lot all right, but the date and time stamp on the ticket is a whole twenty-four hours after the guy and his wife landed in Paris. When the crime lab went over it, the interior had been wiped down pretty thoroughly, but they did find pieces of Juan Carlos still stuck to the front end and undercarriage.'

'What about the nun?' I asked. 'Did you ever find her?'

'Look,' he said, hedging, 'this is a small town. I'm not sure I should go into all this.'

After blithely spilling his guts about Escobar, I found Donner's sudden reticence mystifying.

'Come on, Detective Donner,' I urged. 'Did you find her or not?'

'We never found her,' he said. 'But nobody ever reported her missing, either,' he hurried on. 'We never found a body. Never found any remains or any blood evidence. So we didn't have any way of knowing if we even had a second victim. The chief made the call. Said we were keeping it under wraps until we had an actual ID or a missing persons report to go on.'

'Wait a minute,' I said. 'What are you saying?'

Donner sighed. 'When the crime lab went over

the Buick, they found a single thread — a long black thread. The guy who owned the car didn't own anything black like that and neither did his wife.'

'So the nun was in the car.'

'That's what we think, but we have no idea what happened to her afterward.'

'The thread's still there?'

'As far as I know.'

'Did you do composites of her?'

'I think so,' Donner said. 'They're probably locked away in the cold case room. Why?'

'I'd like to get a look at them, if I could. Maybe you could fax them over to me.'

'But . . . ' he began.

'Look,' I said. 'I know you went out on a limb here by telling me this. If you like, you don't even have to fax them to my office. If I give you my home number, we can keep this off everybody's radar, right?'

'Right,' he said. 'That would be a big help. What's your number?'

18

What's going on?' Mel asked as I hung up with Donner.

'The cops in Bountiful had reports that Escobar spoke to a nun shortly after his release and just before his disappearance. There's some evidence that the nun was in the car that ran down Escobar.'

'She's dead, too, then?'

'No evidence one way or the other,' I returned. 'And without a missing persons report or any evidence of foul play, Bountiful sat on that part of the case. I've asked him to fax over a composite sketch, but we won't get that until after Detective Donner goes into work tomorrow — if then.'

The phone rang. It was the doorman calling to say Ralph Ames was on his way up.

Even late on a Sunday evening, Ralph arrived looking like someone who had just stepped out of a Brooks Brothers ad. Under the best of circumstances I look like your basic rumpled bed — tux-wearing occasions excepted. Fortunately our friendship is more than skin-deep.

'Good evening,' he said. 'Although, from the sound of things, there's not much good about it.'

Mel gave him a wan smile. 'Not much,' she agreed. 'Should I get my checkbook?'

'Definitely,' he said. 'Then let's go over this whole thing again, from beginning to end. I've got a call in to Lucinda Reyes down in Arizona. She's a retired Phoenix cop, and she's the best translator in the business when it comes to talking with *federales*.'

We spent the better part of the next two hours bringing Ralph up to speed on everything we had learned not only about the Matthews case but about Juan Carlos Escobar as well. In the end, Ralph seemed to agree with us.

'Yes, it is a bit much to think that these are unrelated,' he said. 'The fact that you and Ms. Hennessey are both involved in the same organization would seem to indicate some kind of connection. Are you finding any similar cases among those essays you mentioned?'

'I've only checked out four of them so far,' Mel said. 'One of those was a grandfather, a pedophile who died, reportedly of natural causes, thirty years ago. That's approximately twenty-five years before SASAC was a gleam in Anita Bowdin's eye, so I doubt that one has anything to do with this. One was a bar pickup scene date rape where no assailant was ever named, apprehended, or charged. The other two are still locked up in prison. One of those raped and murdered Professor Clark's eleven-year-old granddaughter. The other attacked Justine Maldonado's younger sister.'

'And both of those are still alive?' Ralph asked.

'Alive and kicking,' Mel said. 'I already checked.'

It struck me as interesting that in almost every case, with the possible exception of the date rape scenario, the women had all been galvanized into

282

taking action — and joining SASAC — by an attack on someone other than themselves. Before I could make that observation, though, the phone rang.

By then it was late enough in the evening that I expected it to be Scott telling me that he and Cherisse were safely home or Jeremy calling to give me the latest update on Kelly. Or maybe even Thomas Dortman finally getting around to returning my call. It wasn't.

'Mr. Beaumont?' a tearful female voice asked when I answered.

'Yes.'

'It's me, DeAnn Cosgrove. I need to see you. Right now.'

'Why? What is it? What's going on? If it's an emergency, you should probably hang up and call 9-1-1.'

'No. I need to talk to you. Please.'

Taking the hint, Ralph was already gathering up his things in preparation for leaving. DeAnn sounded utterly frantic, making me think that I was being invited into some kind of domestic dispute.

'Is your husband there?' I asked. 'Is there some kind of problem?'

'Donnie's not here,' DeAnn answered. 'That's why I need to talk to you.'

Talking to hysterical women has never been my strong suit, and DeAnn definitely sounded hysterical.

'All right,' I said, 'but if you don't mind, I'd like to bring my partner along. We'll be leaving downtown Seattle in a matter of minutes.'

DeAnn didn't wait around long enough to reply one way or the other. She simply hung up. Before I could do the same, Mel was slipping her shoes back on her feet.

'Wait up,' she said to me. 'My Glock's down the hall. So's my jacket.'

Ralph, Mel, and I rode down in the elevator together. Ralph exited at the lobby and Mel turned to me. 'Who was that on the phone?' she asked. 'Where are we going and why?'

'DeAnn Cosgrove is a woman whose father disappeared in the Mount Saint Helens eruption in 1980. She lives in Redmond, and that's where we're going. As to why? I have no idea. She said she needed to talk to me, and waiting until morning evidently isn't an option. The other problem, of course, is that her parents were gunned down last night up in Leavenworth. The last thing her husband said to me on the phone was that he was going to rip the stepfather's head off. Not surprisingly, Detective Lander, the guy working the Leavenworth homicides, is wondering if DeAnn's husband may have had something to do with the shooting.'

'Do you think he did?' Mel asked.

'Donnie told Detective Lander he was out drinking with his pals last night,' I replied. 'But at this point, I don't have enough information on Donnie Cosgrove to think one way or the other.'

'But he isn't home right now, is he?' Mel ascertained.

'Right,' I told her. 'That's what DeAnn said on the phone.'

We drove for a while in silence. The clearing

that had happened earlier was now a thing of the past. The wind was coming in sharp gusts and it was spitting rain as we headed for the bridge. I knew I should keep my mind on the Cosgroves and what was happening there, but it kept coming back to Mel.

'What's Anita's deal?' I asked.

'Anita's?' Mel returned. 'What do you mean?'

'The other women you were telling us about, the ones on the board, all but one of them — you included — got involved because of something that happened to someone else — a friend or a relative. Since Anita's the mover and shaker behind all of it, I'm just curious about what set her off. Did something happen to her? Did it happen to someone she cared about?'

'I don't know,' Mel said. 'I don't think anyone's ever said. Why?'

'Just curious.'

'Now that you mention it,' Mel remarked, 'I am, too.'

By the time we parked in Donnie and DeAnn Cosgrove's driveway, the sprinkles had changed into a hard rain. The porch light was on. The moment we pulled into the driveway the front door opened and DeAnn came dashing out to meet us. Her hair, hanging loose, seemed to stand on end in the blowing wind and rain.

'I'm sorry about your mother,' I said at once.

'Thank you,' she said, stepping forward to meet me. 'And thank you for coming. I didn't know what else to do or who else to call. And with the kids already asleep, I couldn't just throw them in the car and go traipsing all over God's

285

creation looking for him.'

'Looking for Donnie?' I asked.

She nodded. 'He left the house a little while after Detective Lander did. I was so upset about my mother that I couldn't think straight. I really needed him here with me, but he said he had to go out, that he'd be right back. But it's been hours now, and I have no idea where he is. I've tried calling his cell and his office phone, but he isn't answering. I even tried calling his friends, the ones he said he was with last night.' She paused.

'And?' I prompted.

'They hadn't seen him,' she said. 'They hadn't seen him today — or last night either, Detective Beaumont. What does it mean if he wasn't where he said he was?'

Mel rounded the back corner of the car. Neither she nor I answered, but we both knew what it meant: Donnie Cosgrove's alibi was out the window.

'I even called some of the local hospitals,' DeAnn continued distractedly. 'But then, when I found the note . . . '

'What note?' Mel asked, speaking for the first time.

DeAnn wheeled and turned on Mel. 'Who are you?' she demanded.

Obviously a good part of what we'd said on the telephone hadn't penetrated DeAnn Cosgrove's frantic concern.

'I'm Detective Beaumont's partner, Melissa Soames,' Mel explained. 'He asked me to come along and see if I could help. Since it's raining so hard, maybe it would be best if we went inside.'

Nodding, a distraught DeAnn Cosgrove led us into her house. The place looked entirely different from the way it had looked on my previous visit. The living room appeared to have been cleaned within an inch of its life. There were fresh vacuum cleaner tracks on the rugs. The dining room table had been cleared of almost all paper debris, and no toys at all were anywhere in evidence.

'After Detective Lander left, he did, too,' DeAnn went on. 'I mean, how could he do that, leave me here alone with my mom dead and everything? After a while I called some of my friends from church, just so I'd have someone here with me, so I wouldn't be alone. They came over and helped with the kids. Helped get the house cleaned up. They finally left a little while ago. I knew I needed to get some rest whether Donnie came home or not. That's when I found the note — when I was getting ready for bed.'

'What note?' Mel prompted.

DeAnn hurried over to the dining room table and picked up a single three-by-five card. On it was written: 'I'm sorry. I love you. Donnie.'

'Sorry for what?' I asked.

DeAnn shrugged. 'About my mother, maybe? I guess that's what he meant.'

I couldn't help but feel sorry for the poor woman. Her mother and stepfather had both been murdered, but at this juncture she was so concerned about her missing husband that grief for the two homicide victims had yet to gain any real traction.

'And the note,' Mel said, 'where did you find it?'

'Folded up in my nightgown, under my pillow. Donnie would have known I wouldn't find it until I started getting ready for bed. I understand that now. It means he knew he wasn't coming back before bedtime. But why? Why would he do that?' DeAnn wailed. She was crying in dead earnest now.

'You hadn't quarreled?' Mel asked when DeAnn quieted down some.

'Well, maybe a little,' DeAnn admitted. 'I was really mad at him for staying out so late last night. I'm here with the kids all day every day. I expect us to be together on weekends, and usually we are. But last night he said he needed to meet some guys from work. We had a fight about it before he even left.'

'What time did he come home then?' Mel asked.

'Late,' DeAnn answered. 'And I mean real late. After the bars closed. He didn't think I'd be awake, but I had been up with the baby. He parked on the street and then came sneaking in through the garage wearing nothing but his underwear. Said one of his buddies had gotten drunk and barfed all over him, so he put his clothing in the wash before he ever came into the house. That seemed really strange to me because, barf or not, doing laundry isn't Donnie's thing. And this morning, when I went out to the garage to do a load, I saw that he'd washed everything, even his sneakers — washed them and put them in the dryer. I don't know what he was thinking. They came out of the dryer completely wrecked. I had to throw them away.'

'What happened then?' Mel inquired.

'He was really quiet all morning,' DeAnn answered. 'I kept asking him what was wrong — if he was sick or hungover or what. I even went out and checked on his car. I was afraid he had wrecked it or something and was scared to tell me about it. Then, when Detective Lander was here, it was like Donnie was . . . ' She paused, as if struggling to find the right word.

'What?' Mel asked.

'I don't know,' DeAnn said. 'Just weird. I mean, my mother was the one who was dead. I needed him to be here for me, but it was like he was out of it or something. And, of course, the kids picked right up on it. Since we were both upset, they were upset, too. It was all I could do to concentrate and answer Detective Lander's questions. Then, as soon as the detective left to meet you, Donnie left, too. He told me that he had to go out, that he'd be back later.'

'And you haven't heard anything from him since?' I asked.

DeAnn Cosgrove's eyes filled with tears. 'Not a word,' she said, shaking her head. 'Except for the note. What does it all mean?'

'After your stepfather came by here the other day and after Donnie called me, did he go to Leavenworth?'

'He talked about it,' DeAnn allowed. 'Donnie was livid Jack had come here to cause trouble. He said he was going to go to their house and do the same thing, but I told him not to. I told him two wrongs don't make a right and that we're supposed to be big enough to turn the other cheek.'

I had a feeling that Donnie had been focused on something far more Old Testamenty — an eye for an eye, for example.

'You said you'd done some calling around, looking for your husband,' Mel said. 'Where all did you check?'

'He sometimes works weekends, so I thought he might have gone to his office,' DeAnn said. 'But I called and checked with the guard shack where people have to sign in and out. Nobody there had seen him. When I found out his friends hadn't seen him, either, that's when I finally called you. I didn't know who else to ask. Should I file a missing persons report now, or is it too soon?'

Under the circumstances, it seemed unlikely that a missing persons report would be needed to jump-start a search for Donnie Cosgrove.

'Does your husband have access to any weapons?' Mel asked.

DeAnn stared at her. 'You mean, like a gun?'

Mel nodded.

'Donnie does have a gun,' DeAnn conceded. 'It belonged to his father. He keeps it locked in his desk in the bedroom. But why . . . ?'

'Is it there now?'

Without a word, DeAnn left the room. When she returned a few moments later, her face was pasty white. 'It's gone,' she whispered, sinking onto the couch. 'You don't think he's the one who did it, do you? I mean, it's not possible!'

But of course it was all too thinkable and all too possible, although I'm sure that was the very first moment it ever crossed DeAnn's mind that her beloved Donnie, the father of her children, might have murdered her mother and stepfather.

'What kind of gun is it?' Mel asked.

'I have no idea,' DeAnn managed. 'I don't know anything about guns — anything at all. I just know I didn't like him having one.'

'But it was a handgun of some kind?' Mel persisted. 'Not a rifle or a shotgun.'

'Yes, I guess that's what you'd call it — a handgun. I think Donnie said it was a .357, but I'm not sure.'

Had I been asking the questions right then, my face probably would have given away the game. Mel's didn't. 'I'll go ahead and take down that missing persons information, then,' she said smoothly. 'What kind of vehicle did you say your husband drives?'

It was a deft pivot on Mel's part, and DeAnn Cosgrove clung to that disarming piece of fiction as though her life depended on it. Maybe it did. Without being able to believe we really were taking a missing persons report, DeAnn might have fallen apart completely.

'A Chevrolet Tahoe,' she answered. Surprisingly enough, the woman was still able to reel off Donnie's plate number from memory. For the next several minutes, she located and supplied all the necessary info about the clothing her husband had been wearing when he left the house. She gave us his contact information at

291

work as well as the names, addresses, and phone numbers of friends and relations.

'Now what?' DeAnn asked when Mel finally put her notebook and pen away.

'We're going to try to find him,' Mel said.

'But not hurt him, right?' DeAnn said. 'I'm sure he hasn't done anything wrong. He wouldn't have.'

I think she was trying to convince herself even more than she was us.

'We'll do everything in our power to see that no one gets hurt,' I told her.

'Thank you,' DeAnn said gratefully. 'Thank you very much.'

She stood on the front porch as we made our way out the gate, down the driveway, and back to the sidewalk. At the end of the driveway a rolling garbage bin had already been hauled out to the street. Mel and I exchanged glances as we walked past it. She held out her hand. 'I'll drive,' she said.

Gentleman that I am, I handed over the keys and climbed into the passenger seat. DeAnn watched while we fastened our seat belts and Mel started the engine. Only when we actually pulled away from the curb did DeAnn disappear into the house, closing the door and turning off the porch light. At the end of the block Mel negotiated a quick U-turn and then brought us back to the garbage bin parked at the end of the Cosgroves' driveway.

Garbage hauled out to the street no longer has the expectation of privacy. Since the Dumpster in question came from a house awash in toddlers and disposable diapers, opening the lid was not for the faint of heart. I can handle crime scenes. I can handle the stench of death. The odor of several dozen moldering dirty diapers, however, left me gagging.

The top layer consisted of two large white plastic bags, carefully tied shut. For a time it looked as though I'd have to untie the bags and go pawing through them — not a pleasant thought. I hauled them out and placed them on the curb beside me. Then, to my immense relief, visible in the pale glow of a rain-drenched street lamp was exactly what I was looking for — a pair of mangled man's sneakers. They had clearly been run through both a washer and dryer and looked as though they were no longer wearable.

Triumphantly I grabbed them up, threw the trash bags back inside the container, and hurried back to the car with my booty.

'Got 'em,' I told Mel. 'Now drive. Next stop is the crime lab. Let's see what, if anything, Luminol can tell us.'

Mel, driving like a maniac as usual, steered us straight to the Washington State Patrol Crime Lab on Airport Way south of downtown Seattle. There it took only a matter of minutes for Rena Bullworth, one of the criminalists specializing in blood evidence, to confirm what Mel and I already suspected. The Cosgroves' Maytag may have done its darnedest to clean up the mess, but the Luminol's telltale blue told us that there were still tiny traces of human blood lingering on the seemingly white shoelaces and seams of Donnie Cosgrove's Reeboks.

Seeing blood there was one thing. Being able to know whose blood we were seeing was another problem entirely.

Moments later I was on the phone with Detective Lander up in Leavenworth telling him about this latest development.

'So you think I'm right and the son-in-law could be our shooter?' he wanted to know.

'Maybe,' I said. 'The lady here at the crime lab isn't very hopeful about being able to extract a DNA profile from what little blood is left on Donnie Cosgrove's shoes, but she's going to try.'

'Even if the blood evidence isn't there, we've got footprints,' Lander said. 'If your shoes match our prints, we can at least put him at the crime scene.'

'Fair enough,' I said. 'In the meantime, what kind of shell casings were found?'

'Just a minute,' Lander said. 'Let me check the log.' It took a while for him to come back on the line. 'Here it is. A nine-millimeter Golden Saber. Why?'

'Donnie Cosgrove's wife told us he owns a handgun of some kind — a .357, she *thinks*,' I said. 'But considering what she knows about guns, it could very well be a nine millimeter. Whatever kind of gun it is, it's currently missing from its usual spot in their bedroom.'

Lander whistled. 'Sounds like we need to have a sit-down with this guy.'

'Yes,' I said. 'We do, but good luck finding him. He took off this afternoon after you left without telling his wife where he was going and hasn't been seen since. He isn't answering his phone.'

'You want to post the BOLO on him, or should I?' Lander asked.

In cop parlance, a 'be on the lookout' is one step under an all-points bulletin, but it means pretty much the same thing. An unwitting DeAnn Cosgrove had willingly supplied all the necessary information.

'Not to worry,' I said. 'My partner's doing that right now.'

'Back to Redmond?' Mel asked as we left the crime lab.

'I don't see any way around it,' I said. So back to Redmond we went. When we arrived at the Cosgroves' little rambler a second time, the porch light was still off but interior lights showed at the windows. A fully dressed DeAnn responded to the bell. She came to the door with a sleeping baby cradled in her arms.

'Did you find him?' she asked anxiously. 'Is he all right?'

'No,' Mel said. 'We have yet to locate your husband, but we did find something else. We need to talk to you about it.'

By then DeAnn Cosgrove must have cried herself out and reached her own conclusions about our earlier visit. She listened to everything Mel and I had to say with dry-eyed concentration.

'You're telling me he's a suspect, then?' DeAnn asked.

Mel nodded.

'So what should I do? When Donnie comes

home, should I try to talk him into giving up? Tell him that he should turn himself in?'

'No!' I interjected, probably more forcefully than I should have. 'Absolutely not. Don't even think about it. Convincing armed suspects to surrender is dangerous work even for trained emergency response teams.'

I could have added that unarmed wives are notoriously bad at it, but I didn't. Even fully armed, Sue Danielson had been no match for her ex-husband. She hadn't been able to convince him to lay down his weapon and stop shooting. I didn't want DeAnn Cosgrove and her children to suffer the same fate. Neither did Mel.

'It's always possible that your husband had nothing to do with what happened up in Leavenworth,' she said in a far more conciliatory tone than the one I had used. 'But I think we can all agree that his behavior today is unusual. Until we can locate him and sort this all out, our first concern has to be keeping you and your children safe. I think you should take the children and leave.'

'Leave?' DeAnn repeated dully. 'You mean run away?'

Yes! I wanted to scream at her. *Get the hell out of Dodge!*

'It's the middle of the night,' DeAnn objected. 'The kids are asleep,' she added. 'I'd have to wake them up and load them into the van. Where would I take them?'

'You said earlier that some of your friends from church came over this afternoon and helped you. Do you think you could stay with one of them?'

Mel met and held DeAnn's gaze for a period of several long seconds. When DeAnn looked away first, I knew Mel had her. Give a mother a choice between her babies and her husband, and most women will take the former.

'I'll call Mary Jane,' she said.

Mel and I stayed around while DeAnn packed up a vanload of food, clothing, and toys. Once the child gear had been loaded into the Dodge minivan in the garage, Mel and I helped carry the three sleeping kids out to the car and strap them into their car seats.

With the engine running, DeAnn backed out of the garage and closed the garage door behind her. In the driveway, though, she paused and rolled down the window. 'Shouldn't I leave Donnie a note?' she asked. 'What if he comes home and we're not here? Won't he be worried? Shouldn't I let him know where we are?'

I was afraid that if she went back into the house, we'd never get her to leave a second time. Mel must have shared that concern.

'You have a cell phone, don't you?' she asked.

DeAnn nodded. 'Yes, but — '

'You can talk to him on the phone if he calls you,' Mel advised. 'Tell him you and the kids are fine, but don't tell him where you are or how to find you, and whatever you do, don't agree to meet him. If he contacts you — if he tells you where he is — you call us. We'll negotiate with him, not you.'

'All right,' DeAnn agreed at last, putting the

minivan in gear. 'If you think that's the best way to handle it . . . '

Mel and I stood in the street and watched until DeAnn's tail-lights disappeared around the next intersection. The process of talking her into leaving had left me drained.

'Can we go home now?' I asked Mel. 'This has been a very long day.'

19

You did a good job with DeAnn,' I told Mel as we headed back to Seattle.

'Thanks,' Mel said.

We didn't know it yet, but our self-congratulations at rescuing DeAnn Cosgrove were more than slightly premature. We went home. We went to bed. Breakfast at Fisherman's Terminal seemed eons in the past, and we had missed having dinner altogether, but I was too tired to be hungry. I fell into bed and was asleep almost immediately. When the phone rang at two-twelve I was so far off in la-la land that I tried to shut off the alarm instead of answering the phone.

'Mr. Beaumont?'

I hadn't spoken to DeAnn Cosgrove all that often, but even half asleep I recognized her voice in the urgent whisper on the other end of the line. 'Are you all right?' I asked at once.

'I'm at the house,' she said. 'Donnie's here, too. I can see him through the window. He's asleep on the couch.'

My heart constricted inside my chest. DeAnn was at the house and so was Donnie. In my mind's eye I could foresee the worst of all possible outcomes.

'What in the world are you doing there?' I demanded. 'I thought I told you — '

'I was worried about him,' DeAnn continued

299

hurriedly. 'I left the kids in Issaquah and drove by the house just to see if Donnie might have come home. And he did. His Tahoe is right here on the street where he usually parks it. His gun's there, too — locked inside. I can see it on the front seat, but I don't have my own key to the Tahoe. It's still in the house. I thought about breaking the window to get at the gun, but I'm afraid that will set off the car alarm and wake him.'

Mel sat up next to me. 'What is it?' she asked.

'You say Donnie's asleep on the couch?' I said as much to Mel as to DeAnn, trying in that one sentence to calm DeAnn while at the same time bringing Mel up to speed. 'Hang up the phone, DeAnn,' I ordered. 'Get in your car and drive away. I'll call 9-1-1 and have them send someone to — '

'No,' DeAnn whispered to me. 'No way. I'm not leaving and don't call 9-1-1, either. Please. If armed cops show up here, they won't think of Donnie as the man I love or the father of my children. They'll only see a suspected killer.'

Which he is, I thought.

'Please, Detective Beaumont,' DeAnn continued. 'If you'll just talk to him, I'm sure he'll listen to you.'

I wasn't nearly as convinced of that as DeAnn was, but by then I was already pulling on my pants. Mel scrambled out of bed after me and padded down the hallway to dress.

'All right,' I agreed finally. 'I'm coming. We're coming,' I corrected. 'Mel Soames and I both. If you don't want us to call anyone else to meet us there, you have to promise me one thing.'

'What's that?'

'That you won't stay there with him by yourself. Drive down the street. Pull into someone else's driveway. You can stay close enough to keep the truck in view so you can let us know in case he wakes up and starts to leave. But you cannot — you must not — be there in the house with him alone. Understand?'

'I already told you. It's okay. His gun's out in the Tahoe in plain sight.'

I reminded myself that this was a woman who probably wouldn't know the difference between a .357 sidearm and your basic firecracker.

'What makes you think that's the only gun he owns?' I demanded. *And what about knives? I asked myself silently. How many of those does he have?*

DeAnn started to reply, then stopped. 'Donnie's my husband . . . ' she declared finally.

'Look, DeAnn,' I said, struggling to sound reasonable. 'I know he's your husband and I know you love him, but in Donnie's current state of mind, armed or not, there's a good chance he poses a danger to himself and others — you included.'

'But Donnie loves me,' she insisted. 'He'd never hurt me.'

'Don't bet on it,' I said.

Of course she was betting on it — betting her entire existence — or she would never have returned to the house in the first place.

'What becomes of your children if something happens to you?' I demanded. 'What happens to

301

them if both their parents turn up dead? Your mother's not here to step in. Do you want the state looking after your babies? Do you want Child Protective Services calling the shots for them? Think about your kids, DeAnn. They need you a whole lot more right now than Donnie does.'

I held my breath and hoped I'd made a convincing argument. About then Mel returned to the bedroom. Completely dressed, she was already wearing her Kevlar vest. She tossed mine onto the bed.

'I'm hanging up now so I can get dressed,' I told DeAnn. 'Promise me you won't go anywhere near the house. Promise?'

For an answer she pushed the button and ended the call. I threw my phone onto the bed in utter frustration while I buttoned up my shirt. 'What the hell is the matter with that woman?' I demanded. 'What does she use for brains?'

Mel ignored my outburst. 'Where's Donnie Cosgrove and where's his gun?' she wanted to know. 'And how are we going to play this?'

'Donnie's asleep on the couch. At least DeAnn *thinks* he's asleep. She claims his gun is locked in the car out on the street, but we have no idea if the one she's seeing in the vehicle is his only weapon. As far as your question about how we should play this is concerned? You tell me.'

'The way I see it, smaller is better,' Mel said. 'I'm all for understated elegance. Come on.'

In one way, she was right. Summoning an emergency response team to a quiet residential neighborhood in the middle of the night is a lot

302

like putting a huge locomotive in gear, sticking the throttle to the floor, and sending the train roaring down the rails. Like high-speed trains, once ERTs are in motion it's hard as hell to stop them. Or change their direction. Or purpose. I didn't want DeAnn's cozy little home shot through with bullets or permanently damaged with a lobbed canister of tear gas. And regardless of what he'd done, I didn't want Donnie Cosgrove shot full of bullets, either.

On the other hand, approaching a possibly armed and dangerous suspect with too little firepower and no backup is one of those fatal errors cops can make — one many officers make only once. Just ask Seattle PD's Paul Kramer.

On the way down in the elevator, Mel held out her hand. 'Give me the keys,' she said. 'I'll drive. DeAnn called you. Try to get her on the phone and keep her there. At least that way we'll know, minute to minute, exactly where we stand and can call in reinforcements if we need them.'

Mel pulled our bubble light out of the glove compartment and slapped it on the roof of the Mercedes before she even pulled out of the parking space. We exited the garage. Half a block later we turned north on First Avenue. A rain-shrouded Queen Anne Hill loomed ahead of us. Seeing it, I couldn't help but remember the last time Mel and I had set off on this kind of a fool's errand. When it was over, Heather Peters's boyfriend had been fatally wounded. It was only pure luck that Heather herself wasn't killed that night.

I glanced over at Mel as she turned onto

303

Broad. 'If you're having second thoughts . . . ' I said.

'I'm not,' she said. 'We're a lean, mean force.' With that she slammed on the accelerator and sent us racing through four stoplights in a row, clearing each intersection as the light changed from yellow to red.

'Besides,' she added, circling around to turn onto Mercer, 'if it's a choice between having you at my back or having a bunch of gun-happy SWAT guys, I'll take you any day of the week. Now get DeAnn on the phone. Let's find out what's going on.'

I picked up the phone. With Mel at the wheel, we'd either get to Redmond in a hell of a hurry or we wouldn't get there at all. I knew I was better off manning the phone than I was watching the speedometer.

'Where are you?' I asked when DeAnn Cosgrove came on the line.

'I'm doing what you said,' she told me. 'I moved my car down the street. Are you coming?'

'Yes,' I said. 'Yes, we are. We're on Mercer now, heading for 1-5.'

There was a pause before DeAnn said, 'Just because you found blood on his shoes doesn't mean he did it, you know. Isn't there such a thing as innocent until proven guilty?'

Sitting alone in the dark, I'm sure DeAnn had been replaying everything that had happened in the course of the last several days, everything that had been said.

'Yes,' I said. 'Maybe he didn't.' I was agreeing for form's sake and to keep DeAnn talking. The blood on Donnie's clothing, his bizarre behavior, his going missing. None of those spoke of innocence, but I didn't say that aloud.

'What if he goes to prison?' DeAnn asked with a despairing catch in her throat. 'What will happen to the kids and me then?'

I wanted to say, *You'll do what you have to do.* But I didn't say that, either. The idea that Donnie Cosgrove was on his way to prison was a likely possibility.

'Let Mel and me talk to him first,' I said, throwing DeAnn a reassuring bone. 'Let us get his side of what happened.'

'Just don't hurt him,' DeAnn said. 'Please don't hurt him. I don't care what he did. I still love him.'

'You've got to let us handle this, DeAnn.'

'I'm hanging up now,' she said. She did. When I tried calling back, she didn't answer.

Sick with worry and a short fourteen minutes after pulling out of the parking garage at Belltown Terrace, we turned onto the Cosgroves' quiet cul-de-sac. Unplugging the flasher, Mel pulled in front of Donnie Cosgrove's SUV and shut down the engine.

Before the Mercedes could come to a complete stop, I was out the door and racing back toward the Tahoe. There I was relieved to see for my own eyes that DeAnn was right. The blued-steel handle of a .357 Magnum lay partially visible under a folded newspaper that had been left on the passenger-side front seat. As soon as I saw the revolver, I knew for sure it wasn't the weapon that had left behind the shell

305

casing that had been found at the scene of the Lawrence double homicide. Revolvers don't eject their brass.

By then Mel had joined me on the sidewalk. 'His gun's here,' I whispered to Mel. 'As least we've got that much going for us.'

Just then there was a single flash from a pair of headlights on a car a block or so down the street. A car door slammed some distance away and running feet splashed toward us on the rain-soaked pavement.

'Thank God you really did come alone,' DeAnn said, gasping. 'I was afraid you were lying to me, that you'd bring a whole army along with you.'

I had given DeAnn Cosgrove the benefit of my very best advice. She wasn't listening to any of it. 'Go back to your vehicle,' I whispered urgently, catching DeAnn by the arm and bodily turning her. 'Or else go sit in ours and stay the hell out of the way. Let us do our jobs. Is the front door locked or unlocked?'

'It was locked when I left it,' she said, 'but I don't know if it's locked now.'

'Give me the key.'

She hesitated, so I said it again. 'The key. Give it to me.'

Reluctantly she reached into her jacket pocket and handed it over. 'This one,' she said. 'The Schlage.'

'Now get out of the line of fire.'

'What do you mean, 'line of fire'?' she yelped, her voice rising. 'You said you wouldn't hurt him. You promised. I checked on him just a minute ago. He's still sleeping. He hasn't moved.'

'Shut up!' I ordered. 'Stay the hell out of the way!'

There are essentially two ways for police officers to approach a sleeping subject. In one, you sneak up on him and try to catch him completely unawares. In the other, you come on like gang-busters. You burst in with guns drawn, breaking down doors and screaming, 'Police! Police! Get on the ground! Get on the ground!' at the top of your lungs. The second method is generally used when you have overwhelming firepower to back you up. The god-awful racket is calculated to do two things — to ratchet up the courage for all arriving officers and let them know where all the good guys are and to scare the living crap out of the unsuspecting suspect.

On the way to Redmond, Mel and I had discussed which strategy was called for in this particular situation. In view of DeAnn's claim that Donnie's gun was safely locked in his car and assuming — hoping — that was the only weapon involved, we had come down on the 'let sleeping dogs lie' side of the equation. If Donnie really was sound asleep and since we'd be entering the house with DeAnn's permission, it wasn't necessary to go breaking down doors in the process. And if we came upon Donnie quietly enough and fast enough, it seemed likely that we'd be able to subdue the man before he woke up fully and knew what was happening.

We had determined that Mel would go around to the back of the house and wait on the far side of the patio doors in case he made a break for it and tried to exit that way. Once she was in place, I'd go in through the front door and tackle him wherever he was sleeping.

That was the plan, at least. Once we arrived, we didn't stand around jawing about it before putting it into play. I nodded to Mel and off she went.

I suppose there are those who think I shouldn't have sent Mel off like that. Some people are of the opinion that if I really loved her, I would never have put her in jeopardy. The reality is this: I had and have one hundred percent confidence in Melissa Soames and her abilities. I know what she's capable of, and I know I can count on her.

With one hand resting on her Glock, she set out through the side yard to circle around to the back of the house. Rain was falling at a steady enough clip that it thrummed on the rooftops and dripped out of the gutters. I hoped the noise of the rain would help muffle the sounds of our moving footsteps. The front yard was a minefield of scattered Big Wheels and toys, and I hoped there weren't more of the same waiting in the side- or backyard to send Mel ass over teakettle. In this kind of life-and-death situation the last thing I needed was to have my partner taken out by somebody's toy fire engine or dump truck.

Wanting to give Mel plenty of time to get into position, I stayed where I was and counted to one hundred — very slowly. Only then did I move forward. Carefully. Quietly. One silent step at a time.

I eased my way up onto the porch where glass sidelights on either side of the front door offered a narrow glimpse of the living room. Pressing up to one of the windows, I saw the figure of a man lying sprawled against the back of the living room couch. One arm dangled limply over the end of the armrest with no sign of movement. On the coffee table I glimpsed the outline of a spilled booze bottle, which probably accounted for why Donnie Cosgrove was sleeping so soundly despite all the unusual activity in front of his house.

As I reached for the doorknob I knew there was a fifty-fifty chance that the door would be locked, but it wasn't. The knob turned easily in my hand. The latch let go with what was probably only a tiny click, but the sound bore an ominous resemblance to a bullet dropping into a chamber. I waited for a moment to see if Cosgrove had heard it, but there was no movement from the couch, none at all.

Grateful that the Pergo flooring didn't sag or squeak under my weight, I stepped into the tiny vestibule. On the far side of the living room I caught a glimpse of Mel through the glass of the patio door. She had yet to draw her weapon, and neither had I. If we could do the takedown without unholstering our weapons we'd all be better off — and a hell of a lot safer. Being shot by friendly fire is no benefit, especially if you're dead.

I was within three steps of the couch when DeAnn Cosgrove took Mel's and my well-thought-out plan and smashed it into a million pieces. Without any warning, she darted past me, screaming like a banshee. 'Donnie, wake up! You have to wake up!'

I tried to grab her, but she dodged out of the way. Despite the racket, though, Donnie Cosgrove didn't move; didn't even budge. And that's when I saw several empty prescription-drug containers next to an almost empty vodka bottle that had spilled most of its remaining contents on the coffee table.

Mel popped the flimsy lock on the patio door, shoved it open, and burst into the room. Kneeling beside the couch, she grasped Donnie's loose wrist. By then I had managed to grab DeAnn and hang on to her. She was screaming frantically when Mel turned to us. 'He's still alive,' she said. 'Barely. Call 9-1-1.'

From the look on Mel's face I knew the situation was serious, and there wasn't much time. I can tell you straight out that it's impossible to hold a desperately struggling woman with one hand while dialing a cell phone with the other. I finally gave up and let DeAnn loose in favor of calling the EMTs. DeAnn raced around the coffee table and fell to her knees at her husband's side, shaking him and begging him to wake up. He didn't stir.

By then it was almost three o'clock in the still of a cold March morning. I'm guessing the ambulance crew was thrilled to have something happening on their watch. They showed up in their rubber boots and waterproof jackets in something less than three minutes. When they arrived, my heart was still pounding with post-incident jitters. While I attempted to keep a shaken and sobbing DeAnn out of the EMTs' way, they slapped Donnie onto a gurney. They wheeled him out to the waiting aid car. With a burst of noisy sirens the ambulance took off, headed for Evergreen Hospital a few miles away.

At the time they were leaving, there was no way to know if a stomach-pumping procedure would do the trick or if Donnie Cosgrove was a goner.

'I'm going, too,' DeAnn insisted. She pulled away from me, and I let her go.

Moments later Mel and I were alone in a living room littered with the ambulance crew's debris — muddy boot prints and discarded latex gloves.

'Are you okay?' I asked.

Mel nodded. 'But you'd better take a look at this,' she said.

She was pointing at the coffee table. Next to the vodka bottle and under one of the empty prescription bottles lay a page of notebook paper covered with writing.

'Suicide note?' I asked.

'Looks like,' she said.

I moved over to the table and examined the paper without actually touching it. At the beginning of the note the penmanship was reasonably legible. Toward the bottom of the page it devolved into an illegible scrawl. The ballpoint pen still lay on the floor where it had fallen.

Honey Bun,

I didn't do it, but they'll think I did. That cop I talked to will think I killed them because I told him I was going to. I even had the gun along. My gun. But that was only because I wanted to scare the shit out of Jack Lawrence. I wanted him as scared as you were the other day. But mostly I took the gun along for protection. I was there when it happened, or right after, and the cops will be able to figure that out. They'll find my footprints there. There's blood on my clothing and on my shoes. I never knew there could be so much blood. It was awful.

I saw the car of the guy who did it — at least I think it was his car. I watched him drive away. You've got to believe me when I tell you they were already dead when I got there. I checked. That's how the blood got all over me, but there was nothing I could do to help them, God help me. Nothing.

I know I should have called right then and reported it. But there was so much blood that I just panicked. I was scared and couldn't think straight. I just wanted to get away. And when that detective came to the house this morning to tell you what had happened, it just got worse and worse. By not reporting it to begin with, that was one lie. And by not saying anything then, that was another.

I'm sorry . . . and you and the kids . . .

The note ended its illegible scrawl in midsentence. It was unsigned.

'What do we do about this?' Mel asked.

'We call Detective Lander over in Chelan and let him know that we've got Donnie. He may not be our suspect, but he is a potential eyewitness.'

'If he lives,' Mel muttered. 'And if DeAnn had listened to us and stayed away from here, he'd be dead for sure.'

About that time there was a knock — a firm, businesslike knock — on the door and a uniformed Redmond cop entered the room.

'We understand there's been a disturbance here,' he said. 'Maybe you two would like to tell me what's been going on.'

That took time. Local jurisdictions do not look kindly on other law enforcement agencies conducting raids or investigations of any kind on their turf without letting the home team know what's happening. We showed the patrol officer our SHIT ID. We told him what had transpired. It made no difference. Not only was the responding officer not impressed, he was offended. The patrol officer's supervisor, when he arrived, was also offended. And when the desk sergeant heard about it, he was really offended. We tried explaining why DeAnn Cosgrove had summoned us instead of them, but to no avail. Nothing was going to fix it since DeAnn wasn't there to vouch for us.

At three forty-five I finally admitted defeat and did what I should have done to begin with. I called Harry I. Ball at home and woke him up.

He arrived on the scene in fifty minutes flat — all the way from the far side of North Bend. We gave him the shorthand version of what had happened.

'Fair enough,' he said. 'You've told them all this?' he asked, nodding in the direction of the assembled local yokels.

'Several times,' I answered.

'You two go on home, then,' Harry told us. 'Leave this to me. I'll kick ass and take names later.'

Mel and I retreated to the Mercedes. As we drove away we could hear Harry bellowing into his cell phone at some poor hapless soul or other.

'There are occasions when Harry I. Ball can be annoying as hell,' Mel observed, 'but there are other times when you've gotta love the guy.'

This was definitely one of the latter.

20

As we drove across the 520 Bridge, it was 5:00 A.M. The early-bird morning commute was already under way, and Mel and I were both starving.

Twenty-four-hour dining has almost gone the way of the dodo bird in downtown Seattle, with the notable exception of the Five Point Café at Fifth and Cedar. Smoking may have been abolished in Washington restaurants, but there's enough residual smoke lingering in the Five Point to make an old Doghouse regular feel right at home.

While we waited for our breakfasts I dialed DeAnn's cell phone number just to see if she had any update on Donnie's condition. She didn't. I also called Detective Lander across the mountains in Chelan to let him know what the deal was. We ate breakfast — no coffee — and then staggered home to bed. At six. In the morning. To say we were both beat is understating the obvious.

Harry I. Ball called at nine and woke us up, and I was something less than cordial. What had been downright endearing at 5:00 A.M. was a lot less lovable on three hours of sleep. When the phone rang Mel didn't even wiggle. Answering it was my responsibility.

'Time to rise and shine,' Harry bellowed into the phone, breaking my eardrum.

315

'Come on, Harry,' I said, 'have a heart. I barely got my eyes closed.'

'And I haven't closed mine at all,' he returned cheerily. 'So stop complaining. This BOLO that just came across my desk. That would be on the guy who went off to the hospital to have his stomach pumped. Right?'

'Right,' I said.

Mel turned over on her side and buried her head under her pillow.

'And what about these phone records, the ones that were faxed to me this morning? They're for Jack and Carol Lawrence up in Leavenworth — the two victims, presumably. What do you want me to do with those?'

I sure as hell didn't want to drive across the water to pick them up. 'How about faxing them over to me here in Seattle?' I asked.

'Barbara isn't here,' Harry said with a growl. 'Has to take her kid to the dentist. Faxing'll have to wait until she gets in. That probably won't be before noon.'

The truth is, Harry is one of the world's greatest technophobes, a guy who has never sent a fax in his life. His ineptitude makes me feel like a telecommunications genius. Besides, right about then, noon didn't sound half bad.

'Fine,' I said. 'Whenever.'

I put down the phone. It immediately rang again. 'This is the doorman,' Jerome Grimes told me. 'I have a Mr. Hatcher down here to see you.'

The very last thing I wanted right then was an in-house visit from Ross Connors's pet economist, but he was already there. 'All right,' I said.

'Tell him to go to the deli next door for some coffee and a bagel. Tell him we'll see him in fifteen minutes.'

Mel groaned. 'See who?' she mumbled from under her pillow.

'Todd Hatcher,' I told her, giving her a whack on her down-comforter-shrouded hip. 'Up and at 'em. The world awaits. Todd'll be here in fifteen.'

He was, too, bringing with him two extra toasted onion bagels with cream cheese — in case we were hungry. We weren't. I went to the door to let him in. Mel was still in the shower.

'You did tell me to come back on Monday, didn't you?' Hatcher asked uncertainly.

'Yes,' I said. 'I just didn't know we'd be out all night working a case, is all. Come on in and get set up. Mel will be out in a minute.'

While Todd went about taking over the kitchen counter I muddled around making coffee. Mine isn't as good as Mel's, but it's drinkable, and that's what was called for that particular Monday morning — gallons and gallons of coffee.

Mel emerged from the bedroom fully dressed, made up, and looking far better than she should have under the circumstances.

'Didn't mean to wake you,' Todd Hatcher apologized. To her. I noticed he hadn't bothered apologizing to me.

'It's okay,' Mel said. 'We had to get up anyway. What have you got?'

'I spent most of the weekend working on my copies of the abstracts,' he said. 'I've gone over all but two of them and input most of my

317

observations. If you two could sit down and work on the rest of them this morning . . . '

That seemed unlikely to me. On less than three hours of sleep, I wasn't going to be in the best condition to go searching for tiny discrepancies in a stack of old dead files. Mel gave me a look, took her stack of paper and her cup of coffee, and settled down in the window seat to go to work. I was saved by a phone call from Detective Lander over in Chelan.

'Any word on Donnie Cosgrove?' I asked.

'Not since he got to the hospital. I tried checking, but the hospital wouldn't give me any info.'

Welcome to the world of patient privacy.

'I have DeAnn's cell phone number,' I told him. 'I'll try reaching her. When they hauled Donnie away in the ambulance, it didn't look too promising.'

'What do you think about this supposedly suicidal non-confession?' Lander asked. 'Do you think he really wasn't involved in the Lawrence homicides, or was he just trying to throw us off?'

I had been in the room and had seen the note Donnie had left behind as the drugs and booze took effect.

'I think Donnie Cosgrove really did mean to kill himself,' I responded.

'Does that mean he meant the rest of the note as well?' Lander asked.

'Maybe,' I said. 'He doesn't claim to have witnessed the actual shooting. He says he saw a vehicle that could have been the killer's drive away. At this point, even a description of the vehicle would give us a big leg up.'

'You'll check on Cosgrove and let me know if and when I can come talk to him?' Lander asked.

'Will do,' I said.

'In the meantime, Ross Connors came through like a champ. The phone records we ordered yesterday were on my desk when I showed up this morning. Have you seen yours yet?'

The fact that Tim Lander was absolutely focused and on task annoyed the hell out of me. Obviously he hadn't spent the whole night traipsing back and forth across Lake Washington.

'Not yet,' I said.

'They're pretty interesting,' he continued. 'They go along in a pretty predictable pattern. Most of the time the Lawrences were calling the same numbers and the same people over and over. That lasted right up until early last week. After that, we've got a bunch of calls that haven't shown up on the records before. Who was that guy you mentioned to me yesterday, the one you'd said you'd left a message for but he hadn't called you back?'

'Dortman,' I said. 'Thomas Dortman. Why?'

'Because I have a whole series of calls from Jack Lawrence to Thomas Dortman starting first thing on Tuesday morning.'

'That would be the day after I first talked to DeAnn.'

'Like I said, there are no calls at all to this Dortman character until Tuesday morning. Then there are eight, nine, ten calls altogether from

Jack Lawrence's cell phone. Why were you looking at Dortman again?'

'Because in the process of reexamining Tony Cosgrove's disappearance, I came across an article by Dortman that mentioned Tony by name.'

'This Tony guy is DeAnn's father, the one who disappeared back when Mount Saint Helens blew?'

'That's right,' I replied. 'Dortman mentioned Tony as a possible whistle-blower. I wondered if there might be some connection between them. They both worked at Boeing around the same time, so I thought maybe they knew each other there or worked in the same department. I also wondered if there might be a relationship between Tony's possible whistle-blowing activities and his disappearance.'

'Which you're thinking may not have had anything at all to do with a volcano?' Lander asked.

'Exactly. So we probably do need to talk to Dortman. I have a phone number but no street address.'

'I have his number, too,' Lander said. 'In fact, I already tried calling it. No answer. I left a message. If he didn't get back to you, I probably won't hear from him either. I have his street address, but I don't know how much good that'll do. The one other oddball phone call was placed to a number in Portland to a phone listed to someone named Kevin Stock. That one — and there was only one — was made on Saturday morning from the Lawrences' home phone.'

I know Tim Lander was talking, but I wasn't really paying strict attention. Suddenly I had another idea.

'Hold on a second,' I said into the phone. Then I called over my shoulder to Mel. 'Hey, Mel, when you looked up Thomas Dortman the other night, didn't you tell me he had a book coming out sometime soon?'

'Something about whistle-blowers,' Mel replied. 'You're right. I think it's due in bookstores sometime in the next several weeks. If you need the exact date, you can always check on Amazon.'

'Give me a little time,' I told Lander. 'Maybe I can figure out a way to get in touch with our friend Dortman.'

When I put down the phone, Mel was staring at me. 'What?' she said.

'Supposing you were someone who had cut a corner here and there in the past. Supposing you'd done something really wrong, but as far as the world was concerned, you'd gotten away with it clean. So you're free as a bird, with nothing but a guilty conscience. Then, all of a sudden, out of the blue, you get a call from some guy who says he works for the Washington State Attorney General's Office. Would you be eager to call him back?'

'Not me,' Mel said.

'Me either. But what do authors need more than anything else?'

Mel wasn't at the top of her game either. 'I give up,' she said finally.

'Publicity?' Todd Hatcher asked.

'Bingo,' I said. I scrolled down my outgoing calls and handed Mel my phone. 'Here's the number, but call him on your phone, not mine. Tell him you're writing a magazine article or a newspaper article or something and you want to review his book. Tell him you're working on a deadline and don't have time to go through his publicity department.'

'What good will that do?' Mel wanted to know.

'You make an appointment to talk to him, only we show up instead.'

Mel was shaking her head and giving me one of her glowers when Todd took the phone from me and said, 'I'll do it.'

He did, and he did a credible job of it, too, leaving a message that was flattering enough that I figured no author in his right mind would be able to resist. In the meantime I took my own phone back and called DeAnn Cosgrove. She sounded more with-it than I would have expected, and certainly more connected than I was feeling about then.

'J. P. Beaumont,' I said when she answered. 'How are things?'

'Better,' she said. 'The doctor was here just a little while ago. They're going to keep him until later on today, maybe even until tomorrow. For observation.'

For a psychological evaluation, I thought. That's standard procedure with attempted suicides.

'Is he well enough to answer questions?' I asked.

DeAnn stalled. 'I don't think — '

'You know about the note he left, don't you?' I interrupted.

'I know there was a note,' she said. 'I haven't seen it.'

'Your husband admitted being at the scene of the crime,' I said. 'It's possible he saw the killer drive away after that person shot your mother and stepfather. We need to talk to Donnie. We need him to tell us what he saw.'

'This isn't some kind of trick? I mean, if he's still a suspect, shouldn't he have a lawyer here when he talks to you?'

'Your husband isn't a suspect at this point,' I said. 'He's not even a person of interest. As a potential witness he doesn't need a lawyer.'

'You're sure? I mean, he had his gun there and everything.'

I was losing patience. 'Whoever killed your mother and stepfather fired a pistol,' I said. 'Your husband's .357 is a revolver. Unless Donnie has another weapon none of us knows about, he can't have been the shooter. Now, can Mel and I come over and ask him some questions?' I asked. 'Please?'

'Okay,' DeAnn said at last. 'I guess it'll be all right.'

I closed the phone. 'Okay,' I said to Mel. 'Come on. Let's go talk to Donnie Cosgrove.'

'What about me?' Todd asked.

'Keep working,' I said. 'There's fresh coffee in the pot. We'll be back.'

'And what if that Dortman guy calls to set up an interview?'

'Tell him where and when and then call us,' I

said and gave him the number.

It was daytime. Since we didn't need to get to Kirkland in a hell of a hurry, I drove. At the hospital, when we located Donnie Cosgrove's room, he was still hooked up to an IV. Looking haggard, DeAnn hovered on the far side of the bed.

'This is Mr. Beaumont,' she said as we approached. 'I think you talked to him on the phone. And this is his partner . . . '

'Melissa Soames,' Mel supplied easily, holding out her hand. 'Most people call me Mel.'

In the heat of the moment, when we'd been milling around in the Cosgroves' living room, summoning EMTs and trying to determine whether Donnie Cosgrove was going to live or die, I hadn't taken the time to look at him very closely. Now I did. Propped up in his hospital bed, I realized he was a big man, in a flabby, flaccid kind of way. And the distended veins on his nose spoke of a man with a more-than-nodding acquaintance with the sauce. I've spent enough time with boozers and ex-boozers to read the signs — as in, it takes one to know one.

'They're the people who saved your life last night,' DeAnn continued.

'No,' Mel corrected. 'That's not true. The person who saved your life is your wife. When everyone else was busy giving up on you, when everyone else was telling her to stay away, DeAnn insisted on coming back to check on you. If she hadn't, we'd be talking about a successful suicide here, not an attempted one.'

'I'm sorry I made such a mess of things,'

Donnie said to DeAnn. 'Sorry I put you through so much . . . '

'Hush,' she said. 'It's okay. It doesn't matter. They need to talk to you is all. Need to ask you a few questions.'

'What kind of questions?' Donnie asked.

'Tell us about Saturday — everything about Saturday.'

'I'd been thinking about Jack ever since he showed up at the house on Thursday. It just burned me up that he could come over and raise hell like that and get away with it. I wanted him to know that wasn't okay, and I wanted to get a little of my own back. Saturday I decided I was going to go give him a piece of my mind. I told DeAnn that I had some work to do at the office, even though I didn't, and when I left the house I put my .357 in my pocket. Did you ever meet Jack Lawrence?'

The question seemed to be directed at me. 'No,' I said. 'I never met the man.'

'He was a big guy — bigger than me — and very tough. I'm not exactly awash in muscles. I may not be a ninety-pound weakling, but close enough. So I took the gun along, sort of to even things out between us, if you know what I mean. To buck up my courage a little bit. And on my way there I stopped off a couple of times for a beer or two.'

'As in liquid courage?' I asked.

He nodded. 'But it didn't work. Not really. When I got there I was so nervous I couldn't drive up the road. I parked at their turnoff instead.'

'Parked and chewed gum?' I asked.

'Nicorette,' he said. 'I'm trying to stop smoking.'

So much for our possible DNA ID from the chewing gum, I thought. 'What happened then?' I asked.

'The beer,' he said. 'I was just sitting there thinking about him and then I fell asleep. Something woke me up — I'm not sure what. Maybe it was the gunshots. Anyway, I woke up with a start and was sitting there trying to get my bearings and think what to do next when this car comes barreling out of Jack and Carol's driveway. Scared the crap out of me. I thought Jack had seen me and was coming out to clean my clock. I was grabbing for my gun to defend myself when the driver turned in the other direction and took off like a bat out of hell.'

'What kind of car?'

'An '04 Lincoln LS,' Donnie said. 'Silver. I didn't see the plates.'

I was surprised. Most people are lucky to remember the color. The make, model, and year was way more than I expected.

'Donnie knows cars,' DeAnn put in. 'He's already teaching the boys which are which when they come on TV.'

'What happened next?' Mel asked.

Donnie bit his lip, and for the first time in the whole encounter he clearly didn't want to talk anymore.

'What?' I pressed.

'Nothing,' he said finally, not looking at DeAnn when he answered. 'That's what's so bad

— why I feel so guilty. I sat there in the car for a while. I mean, I didn't have any way of knowing something awful had just happened, so I sat there and had another beer or two — thinking things over. If I had gone right then, when it first happened, maybe I could have helped them. Maybe it would have made a difference. But when I got there and found them, it was too late. There was so much blood that I just couldn't think straight.'

And suddenly, like a flashbulb going off in my head, I knew why Donnie Cosgrove hadn't come forward at the time, why he had staggered around in Jack and Carol Lawrence's blood without bothering to report the shootings to anyone. He wasn't thinking straight because he was drunk.

'And you were afraid if you called the cops they'd either think you had done it or give you a DUI,' I said accusingly. 'Or both.'

Donnie Cosgrove gave me a baleful look and nodded. 'I already have one,' he admitted.

Even though I had already figured out the lush part, his admission made me mad as hell. DeAnn deserved better. Their three kids deserved better. It made me want to pick Donnie up out of his sickbed and toss him through the nearest window.

'I think we're done here,' I said.

With that I turned and left the room. A few minutes later Mel joined me in a covered breezeway.

'What the hell were you thinking walking out like that? You didn't even bother asking him if he'd seen the shooter.'

'Had he?' I asked.

'No, but — '

'That's what I figured. That's why I left — and to keep me from flattening the drunken bum's nose.'

'I don't understand . . . ' Mel began.

'Of course you don't. But I do. Donnie Cosgrove is a self-important bastard with a gorgeous wife and three little kids who all think he walks on water. And why shouldn't they? He's told them so. He's got an education and a good job. But he's too busy drowning his nonexistent sorrows on the weekends to pay any attention to them. And when he came across Jack and Carol Lawrence's bodies, he was too damned drunk to do the right thing.'

'But I thought DeAnn told us he hardly ever went out drinking like that,' Mel said. 'That he loved spending time at home with her and the kids.'

'Of course she told us that,' I said. 'She wants to convince everyone her life is perfect, even if the first person she has to convince is herself. As for Donnie, he'd rather commit suicide than face up to his own mistakes. Talk about a worthless excuse for a human being.'

We were out in the parking lot by then. Naturally it was raining. Again.

'Don't you think you're being a little harsh about this?' Mel wanted to know. 'A little judgmental?'

Maybe she was right. Maybe Donnie Cosgrove's failures as a husband and father too

328

closely mirrored my own. Maybe that's what set me off.

'Not nearly judgmental enough,' I shot back at her. 'Believe me, I recognize the symptoms. I've been there, done that, and I've got the T-shirt.'

21

We were almost back to 405 before either one of us spoke again. Mel was the one who broke the silence. 'If Cosgrove was that drunk, do you think there's any validity to the vehicle description he gave us?'

I could remember having momentary flashes of clarity like that in the middle of royally tying one on. I also knew there were times when I had driven home blind drunk with no memory of how I got there. It's not something I'm proud of, and it's something I make an effort to remember rather than forget.

'The man's an engineer,' I said. 'The vehicle ID may very well be accurate.' I tossed Mel my phone. 'We'd better let Tim Lander know. His number is in there somewhere. Look for a 509 area code in the dialed calls.'

Detective Lander didn't answer, so Mel left a message.

'Try Todd,' I suggested. 'Let's see if Dortman called him back.'

'He did,' Hatcher was saying when Mel turned my cell phone on speaker. 'I just got off the phone with him. He said he couldn't do an interview today because he's been called out of town and is on his way to the airport. He gave me the number for his publicist in New York and suggested we arrange to do what he called a 'phoner' later. Sorry I didn't do better,' Hatcher added.

'Wait a minute,' I said. 'He called you from a cell phone?'

'Yes. Like I said, he's on his way to the airport.'

'Give me that number.'

Mel pulled out her own phone. Because she's a woman and, as she's told me many times, can do more than one thing at once, she held one phone to her ear with her left hand and keyed the number into her own phone with the other.

'Mr. Dortman,' she said when he answered, 'Melissa Soames with Special Homicide. We're looking into a pair of homicides that happened up in Leavenworth over the weekend. If you don't mind, we'd like to ask you a few questions.'

Sugar wouldn't have melted in her mouth. 'Oh, that's quite all right, Mr. Dortman. We're near the airport right now. Tell us where we can find you. Just a few questions. I'm sure you'll have no problem making your flight. In the Alaska Board Room? Sure. That's great. I know where it is.'

I had already hit the gas pedal. We were in fact nowhere near Sea-Tac Airport, but we would be soon.

'He couldn't resist,' Mel said. 'I love crooks. They always think they're smarter than we are, and they always want to know what we know.'

My phone rang. Mel put it on speaker before she answered. 'Bingo!' Tim Lander shouted. 'Dortman has an '04 Lincoln LS. How did you figure that out?'

'Donnie Cosgrove,' I told him. 'That's the vehicle he saw driving away from the crime scene in Leavenworth on Saturday. Dortman is on his way to the airport right now, and so are we. Do some digging on him if you can. Call us if you find out anything more.'

Sometimes I long for the old days when telephones couldn't touch you in a vehicle. On the other hand, I'm glad we have them. I was especially happy about that when Tim Lander called back a few minutes later, long before we'd even reached the S Curves in Renton.

'I'm headed over the mountains right now,' Lander said. 'Guess who has a license to carry? Our friend Dortman is the proud owner of a nine-millimeter Beretta, which would be consistent with that one piece of brass we found.'

'Which, with any kind of luck,' Mel said, 'he won't have on him at the airport.'

One can always hope. Even sworn police officers have a tough time getting through security with handguns these days.

'I'm in my car and headed in your direction right now,' Lander said. 'When I get to Sea-Tac, I'll call for an update. Or you call me.'

'What are we going to ask Dortman once we find him?' Mel asked me.

'We try to catch him in a lie. First we ask him whether or not he was in Leavenworth on Saturday night. Depending on how he answers the first one, we ask him whether or not he knew Jack and Carol Lawrence. If he lies about either one, he's not flying today. But what do you think are the chances that he won't be waiting for us in the Board Room?' I asked.

'I think the chances for that are excellent,' Mel returned. 'So we won't bother looking for him there. We'll find out which plane he's due to fly out on and catch up with him at the gate.'

That seemed unlikely. I've tried to get information out of airlines before. I've tried getting information about my own kids. Good luck with that. Airline personnel do not like giving out information of any kind. At least they don't like giving it to me. Which is why I let Mel out at the departing passenger door and went to park. If gaining passenger information was a tough score, I knew that convincing a ticket-happy port police officer that my Mercedes 500 was parked in the curb lane on official police business was even less likely.

Bent on catching Mel, I was hotfooting it across the sky bridge toward the terminal when my phone rang. I grabbed it out of my pocket, thinking it would be Mel telling me where she was and where I should go. It was Ralph Ames.

'It's taken me all morning to finally put together a conference call with the detectives down in Cancún and my translator in Phoenix,' he told me. 'You'd think I was trying to broker a Middle East peace agreement.'

'I'm a little busy right now, Ralph,' I said. 'Can I call you back?'

'Sure, but here are the high points. I've talked them into faxing you a copy of the ballistics information on the bullet taken from Richard Matthews's body. They'll be sending that to you at your office. But here's the kicker. You'll never guess who their main person of interest is. The cops in Cancún say they're looking for a nun, a Catholic nun. Matthews and an unidentified sister were seen walking together on the beach shortly before he disappeared.'

Another nun! I stopped in midstride. A woman behind me, pushing an overloaded luggage cart, almost ran me down. 'Did you say a nun?'

'Yes,' Ames answered. 'A fairly young nun, early thirties at the most. I thought you'd be glad to hear it. You can call Mel Soames a lot of things, but a nun isn't one of them. I asked for a composite, but they evidently don't have one.'

At the moment I seemed to have unidentified nuns coming at me from all directions, and call waiting was buzzing in my ear.

'Look, Ralph, I've gotta go. But thanks. I'll get back to you as soon as I can.' I switched over. 'You found him?' I asked.

'Come to security at the main C Concourse gates,' Mel said. 'Look for the first-class passenger and crew line. I've got someone here from TSA who'll walk us through.'

If I had been with Mel instead of parking the car, I might have discovered how she worked that incredible piece of public relations magic. Not only had she charmed Dortman's flight information out of someone at the ticket counter, she had also enchanted a member of one of the least cooperative law enforcement agencies on the planet, the Transportation Security Administration, into helping out as well. That wasn't magic — it was downright miraculous.

When I came into the ticketing concourse, my heart fell. The crush of people waiting to clear security stretched all the way across the lobby. But I did as I was told and looked for the first-class line. There, next to a much shorter but still long line, I found Mel standing beside a wiry old geezer who looked more like a Wal-Mart greeter than a law enforcement officer.

When I caught up to them, Mel introduced him as Darrell Cross. Cross nodded curtly in my direction, spoke briefly into his walkie-talkie, and then opened a chain into one of the maze-like sorting areas and led us straight to the front of the line. While we were placing our shoes and weapons in the security trays, I leaned over to Mel. 'Lady, when you're good, you're good. How the hell did you pull this off?'

'If I told you, I'd have to kill you,' she said with a smile.

We did have to show our IDs, but to my amazement there was no hassle about our carrying weapons or handcuffs, and not a word was said about our not having boarding passes.

'Okay,' Mel said once we had our shoes back on. 'Dortman's on the eleven forty-five flight for LAX. When he gets there, he's scheduled to connect with an overnight Copa Airlines flight to Caracas, Venezuela. Booked his tickets yesterday. Paid full fare.'

'In a hurry to get out of town?' I asked.

'Do you think?'

The whole time we'd been going through the search procedure, Mr. Cross had been speaking into his walkie-talkie. 'Okay, Ms. Soames,' he said, leading us in the direction of the D gates, 'I've talked to baggage. They've got Mr. Dortman's baggage isolated. If he doesn't fly, neither will his luggage.'

A guy from TSA was doing all this? That absolutely put me in my place and made me realize Mel Soames was even more out of my league than I had thought.

As we approached the gate area I didn't think it would be difficult to recognize Thomas Dortman. I had never seen any of his on-air commentary, but he had posted his photo all over his Web site. He was seated at the end of the bank of seats nearest the ticket agent's counter and the door leading out to the jetway. He huddled there with his back to the window, looking as inconspicuous as possible.

His Web site photos must have been either very old or Photoshopped into the male equivalent of Glamour Shots. The man depicted there had been younger and far leaner than this one. He also had a full head of hair. This one was jowly and slightly balding. He also looked haggard and bleary-eyed — as though he hadn't slept in several days.

I could see we were arriving just in time. The departure door was already latched open and the gate agent was preparing to make her first boarding announcement. The nod she gave to Mr. TSA Walkie-Talkie indicated he had been in contact with her as well. Despite his unassuming appearance, Mr. Cross was obviously a go-to kind of guy.

Without any discussion, Mel and I approached

Dortman from either side, effectively boxing him in.

'We somehow missed each other in the Board Room, Mr. Dortman,' Mel said, casually flashing her ID in his direction. 'I must have misunderstood.'

The gate agent made her announcement. Dortman started to rise. 'You'll have to excuse me,' he said. 'They're calling my flight.'

'Have a seat, Mr. Dortman,' Mel said. 'You paid full fare. If you miss this flight, you can always rebook.'

Unhappy about it, Dortman sat while nearby passengers studied us with open curiosity. Beads of sweat suddenly popped out on the man's forehead.

Mel slipped onto the seat next to him. 'So is your publisher putting out a Spanish edition of *The Whistle-blower's Guide?*' she asked conversationally.

Dortman looked at her as though she were nuts. 'No,' he said. 'Why?'

'With a book coming out a few weeks from now, I'd think you'd need to be available for interviews and appearances. Won't that be difficult to do from so far away, especially since you didn't bother to book a return flight?'

'I have a meeting with a source in Caracas,' he said indignantly. 'For my next book. In addition, my flight information is supposed to be confidential. You have no right to — '

It was time for me to step up. 'When's the last time you saw Carol and Jack Lawrence?' I asked.

'Who?' he returned.

337

'Wrong answer, Mr. Dortman,' I said.

I nodded toward Cross, but it wasn't necessary. He was already picking up his walkie-talkie. 'Okay with the luggage,' he said. 'Take it off the cart and bring it to my office.'

'My luggage!' Dortman yelped. 'You can't touch my luggage. You don't have a warrant.'

'*They* can't touch your luggage,' Cross said pleasantly, glancing at Mel and me. 'But I can, particularly if there's a chance a traveler's luggage will be on a flight when he isn't.'

'But I haven't missed my flight,' Dortman objected.

Darrel Cross smiled. 'I believe you're about to,' he said. 'You need to come with us, Mr. Dortman.'

For a second or two, I thought Dortman was going to bolt and make a run for the jetway. Not that it would have done him any good, but desperate people can make some pretty stupid decisions at times. In the end he thought better of it. He shrugged and stood.

I was about to ask him to put his hands behind him. 'This is my jurisdiction, Mr. Beaumont,' Cross said. 'If you don't mind, we'll do the honors, but you're welcome to read him his rights.'

Two more TSA agents appeared out of nowhere, patting Dortman down and cuffing him. You would have thought that, having cleared airport security, Thomas Dortman would have been unarmed. That wasn't true, however. In the pocket of his jacket they found a plastic cheese knife that, wielded properly, could have done a good deal of damage to soft body tissue.

Dragging Dortman's two fully loaded pieces of carry-on luggage with us, Mel and I followed Dortman and his TSA contingent back down the concourse and out past security. On the way, my phone rang. It was Lander.

'What's happening?' he asked.

'We've got him,' I said. 'He's in custody. TSA has him for carrying an unauthorized weapon through security, but you'd better come up with probable cause pretty damned quick. I'm guessing he'll be lawyered up before we ever get to the TSA office. That's where we'll be talking to him.'

I've seen jail cells more welcoming than Darrell Cross's windowless hole of an office. It was carved out of otherwise wasted space between a men's restroom and the back of an abandoned ticket counter and furnished with grim gray-green federal building castoffs. Two enormous suitcases were tucked into one cramped corner of the room. We took seats around a scarred Formica-topped conference table. One of Darrell Cross's TSA minions removed Dortman's cuffs.

Had he called for a lawyer, we would have gotten him one. And had an attorney appeared, his first bit of advice would have been for Dortman to shut the hell up. But no attorney had been summoned, and by the time we seated ourselves around the battered tabletop, Dortman was in tears.

'I didn't mean to,' he blubbered, lowering his head onto his arms.

Sure, I thought. *Firing off that whole barrage of shots was an accident. So was going around the crime scene collecting your brass.*

Fortunately for all concerned, I kept my mouth shut. Sitting behind his battle-worn desk, Darrell Cross seemed content to let Mel and me take over the questioning process. 'Maybe you'd like to tell us about it,' she suggested.

'Jack was going to go public,' Dortman said. 'He was going to spill his guts.'

'About what?' Mel asked.

Here it comes, I thought. *I'm finally going to find out what really happened to Tony Cosgrove.*

'Jack was completely paranoid,' Dortman continued. 'Once someone started looking into his wife's ex-husband's death, Jack said he was sure they were going to come after us, too. I tried to tell him that the statute of limitations had run out long ago and there was no way for anyone to lay a glove on us. He was retired. Since I'm still working, I was the one who'd get hurt in the deal. If I got linked back to that whole scandal thing, that would be the end of my credibility.'

'What scandal thing?' I asked.

Dortman shook his head. 'There was so damned much money floating around,' he said. 'Those were the days when planes didn't get sold unless someone's palm got greased. Since Jack was in sales, he knew all about the kickbacks. We figured out a way to skim some off the top. Not very much, in the big scheme of things, but enough.'

'Enough for Jack Lawrence to retire early?'

340

Dortman nodded. 'I would have been all right, too, but I got caught up in the dot-com bubble. Lost my shirt. And I'm still working. So when Jack threatened me, I had to do something. I tried to convince him to keep quiet. When I went to talk to him about it, he came after me. What happened was really self-defense. All I was doing was protecting myself.'

That's why Carol Lawrence was shot in the back, you little shit, I thought. *You were protecting yourself.*

'What about Tony Cosgrove?' I asked.

'What about him?' Dortman returned. 'He went fishing. The mountain blew up. End of story.'

'Was he involved in the skimming?' I asked.

'He figured it out,' Dortman said.

'And he was going to tell? I believe that's what you said in the article you wrote. I read it in some obscure engineering magazine or other.'

'I never should have mentioned his name,' Dortman murmured.

'True,' I agreed. 'You shouldn't have, but you did. So what happened?'

'I was out of the country when that all came down. For all I know, maybe Jack did get rid of him, but I had nothing to do with it.'

Being accused of three homicide charges is only marginally worse than two. I let that one go.

'What about Kevin Stock?' I asked. 'Who's he?'

Dortman shook his head. 'I have no idea,' he said. 'Never heard of him.'

A laser printer sat behind Mel. She reached

around to it and removed a blank sheet of paper, which she slid across the table so it came to a stop directly in front of Thomas Dortman.

'Maybe you'd like to write some of that down for us,' she said, passing him a pen as well. 'Just to be clear.'

That little byplay seemed to be enough of a reality check to snap Dortman out of his spasm of stupidity. 'You mean, like write down a confession or something?' he asked.

Like a confession exactly, I thought.

Mel didn't reply because Dortman was already shaking his head. 'I'm not confessing to anything,' he declared. 'I want a lawyer. Now. You have to let me go.'

Darrell Cross had maintained his silence throughout the process. 'No,' he said. 'Actually we don't. Not only did you have a dangerous weapon in your possession that you carried through security, we've now x-rayed your checked luggage. We know that there's at least one weapon in there as well.'

'I have a license for that,' Dortman objected. 'A valid license to carry. I want a lawyer.'

We all knew it was a little late for a lawyer, but Darrell Cross was entirely agreeable about it. 'And you'll have one,' he said. 'With any luck, he'll arrive about the same time we have the warrant to search your luggage. You're welcome to use my phone here to call your attorney if you like. Have him meet you at the King County Justice Center down in Kent. Or, if you'd rather, you can call him from there — your choice.'

'I'll call from there,' Dortman said.

'As you like,' Cross responded.

He pressed a button on his phone console. The door opened and the two TSA officers who had brought Dortman into the office appeared once more. 'I believe Mr. Dortman here is ready to be transported.'

The guards led him away. I couldn't help feeling let down. 'I thought we were going to come out of here with a confession,' I groused. 'Right up until you passed him that paper. Then he freaked.'

'Not to worry,' Darrell Cross said with his Cheshire-cat smile. He motioned toward the clock behind him. Only then, upon closer examination, did I notice the camera lens that had been discreetly concealed inside the face of it.

'You recorded it?' I asked.

'Every bit of it,' Cross replied. 'Every single word, in full video and audio. Whenever we bring people in here, they're always complaining that we're abusing their rights. I've found it helpful to be proactive about that — to take preemptive measures, if you will. With all of us visible in the room, I think Mr. Dortman will have a hell of a time convincing anyone that it was a forced confession. Copies, anyone?'

'Yes, please,' Mel said.

And while Darrell Cross went to fetch ours, I sat there in his office and decided perhaps it was time to rethink my long-standing contempt for the TSA. Maybe Homeland Security wasn't in such bad hands after all.

22

Darrell Cross remained pleasant and cordial enough, right until Tim Lander showed up. He arrived with his legally executed search warrant in hand about the same time Darrell Cross's warrant appeared. That was when some old-fashioned TSA rigidity and noncooperation arrived on the scene as well.

Before the situation devolved into open warfare, Mel was able to finesse things enough that we were finally able to open Thomas Dortman's assorted luggage. The lid of one carry-on was stuffed with packets of hundred-dollar bills.

'Looks like he stopped by his bank this morning and closed out his accounts,' I said.

Mel nodded. 'That's probably why he hung around until Monday,' she said.

In the end Detective Lander settled for walking away with Dortman's 9-millimeter Beretta while Darrell Cross took control of everything else.

As far as Dortman's Lincoln was concerned, however, Lander held the trump card. The LS was specifically listed on his search warrant. It wasn't mentioned on Cross's. So after we left the TSA office, Lander, Mel, and I spent the next half hour walking through Sea-Tac's massive parking structure searching for the vehicle. Because local spring breaks were already in process, the garage was packed to the gills. My idea was to start on the top floors and work our way down. It was a logical-enough choice but a bad one. It turned out Dortman had used valet parking. And why not? It didn't matter how much it cost. Dortman wasn't planning on coming back, so he wasn't ever going to pay the bill, either.

In the long run, that was a benefit. Once we located the vehicle and showed the parking attendant the search warrant, he produced the keys. Lander opened the driver's door, bent down, and peered at the floor. Then he stepped back. 'Take a look,' he said.

Mel took a look herself. 'Looks like dried blood to me,' she said.

'That's what I thought,' Lander replied.

He had summoned a tow truck. He and the attendant were arguing over payment of the parking fee when my phone rang.

'You never called me back,' Ralph Ames said accusingly.

Ralph isn't someone who gets his nose out of joint easily, but this time he did sound miffed.

'Sorry,' I said. 'Mel and I have been caught up in a situation that's just now settling down.'

'So did you tell her — about the nun thing?'

'No,' I said. 'I didn't have a chance. Why don't you?'

The look on Mel's face was thoughtful as she finished the call and handed me back my phone. 'Two unidentified nuns,' she said. 'That pretty well spells it out. Richard Matthews's murder and Juan Carlos Escobar's have to be related.'

'Not two unidentified nuns,' I told her. 'Three.'

'Three,' she said. 'What are you talking about?'

'LaShawn Tompkins. Shortly before he was gunned down at his mother's front door an unidentified nun was seen lurking in the neighborhood. She was seen, but no one's been able to find any trace of her. Initially I thought she was an eyewitness, but maybe now . . .'

'A nun who goes around shooting people or running them down?' Mel asked. 'That's ridiculous.'

But I'm older than Mel Soames, and maybe I'm more cynical. Not only that, I've met enough religious nutcases that the idea of an unhinged nun didn't sound at all beyond the realm of possibility.

'It makes no sense,' Mel insisted.

'It's still a possibility,' I told her. 'And even if it's a long shot, with both you and Destry Hennessey involved, we'd better give Ross Connors a heads-up on this, too.'

She nodded. When Ross didn't answer his cell I called his office, only to be told he was locked up in a series of meetings. When those ended, he was scheduled to speak at a dinner meeting in Tacoma. I had to summon a full dose of blarney before I was able to wheedle the location of said meeting out of his secretary, but with Mel's Sea-Tac performance as inspiration, I hung in there until I finally had the name of the restaurant — Stanley Seaforts.

It's actually Stanley & Seaforts, but I didn't correct her. By then Mel and I were running on empty on both food and sleep. We had planned to go back to Belltown Terrace and call it a day. Instead we left the airport, hit I-5, and headed south smack in the middle of rush-hour traffic.

'Can't we stop somewhere and get a sandwich?' Mel complained. She was hungry enough to be downright whiny.

'Wait,' I told her. 'You'll thank me later.'

'I doubt that,' Mel said. Sulking, she folded her arms across her chest, settled into the far corner of the passenger seat, and soon nodded off, leaving me alone to do both the driving and the thinking.

The problem with tying the three cases together was that, an unidentified nun aside, they were still very different. Juan Carlos Escobar had been guilty and punished some, if not enough to satisfy some of his victim's survivors. Richard Matthews had been guilty and punished not at all — unless the bullet in his chest was some kind of latter-day payback for molesting his daughter. Fair enough. But LaShawn Tompkins hadn't been guilty at all, although now he was just as dead as the other two. There again, like it or not, another unidentified nun had been seen in the vicinity of the crime. And what about the black cloth they had found in the door of the vehicle they had dredged out of the water up by Chuckanut Drive? Surely these weren't all connected. That couldn't be.

By the time we finally exited the freeway and made our way up the hill to the restaurant, the rain had stopped and an afternoon sun break had burned through the gloom. Inside, they had started serving dinner and the early dining crowd was lining up for the cheap eats. I guided Mel into the bar, hoping that from there we'd be able to spot Ross on his way into the restaurant. As we mowed our way through two orders of crab cakes, a side of pea salad, and several cups of coffee, Mel was almost civilized again. She was also puzzling over the same question that was bothering me.

'Okay,' she said. 'Matthews clearly got away with something. To a lesser degree, so did Escobar, since the punishment didn't exactly suit the crime. It makes sense that we're dealing with a vigilante action of some kind. Other than the involvement of a nun, the only other connection between those two cases is that Destry and I are both involved in SASAC.'

I had already come to that same conclusion, and I was glad to hear Mel arrive there on her own. Under the circumstances it seemed wise to nod and say nothing more.

'But LaShawn Tompkins was exonerated,' Mel continued.

'Of that particular crime,' I said. 'What if there's another crime we don't know about? What if he got away with that one?'

'The problem with that is, if we don't know about it, how would anyone else?'

Just then a chauffeur-driven limo stopped at the front entrance. Ross Connors emerged and entered the lobby. Three stylishly dressed, power-suited women greeted him there and were about to lead him off toward a meeting room when I managed to snag him away from them.

The ladies weren't pleased to let him go, but he excused himself. On his way to join us he ordered a single-malt from the bar.

'I saw that you called,' he said. 'What's up?'

We told him what was going on. All of it, from Donnie Cosgrove and Thomas Dortman right through to our unexpected but possible linking of those three very disparate cases. When we got to the part about LaShawn Tompkins, he stood up abruptly, walked over to the bar, and ordered another drink. By the time he returned to the table he seemed to have made up his mind about something.

By then one of the ladies had returned to retrieve Ross and was standing impatiently at his shoulder. Taking the paper cocktail napkin from under his drink, he jotted a name onto it and then dropped it on the table in front of me. Two words were written there: Analise Kim.

'She works at the Crime Lab in south Seattle,' Connors said. 'We may have an evidence-handling problem there. Go talk to her.'

'Mel and I were actually talking about going on down to Olympia to see Destry — '

'No,' Connors barked, cutting me off. 'Not at this time.' With that he turned and gave his hostess a bland smile and allowed himself to be led away.

'Whoa,' Mel observed. 'Who pushed his button?'

'We did, evidently.'

Mel picked up the napkin. 'Who's this?'

'I'm not sure. I think she's an evidence clerk.'

349

'I guess we'd better go see her.'

Which we did. Once again, I drove while Mel ran the phone. We were headed for the crime lab, but fortunately she called ahead and learned that Analise Kim was currently off on leave. Nobody said what kind of leave, but the answer Mel was given raised enough red flags that she didn't hang up until she had Analise's home phone number and address. When Mel phoned there, she spoke to a Mr. Kim, who told us that his wife volunteered at the Burien Public Library Branch on Monday evenings. So we went there instead.

Walking into the library, we went straight to the lady stationed at the reference desk. It was just past seven o'clock.

'I'm looking for Mrs. Kim,' I said.

The woman smiled and nodded in the direction of one of the book stacks. 'She's over there,' the woman said. 'The woman with the cart who's shelving books.'

Partway across the room a small woman with iron-gray hair and decidedly Asian features was pushing a heavily laden wooden book cart that was nearly as tall as she was. As we approached her she pulled a Rubbermaid footstool from the bottom shelf of the cart and climbed up to return a book to a spot that was far beyond her normal reach. She was still on the stool and at my eye level when we reached her.

'Mrs. Kim?' I asked, pulling out my ID. 'I'm J. P. Beaumont with the Special Homicide Investigation Team. This is my partner, Mel Soames. Ross Connors suggested we get in touch with you.'

'That didn't take long.' She climbed off her perch, returned the stool to her cart, and shelved the next several books without needing the stool's extra elevation. Not only did she shelve returning books, Analise straightened the spines of all the other books as she went along. Clearly the woman was a perfectionist.

'Didn't take long?' I asked. 'Sorry, I'm not sure what you mean.'

'I've been complaining about this for months, but as soon as I send an attorney around, well, that gets a reaction, doesn't it.'

'Complaining about . . . ?' Mel said.

Analise Kim moved to the next section of shelves, retrieved the stool, and once again clambered up high enough to reach the topmost shelf. She returned two books and then sorted and reshelved several that must have been put away in the wrong order.

'About the hostile work environment at the crime lab,' she said in answer to Mel's unfinished question.

'Mrs. Kim,' Mel said, 'we seem to be coming in in the middle of something. If you wouldn't mind bringing us up to speed . . . '

'I like order,' Analise declared. 'I like order at work, at home, and here. That's why I come here once a week to do what I'm doing now — putting books away. I like to know that every book is where it belongs. If I don't put a book away properly, then the next person who needs it won't be able to find it. If books are just put away anywhere, what you have is chaos.'

I couldn't tell if Analise Kim was giving us a

glimpse into her basic philosophy of life or if this was something else.

'Some people aren't interested in keeping things in order,' she continued. 'Or in doing them in a timely fashion.' Pausing to straighten the spines of books that were less than properly aligned, she muttered, 'LIFO,' almost under her breath. 'That's the way we used to do it, before . . . '

I glanced at Mel, who seemed to be as mystified about all this as I was. 'Excuse me?' she said.

'LIFO,' Analise said impatiently, as though we were dim beyond bearing. 'As in Last In First Out, as opposed to FIFO — First In First Out. LIFO is how we do things here, too. When I come in, the returned books are stacked right there under the counter. The last ones to come in go back on the shelves first. And when I get to the last stack, the one in the back, I know I'm catching up. I like that. It makes me feel as though I'm accomplishing something. Not only that, the last books that come in are often the newest and the most popular — the ones with the biggest demand — so it's important to get them back out first thing.'

That pretty well clarified one thing. We really were talking about Analise Kim's philosophy of life, but we also needed to get her back on track.

'To go back to what you said before. I'm assuming LIFO is how you used to do things at the crime lab, but now something has changed and you don't do things that way anymore. Is that correct?'

'What changed is *she* came along,' Analise declared. The vehemence she put behind that single 'she' said volumes.

'By 'she,' you mean Destry Hennessey?' Mel asked.

'Oh, no. Not her,' Analise said quickly. 'But since she's in charge, she's the one who could have fixed it — the one who should have put a stop to it.'

'Who then?' I insisted.

'Yolanda Andrade,' Analise replied.

'One of your coworkers?'

'Not exactly. I'm just a clerk. Yolanda's an actual DNA analyst. So even though she's much newer, she thinks she's better than I am and she wants everyone to do things her way. When I told her that was wrong, that's when it started.'

'What started?' I asked.

'Yolanda likes to mess with me. She puts evidence kits back in the wrong place, just because she knows it drives me crazy. When I come to work she'll have moved things around on my desk — my stapler; my tape holder; my pencils. She'll put them in different places on my desk or in different drawers. Sometimes, when I put my lunch in the refrigerator in the morning, I'll come back at noon and it'll be on a different shelf. Or in the garbage.'

Watching Analise's fierce dealings with unaligned library books, I could see how this kind of harassment would drive her absolutely nuts. She was someone who required order as much as she did air to breathe.

But Ross had mentioned something about

evidence-handling irregularities.

'About the LIFO thing . . . ' I suggested.

'Yolanda is supposed to develop profiles on the most recent cases,' Analise returned. 'That's the whole reason they hired her, so the newest cases could be run through those new violent offender DNA databases. But she keeps rummaging around in the old stuff. I know, because she takes kits out of cold storage and then she doesn't return them to where they're supposed to go.'

Mel had been quiet for a while. Now she spoke up. 'What do you mean, old stuff?' she asked.

'Before the crime lab moved into the new building, they had storage facilities here, there, and the next place, and things were a mess. No one could find anything. Once we had everything gathered in one spot, it was my job to organize it. And I did. Working with years of unprocessed rape kits was no fun. I developed a system and was starting to get it organized, but then Yolanda came along and started messing around with those old evidence kits, ones from ten or fifteen or even twenty years ago. And even though I've tried talking to her about it, she hasn't stopped, and Mrs. Hennessey won't make her stop, either, probably because Yolanda is free and I'm not.'

'Free?' I asked.

'Right,' Analise said. 'Someone else, I'm not sure who, is paying her wages. Mine come out of the crime lab budget. But I'll be a lot more expensive when this is all over. I'm on leave to

354

use up the rest of my vacation. After that, I'll quit. Then I'm going to court.'

I made the connection then. Yolanda Andrade had to be the DNA profiler SASAC was paying for, the one I'd heard about on Friday night at the fund-raiser. When I glanced in Mel's direction, she was grim-faced. And I knew why. If you're going to launch a vigilante action, how much better to do it against people the cops didn't know they were looking for. Those long-stored rape kits, with their unidentified DNA profiles, would be an open book. One of those could very well lead back to LaShawn Tompkins, for example, and to many others as well. Like to any number of ex-cons whose DNA profiles had been entered into the CODIS system or into our statewide DNA database simply because they'd been locked up in our prison system. Knowing we had stumbled into something important, I felt the hair rise on the back of my neck.

'Did she ever get any hits on those old cases?' Mel asked. Her tone was easy, conversational, but I knew she was as on edge as I was.

'I never saw any,' Analise answered. 'Getting a hit is a big deal, you see. We mark them off on a board and everything. We're at 406 right now — 406 hits, that is. And once there is one, the kit is moved to a different section in the evidence room — from cold case to pending.'

'Another part of your filing system?' Mel asked.

Analise nodded.

'Tell us about it,' Mel said.

'The filing system? It's really nothing more or less than a shelf list, like the shelf lists kept by libraries everywhere. It's an inventory system — a way to tell what's missing and what isn't.'

'Except this one isn't about books,' I suggested.

'I added a few bells and whistles,' Analise said modestly.

'What kinds of bells and whistles?'

'The kits are filed by year and date,' she said. 'A year or so ago, once I got wise to what Yolanda was doing, I started keeping track. I assigned each kit its own separate number — a sort of Dewey decimal number of rape kits. And that's one of the things I did every single day — checked the shelves to see if any of my control numbers were missing.'

'And if they were?' Mel asked.

'I wrote down the kit number, noted when it left the shelf, when it came back on its own, or when I found it somewhere it didn't belong.'

'You don't still happen to have that list, do you?' Mel asked.

'Of course I do,' Analise returned. 'Not here, not with me. But at home. Would you like to have a copy?'

'Yes,' Mel said. 'It would be really helpful.'

'Fine, then,' Analise told us. 'Once I finish here we can stop by the house. But I have to finish shelving the rest of the books.'

I had just that moment fallen in love with Analise Kim and her insatiable love of order. In fact, I had to resist the temptation to reach out and smother that incredibly wonderful record-keeping woman in an old-fashioned bear hug, but that might have been as unwelcome as an improperly aligned book spine. 'We wouldn't even consider taking you away from that,' I said.

At which point my phone rang. The withering look Analise sent in my direction made it clear cell phones were an unwelcome intrusion in *her* library. I raced for the door.

'It's me,' Todd Hatcher said. 'I was hoping to talk to you. I've turned up some pretty interesting stuff today, but it's getting late. I'm about to head home.'

'You're still at Belltown Terrace?' I asked.

'Yeah,' he said. 'I ordered a pizza for dinner. Hope you don't mind.'

'I don't mind at all,' I said. 'Hope it was good. Now, did Ross Connors happen to give you access to the SHIT squad's Lexis-Nexis program?'

'No,' Todd said. 'He didn't need to. I have my own. Why?'

'Because neither Mel nor I have our computers with us at the moment, and we need a whole batch of research done in a hell of a hurry.'

'When it comes to research, I'm your guy,' Todd said. Coming from someone else it might have sounded conceited. Coming from him I suspected it was absolutely true. 'What do you need?' he asked.

'Every single thing you can find on both Destry Hennessey and Anita Bowdin. Two esses on Hennessey, and Bowdin is B-O-W-D-I-N.

357

Find whatever you can and print it.'

'No problem,' Todd said. 'I'll get right on it. When do you think you'll be here?'

'That remains to be seen,' I said. 'We've got a few things to handle on the way.'

23

I was fine while we hung around the library waiting for Analise Kim to finish her volunteer shift of shelving books. I was fine while we drove to her house to pick up a copy of her 'shelf list.' But after that, on the way back to Belltown Terrace in downtown Seattle, I fell off the cliff.

Once upon a time I could do all-nighters. I used to be able to go without sleep for seemingly days on end without it bothering me, but time has a way of catching up with a guy. On the drive north from Burien, as I fought to stay awake, I was forced to confront the fact that J. P. Beaumont is no Jack Bauer from *24*. It helped my ego that, despite Mel's relative 'youth' and the nap she had grabbed earlier in the day, Mel was struggling to stay awake, too.

The only thing that helped was talking. 'So what do we do?' Mel asked. She was clutching the papers Analise had given us.

What they contained was more a series of diagrams than an actual list. Each sheet represented one year and was covered with consecutively numbered boxes. I could see how numbering each of the rape kits in that fashion would have made it easy for Analise Kim to scan her shelves each day to see what, if anything, was missing. Annotations in some of the boxes, 'out' or 'in,' followed by dates, showed when the kit had disappeared and returned.

'As in?'

'Do we call Ross, have him send someone in to isolate all the kits that have been tampered with so they can be analyzed, or, more likely, reanalyzed?' she asked.

'Bad idea,' I said. 'As soon as we do that, we tip our hand. Once Yolanda Andrade knows we're looking into this, you can bet everyone else involved will know, too. I'm sure that's why Ross didn't want us talking to Destry, either.'

'It hurts me to think that Destry's crooked,' Mel said.

'Me too,' I said. The very idea left me feeling half sick.

'And if there have been evidence-handling irregularities in the crime lab . . . '

She didn't finish the sentence and she didn't need to. I knew exactly what she meant. That kind of scandal could jeopardize convictions that were years in the past.

'Todd's on it,' I said.

'On what?'

'He called while we were at the library. Since he was still at the house, I put him to work tracking down information on Destry Hennessey.' I paused, worried that I was venturing onto thin ice. 'I also asked him to track down whatever he could on Anita Bowdin.'

'Good idea,' Mel said, and that's all she said.

When we got to the condo Todd greeted us like an eager puppy that's been left on its own all day long. He had a fistful of papers to show us. He had stuff he wanted to talk about, and he was disappointed when I waved him off.

'Sorry, Todd,' I told him. 'Mel and I are both working on two hours' worth of sleep. Talking to us now would be a waste of breath and effort. You're more than welcome to stay over. The guest room's made up and available. Help yourself.'

And off to bed we went.

Women perform these mysterious but invisible rituals that men mostly miss. For instance, I never really understood that when Mel goes down the hall every night before we go to bed, she uses some potion or other to remove her makeup. That night, tired as she was, she went to bed without performing that little chore. And since she's usually up before I am and down the hall in her bathroom, it's usually a nonissue.

The next morning, though, I happened to wake up first, and I was shocked. Mel looked like a raccoon.

'Are you all right?' I asked when she finally blinked awake.

'Sleepy,' she said. 'Why?'

'You look like someone blacked both your eyes.'

She uttered a strangled little sound that was halfway between a whimper and a legitimate *eek*. Then she leaped out of bed and, stark naked, raced down the hall to her bathroom. The guestroom bathroom. She came back a few minutes later wrapped in a robe, carrying her clothing, and absolutely furious — at me.

'Why didn't you *tell* me Todd was sleeping over?' she demanded.

'You were right there when I told him he was

welcome to stay,' I countered.

'Yes,' she hissed back. 'But you never told me he'd *accepted!*'

In other words, the Ides of March didn't get off to the most auspicious of starts around our place. While Mel showered in my bathroom, I went out to the kitchen to make coffee. Todd was there, eating cold leftover pizza. He didn't say a word about Mel, and neither did I.

Todd gave me a choice of two different stacks of paper, one with reprints of articles on Destry Hennessey and the other, far larger, devoted to Anita Bowdin. I picked the Anita option and retreated to my recliner to go to work.

What I read to begin with was mostly one puff piece after another, many of them dealing with Anita's work in founding and maintaining the SASAC. Tired of reading the same thing over and over, I skipped to what Analise Kim would have referred to as the FIFO — First In First Out — program and skipped back to the earliest one I could find, a *New York Times* feature article that profiled a group of six exceptionally brilliant female students, all of whom had enrolled in prestigious colleges at a time when most of their contemporaries were just venturing into high school.

Anita Bowdin, daughter of a university physics professor and an insurance executive, was one of the six very young women. All of them came from upper-crust, privileged backgrounds. All of them voiced concerns about whether or not they'd be able to fit in with the older students around them. All of them expressed some worry about being able to keep up with the course work. All of them credited teachers for encouraging them to strive. I was struck by the one Anita Bowdin mentioned — Sister Helen Thomas of Sisters of the Sacred Heart School, Ann Arbor, Michigan.

So Anita Bowdin had attended a parochial school. Was that a connection? Did the fact that Anita Bowdin had attended Catholic schools as a child have something to do with the fact that a mysterious nun was somehow involved in our series of homicides?

The next media mention of Anita Bowdin came two years later, in the July 7 issue of *Ann Arbor News*, where she was mentioned in her father's obituary.

Private funeral services will be held today at 2:00 P.M. at St. Claire Catholic Church for noted University of Michigan physics professor Armand P. Bowdin, who died unexpectedly in his home late last week.

Died unexpectedly in his home. In the old days, when journalism was a more gentlemanly pursuit, those words constituted media shorthand and media newspeak for suicide. They were used primarily when either the deceased or his survivors had enough media pull that no one wanted to mention that the dead guy pulled his own plug.

The rest of the article was a mostly laudatory recitation of his educational and employment background. Anita's name came at the very end,

363

where she and her mother, Rachel Bowdin, were listed as survivors.

Those two snippets of Anita Bowdin's history were as far as I'd managed to make it when Mel finally emerged from the bedroom. She was not only dressed — she was dressed to the nines: heels, panty hose, skirt, silk blouse, and blazer. Every hair was in place. Her makeup was impeccable. In other words, she was clothed in the full armor of God and ready to take on all comers.

'All right,' she said coolly, ignoring me and looking Todd straight in the eye. 'What have we got?'

Wordlessly he passed Mel the Destry Hennessey file. She took that and a cup of coffee and headed for the window seat. For the next several mintues the atmosphere in the room was thick with tension. It was a relief when my phone rang.

'Detective Beaumont?'

'Yes.'

'Detective Donner here, Ambrose Donner with Bountiful PD. Sorry I wasn't able to get that composite from the Escobar case off to you yesterday like I said I would. Turns out I ran into, shall we say, a few difficulties.'

'I know how that goes,' I said, and I did. He meant that somebody with a wad of brass on his uniform had decided sending the composite wasn't going to happen. 'That's all right,' I added. 'I was tied up all day yesterday on another case.'

'I can send it now,' Donner said. He sounded pissed. 'Is that fax number you gave me still good?'

'Sure,' I said. 'Send away.'

'While I was at it,' Donner continued, 'I read through the case file, just for the hell of it. Did I tell you about the thread?'

'The black thread?' I asked. 'Yes, you mentioned it.'

'The Utah State Police Crime Lab did some analysis of it. They sent word to all convents operated by the Catholic Church in the state of Utah, asking whether or not one of their members had gone missing and also asking for samples of fabric used in the sisters' habits. Every single convent responded. None of them reported any of their members to be missing. There are only a few convents — eighteen, to be exact — where the nuns still wear habits. All eighteen sent fabric samples, but there wasn't a single match. Not even close. So what I'm asking is this, Detective Beaumont. Are you looking for a Catholic nun who's been reported missing? There's nothing I'd like more than to clear this case and tell the guy who's running the show here that he's all wet.'

Working with other jurisdictions involves a lot of horse-trading. They give you something, you give them something in return. Donner deserved to get something back.

'We're actually looking at the nun more as a possible doer than we are a missing person,' I said.

'No kidding,' Donner murmured.

'We've got a couple other cases here on our end where an unidentified nun has been seen in the vicinity of a homicide.'

'That would shed a whole new light on things, wouldn't it,' Donner said. 'So I'll ship you that composite as soon as we're off the phone. If you need anything else, just let me know.'

'What about the Escobar file?' I asked.

'I'll copy what I can and ship that to you as well. What about Hammond?'

'Hammond?' I asked.

'Phyllis Elaine Hammond, the old lady Escobar killed. I've got some friends at Salt Lake PD. I might be able to get that file sent to you as well.'

'That would be great,' I said.

'On one condition. Promise me that if and when you resolve this thing, you'll keep me in the loop.'

'Not only in the loop,' I said. 'I'll make sure you get credit where credit is due.'

I put down the phone and sat there waiting for the fax machine to come to life. 'Did you call Ross yet?' Mel asked.

'I was stalling on that,' I admitted. 'I'm not wild about telling him one of his favorite people, a criminalist he personally hired and mentored, is bent.'

'You'd better call him all the same,' Mel told me. 'We may think confiscating those tampered rape kits is a bad idea, but Ross Connors may think differently about that.'

'Wouldn't you like to make the call?' I offered.

'Do I look stupid or something?' Mel returned. 'Not on your life. You do it.'

So I did. While the fax machine began clicking and clacking, I dialed Ross's office and was thrilled to be told the attorney general was in a meeting.

'Any message?' his secretary asked.

'Naw,' I said. 'I'll get back to him later.'

'Coward,' Mel said when I hung up the phone.

I waited until the fax machine shot the piece of paper into the tray. Then I picked the composite up. Beneath it was a second fax, the ballistics information Ralph had managed to wheedle out of the authorities down in Cancún. I took both faxes along with me as I headed to the kitchen for a coffee refill. Mel must have emptied her mug at about the same time. I had put the composite down on the counter and was pouring my coffee when Mel joined me. She set her cup down and picked up the piece of paper. What I heard next was a sharp intake of breath.

'Damn!' Mel muttered.

'What's the matter?' I asked.

'I know her,' Mel said. 'I've seen this woman before.'

'Where?' I demanded.

'On the trip to Mexico.'

'She was there?' I asked. 'She's one of the board members?'

'No,' Mel answered. 'She's one of the pilots — one of the two pilots on Anita Bowdin's private jet.'

Life keeps reminding me that things have changed. 'The pilot was a woman?' I asked, blurting out the question without even thinking.

'Both of the pilots were women,' Mel said pointedly.

My mistake! 'What's her name?' I asked.

'I have no idea,' Mel said. 'We may have been introduced. If we were, I don't remember. A pilot is a pilot. There were two of them. They were both wearing uniforms.'

Yes, I thought, a pilot in a uniform is almost as invisible as a nun in her habit.

There were official ways to get the information I needed — grindingly slow bureaucratic ways. The situation required speed. Later on I could go back and cross the official *t*'s and dot the *i*'s. In the meantime I opened my cell phone and dialed Ralph Ames. 'Any word on the ballistics stuff I sent you?' Ralph wanted to know when he answered.

I didn't have the heart to tell him I'd only just that moment seen it. 'Not yet,' I said, 'but remember the other day, when I asked you about that flight into Cancún?'

'Sure,' Ralph said. 'What about it?'

'Can you get back to whoever gave you that information and ask for a little more?'

'That depends,' Ralph replied. 'What kind of information?'

'I need the tail number on the plane,' I said. 'I also need to know the names of the pilots — names and addresses, too, if you can get them.'

'That might be a little more difficult,' he allowed, 'but I'll see what I can do and get right back to you.'

I closed my phone. 'I don't remember asking Ralph about the flight to Cancún,' Mel said absently.

It was, as I mentioned earlier, the Ides of

March. 'It was when we were talking to him about everything else,' I said. 'It must have slipped your mind.'

Before anything more was said, Ross called me back. Now the conversation with him, one I had dreaded, came as a welcome diversion. I spent the next ten minutes telling him what I could about what was going on in the Washington State Patrol Crime Lab under Destry Hennessey's dubious leadership.

When I finished, he let out a long sigh. 'Damn,' he said. 'But you and Mel are right. Doing anything to try to secure those rape kits right now is going to set off alarms for whoever's involved. We're just going to have to leave them for the time being. And maybe when some of the dust settles, we'll be able to talk Mrs. Kim into coming back and helping us sort it all out.'

'If it gets rid of whoever's been responsible for moving her stapler, I'm sure she'll be happy to.'

'Her stapler?' Ross asked.

But call-waiting was calling. 'Sorry, Ross,' I said. 'Gotta go.'

Ralph Ames was on the other line. 'Here are the names of the pilots,' he said. 'Diane Massingale and Trudy Rayburn. The plane's a Hawker 800XP. Tail number is N861AB — that's November eight six one Alpha Bravo.'

'Excellent, Ralph,' I told him. 'What about addresses on the pilots?'

'Didn't get those,' he said. 'The FBO in Cancún might have some information on that.'

'FBO?' I repeated. 'What's that?' It sounded as though we had landed back in Analise Kim's

369

world of LIFO/FIFO.

'FBO stands for Fixed Base Operator,' Ralph explained. 'They handle ground operations for general aviation — fuel, catering, landing facilities, ground transportation, car rentals, all those kinds of things. The FBO in Cancún is called ASUR. Again, that's A-S-U-R. Got it? If the pilots purchased fuel there, they probably have a record of the credit card transaction. They would also know if there was a rental car involved and maybe even what hotel was used.'

'So FBOs are all over?'

'Sure,' Ralph said. 'There are only about three hundred airports in this country that handle commercial jet traffic, but there must be at least five thousand that serve the private, corporate, and charter-jet end of the business. Every one of them has at least one FBO. Some of them have several.'

'And they keep a record of planes that land and take off under their auspices?'

'Especially if landing fees or fuel purchases were involved,' Ralph said. 'Why? What does any of this have to do with the price of peanuts?'

'I'll tell you later, Ralph. Right now I've got to go.'

I closed the phone and turned to Todd Hatcher. 'Do you happen to have your spreadsheet handy?' I asked.

'Sure,' he said. 'Why?'

'You know what an FBO is?' I asked.

'I have no idea,' he returned.

So I explained it as well as I could, bearing in mind that I had only heard the term for the first

370

time a few minutes earlier. 'I want you to go to each of the crime scenes we know about, the ones you've been putting in. Then I want you to locate all the FBOs in the area and find out if a plane with the tail number November eight six one Alpha Bravo was anywhere in that vicinity at the time of any of our mysterious deaths. Ditto the case in Salt Lake City,' I added.

'The one I read about in the Destry Hennessey stuff?' Todd asked. 'The Escobar murder?'

'That's the one.'

'What do I say if they ask me who I am or what right I have to ask for any information?'

'Tell them you're a cop,' I told him. 'You work for the Special Homicide Investigation Team, an arm of the Washington State Attorney General's Office. And if they give you any trouble, tell them to call Ross's office and check. Tell them to call collect.'

While I had been talking to Todd, Mel had located a phone book. 'Here,' she said. 'T. Rayburn. She lives in Kent.'

'Don't pilots all have licenses?' I asked.

'I'm sure,' she said. 'They're handled by the Federal Aviation Administration. Want me to see what kind of information we can come up with? If nothing else, it would be helpful to know which is which.'

Suddenly my Belltown Terrace apartment was a beehive of activity as our mini 'task force' swung into action. With Todd using the landline to track FBOs, Mel got on her cell phone to start working her way through the powers that be at the FAA. Meanwhile, I poked away at my cell phone to dial my own favorite weapons analyst, a self-described 'gun guy' down at the crime lab, one Larry Crumb.

Larry and I go back a long way. We used to be pals — drinking buddies. And for a while, back when we were both still married, we were on each other's Christmas card list. Every year, Larry's card was a photo featuring Larry posing with some outrageous weapon or other.

'Hey, bro,' Larry said, when I identified myself. 'How's it hanging?'

Typical drinking-buddy BS. And typical drinking-buddy conversation — never say anything real.

'I'm working on a case,' I told him.

'This is not news,' he replied.

'The problem is, it crosses a few international lines,' I explained. 'Like between the U.S. and Mexico. I have the ballistics workup that was sent from the crime scene, and I'm trying to figure out a way to run it through NIBIN.'

'No can do,' Larry returned. 'NIBIN would be the National Integrated Ballistics Information Network. Nobody's calling it the International Whatever, if you get my meaning.'

'I understand that,' I said. 'And I don't want to rattle cages, but I think the case from Mexico leads directly back to at least one case and maybe several more here in the States. If you could just walk this past — '

'Look, Beau,' he said. 'You don't hang around the crime lab much these days, but I can tell you, it's hell. When Destry Hennessey comes riding through here on her broom, we all run for cover. If she finds out I'm doing an unauthorized analysis on her equipment and on her watch, she'll have my balls — and my job.'

In other words, Analise Kim wasn't the only pissed-off employee at the Washington State Crime Lab. There were other avenues I could have used, but those would have taken more time. And lots more documentation. The material I had in hand through Ralph's unofficial efforts would have to be reobtained, this time going through channels and across desks, something that would take time — a commodity we didn't have. So I punted.

'As it happens,' I said, 'Destry Hennessey could be part of the problem.'

'Whoa!' Larry Crumb exclaimed. 'Bring down what you have, then. Let's see what I can do.'

24

Because Mel had commandeered my bathroom, I had been trying to work while still lounging around in my robe — not a good plan. Now I went to shower and dress. By the time I emerged, Mel was still arguing with the FAA, but Todd had a hit.

'I'm on the phone with Million Air in Salt Lake City,' he said gleefully, holding one hand over the telephone receiver as he spoke to me. 'Their records show tail number November eight six one Alpha Bravo was tied down there from October 9 through October 11, 2003. They flew out the morning of October 12.'

I couldn't help but notice how quickly Todd Hatcher had caught on to the FAA lingo, and we both knew that Juan Carlos Escobar had been released on his twenty-first birthday, October 10, 2003. 'Do we have any idea who all was on the plane?' I asked.

Todd held up his hand. 'You can't?' he said. 'I just want to . . . But . . . All right, then. Someone will have to get back to you.'

'What happened?' I asked.

'They blew me off. I wanted to know if they had any details about the passengers or pilots, but they said they can't or won't provide that information, not without a warrant.'

'When Mel finishes with the FAA, put her on it,' I advised. 'Either she'll figure out a way to

374

worm the information out of them, or she'll figure out a way to come up with enough probable cause to get a warrant.'

'Where are you going?' Todd asked.

'I'm on my way to the crime lab with the ballistics stuff. You keep tracking on FBOs.'

I started for the door, but Mel waved me down, signaling for me to wait.

'Thank you so much,' she was saying into the phone. 'Yes, I can hear it. The fax is coming through right now. You've been a huge help, David.'

Mel hurried over to the fax machine and then had to stand and wait until the documents finished printing. She handed the first one to me and I saw it right away. Whoever had drawn the composite had done a wonderful job, Diane Massingale and the nun in the composite from the Bountiful Police Department were clearly one and the same.

'So Diane it is, then,' I said.

'Maybe it's both of them,' Mel replied. 'They both trained with the Air Force in the first Gulf War. Both left under less than optimal circumstances — as in don't-ask-don't-tell.'

'The FAA told you that?'

'Not the FAA per se. David told me that. He just happens to work for the FAA,' Mel answered. 'Anyway, after that they both worked for commuter airlines, then they flew charters. They've worked exclusively for Anita Bowdin since 2002. And they both live at the same address in Kent, the one we found for T. Rayburn. Now where do you think you're going?'

'The crime lab, to drop off the ballistics info.'

'I'm coming too,' Mel said determinedly.

'But Todd needs you to work on the FBO situation,' I objected.

'Todd has a telephone,' Mel declared. 'And I have a telephone. If Todd needs me to do something, he can call. Right, Todd?'

'Right,' Todd said, ducking his head into his computer screen and not meeting her eye. I suspected that he had seen more of Mel Soames than he expected that morning. She seemed to be coping with the situation far better than he was. And leaving them alone to work together clearly wasn't an option.

'Okay, then,' I said. 'Come on. Bring along our Destry and Anita info. That'll give us something to read if we end up having to sit around somewhere and cooling our heels.'

The Mercedes was almost out of gas, so we took Mel's BMW. She drove. When my phone rang I expected the caller to be Todd Hatcher or Ross Connors. It was Harry I. Ball.

'You don't call,' he said. 'You don't write. And considering I bailed your butts out of hot water yesterday morning you'd think you could be bothered to pick up the phone and say thanks a bunch.'

'Sorry, Harry,' I said. 'We've been busy.'

'Hah!' he said. 'I'll bet. Now are you two ever coming back or should I just sublet your space and get it over with? No sense sitting here with empty offices going to waste.'

'We're working, Harry,' I said. 'We're making progress.'

'But I shouldn't hold my breath waiting for you to send me an actual report on what you're doing. Brad and Aaron are a little pissed about this, you know. Barbara, too. They come in every day, punch the time clock, put in their hours, while you and Mel are wandering around free as a couple of birds.'

Brad Norton and Aaron Oliver were two of our SHIT Squad B teammates.

'Sorry to leave you out of the loop, and I'll shoot you an update,' I promised, 'as soon as we get within shouting distance of our computers.'

'You do that,' Harry said. 'But I'm not holding my breath.'

When we reached the crime lab parking lot, I thought Mel would want to come in with me.

'You go on,' she said. 'There are a couple of things I want to check out.'

I went. I've been to the crime lab countless times without ever catching sight of Destry Hennessey, but as I pointed out earlier, this was the Ides of March, and the stars were not in our favor. She was down in the lobby, talking to the lady in charge of handing out visitors' badges.

'Hey, Beau,' she said. 'What are you doing here?'

She seemed happy enough to see me. She wouldn't have been had she known what I was up to.

'Ballistics,' I said. 'Need to see Larry.'

'Your old bud,' she said. 'This about the double homicide up in Leavenworth?'

'Yup,' I said. 'That's the one,' making a mental note to be sure Tim Lander sent Larry something about that Golden Saber shell casing that would keep everyone out of trouble.

'Good work,' she said. 'Sounds like you cleared that one up in a hell of a hurry.'

I took my visitor's badge and rode the elevator upstairs. Larry was aghast when I told him I had run into Destry herself in the lobby. 'Don't worry,' I said. 'Put in a call to Tim Lander at the Chelan County Sheriff's Department and make sure he sends you everything there is to know about the weapon involved in the double homicide up in Leavenworth.'

'But he already did,' Larry said. 'That's what I'm supposed to be working on this morning.'

'We're covered then,' I said. 'Not to worry.'

I gave him what I had. He looked it over, sniffing his disapproval. 'This isn't all that good,' he said. 'But it may be enough. Give me a number so I can get back to you.'

I did and then headed back down to the car, where I found Mel talking on her cell. When I got into the car, she handed me a scrap of paper. On it she had scribbled something that looked like 'Wingnuts and Butte Av.' She hung up.

'Who was that?' I asked.

'Ross Connors,' she said. 'I just finished telling him that his boy wonder economist, Todd Hatcher, is in fact a genius. He's located two more FBOs — Wingnuts is in Roseburg. Butte Aviation is in Butte, Montana. The dates Anita's plane was in those areas coincide with two of my sexual offender 'mysterious deaths.''

'So they are connected?'

'Looks like,' Mel said.

'And we're dealing with serial killers.'

'That, too,' Mel agreed.

'So what's the next step?'

'Ross has the whole Olympia squad working the problem as well — checking out the plane, where it's based, flight plans, all that kind of thing. Since we can put the plane in the vicinity at the time of four homicides, three in the U.S. and one in Mexico, he's also looking into whether or not we have sufficient probable cause to get a search warrant.'

'I don't think so,' I said.

'That's what I told him,' Mel agreed. 'He said it depends on the judge, and Ross Connors knows a lot of judges.'

'So what's the next step for us?' I asked.

'Breakfast,' Mel said. 'Cold pizza doesn't do it for me. Then what say the two of us head out to Kent and have a chat with Diane Massingale or Trudy Rayburn? An unexpected visit from us might force them into making some kind of error.'

'If we spook them, what if they just jump in the plane and take off?' I asked.

'If they try that, we'll know where the plane is, won't we,' Mel said with a smile. 'And if they're apprehended while attempting to flee, we'll have probable cause for sure.'

Which is exactly why Mel Soames is my kind of girl.

We stopped off at the Yankee Diner in Renton on our way to Kent. Mel ordered breakfast; I ordered lunch. We had taken the Destry/Anita papers in with us. While we waited for our food, we tried to work on them again, but Mel pushed hers away after only a minute or so. Glancing at her face, I saw she looked troubled.

'I thought these women were my friends,' she said. 'And I thought the whole purpose of SASAC was to help people — to accomplish something worthwhile.'

The comment made me revisit the betrayal I had felt when I learned Anne Corley wasn't at all who or what I had thought her to be. Not knowing exactly which way Mel was leaning, and not wanting to make the situation worse, I tried to soft-pedal Anita Bowdin's involvement.

'We don't know for sure Anita Bowdin did this,' I said. 'Maybe her pilots were acting on their own.'

Mel remained unconvinced. 'We don't know that she didn't, either. If she wanted to find unconvicted and anonymous sexual offenders, the crime lab was the perfect place to go hunting,' Mel declared. 'I know for a fact that Anita was bound and determined to place someone inside the DNA profiling lab. That was a major goal when I turned up on the scene. She may not have pulled the actual triggers, Beau, but I know Anita Bowdin is involved. I'm guessing the pilots are the puppets while Anita controls the strings.'

'But we still don't know why.'

'One way or the other,' Mel said determinedly, 'we're going to find out.'

By the time we arrived at Trudy Rayburn and Diane Massingale's neatly rehabbed 1920s bungalow on the edge of downtown Kent, Mel and I had come up with a suitable fiction and with the decision that, in this instance, Mel would do all the talking. We parked Mel's BMW three blocks away and almost out of sight of Trudy Rayburn's house. Mel opened the trunk and removed the his-and-hers Kevlar vests we keep there. Only after donning them did we walk back to the house. A blue Ford Freestyle minivan was parked in the driveway. We walked past it and stepped up onto the low porch. Then Mel rang the bell.

As soon as Trudy answered the door, Mel put our game plan into action. She greeted the woman with a handshake and a warm smile. 'I don't know if you remember me or not,' Mel said, 'but I flew with you on a trip to Cancún last fall.'

'Oh, sure,' Trudy answered. 'I remember now. What can I do for you?'

Once Mel handed over her business card, Trudy was a lot less welcoming. 'What's this about?' she asked.

'Your boss,' Mel answered. 'Anita Bowdin.'

'What about her?'

Mel sighed — very convincingly, I thought. 'We really can't go into any great detail right now,' Mel said. 'It's an ongoing police matter and obviously we can't comment, but we understand that you and your partner have worked for Ms. Bowdin for several years. We wondered if, in the course of your employment, you've ever noticed anything suspicious — anything out of line?'

'You mean like some kind of illegal activity,

like transporting drugs or something?' Trudy asked.

'That would work,' Mel said with another smile.

Trudy had been standing in an open screen door. Now she moved back into the house and let the screen door close between us. 'Look, Ms. Bowdin has been wonderful to us,' she declared, standing with her arms folded. 'I can't imagine her doing anything 'out of line,' as you call it. So, no. In answer to your question, I haven't noticed anything at all.'

I for one was delighted to see Trudy Rayburn exhibiting such classic defensive behavior, and I was sure she wasn't doing it out of concern for Anita Bowdin, either. This was a lot more personal.

'When was the last time you flew Anita somewhere?' Mel asked conversationally. 'Where did you go and when did you return?'

'I'm sure I shouldn't be answering these questions,' Trudy said.

'It's really more a matter of corroboration than it is answering questions,' Mel returned. 'We know what Anita told us about her recent travels. We're simply trying to confirm what she told us from an independent source, but that's all right, Ms. Rayburn. Not to worry. I'm sure we'll be able to check out your aircraft's past flight plans with the FAA. That'll take some time, but it will accomplish the same end. In the meantime, though, go ahead and keep my card,' Mel added, 'just in case you or Ms. Massingale decide there is something you'd like to tell us about. And don't forget, if the plane has been used in the commission of any crime, the two of you, being the pilots, could well be implicated as coconspirators.'

Mel turned and sauntered off the porch, with me trailing discreetly behind her. We were all the way to the sidewalk before the interior door closed behind us. 'Now we wait,' Mel said as we headed back to the BMW.

'What if she calls Anita?' I asked.

'That's a risk we're going to have to take.'

We had just settled into the car when Mel's phone rang. 'Okay, Roy,' she said after listening for several seconds. 'Good work. Thanks for letting me know.'

'Who was that?' I asked. 'And thanks for letting you know what?'

'Roy Porter,' Mel answered. 'He's an inter-agency information officer for the King County Sheriff's Office. Ross asked him to do some background work for us. According to him, Trudy Rayburn has a CPL.'

That was bad news. It meant King County had issued a concealed pistol license to Trudy Rayburn. It's one thing to do an ounce of prevention and put on a Kevlar vest to go chat up a suspect who may or may not be armed. Once you know for sure the suspect is carrying, though, it's a whole other can of worms.

'Great,' I said. 'That's just what I want to know.'

'And they've located Anita's plane,' Mel added. 'At least they've established that she rents a hangar at the Renton Municipal Airport. They're still working on getting a search warrant. If they can get it, it'll include the house here, the hangar, the plane, and the minivan. The problem is, even if a judge grants it, how long will it take to get it here?'

'Good question.'

We settled in to wait. Stakeouts can be incredibly boring. We didn't try to catch up on our reading for fear we might miss something, but there was plenty of time for thinking and for considering the very real difference between 'bulletproof' vests as the public thinks of them and the far less definitive reality of 'bullet-resistant.' And then there's the problem of how much of the human body a Kevlar vest doesn't cover — Captain Paul Kramer's life-threatening injuries being a prime case in point.

So Mel and I sat there side by side thinking but not talking. In that tense silence I found myself grappling with some serious life-and-death issues — and contemplating what's important and what isn't. Once I came face-to-face with what I was really thinking, I went ahead and said what was on my mind.

'Will you marry me?' I asked. 'I know there should be hearts and flowers and moonlight and all that other stuff, but . . . '

Mel didn't reply right away. She just looked at me. 'Yesterday you thought I was responsible for Richard Matthews's death,' she said finally. 'And today you're asking me to marry you?'

If this was an answer, it wasn't the one I wanted.

'What can I tell you?' I said. 'I'm a hopeless romantic.'

Which is precisely the moment Trudy Rayburn chose to appear at the end of her driveway lugging a pair of heavy-looking suitcases. She opened the back of the minivan and hefted those inside. Then, leaving the cargo door open, she hurried away, most likely back into the house to fetch another load.

'Showtime,' Mel said, which was true, but it wasn't an answer to my question at all. 'The bad news is, she's wearing her uniform. And where's Diane?'

After the minivan left the driveway, Mel gave Trudy a several-block head start before she pulled out after her. I called Olympia and talked to Don Hastings, Harry I. Ball's Squad A counterpart. 'What's the story on that warrant?' I asked him. 'We don't have much time.'

'We've got it,' Don told me. 'A judge in Tacoma finally issued it a few minutes ago. Haley Mitchell is on her way with it. She's just now leaving Tacoma headed for your location in Kent.'

'It's too late for that,' I said. 'We're on the move here.'

'What's that?' Don said. At first I thought he was speaking to me, then I realized he was dealing with a second conversation with someone else at the same time. 'Okay, okay,' he agreed, coming back to me. 'We'll redirect Haley and the search warrant. Did you hear that, Beau?'

'Hear what?'

'November eight six one Alpha Bravo just filed a flight plan leaving from Renton Municipal at thirteen hundred thirty and flying to a place called Puerto Peñasco, Mexico. Flight time approximately four hours.'

The clock on the dash of Mel's 740 read twelve forty-eight. We didn't have much time at all.

'How many passengers?' I asked.

'Two souls on board indicated.'

That meant it was most likely the pilots only. Trudy and Diane hadn't alerted Anita Bowdin after all. They were meeting up, taking the plane, and making a run for it on their own.

'Where are you now?' Don asked.

Trudy's blue minivan had pulled off Kent's main drag and into a Wells Fargo Bank branch. Mel switched on her signal and parked at the edge of a Safeway parking lot across the street. We sat with the engine idling and watched while Trudy, carrying a briefcase, hustled into the bank.

'The suspect just went into a bank branch here in Kent,' I told him. 'Most likely picking up some cash.'

'All right,' Don said. 'SHIT's got a standing mutual aid agreement with Renton, so I'll let them know what's up and that we'll need units on the ground there at the airport. And Haley wants you to know she just passed the Kent/DeMoines Road exit coming north, so she's making good progress.'

I rang off and gave Mel the lowdown on what Don had told me. Then, silent once more, Mel and I sat and waited. Again. She hadn't given me an outright no to my impulsively impromptu proposal, but she sure as hell hadn't said yes, either, and I had far too much male pride to bring it up again. Instead I sat there and wondered how slow the bank tellers could possibly be and wished to hell I hadn't had so much coffee earlier in the morning.

When my phone rang again, I expected it would be Don Hastings, calling to give me a minute-by-minute update on Haley Mitchell's progress. It wasn't.

'You son of a bitch,' Detective Kendall Jackson said. 'You've been holding out on me.'

'What do you mean?' I asked. 'What's wrong?'

'Just had a call from Larry Crumb at the crime lab. He got a hit.'

'A hit on what?'

'On the weapon that killed LaShawn Tompkins. And guess what? Where do you think it came from? From you, you worm. From a case in Mexico! What the hell — ?'

'Sorry, Kendall,' I told him. 'Gotta go.'

I dialed Don back. 'Is Ross Connors there?' I asked.

'No, but — '

'Never mind.' I hung up and dialed Ross Connors's cell. He answered after only one ring. 'What?' he asked. 'Is there some other problem besides the plane?'

'We've got to move on those rape kits,' I told him. 'Now! If there's any media coverage at all of the plane takedown, it'll be too late.'

'Done,' he said. 'I'll put the DNA lab on an

immediate lock-down. No phone calls in or out. No e-mails, either. Now where's that blasted list thing you were telling me about?'

'Todd Hatcher has our copy.'

'How soon can he have it there?'

'I have a better idea,' I said. 'Send someone to pick up Analise Kim at her house and take her to the lab. It's her list — the one we have is only a copy. She's the one who organized the whole storage system, and she's the one who'll be able to find what we need.'

'All right,' he said. 'I'm on it. Where are you?'

'In Kent, waiting for Trudy Rayburn to finish up in the bank.'

Which happened almost at the same time I said the words. Trudy emerged and headed for her van. Once Trudy's vehicle had merged into traffic, Mel pulled in behind her. The minivan was tall enough that we were able to stay several car lengths back. Within a matter of seconds it was clear Trudy was headed for Highway 167.

'What was that all about?' Mel wanted to know.

'Larry Crumb got a hit. The gun that killed Richard Matthews is the same one that killed LaShawn Tompkins.'

Without warning, Mel jammed her foot on the accelerator. The BMW shot forward, passing several of the intervening vehicles and putting a permanent whiplash-style crink in my neck.

'I hate vigilantes,' she muttered.

'So do I,' I agreed. 'But please don't kill us in the process.'

She eased off on the gas, slowing a little and

dropping back into the right-hand lane behind the minivan. 'Okay,' she said.

I thought she meant okay, she would slow down. I didn't get it at first.

'I meant okay, I'll marry you,' Mel explained.

'Oh,' I said.

Don't think I wasn't grateful — ecstatic would be a better word — but Mel Soames is not the world's best driver.

'Great,' I told her. 'But how about if we discuss this later? Right now, shut up and drive.'

25

In the world of law enforcement, takedowns can go either way, very good or very bad. The one at Renton Municipal Airport went off without a hitch. The blue van pulled up to the security gate, and after a pause was allowed onto the tarmac. Soon the van disappeared behind a long line of hangars, but I wasn't overly concerned. Once the gate closed behind her, I knew for sure we had her. In a post 9/11 world, the Freestyle wouldn't be coming back through that secured gate, not unless someone opened it for her. And I knew their plane wouldn't be taking off, either, not without clearances from the FAA, which, I was sure, wouldn't be forthcoming.

Haley Mitchell, waving frantically, pulled up behind the BMW in her Jeep Cherokee. I hopped out and hurried back to collect the search warrant, which she held out the window for me. As I started back to the BMW, another vehicle pulled into line behind hers — a Suburban — and I was gratified to see the remainder of Squad B — Harry I. Ball, Brad Norton, and Aaron Oliver — come spilling out of it.

Harry strode up to the BMW. 'Where are these turkeys?' he demanded.

'They went around the building.'

By then Mel had negotiated with the keeper of the gate. And, because she's a female, she had asked for and received directions. 'We go around the end of this building and then turn right,' Mel said. 'Anita Bowdin's hangar is at the far end.'

'Okay,' Harry announced. 'I'm in charge here. Renton already has units inside the airport grounds, but they're waiting for me to give the word. If necessary, they'll surround the aircraft and make sure it doesn't go anywhere.' He looked back at his little band of SHIT squad soldiers. 'Everybody wearing vests?' We all nodded, Haley Mitchell included. 'Okay, boys and girls,' Harry said. 'Lock and load, back in your vehicles, and let's hit it.'

The gate opened — with an astonishing lack of speed or urgency, but in the long run, I think slowing our approach actually worked in our favor. There were no sirens and no lights, nothing to alert Trudy Rayburn and Diane Massingale to our impending arrival. Once we came around the near end of the building we could see the van parked at the far end, where two people were engaged in hauling things out of the back and carrying them into the hangar. They never saw us coming.

Because Mel and I were leading the way, we got there first. In the movies and on TV, cops always arrive in a squeal of tires and a spray of gravel. Mel brought the BMW to a smooth and silent stop directly behind the van where Trudy Rayburn was leaning deep inside to pull something from the far end of the cargo area. Trudy was the one with the concealed weapon permit, and I didn't want to take any chances. I tackled her and brought her down before she ever knew what hit her. Once she was on the ground, Mel removed her weapon.

By then Haley, Brad, and Aaron were out of the Suburban. They rushed into the hangar, where Diane was coming back from the plane for another load of luggage. She hit the tarmac when ordered to do so and placed her hands on the back of her head. It was a by-the-book operation, over almost before it started, which was fine by me. Kevlar vests are okay in their place and in theory, but I prefer not to field-test them if at all possible.

One of the things we good guys have going for us is that most crooks are under the mistaken impression that all cops are stupid. Trudy Rayburn and Diane Massingale were true to type. They both seemed thunderstruck to think someone had actually caught on to them. As the ranking officer present, Harry enjoyed introducing himself and taking charge of the two suspects. Their consternation at hearing his name was well worth the price of admission. As I've said before, people who regard Harry I. Ball as some kind of joke do so at their peril.

By then a whole phalanx of Renton PD patrol cars had appeared out of nowhere. Harry ordered the handcuffed suspects into two of them. Then, with Harry leading the way in his Suburban, a mini-motorcade set off for the King County Justice Center, where the suspects would be held for questioning.

Armed with our search warrant and several eager helpers, Mel and I turned our attention to Anita Bowdin's slick jet — November eight six one Alpha Bravo. We emptied the Hawker's cargo hold. One by one we went through all the pieces of luggage we found there and inventoried the contents. From the amount of clothing we found there and from the amount of money stashed in Trudy's confiscated briefcase, it soon became clear that their trip wasn't planned as a short south-of-the-border getaway. It was a real getaway. Trudy and Diane had expected to go to Mexico and stay there.

For a while it seemed as though our search wasn't going to uncover anything particularly incriminating. By the time we had finished sorting through the plane and its contents, I was growing discouraged. That was when I turned my attention to an unlocked footlocker in a relatively dim far corner of the hangar.

When I pulled up the lid, the first thing I saw was a cardboard box — a large shipping box. The printed label was still visible: 'Display and Costume Supply.' I recognized the name at once. When I first moved to the city, Display and Costume Supply was located in the Denny Regrade neighborhood, just down the street from my first condo in the Royal Crest. Years later, as the neighborhood changed, they moved their operation out to the burbs somewhere, and I lost track of them.

But I still have happy memories of the owners, Dallas and Suzie Carlton. Back when I was newly divorced and the Doghouse Restaurant was my home away from home, they tended to show up there around Halloween — and the Fourth of July, Saint Patrick's Day, and Easter

— dressed in costumes from their apparently never-ending supply and bringing their unfailingly good spirits with them.

So I knew something about Display and Costume Supply before I ever lifted the lid on the box. That corner of the hangar wasn't well lit. And when I first opened the box, it was almost like looking into a black hole. When I reached inside, I touched fabric — black fabric — yards of it. And when I pulled some of it out, I knew at once what it was — a nun's habit. Not a real nun's habit, a phony nun's habit. No wonder none of the samples from the various convents in Utah had matched up with the black-thread trace evidence. Those were real. This was a costume, a disguise.

Mel came up behind me. 'What in the world . . . ?'

But by then I already had my phone in my hand and was dialing information. Within seconds I had Dallas Carlton on the phone. With a little prodding he remembered me — or at least he claimed to — and when I told him I was looking at a shipping box loaded with nun's habits, he knew right away what I was talking about.

'Oh, those,' he said.

'So you know about them?'

'Of course. We usually get orders for five or six nun's habits at Halloween. Fewer of them now that that popular Capitol Hill production of *The Late Night Catechism* closed. But I do remember ordering that one whole carton. It was a special order — the only one I've ever done.'

'You wouldn't happen to remember who was it for?' I asked.

'Sure,' Dallas said. 'Anita Bowdin's a good customer of ours. She said she was working with a school somewhere that was putting on a production of *The Sound of Music*. I was able to get her a really good price.'

'Thanks,' I told him. 'Thanks so much.'

I turned to Mel. 'Guess who ordered a case of phony nun's habits?'

'Who?'

'Your friend and mine, Anita Bowdin.'

'Let's go get her, too,' Mel said. 'She lives in Laurelhurst.'

'Do you have the address?'

'I don't need the address,' Mel returned. 'I've been there.'

Ross called while we were on the road and brought us up-to-date. 'The DNA lab is secure. With the help of several Washington State Patrol Internal Affairs officers, Mrs. Kim is in the process of gathering up the rape kits in question. Yolanda Andrade is in custody for possible evidence tampering. Destry Hennessey has been relieved of her duties, and she's in custody as well. I've asked for the suspects to be housed separately at the Justice Center until we have a chance to interview them. So far Destry is the only one calling for a lawyer. What about you?'

'We've found a whole boxful of fake nun costumes, purchased by Anita Bowdin and stored in her airplane hangar at Renton Municipal Airport. Mel and I are on our way to pick her up.'

'Excellent,' Ross said. 'Once you have her in custody we'll settle in for a game of *Let's Make a Deal*, and we'll see which of these ladies is interested in spilling the beans.'

We drove to Anita's humongous waterfront villa on the edge of Lake Washington in Seattle's tony Laurelhurst neighborhood. Just as at Renton Municipal Airport, we entered Anita's property through a remote-controlled security gate. When we rang the front door a uniformed maid greeted us and then led us through to the back of the house. (Or the front. With waterfront houses I'm never sure which is which.)

There, on a sun-drenched sunporch, we found a sweats-clad Anita, iPod earphones clapped to her ears, jogging along at a very fast clip on a high-tech treadmill.

'Mel, Beau,' she gushed, taking off the earphones. 'What a pleasant surprise. Have a seat. I'll be done in a minute. Dory,' she added for the maid's benefit. 'Do bring our guests something to drink.'

Her arrogance was such that I don't believe it occurred to her for one moment that we were onto her or that the jig was up. When Anita finished her workout she grabbed a towel, slapped it around the back of her neck, and then came toward us smiling.

'To what do I owe the honor?' she asked.

'I'm sorry, Anita,' Mel said. 'You're under arrest on suspicion of murder.'

Anita Bowdin was shocked. 'No!' she exclaimed. 'I'm under arrest? That's insane. What for? You can't possibly mean — '

'Oh, but I do mean it,' Mel said grimly. 'Hands on your head. Now!'

Anita Bowdin did as she was told without further protest. By then I think she knew we knew and there was no need for any further discussion.

Halfway between the sunporch and the front door we met up with Dory. She was carrying a silver tray laden with a complete coffee service along with an ice bucket, glasses, and a selection of sodas.

'Call Calvin,' Anita snapped at the maid as we went past. 'He's at the office. Tell him I need him.'

We walked on. Behind us we heard the tray crash to the floor, glasses and cups shattering as they fell.

26

Mel Soames and I had both worked high-profile cases before, but nothing could have prepared us for the storm of controversy we'd fallen into this time. It's one thing for a derelict pig farmer to be murdering folks society is ready to label throwaway prostitutes. Cops who bring down a guy like that are heroes while, through some warped logic, society views those kinds of victims as somehow complicit in their own deaths — as in, they were asking for it. As for the killer? He's a nutcase, to be sure, but he was also doing some of society's dirty work, so let's put him away somewhere and move on.

Anita Bowdin and her gang of female vigilantes turned that whole scenario on its ear. She and Destry Hennessey were and are well known and ostensibly respectable women in Washington State, with plenty of people who, without knowing any of the story, were ready to back them to the hilt. As far as those folks were concerned, the two of them could do no wrong, whereas Mel and I were nothing but a pair of malcontents who should never have brought any of this up. Ditto Todd Hatcher, who, I learned much later, did indeed turn his fifteen minutes of fame into a whopping two-book publishing contract.

What really ended up pulling all the various threads together, however, was a young IT wizard, also a friend of Todd Hatcher, who, search warrant in hand, went on a mission through Anita Bowdin's computer's hard drives. The information he uncovered there was nothing short of a gold mine.

Destry Hennessey's initial position — that she had been duped the same way Mel had — went bye-bye when we uncovered and decoded a secret recording Anita had made of a telephone conversation between her and Destry. In it the two women not only discussed exactly when Juan Carlos Escobar was due to be released from jail but also how serendipitous it was that both Destry and her husband would be in Washington, D.C., at the time. Ambrose Donner of Bountiful, Utah, was especially pleased to hear about that one.

Anita was someone who liked to keep score. Several weeks into the now-public investigation, Mel and I found ourselves scrolling through one of Anita's files that the IT guy had lifted from her computer. It was a chilling rogue's gallery of the people she had successfully targeted and had taken out. With the exception of Richard Matthews, who had never been arrested, the record for each man came complete with mug shot, copies of fingerprints, and rap sheets. No doubt all that official information had been obtained with the help of Destry Hennessey. And side by side with each mug shot was a second photo of the same face, often a postmortem one, taken by a grainy cell phone camera and annotated with a caption that listed the date of death.

As we worked our way through the list by Analise Kim's preferred LIFO fashion, the names we saw were far more familiar to Mel than they were to me. After all, these were 'her guys' — violent sexual predators — who were dead now for crimes they had committed but for which they had never been either officially tried or convicted. It was only when we scrolled down to the last one — the earliest one — that we found another record missing its mug shot.

'What's he doing here?' Mel demanded.

I had gone to refill our coffee cups. When I returned I was looking at the head-shot photo of a pleasant-faced balding man in a jacket and tie. The caption beneath it read: 'Professor Armand P. Bowdin.'

'I thought he committed suicide,' Mel added.

'So did I.'

We went back through the now dog-eared collection of papers Todd Hatcher had amassed for us the day we started closing in on the truth. Searching through them all, we came up with nothing more than 'died unexpectedly in his home.' A call to the Ann Arbor Police Department didn't add much to what we'd already surmised. Armand P. Bowdin had committed suicide by taking an overdose of prescription medications.

'That doesn't change the fact that his picture is here,' Mel said determinedly.

And off we went on the trail of Anita Bowdin's mother Rachel. It took time for us to bring her to ground. Widowed for a second time, Rachel

A. Trasker lived in a retirement compound near Tampa, Florida.

'This is about my daughter?' Rachel asked warily once we finally had her on the phone. 'If you're a reporter . . .'

Clearly we weren't the first people to make the connection between Mrs. Trasker and her errant daughter.

'I'm definitely not a reporter,' Mel corrected. 'I'm an investigator for the Washington State Attorney General's Office. We're calling about your husband — your first husband.'

Mel's remark was followed by a long period of dead silence. 'What about him?' Rachel asked finally.

'Did he commit suicide?'

'Why do you ask?' Rachel wanted to know.

'Did he?' Mel insisted.

There was another long pause. 'What if she comes after me?' Rachel asked finally.

'What if Anita comes after you?' Mel clarified.

'She always said she would. If I ever told anyone, she said she'd get rid of me, too. I happen to believe her.'

'Your daughter is an accused serial murderer. She's in jail awaiting trial on twelve cases of homicide. She isn't getting out anytime soon.'

'Armand never did any of the things Anita said,' Rachel declared after a time. 'He wouldn't. He was a nice man. She tried to tell me that he did things to her, messed with her, touched her. It was just too crazy. I never believed a word of it. But she told me she gave him a choice, either take the pills or she'd go to the police. She told

401

me she sat right there and watched him do it. How could her father and I have raised such a monster?'

Unfortunately, the answer to that question was all too apparent — to everyone but Anita Bowdin's mother. And now we knew why Armand's picture was the very first entry on Anita's scorecard.

Meanwhile the case kept grinding on in other people's hands. In the end, Yolanda Andrade turned out to be the weakest link. She had come to the crime lab with a phonied-up résumé after being fired from working at CODIS, the national DNA database. With her expertise it had been simple enough for her to make inroads into Washington State's far less secure DNA database — the shortcomings of which Ross Connors is even now working to fix.

I think it was shocking for the whole law enforcement to realize that this invaluable crime-fighting tool, DNA profiling, had been perverted into a targeting device for murder. But once Yolanda confessed to her part in the scheme and agreed to testify against the others, other guilty pleas started falling into place. Eventually Destry and Anita will either cop pleas as well or else stand trial. When that will happen is anyone's guess.

As the investigators closest to the case, Mel and I were put in charge of victim and family notifications. Every single case was one of justice denied. Talking to those folks was grueling, emotional work — some of the hardest police work I've ever done. With the notable exceptions of Richard Matthews and LaShawn Tompkins, all the victims were either convicted sexual predators or else convicted felons. That made them a less than sympathetic lot, but the same wasn't true of their survivors. For the parents or grandparents or siblings or wives or girlfriends of all these bad boys, the murdered victim was still *their very own* bad boy. Regardless of what crimes he may have committed as an adult, he had been little once — little, innocent, and loved.

Of all of those family notifications, the hardest for me was the one with Etta Mae Tompkins. In the intervening months she had become far frailer. She sat quietly in her corner chair and listened to what I had to say. When I finished, she nodded.

'It's all right,' she said. 'My Shawny's in heaven now. I pray to Jesus every night that he'll come soon and take me, too. With LaShawn gone, I've got nothing else to live for.'

I felt honor-bound to go back to King Street Mission to tell Pastor Mark I had been wrong and he was off the hook as far as LaShawn Tompkins's murder was concerned. When I got there, though, the building was gone — demolished. What I found instead was a hole in the ground with a construction crane parked in the middle of it. I never found Pastor Mark again, and I never found Sister Elaine Manning, either.

Then there was the matter of dealing with the victims of all those long-ago, never-solved rapes. As the rape kits were tested, or rather, as they were retested, results led back to one or another

403

of Mel's dead sexual offenders. And one by one we located the rape victims involved to let them know that their cases were now considered solved and closed, even though they would never have the benefit of a trial to help put the attacks behind them.

For a long time I wondered if LaShawn Tompkins's case would ever surface. One of the last profiles developed was that of a fourteen-year-old rape victim, Jonelle Lenora DeVry, who claimed she had been attacked and raped on her way home from school by an unidentified gangbanger.

It took us a while to track down Jonelle DeVry Jackson, but we finally did. That was how, two months later, Mel and I came to be sitting across from a young black woman in the neat living room of a small house on the outskirts of Ellensburg, Washington, where Jonelle now works in the admissions office for Central Washington University.

'We wanted you to know the case is finally resolved,' Mel said tentatively. 'That we've finally learned the identity of the boy who raped you.'

Jonelle studied Mel for a long hard minute. 'Is this going to come out in the newspapers?' she asked.

'No,' I said. 'Not at all. You were a juvenile at the time. There's no reason to reveal your name now.'

'Good,' Jonelle said with a relieved sigh. 'I always knew who raped me,' she added. 'And it wasn't rape, either. LaShawn Tompkins was five years older than me, but I loved him to distraction, and I thought he loved me, too. I told my parents it was somebody else because I knew my daddy would have killed LaShawn if he'd known. And then, about the same time, LaShawn got caught up in that other case . . . '

'The one he went to prison for?' Mel asked.

Jonelle nodded. 'Yes,' she answered. 'But once he went to jail for that, I knew not telling had been the right thing to do. And it still is. DeShawn has no idea who his father was. I want to keep it that way.'

That stopped me. 'DeShawn?' I repeated. 'You had LaShawn's baby and kept him? You named him after LaShawn, but you raised him without ever telling him who his father is?'

'My parents raised him,' Jonelle corrected. 'They raised both of us. They helped me get through school, the same way I'm helping DeShawn right now. It hasn't been easy, but he's a smart boy. He earned a full scholarship to Gonzaga. He's studying premed. With all that, what was the point of telling him his father was in prison? And by the time LaShawn was released . . . ' She paused and shrugged. 'There wasn't any point then, either.'

'You knew LaShawn was raised by his grandmother?'

'I knew Etta Mae,' Jonelle replied. 'Our old house is gone now. They tore it down and built an apartment building there, but we lived on Church Street, too. Etta Mae and my mother were good friends.'

'You knew LaShawn turned his life around while he was in prison?'

'I guess,' Jonelle said.

'And Etta Mae stood by him the whole time, believing in him, loving him.'

A single tear slid out of the corner of Jonelle DeVry's eye and trickled down her cheek. 'She would do,' she said. 'That's Etta Mae.'

'She's an old lady now,' I continued. 'She's old and frail, and she's lost LaShawn, the boy she raised from a baby.' I left the sentence hanging in the air and waited.

'And you're thinking I should tell her?' Jonelle retorted angrily. 'You think I should drag my DeShawn over there to Seattle and tell him here's your other grandmother — your great-grandmother — and sorry I didn't tell you because your real father was locked up in prison and now he's been murdered and have a nice day?'

'I'm not telling you what you should or shouldn't do,' I said. 'But it sounds like you've raised a good kid, and I think knowing DeShawn exists would give a dying old woman a precious gift beyond her wildest imaginings.'

Jonelle studied me for a very long time. 'I'll think about it,' she said finally. 'But I'm not making any promises.'

A week or so after that, I was due to go to court for a hearing in the Thomas Dortman matter. In the corridor outside the courtroom I ran into DeAnn Cosgrove. The ponytail was gone. Her hair was cut short and her makeup was deftly applied. She was wearing heels and a skirt and blazer. There was only the vaguest resemblance to the overwhelmed young woman I had seen juggling her three children in that messy living room or standing angry and silent next to her husband's hospital bed.

'DeAnn,' I said, taking her hand. 'I almost didn't recognize you.'

She smiled. 'I'm working,' she said. 'At Microsoft, so it's practically just up the street.' She paused and then added, 'Did you know Donnie's moved out?'

'No,' I said. 'I'm sorry to hear that.'

'I kept trying to pretend he didn't have a problem,' she said. 'But that day in the hospital you knew, didn't you.'

'Yes,' I said. 'I guess I did.'

'Finally I just couldn't pretend any longer. If he was so drunk that he'd just leave people to die, I had to give him a choice. Us or booze.'

'I see,' I said, knowing without having to be told which choice he had made.

'But don't worry about the kids and me, Mr. Beaumont,' DeAnn continued brightly. 'I have a roommate now, to help with the kids and expenses. And once Jack's and my mother's estate is settled, we'll be fine.'

She started to walk away then, into the courtroom, when I remembered something else.

'There was one other person your mother was in touch with that weekend, someone down in Portland. Do you remember any friends she might have had down there, someone she might have turned to in a crisis?'

DeAnn shook her head. 'Not that I remember.'

And so, because I was curious, I called Barbara Galvin and had her dredge Kevin Stock's name out of the file. But when I called DeAnn that evening and asked her about him, he still didn't ring any bells.

A few days later, Mel and I drove to Vancouver, Washington, to meet with the family members of one of the last men to die at Anita Bowdin's behest — a man who had been placed in a vehicle with the engine running and asphyxiated in his own two-car garage. We finished meeting with the family earlier than we had expected. Mel was anxious to head back north. But Vancouver, Washington, is right across the river from Portland.

'If you don't mind,' I said, 'there's one more stop I'd like to make.'

'Where?' Mel asked.

'In Portland.' And I gave her Kevin Stock's address, which I had looked up before we ever left Seattle.

'You just happen to have his address with you?' Mel asked.

'It's a coincidence,' I told her.

Kevin Stock lived in a small condo overlooking the Willamette River near downtown Portland. I saw the family resemblance as soon as he answered the door. Kevin Stock may have aged twenty years, but he was still Tony Cosgrove. His daughter looked just like him.

'Anthony Cosgrove?' I asked.

'No,' he stammered. 'You have me mixed up with someone else.'

'I don't think so,' I said, handing him my card. 'We need to talk.'

Just then a second man appeared in the doorway behind him. 'What is it, Kev?' he asked. 'What's wrong?'

Tony shook his head and sighed. 'All right,' he relented. 'I guess we do need to talk.'

It took the better part of an hour. Sometimes it's hard to realize how much things have changed since the early eighties. Then, on the other hand, many things have remained the same. Tony Cosgrove had fallen in love with another man. He was also a devout Catholic who didn't believe in divorce or suicide. So he had chosen to disappear.

'I loved Carol,' he said, 'And I told her if she ever needed me, to call. I always made sure she had my number, just in case. But she only called me once,' he added accusingly. 'To tell me about you. She was afraid you were going to upset things. And you did, and you're still upsetting things. Why are you here? What do you want?'

'I want you to think about your daughter,' I said. 'And your grandchildren.'

'I think about DeAnn every single day,' he returned. 'But at this point, she's far better off without me.'

'I'm not so sure,' I said. 'Her mother's dead. Her husband's moved out. She's on her own with three preschoolers. And no matter what happened, Tony, she never once believed you were dead. She's been waiting all this time for you to come home.'

'I can't,' Tony said hopelessly. 'Think about the insurance. If I turn up alive, she'll have to pay it back.'

'Between having the money and having her father?' I asked. 'For the DeAnn Cosgrove I know, there's no question how she'd choose.'

EPILOGUE

While we were knee-deep in investigative alligators, though, neither Mel nor I lost sight of her one-word answer: 'Okay.'

By now I'd had extensive experience with weddings. As the groom, I had survived the full-court-press June aisle-walker that had been my wedding with Karen and the three-day rush to judgment with Anne Corley. I had been the father of the bride for Kelly and the father of the groom for Scott. When it came to how Mel wanted to do this, I left the arrangements entirely in her capable hands. The resulting ceremony turned out to be a happy medium of all of the above.

We got married in Vegas at Treasure Island. Scott was the best man. Kelly, having recovered her equilibrium, was the matron of honor. Kayla was the flower girl and ring bearer both. Mel doesn't do sexism even for weddings. In addition to the kids, the only other guests were Lars — and, Lars being Lars, the joke-wielding Iris Rassmussen. Ralph Ames convinced me to charter a jet and fly everybody in, and that's what I did.

The wedding was in late afternoon. Mel wore an ivory silk suit and was absolutely stunning. I wore my tux. After all, I had already paid for the damned thing and it seemed reasonable to get a few wearings out of it. I had fairly low expectations about the kind of wedding ceremony we'd have at a Vegas hotel, but I shouldn't have worried. Vegas is full of showmen, and the hired reverend delivered his memorized lines with a kind of heartfelt sincerity that left everyone in attendance in tears — well, almost.

The wedding supper was next door in a small private room at Morton's. Then, while everyone else went out to party, Mel and I returned to our bridal suite, where someone had strewn our bed with rose petals, for Pete's sake!

I was lying in bed when Mel emerged from the bathroom, having removed her makeup. She flopped onto her side of the bed.

'Ouch!' she exclaimed, sitting up and rubbing her head. 'What the hell's wrong with the pillow?'

I love being married to a plainspoken woman.

Reaching under the pillow, she removed the small gift-wrapped box I had hidden there. 'What's this?' she asked.

'Open it and find out,' I said.

Inside was a model car, and not just any model car, either — an arctic silver Porsche Cayman.

'What's this?' she asked.

'It's a wedding present,' I told her. 'Some people register at Macy's. When I get married, I prefer to give and receive Porsches. So that's your present. A Cayman. It's on order. We're scheduled to take European delivery in Stuttgart in early September. I already cleared it with Harry so we can both have the time off.'

Mel looked both astonished and bemused.

'You're really giving me a Porsche for a wedding present?'

'Yes, I am,' I told her. 'Your BMW was starting to look a little worn around the edges.'

'And I get to drive it on the autobahn?'

'Yes,' I said, shaking my head. 'God help us all, you do.'

We do hope that you have enjoyed reading this large print book.

Did you know that all of our titles are available for purchase?

We publish a wide range of high quality large print books including:
Romances, Mysteries, Classics
General Fiction
Non Fiction and Westerns

Special interest titles available in large print are:
The Little Oxford Dictionary
Music Book
Song Book
Hymn Book
Service Book

Also available from us courtesy of Oxford University Press:
Young Readers' Dictionary
(large print edition)
Young Readers' Thesaurus
(large print edition)

For further information or a free brochure, please contact us at:
Ulverscroft Large Print Books Ltd.,
The Green, Bradgate Road, Anstey,
Leicester, LE7 7FU, England.
Tel: (00 44) 0116 236 4325
Fax: (00 44) 0116 234 0205

WEB OF EVIL

J. A. JANCE

The highway from Los Angeles to the Palm Springs desert is parched, unforgiving and deadly. In the suffocating stillness of a car boot, a man — his hands and mouth bound with tape — waits to learn his fate . . . Ali Reynolds is travelling that same blistering, lonely highway, heading for Los Angeles to finalise her divorce and confront the television network that callously fired her. As she passes the site of a horrifying accident, she thanks goodness it's no longer her job to report the news. But suddenly Ali finds she *is* the news . . . for the victim is none other than Ali's cheating husband, and soon she'll find herself the prime suspect at the centre of a terrifying web of evil.

DEAD WRONG

J. A. JANCE.

Juggling a family and a career has never been easy for Sheriff Joanna Brady, so when she's faced with two serious crimes in the same week it's the last thing she needs. One of her deputies has been seriously assaulted and left for dead. Meanwhile, a body has been found in the desert, fingers missing. When it is identified as a convicted killer, whose last movements suggest he may have been stalking a young woman, it seems rough justice has been served. Only Sheriff Brady thinks otherwise. As her department devote themselves to finding the assailant of one of their own, it is left to Joanna to avenge the dead man and find out why he was killed.